Praise for El...

"Beautiful and important."

—*New York Times* b........... ....nor Julia Quinn on
The Love Remedy

"Smart is the new sexy, and Elizabeth Everett does both better than anyone else!"

—#1 *New York Times* bestselling author Ali Hazelwood

"Fizzy, engrossing romance . . . a wholehearted celebration of women who choose to live gleefully outside the bounds of [the] patriarchy's limitations."

—*Entertainment Weekly* on *A Lady's Formula for Love*

"Dazzling. *A Love by Design* is full of heart, brains, and white-hot sizzle." —*New York Times* bestselling author Lynn Painter

"Explosive chemistry, a heroine who loves her science, and lines that made me laugh out loud—this witty debut delivered, and I'd like the next installment now, please."

—*USA Today* bestselling author Evie Dunmore on
A Lady's Formula for Love

"A witty, dazzling debut with a science-minded heroine and her broody bodyguard. Fiercely feminist and intensely romantic, *A Lady's Formula for Love* is a fresh take on historical romance that's guaranteed to delight readers."

—*USA Today* bestselling author Joanna Shupe

"Sparkling, smart, moving, original—just delightful from start to finish."

—*USA Today* bestselling author Julie Anne Long on
A Perfect Equation

"A phenomenally courageous romance with a wonderfully tenacious heroine that also manages to deliver on one of *the* swooniest and most complex heroes I've read in a long time. *The Love Remedy* is a perfect mix of delicious banter, crackling chemistry, and phenomenally cozy moments with Lucy, her siblings, and the deliciously grumpy Mr. Thorpe. A gem of a romance, and a brave one."

—*USA Today* bestselling author Adriana Herrera

"A delightful romp." —PopSugar on *A Lady's Formula for Love*

"A brilliant scientist and her brooding bodyguard discover that love can find you when you least expect it. *A Lady's Formula for Love* is full of wit, charm, and intrigue."

—Harper St. George, author of *The Stranger I Wed*

"Elizabeth Everett's writing absolutely dazzles. Fiercely feminist, deliciously sexy, and bursting with intoxicating enemies-to-lovers goodness, *A Perfect Equation* is an instant historical romance classic and Everett an auto-buy author."

—Mazey Eddings, *USA Today* bestselling author of *Late Bloomer*

"Poignantly feminist and perfectly feisty! Letty and Grey's romance is a delicious journey from sharp-tongued disdain to smoldering desire."

—Chloe Liese, author of the Bergman Brothers series,
on *A Perfect Equation*

"I've always loved Everett's Secret Scientists of London series—historical romances that revolve around the early women of STEM and the men who are either bowled over by their smarts or self-preserving enough to get out of their goddamn way and let them do their thing."   —Paste

"*The Love Remedy* firmly establishes Everett as a trailblazer and truth-teller whose daring historical fiction lights the way forward."   —Joanna Lowell, author of *A Shore Thing*

"A brilliant balance of comedy, sensuous romance, and smashing the patriarchy, the second installment of the Secret Scientists of London is a triumph!"
   —Libby Hubscher, author of *If You Ask Me*,
   on *A Perfect Equation*

"Splendidly entertaining . . . detonates with an ingeniously orchestrated display of wit and whimsy that dazzlingly celebrates the importance of both STEM research and love in a lady's life."   —*Booklist* on *A Perfect Equation* (starred review)

"With sharp wit and a keen eye for matters of social justice, Everett brings the period to life while making clear just how far women's rights have come—and how far they have left to go. This frank, flirty outing will have readers hooked."
   —*Publishers Weekly* on *The Love Remedy* (starred review)

ALSO BY ELIZABETH EVERETT

THE SECRET SCIENTISTS OF LONDON

A Lady's Formula for Love
The Perfect Equation
A Love by Design

THE DAMSELS OF DISCOVERY

The Love Remedy

THE
LADY
SPARKS
A FLAME

Elizabeth Everett

BERKLEY ROMANCE

NEW YORK

BERKLEY ROMANCE
Published by Berkley
An imprint of Penguin Random House LLC
1745 Broadway, New York, NY 10019
penguinrandomhouse.com

Copyright © 2025 by Elizabeth Everett
Excerpt from *The Love Remedy* copyright © 2024 by Elizabeth Everett
Penguin Random House values and supports copyright. Copyright fuels creativity, encourages
diverse voices, promotes free speech, and creates a vibrant culture. Thank you for buying an
authorized edition of this book and for complying with copyright laws by not reproducing,
scanning, or distributing any part of it in any form without permission. You are supporting
writers and allowing Penguin Random House to continue to publish books for every reader.
Please note that no part of this book may be used or reproduced in any manner for the purpose
of training artificial intelligence technologies or systems.

BERKLEY and the BERKLEY & B colophon are registered trademarks of
Penguin Random House LLC.

Book design by George Towne

Library of Congress Cataloging-in-Publication Data

Names: Everett, Elizabeth, author.
Title: The lady sparks a flame / Elizabeth Everett.
Description: First edition. | New York : Berkley Romance, 2025. |
Series: The Damsels of Discovery ; vol 2
Identifiers: LCCN 2024023536 (print) | LCCN 2024023537 (ebook) |
ISBN 9780593550489 (trade paperback) | ISBN 9780593550496 (ebook)
Subjects: LCGFT: Romance fiction. | Novels.
Classification: LCC PS3605.V435 L32 2025 (print) |
LCC PS3605.V435 (ebook) | DDC 813/.6—dc23/eng/20240524
LC record available at https://lccn.loc.gov/2024023536
LC ebook record available at https://lccn.loc.gov/2024023537

First Edition: March 2025

Printed in the United States of America
1st Printing

The authorized representative in the EU for product safety and compliance is
Penguin Random House Ireland, Morrison Chambers, 32 Nassau Street,
Dublin D02 YH68, Ireland, https://eu-contact.penguin.ie.

For my husband, a real-life romantic hero

And to all the girls who are screaming,
I can hear you

Dear Reader,

Before you read this story, know that there is frank discussion of nonsuicidal self-harm within these pages. Tread slowly, and if this is painful, be gentle with yourself.

Phoebe's experience with nonsuicidal self-harm might be familiar to some who have either experienced it themselves or have watched a loved one self-harm.

To anyone who believes a young woman in an abusive household who self-harmed in the eighteen hundreds is historically inaccurate because there are no records of such incidences, I ask you to take a moment and consider whether the men with a stranglehold on recording and retelling our history would know or care about a very real, very frightening coping mechanism used overwhelmingly by adolescent women.

They were there, those girls who couldn't feel until it hurt, who chose to inflict pain on themselves rather than wait for pain to be inflicted by others. They were there, and I honor and respect them and do the same for all of you who walk this path.

Be well.
Elizabeth Everett

THE
LADY
SPARKS
A FLAME

1

I am no poet, but if you think for yourselves, as I
proceed, the facts will form a poem in your minds.

— Michael Faraday

*London
1845*

"HOW DO YOU MANAGE TO MAKE THE WORDS '*YOU*
know best' sound like '*I* know best'?"

"Because . . . I know best?"

Oh, for feck's sake.

A large man sat opposite Sam Fenley at a cheap but polished
wood desk. Sam considered him a friend.

He also considered punching him.

That's how it was sometimes with men. Clap them on the
shoulder one day, punch them the next—no hard feelings.

When Sam was younger, that was how it was with his sisters
until they learned Sam couldn't stand it when they cried. They
would simply wobble their lower lip and he'd wind up punching himself to keep them from sobbing.

"Listen to me, Fenley. I understand your crusade against the Corn Laws." The Earl Grantham rubbed his face with a gloved hand. Dark smudges beneath his blue eyes made him seem older than his two and thirty years.

Sam had bought a newspaper from the earl last year and within six months made enough of a profit to buy a second. It said a good deal about Sam's generosity of spirit that he let the earl sit in his office and tell him what to print after Grantham had gone and sold him *The Capital's Chronicle*. Then again, Grantham was a giant of a man and ridiculously stubborn.

"However," the earl continued. "The last article *The Chronicle* printed has overestimated the scarcity of Britain's wheat crop. Yours and other anti–Corn Law broadsheets will panic the population. More trouble will come from your reporting than progress."

Sam knew Grantham meant well, but this wasn't about the earl's fears. It was about money and power. Or the lack thereof. Pleasure from watching his sales grow leaps and bounds was undeniable, but Sam also gained satisfaction from publishing articles informing regular folk about what their government was doing and why it mattered.

"If I back down now," Sam said, "it gives more fuel to the pro–Corn Law fires. The Corn Laws pour money into landowners' coffers and take it away from the majority of England's working folk."

Sam wasn't telling Grantham anything he didn't know, but he continued anyway, blood boiling as it often did when speaking of the advantages the titled classes held over the rest of the population.

The Corn Laws taxed corn—wheat, barley, and all other cereal grains—from outside Britain. On paper, this appeared to help domestic agriculture, but the taxes made food more expensive for everyone, while political power stayed in the hands of wealthy landowners who profited from the rising price of domestic corn.

"In this great country of ours, if you don't own land, you don't get to vote. How is that acceptable in our day and age?" Simply saying the words out loud angered Sam. The landowners didn't benefit only from the artificial pricing, they also handpicked their Members of Parliament and told them how to vote. "Universal suffrage is the goal, and I'm not above embellishing when it comes to a worthy goal."

Grantham opened his mouth to speak, but Sam beat him to it.

"As *you* are not above embellishing when it comes to stealing women away from other men."

Grantham's jaw clicked softly when he clamped his lips together, and the tips of his ears went red. It said much about the earl's good nature that he didn't fall for the bait.

Sam had tried his hardest to charm the engineer Margaret Gault, but she'd gone and married Grantham, her childhood sweetheart. Why she didn't prefer Sam, a man who had made a fortune of his family's business, turned around a failing newspaper, and set his sights on expanding his holdings even further, was a mystery.

Sam had fallen at Margaret's feet. In the most literal sense, unfortunately. Fallen, tripped, tumbled—a product of Sam's adversarial relationship with immovable objects. Not exactly the stuff of fevered dreams when a man reaches for your hand, loses his balance, and hits the floor with his face.

Huh. Perhaps Margaret's decision was not mysterious after all?

"You are in a terrible mood. What ails you, Fenley?" Grantham asked, stretching out his legs and placing his hands behind his head, the picture of aristocratic indolence.

Sam knew well that Grantham was far from indolent, but the reclined pose annoyed him, nonetheless.

Everything annoyed him these days.

"Nothing ails me, *my lord*."

Sam had meant the honorific as a tease, but the words came out hard and clipped. One long earlish eyebrow lifted on Grantham's face at the tone.

"If I were to guess, I'd say you were in want of one of life's great necessities," Grantham opined.

Jealousy sprang to life deep in Sam's belly, kindled with myriad thwarted ambitions; obstacles a man without title nor a single drop of blue blood in his veins faced every day in this country.

Sam growled. "Simply because women used to fawn over you for the chance at being a countess—"

The pink spread from Grantham's ears to his cheeks as he dropped his arms and sat straight up in his chair. "I'm not talking about sex, Fenley."

What else might constitute one of life's necessities if not sex?

Food?

Wealth?

"I'm not hungry," Sam said. "I've enough money to buy the crown right off Queen Victoria's head, I own two broadsheets now, investments in property, plus half the family business. I'm seldom bored thanks to my four sisters and the never-ending catastrophes those scientists over at Athena's Retreat drag us into. There's not a *single* thing missing from my life."

With a patronizing sigh, Grantham ran his fingers through

his hair, eyes rolling up to the heavens as though he communicated with God on a peer-to-peer level.

"I'm talking about love, Fenley."

What?

Sam nearly fell back out of his chair again.

"What? You're talking about . . . You're talking about sex, you mean," Sam said.

Grantham shook his head slowly, an obnoxious half smile pasted across his face.

"I'm talking about marriage."

Oh, for feck's sake. Sam jumped up from his chair and paced around the desk separating him and Grantham, then to the window overlooking a small courtyard shared by the building next door.

Love.

What nonsense was this?

"You've inhaled too many fumes over at Athena's Retreat," Sam said.

Yes.

Fumes.

That must be the reason those beautiful geniuses at the Retreat fell for Grantham's clumsy charms.

Athena's Retreat, a secret haven for women scientists, was the creation of three brilliant women. One of them was his older sister, Letty, a mathematician who'd *also* married a man with a title. She'd collaborated with her friend Violet Kneland, as well as a woman named Lady Phoebe Hunt.

While Sam knew Violet well enough to use first names, he'd met Lady Phoebe only a handful of times, and she'd provoked an intriguing mix of lust and intimidation. She was as much a genius as Letty and the daughter of a marquess, no less. She and Grantham were almost engaged before Margaret Gault returned to England.

Only a massive inhalation of fumes could delude a group of women with such impressive brains into finding Grantham appealing.

The scientists of the Retreat were a lively bunch, and Sam secretly enjoyed lending a hand when they got into various scrapes and tight corners. Although Letty and Violet were mothers now, they still put time into their scientific studies. Their third compatriot, Lady Phoebe, was no longer a member of the Retreat.

She'd gone and shot Violet's husband, then gotten mixed up with some sinister plots. Did she go to jail for this? No. She was shipped off to America and given a job because of her father's title.

Fecking titles.

What ailed Sam specifically was that his latest attempt to invest in a railway consortium had fallen flat. The consortium he'd approached had been full of second and third sons of barons and earls and that sort. Some secret code passed among them allowing them to recognize one another—a code excluding anyone who didn't bleed blue.

Grantham wanted to talk to him about love?

How about *influence*? That is what Sam needed.

"You remind me of myself before I married Margaret," Grantham said. The stupid half smile grew into a full-blown grin when the earl mentioned his wife's name.

"Carefree and ridiculously handsome?" Sam asked.

"At loose ends and needing to put your energy into something lasting, like a marriage."

"Marry." Sam scoffed. "Why would I want to do something so boring?"

The low throaty chuckle and knowing look Grantham threw him made Sam want to cast up his accounts.

"Marriage is anything but boring," said the earl, his smug tone grating in Sam's ears. "Weren't you lately seen with Flavia Smythe-Harrow? You could do worse than to marry a scientist."

Sam had indeed taken the scientist Flavia Smythe-Harrow out for a drive. Once her father heard of it, his further invitations were declined.

Flavia Smythe-Harrow was the granddaughter of a duke.

Sam was the grandson of an itinerant laborer.

"If marriage to a scientist is wonderful, then why didn't you marry the first one with whom you were engaged, eh? Lady Phoebe Hunt?"

Grantham's smile disappeared like quicksilver.

Sam turned to the window and studied the bark-brown clouds of fog creeping over the buildings' roofs.

"She was a founder of Athena's Retreat, has a more elevated title than yours, and was a villainess of majestic proportions to boot," Sam pointed out.

"Sam—" Grantham began with a warning in his voice.

"That's what's missing in my life. A feckin' title. A man who works as hard as I do gets nothing while Lady Hunt gets away with murder simply because her father's title is older than dirt," Sam continued, warming to the subject.

"Sam—" Grantham's voice rose an octave, and satisfaction washed through Sam. About time Grantham heard a few truths.

"In fact, the only thing a woman with a title is good for—"

"Sam!"

The reflection in the window shifted, revealing a dark figure behind him, backlit by the doorway. A cold brick of embarrassment sent Sam's stomach plummeting to his ankles.

"She's standing behind me, isn't she?"

Phoebe pulled air in through her nose and held it until her lungs hurt, then let it release. This was a trick she learned early on in her sojourn to America. Before then, words would spill from her mouth at the slightest provocation. Words with blades attached, meant to draw blood and flay skin.

Words that got a woman in trouble if she had no protector. Luckily Phoebe had found a profession that taught her how to protect herself.

"Hello, Grantham. Mr. Fenley."

Grantham stood as the Fenley boy turned around, his fair skin scarlet with embarrassment. Phoebe remembered him as being much younger than he appeared now. Life amid the secret scientists of Athena's Retreat must prematurely age a man.

"Lady Phoebe." Grantham was as handsome as ever. More so. It blunted the edges of his anger.

Phoebe was not supposed to be here.

Putting the confrontation off for the moment, she turned to the Fenley boy.

Man.

Man-boy.

"I understand you are the owner of this broadsheet?"

Sam nodded, the blush reaching the tips of his ears, turning them flaming pink. "I must beg your pardon, Lady Phoebe. I meant no . . . disrespect."

A laugh rattled at the bottom of Phoebe's throat, surprising her. She kept it trapped, however. No reason to let the man-boy off easily.

"I like the descriptor, *villainess of majestic proportions*. Makes me sound intimidating," she said.

"Oh, you are indeed," Sam agreed jovially, as though he considered it a compliment as well.

"How can we help you, my lady?" Grantham asked, sounding strangled. This must have been the warring emotions of righteous indignation and his ever-present urge to treat her like a wounded bird.

Irritation itched the back of Phoebe's neck. They had a history, she and Grantham.

She'd spent her last years in England riding a whirlwind of rage. Nothing quenched the anger that had built inside her for twenty-six years, and it had to come out somehow. At first, Phoebe turned the rage on herself; drinking, dancing, fucking— even cutting herself. None of it helped. So, she'd turned her rage outward. Grantham had tried to save her. By offering marriage.

They would both have needed rescuing from that.

If there was one thing that angered Phoebe more than being an object of pity, it was being held an object of pity by a man. Grantham may have had the best of intentions, but the more he tried to reel her in, the further out Phoebe ventured into the extremes.

So extreme, Phoebe had committed treason.

As punishment she'd been exiled from England with the threat of prison if she returned without permission.

One of the delightful parts of Phoebe's banishment to America was a life free of traditional expectations. In America, she was simply Phoebe Hunt, a new employee of a private detective agency—not the wreckage that was Lady Phoebe, the daughter of a marquess. No, a daughter of a marquess didn't ride horses astride while wearing trousers, she didn't carry a gun with her, and she certainly didn't wash her own clothes or cook her own meals.

That, however, was what Phoebe had been doing these last four years in America. Along with learning new hobbies such as how to braid her own hair and sew her own menstrual rags.

Keeping her gaze trained on Sam, Phoebe put off the inevitable confrontation with Grantham.

"I need an advert placed, Mr. Fenley. It should go out with this afternoon's edition and in every edition afterward for one week," she demanded.

Sam's brow quirked. "The clerk at the front desk couldn't help you?"

Like his sister, this one. Not cowed in the least by the presence of the aristocracy. The memory of Sam's sister Letty caught her by surprise and a sharp pain, almost like homesickness, pricked her heart.

Once upon a time, she and Letty had been friends.

"What are you here to advertise?" Grantham asked, bringing Phoebe's attention back to him.

She considered making a joke, but the sight of Grantham's clenched fists kept her from such stupidity. Phoebe was not welcome here anymore—an outsider in a home where she never quite fit.

She had changed.

Everything had changed.

"I was under the impression Mr. Fenley was in charge here now," Phoebe said, taking a few steps farther into the room, sizing Sam up with a glance. "Have you not tutored him in the fine art of servicing the peerage?"

The man-boy had filled out nicely. He was taller than Phoebe in her heeled boots, and his well-cut suit displayed his broad shoulders and strong legs to his advantage. He'd a handsome if unweathered face, white skin that had never seen a desert sun, thick blond hair, and eyes the color of a loch she'd once seen in the northernmost part of Scotland.

Rather like Grantham, when he had been younger and oh so impressionable.

Comprehension deepened the blue of Sam's eyes. "Ah. My apologies, Lady Phoebe. I have been too long away from the pleasures of serving the ton and forgotten how uncouth it would be for you to converse with someone as lowly as a clerk."

Phoebe smiled in appreciation at the line Sam strode between obsequious and mocking. He smiled in return and an understanding passed between them; she would grant him permission to mock her pretensions and he would do exactly as she directed.

"Well done, Mr. Fenley," she said. "As I was saying, I need an advert placed in your broadsheet."

Sam took a seat behind a cheap oak desk and drew a pen from a pewter holder. He stared at Phoebe and raised one brow in expectation.

"Auction to be held for building and furnishings at Hunt House, Number 2 Blexton Place, December first. The auctioneers are Singer and Sons and—"

"What are you saying, Phoebe?" Grantham asked, concern drawing lines across his forehead. "Your mother is selling Hunt House?"

"Mmm." Phoebe made a sound of agreement, certain there

was no expression on her face other than boredom. They might be attacked by a swarm of locusts in the next second and her expression would remain fixed. She'd honed this skill in circumstances far more terrible than biblical catastrophes. "In addition, you may print a notice for sale of Prentiss Manor, North Cumbria."

"You cannot mean to sell your family's estate as well?"

Phoebe leveled a bored stare at Grantham. "I mean everything I say. You should know."

Shaking his head to dislodge her last words from his brain, Grantham spoke to her as though she were simple.

"I know your father died last winter—my condolences—but isn't his estate entailed?"

"It is not," she replied.

Grantham's pity softened the angle of his jaw, but his loyalty to England outweighed his compassion. "You were sent notice of his death eight months ago, yet you arrive now? Unannounced?" He glanced over at Sam and swallowed his next words.

Thoughtful of Grantham not to say anything else in front of the man-boy about Phoebe's ostracism. She'd been assured that only a handful of people knew what she'd done and the extent of her punishment.

No need to set fire to already dry kindling.

That was a handy little Americanism she'd picked up along with a slew of curses that called into question her knowledge of anatomy.

Phoebe again drew breath and held it deep within her. The memories and shame roiling her stomach when she'd caught sight of Grantham—memories of who she'd been and what she'd done the last time she was home—she pushed into a tiny ball beneath her diaphragm.

Ever so slowly, the air trickled out of her nose and a delightful numbness spread through her.

That was how one dealt with a conscience. One strangled it. Time for Grantham to leave.

"What do *you* care how long it takes for me to come and mourn my father, George?" she asked. Grantham's head jerked back when she spoke his given name. Phoebe took a step toward him, boring her eyes into his guileless stare.

"Do you regret having given up on marrying into one of the oldest families in England? Are you second-guessing your match with a woman in trade? I hear your wife works *closely* with her male customers."

If Phoebe hadn't numbed herself, the cold that entered the room with her words would have chilled her. Grantham's sympathetic expression melted into contempt, and Phoebe felt nauseous. He stood, bowed to Sam, turned on his heel, and left the room without giving Phoebe a second glance. His abrupt exit was so cold, there should have been frost on the doorknob when he left the room.

"His wife is a woman beyond reproach."

Sam's eyes had cooled to the color of a winter morning and his hand gripped the pen, knuckles white.

"Yes, I know," Phoebe said. "I've met her on a few occasions. Brilliant woman."

Grantham did have a penchant for women smarter than him. Before he'd reunited with Margaret, he'd considered marrying his best friend, Violet. Before that, he'd wanted to marry Phoebe. Both times, the earl saw himself as saving these women by offering them his protection, literally and figuratively.

His wife, Margaret, was the first woman engineer in England—all of Europe actually—to open an engineering firm. A woman like Margaret didn't need anyone to save her. Instead, from what Phoebe surmised from months-old gossip magazines and the occasional letter home, Margaret was the one to save Grantham in the end.

Sam blinked. "Oh. I see. You wanted Grantham out of your business and instead of telling him politely, you insulted him."

"I am, after all, a villainess of majestic proportions." Phoebe smiled.

Sam dropped the pen, leaned back in his chair, and blatantly studied Phoebe. She held his gaze in return without blinking.

"Didn't you try to kill Violet Kneland?" he asked. "Letty's husband, Lord Greycliff, had you sent to America instead of going to trial."

"I did not try to kill Violet," Phoebe corrected him. "I shot Arthur Kneland instead. By accident, if you must know."

It had indeed been an accident. Phoebe had held a gun on Violet but was about to drop it when Arthur tripped and slammed into her, causing the gun to discharge. Into Arthur's body.

The reason Phoebe was holding a gun in the first place?

The same reason she'd been exiled these last four years. A terrible decision on her part for which she could never atone.

No formal action had been taken against her for the shooting nor for her other crimes. Grantham and the men who looked after the scientists at the Retreat had covered up direct evidence. Phoebe agreed not to return without permission from the Home Office and began a new life; first as an assistant, later as a full private investigative agent. The work could be monotonous, humiliating, and often dangerous. Phoebe loved every second of it.

Her father had explained Phoebe's sudden absence from the country as a conversion from science to religion and a deep desire to spend her life as a missionary.

As if *anyone* who'd met her believed that.

Phoebe cleared her throat and turned her attention back to the problem at hand.

"If you are finished satisfying your curiosity, Mr. Fenley," Phoebe said, sharpening her consonants like darts, "I'm a busy woman."

Clever man, Sam left off his questions and took up his pen again.

"I am forever at your service, my lady. Disposing of the family pile, are we? How sad," he said without a trace of pity.

Phoebe liked what had become of Sam Fenley.

Pity never did anyone any good.

2

⊷≪◆≫⊶

I . . . express a wish that you may, in your generation,
be fit to compare to a candle; that you may, like it,
shine as lights to those about you.

–Michael Faraday

"I DO NOT UNDERSTAND, BEE, HOW WE CAN SHOW OUR faces when strangers have walked through our home and touched our belongings. What would your father say?"

The delicate acidity of brandy fumes tickled inside Phoebe's nose, and she savored the liquid in her mouth before swallowing. Her porcelain teacup held Calvados rather than Darjeeling, for she'd known this conversation would require a cartload of patience.

Since patience was one of Phoebe's missing qualities, she substituted drinking for forbearance.

"Father is dead," Phoebe said.

A quick uptake of breath followed this statement as her sister Karolina turned to stare up at the enormous portrait of the marquess that hung over the pink marble mantlepiece in the center of Hunt House's formal parlor.

"Yes, he is dead," the marchioness repeated, "but we still

live, the three of us. What happens to our consequence now? You will return to the colonies, but your sister and I must remain to . . . continue. Somehow."

Phoebe, Karolina, and their mother sat upon exquisitely embroidered seat cushions, cream silk with blue hyacinths. Their tea tray rested on a low, polished teakwood table. Behind her mother's shoulder, however, the rest of the furniture lay shrouded in dustcloths. There were faint squares of darker color on the walls where paintings had been removed and a lone set of footsteps echoed on the floor tiles outside in the hallway where once dozens of servants had scurried.

It had been years since Phoebe encountered this very British setting of faded luxury, and the contrast with the sensible furniture and hand-braided rugs in her home in America was jarring.

"America is no longer a colony," Phoebe reminded her mother, "but I will not leave until you've enough money to be secure, Moti." Phoebe used the childish form of *mother* as her mother had used Phoebe's childhood pet name.

"If you and Karolina wish to stay in London—" Phoebe began.

Moti set her teacup and saucer down with a discordant clank and rose from the silken settee, wandering to one of the windows that looked out over the square.

"I do not wish for this," she said to the thick blue curtains that blocked most of the wan October sunlight.

Phoebe glanced at Karolina, but her younger sister kept her own counsel, appearing as composed as ever.

Quite a painting they would make.

Still Life with Women on the Edge of Destitution.

Missing from this portrait of the Hunt women were

Phoebe's four other sisters. Two of them were dead and two might as well have been once they married. Death was the last resort; marriage allowed her older sisters to escape, to live, and to never look back. Alice, their oldest sister, had married a Lithuanian count while Mari, the next in age, had married a neighbor's son and moved to France with him. They hadn't even come for their father's funeral. An occasional package and a handful of letters were all Phoebe heard from them after they left England.

She didn't begrudge them.

"Will you return home?" Phoebe asked her mother.

Moti said nothing as she pulled the curtains wide, pressing her forehead against the grimy windowpane. The first six months of mourning were over, thank God, and they all had changed from black dresses to half-mourning colors of purple and gray. Moti looked ethereal in a dove gray day dress with ivory lace at the high neck and bell-shaped cuffs.

"Home to Lithuania?" Karolina cradled a teacup in her slender hand, so pale a white, her skin matched the alabaster sheen of the fine porcelain. She, too, had switched over from her black dresses, for which Phoebe was grateful.

The Hunt women resembled corpses when dressed in black.

"We could stay with Alice and her count," Karolina said.

"I don't want to go home," Moti whispered.

An invisible noose tightened about Phoebe's neck; the sensation of suffocating beneath her mother's misery. Her sight clouded except for tiny sparks of light outlining the furniture and her sister's coiffure while a pinging like the tap of crystal against crystal rang in her ears.

In the past when such a sensation came over her, Phoebe retreated into herself to think about her latest scientific paper.

She took refuge visualizing the various experiments in the induction of electric currents.

As a young woman, she'd been obsessed with the work of Michael Faraday. More specifically, the study of electrical currents; those invisible rivers of charges surging through space. The idea of it made her dizzy and happy at the same time. Energy flowed around her, even though she could not see it. If she could, Phoebe would reach out a hand and dip it into the river of electricity, let it seep into her veins and overwhelm the constant buzzing in her brain.

When the worst times were upon her, she would hide in her dressing room and clutch the velvet box that held her razor.

"My lady, you've a caller."

The words broke her spell, and Phoebe fell back into her body, hard. Her mother dropped the curtain as though it were on fire and Karolina clenched the teacup to her chest.

"This is not a time for callers," her mother said, looking at Phoebe for help. "We are not at home on Wednesdays."

Phoebe knew her mother meant not available for social visits, but the phrase *We are not at home* gave her chills.

"Who is it, Jerome?" Phoebe asked.

The dour butler approached her and held out a silver tray. Upon it rested a rectangle of thick cardstock, gold-embossed printing covering the center of it.

How gauche.

Phoebe took the card and flipped it over in her hands while her mother and Karolina remained frozen.

If she got up and ran away right now, would they stay that way forever?

"Please, have Harriet send up another pot of tea and invite Mr. Fenley in," Phoebe said to the butler.

As if she'd uttered a command to them, her mother and Karolina both began to move.

"Who is this Mr. Fenley thinking he might call at this time of day?" her mother asked, walking away from the windows to collect her gloves.

"Is he a friend of yours, Phoebe?" Karolina asked.

Phoebe ran a thumb over the embossing one more time, then threw the card on the table and put on her own gloves.

"I have no friends anymore, Karolina," Phoebe said. "Only cherished enemies."

Sam knew he had more pride than the average fellow. His early success gave him confidence lacking in most men his age. Occasionally, he'd meet someone like the Earl Grantham or Lord Greycliff, who'd seen organized violence, such as war, rather than the spontaneous violence occurring in the narrow streets where Sam had grown up. Those men's brand of confidence was more polished, closer to the surface.

Sam's certainty was belly deep. The result of pulling himself up from the bottom alongside his father, then reaching heights his father had no interest in attaining. Now, at twenty-five, Sam had made a fortune through his own resolve. That same resolve kept his spine straight and shoulders down as he entered the parlor of Hunt House and met the fierce gaze of Lady Phoebe Hunt.

Whenever Sam had visited Athena's Retreat, he'd watched the lady from the corner of his eye.

Gads, but the woman was stunning.

The first time he'd tried his most persuasive smile on her, she'd frozen him with her icy purple stare, and he'd tripped over an end table. That would have been the end of it if she hadn't attended one of Letty's mathematical lectures wearing a rich, emerald-colored gown. Green gown, amethyst eyes, and a snow-white expanse of neck and shoulder. Like setting lady-bugs out for a hedgehog, that combination had a heady impact on him.

That time Sam had barely said two words to the lady before Grantham knocked into him and Sam tumbled backward over a chair. Grantham had apologized, but by the time Sam righted himself, Lady Phoebe had disappeared. He never saw her again after that. She'd gone and blown things up on purpose and Grantham had her sent away.

Now Lady Phoebe examined him like a specimen as he walked in the room, and Sam stumbled when he saw all three women had the same purple-colored eyes.

They posed with the same grace and dignity; long necks, heart-shaped faces, the astringent smell of nobility, possessed of a beauty only the wealthy attained. Skin unblemished by sun or wind, white teeth from eating healthy food every day, and the absence of worry wrinkles around their eyes. Something else as well, some secret symmetry that made a man's heart beat a little faster.

Who knows?

They might have purchased that secret as well.

"To what do we owe the pleasure of your company, Mr. Fenley?"

Sam bowed to the woman who came toward him. He assumed she was Lady Fallowshall, Phoebe's mother, even though she looked only a few years older than her daughters.

Twin crevices bracketed her mouth and deep horizontal lines bisected her brows.

The marchioness must be a worrier.

"I recently had the pleasure of meeting your daughter Lady Phoebe again after a number of years," Sam explained.

Years in which she'd been hiding out in America.

He flashed to the marchioness and then to Lady Phoebe a smile made brighter by years of Tomas's Tin of Terrific Toothpowder. The other woman, Lady Phoebe's sister, he assumed, flicked her gaze away from Sam to the enormous portrait above the unlit fireplace.

Sam followed her glance.

"What an . . . impressive portrait," he said.

In fact, the painting was hideous. The Marquess of Fallowshall had been a handsome enough man. For some reason, however, he had requested to be painted in profile, accentuating an imposing nose—which he thankfully had failed to pass on to his daughters—his foot atop a dead stag, a hunting rifle raised in his right hand.

The man's thin lips were pursed and his eyes narrow. He looked disappointed, as though there wasn't enough blood or gore, as if the animal hadn't experienced enough pain or terror for his taste.

Sam was not a hunter.

"Have you come to admire our artwork?" Lady Phoebe asked, her smile sharp as a knife. "You could have made an appointment."

The sister mouthed something at Lady Phoebe, then blushed when she saw Sam watching her and dipped her head.

This must be the unmarried youngest sister. Sam had read the society gossip sheets before he came to visit. One sister lived in France, another lived in Lithuania, two were dead, one unmarried, and then there was Lady Phoebe, recently returned from America.

Lady Phoebe stared at Sam with the intensity of her fellow scientists yet managed to appear ambivalent over his existence, like her fellow aristocrats. She was taller than her mother and sister, her heart-shaped face thinner, and her shoulders stood out beneath the fine lawn of her dress. Whatever she'd been doing in America had given her muscles.

"I have come in answer to the advert you placed in my newspaper yesterday," Sam said. Another few steps and he stood at the head of the low table in the middle of a lovely parlor set, two cushioned chairs and a settee. Having traded in such materials for years, Sam cataloged its worth and judged he could fetch a nice price for it.

"An advert?" The marchioness put a hand to her chest as though he'd committed some outrage.

"For the auction, Moti," Lady Phoebe said. No one spoke while an exhausted-looking maid brought in another pot of tea and one more tea setting.

Once the maid left, the sister sitting in the far chair cleared her throat. Blushing, Lady Phoebe performed the introductions. Her blush intrigued him, hinting at a living being behind the mask of perfection she wore.

Sam took a seat. Lady Karolina offered him a biscuit on a delicate plate, then poured him tea. Announcing himself pleased to meet them, he set the plate on the table, biscuit untouched.

"It will be a spectacle, this auction," he said affably.

Lady Fallowshall waved a hand before her face as tears appeared in the corners of her pansy-colored eyes.

"To think strangers here, touching our belongings, looking into our private spaces," she lamented. Her accent pulled at the tops of her consonants; they sounded like raindrops on tin.

Lady Karolina pursed her lips and examined her gloved hands while Lady Phoebe made a *pfft* sound and sat straighter.

"If Father wished us to be spared such humiliation, he should have invested wisely," she said.

To most folks, her words might sound hard, clacking against each other like drumsticks in a march. Sam knew better. He'd heard the same fear in women's voices many times before when bills came due and IOUs were called in.

"Out of respect for you and your family, I have a suggestion," Sam said.

The women stared at him as though he were a ghost.

Had he said something crude?

"Suggest away, Mr. Fenley," said Lady Phoebe with a smile that conveyed only derision. "You must have heard along with everyone in London we have no coin and are forced to sell everything. Our circumstances are such we are willing to entertain even the most outrageous of suggestions."

Ah, but the lady had a way with insinuation; a talent for making it sound as though she were doing Sam the favor.

Lady Karolina peered at him, and for the first time he saw the shadows beneath her eyes were nearly as purple as her irises.

All of London spoke of how Fallowshall had been living off his name for nigh on twenty years. When he died without an heir, these women had lost their protection.

Sam had no title and never would have one. He wanted the grease that came with a title. The way it opened doors otherwise locked to men of common birth. The one thing he could not buy.

Well, not *yet*.

"I don't believe you'll find my suggestion outrageous at all,"

Sam said, smiling directly at Lady Karolina. Her creamy skin flushed beneath his stare. She wasn't as regal as Lady Phoebe, but she didn't scare the bejaysus out of him, either.

She would work.

This would all work.

Sam was convinced of it.

"What if someone took this off your hands?" he asked. "The house, the furnishings—all without having to see a pack of strangers wander through your home?"

Lady Karolina and her mother both looked to Lady Phoebe. Sam did as well in acknowledgment of where the power lay in the room.

Elegant to the point of iciness, she tilted her head a fraction of an inch in a way that conveyed many things without her having to say a word.

Things like, *Continue to speak, for now, peasant.*

Or, *It would amuse me to see your head on a spike.*

Also, *My, what a broad set of shoulders on you. I command you to ravish me here and now.*

Probably not that last bit.

"Mr. Fenley, are you telling us *you* are the answer to our problems?" Lady Phoebe asked, disbelief dripping from every crisp consonant.

Nothing cheered Sam more than a challenge.

"My lady, I'm not telling you, I'm promising you. Trust me and I'll take care of your worries."

3

If in such strivings, we . . . see but imperfectly, still
we should endeavor to see, for even an obscure and
distorted vision is better than none.

—Michael Faraday

"BEE. YOU MUST LOOK HERE."

Phoebe had been combing through the bookshelves in her
father's library. As with most of the ton, the books were for
show. There was no way her father had read *The Elements* in the
original Greek. Not in English, either.

Still, a library was the perfect place to keep a secret, and the
reason Phoebe had returned to England was to protect her
mother and sister from the consequences of her own "secret."

The best protection would be if Karolina married a good
man who had money enough to keep her and Moti in comfort
and shield against scandal if Phoebe's crime were revealed.

With her obligations to family satisfied, Phoebe could take
the next step on the path toward a future less clouded with
shame.

A future of her own making, as plain Phoebe Hunt with
only a handful of dresses and forty dollars to her name.

A woman without a past who might someday earn redemption.

Phoebe leafed through the pages of her father's books, making certain they contained no letters or invoices to set the ton aflutter with gossip. A habit handed down in her family from her great-great-grandfather, who never trusted his sons. Even decades later they would find slips of paper—receipts, promissory notes, even love letters—hidden between the pages of Laurence Sterne's, *A Sentimental Journey Through France and Italy*, or a falling-apart copy of *Moll Flanders*.

Not a single treatise on science stood among the hundreds of tomes.

This was deliberate. Most wealthy families took pains to show off their classical educations, often displaying a collection of Bacon's work or a copy of *Note on the Orbit of Halley's Comet*.

Phoebe's father had removed them years ago when his children first showed an interest in the natural sciences. No daughter of his was going to fill her empty head with *facts*. Too much knowledge rendered a woman infertile or hysterical or whatever state it was women were relegated to when they had learned enough to ask questions.

To say no.

"Come in here instead, Moti. I don't want to lose my place on the shelf."

"Bee, have you seen this?"

Phoebe returned a Bible with its pages still uncut to the shelf.

"No, Moti. What is it?" Phoebe held out her hand and Moti gave her a calling card.

"Yesterday while we were listening to the Fenley man, Mr.

Lionel Armitage stopped to call. When he heard we were with a guest, he left this card and a message, if we please, he will return on Thursday when we are At Home. This is not good, Bee."

Phoebe recalled only one Armitage, Fanny, a terrible woman with horrible taste in clothing who had a great dislike for the women of Athena's Retreat.

"Why are you worried?" Phoebe asked, assuming her mother's concern was rooted in superstition.

It was impossible to predict what Moti might find unlucky as there were as many Lithuanian superstitions as there were stars in the sky. Her skin was nearly translucent in the harsh light streaming through the library's windows. It smelled like paper and mold in here, this room having been mostly unused while the marquess was alive. Her father had never been a loll-before-the-fire-with-a-pipe-and-good-old-Euclid-at-his-side man.

"Lionel has taken over for his uncle, Victor," Moti explained. "He is head of the group, the Guardians of Domesticity."

Ugh. Them.

Lapping at the toes of the aristocracy and blaming women for the ills of society, the Guardians were a group of men who had an unhealthy interest in women. Not a sexual interest, although Phoebe believed frustrated sexual urges did have something to do with their rage, but an interest couched as a celebration of the traditional British family and women's role as keeper of the hearth.

Keepers of the bloody hearth her arse.

They had been peripherally menacing before Phoebe left, hanging about Athena's Retreat and haranguing the women who came to hear lectures on science in the public spaces.

In America, they were occasionally mentioned in the

broadsheets, mostly for riling up male doctors against country midwives or apothecaries who treated women prostitutes or those abandoned by their men. They didn't want women using prophylactics, but they didn't approve of menstrual induction, either.

Did they even understand how babies were made?

"His uncle was disgraced, but the nephew, Lionel, is a hero. He did something brave for the Queen, I can't remember what. They have a magazine, the *Gentlemen's Monthly*," Moti explained.

"I can't imagine Karolina would encourage a suit from a man like *that*." Phoebe grimaced when she realized how that might be taken.

Yesterday, Sam Fenley had made them an offer on Hunt House and left them speechless. He'd taken advantage of the silence and asked Karolina to ride with him in the park the next day.

Karolina's acceptance had been hesitant, and afterward, Phoebe had asked her sister if she already had a favorite suitor. Karolina had only raised and dropped one shoulder the tiniest fraction of an inch, pasting on a false smile.

"I am too busy worrying about Moti to think of marriage," she'd said.

She was difficult to read, since Phoebe did not know her well. Karolina was the youngest by seven years and the favorite of their mother. When her father was in London, Moti and Karolina had often stayed behind at the estate.

Hiding, Phoebe supposed.

The only sister to write regularly to Phoebe in America, Karolina's letters came once every few months; simple recountings of everyday happenings on the estate and in town. She'd an eye for the absurd, however, and Phoebe appreciated the humor when nostalgia made her morose.

Moti flitted about the room with the ribbons of her cap fluttering like cabbage moths, stopping to touch a book spine, then drifting off in her pale gray skirts to touch the frame of a mirror or the top of a chair.

"Lady Tremount has been kind since your father died. She has invited Karolina to dinners and balls and even her country house," Moti said. "Lionel was there, at Tremount's last house party. His wife was still alive then, but ill."

Halting opposite the marquess's chair on the other side of the great oak desk, Moti spoke to the empty chair like a penitent, giving Phoebe chills.

"He paid much attention to Karolina, more than was seemly for a married man. Flattering her, making her laugh and talking about . . . I don't know what. Books?"

What books was Karolina reading that would appeal to a man like Lionel Armitage? Phoebe didn't know her sister well enough to answer that.

"He is not suitable, Bee."

He certainly was not.

"I agree," Phoebe said. "We cannot allow Karolina to marry the head of the Guardians. They are narrow-minded and ignorant."

"Psssht." Moti made a sound that meant she'd decided not to have an opinion on a subject because it was one that invited strong opinions, which meant it was an improper subject for well-bred ladies.

She looked away from the empty chair and whispered, "She cannot marry him because the servants say Lionel . . . *punished* his wife."

Like an avalanche of boulders those words conjured the worst days of Phoebe's childhood when her father had the energy and strength to dole out his own "punishments." Relieved she was already sitting, memories of pain and humiliation washed over her, threatening to choke the breath from her.

They never spoke of it, Moti and her sisters and her. An unwritten rule they'd adhered to even in the worst times. *Never* say aloud that the marquess laid hands on them and others in the household.

They turned their attention to escape because none of them were strong enough to stand up to him.

I don't want to do this, but you've made it unavoidable.

Her father's voice was flat and cold when he meted out his punishments. If they would simply behave as they ought, be silent and comely, know what he wanted before he could say a word. If only they could please him, he wouldn't have to discipline them.

"Simply refuse to see the man," Phoebe said once the room stopped moving and she could breathe again.

"No, Bee. Armitage is too powerful. His magazine is read by the men at your father's club. They have written terrible things about dear Lord Grantham and his new wife. Terrible enough they left London for a time. If he wants to court Karolina and we offend him, he might take his revenge in his magazine."

Ah. The revenge would be an article about Phoebe. She'd left the house only once, but inevitably someone would see her. Four years was not long enough for the gossips of the ton to lose their fascination with her. There would be talk. While Grantham might be persuaded to let Phoebe stay to take care of Moti, the rest of the men who had sentenced her were without sympathy.

If she didn't finish this business fast and return to America as soon as possible, Phoebe would find herself in prison.

"Have you lost all sense?"

Sam assumed his sister Letty's question was rhetorical and did not bother to answer. Instead, he spooned more pudding onto his plate, remembering how still Lady Phoebe had held herself—how still they'd been in that vast parlor they couldn't afford to heat.

Stoic or stupid? He hadn't decided yet.

"He hasn't lost his sense, he's lost his heart," his younger sister Sarah said. "Margaret Gault went and crushed it when she wed Lord Grantham."

Now she was old enough to be employed by the family's emporium, his sister insisted on being called her given name, Sarah, not her baby name of Sadie.

"It is grief, obviously," countered Letty. She crossed her arm over the table to pat Sam's hand. "Fermat has only been gone for three months."

Fermat.

Everyone at the table sighed in commiseration. Except for Mam. Mam sighed in relief. She'd never liked Sam's pet hedgehog.

"It smells like rotting mushrooms, it makes a mess, and it bites you when you pet it," Mam had complained. "What on earth convinced you to bring this creature home?"

Da had looked up from where he sat in a winged chair, holding Fermat close to his chest and cooing at the little beast.

"She has the dearest little nose, Mother. Come look."

Da had been as enamored of Fermat as the rest of them and the hedgehog's death brought tears to the older man's eyes.

Mam made a sweeping motion with her hand as if to dismiss Letty's words to the dust pail. "What nonsense. 'Tisn't grief nor is it a broken heart. Lady Grantham is indeed a lovely woman, but our Sam has a sensible head on his shoulders. He's going to explain himself to us again, this time with more detail, and we will see the genius in his plan."

"Genius," muttered Da. "Don't know many geniuses what mess with nobility and 'spect to get the right side of the deal."

"Letty messed with nobility and now she's a viscountess," said Sarah. "You ask me, Letty got the better of that deal."

"Nobody did ask you, brat."

"You're the brat."

Lucky for them only Letty and Sarah were at the table, or the noise would have risen from loud to deafening.

Letty had indeed had messy dealings with the nobility, but she and her husband, Lord Greycliff, were happily married and had produced the requisite offspring, who napped in the kitchen under the watchful eye of a nursemaid.

Sam considered the dish of pudding in front of him as he made circles in the cream sauce with his spoon. The harsh afternoon light filtered through the yellow curtains that hung over sparkling clean windows and bathed the Fenley family in a softened glow. They sat around an oval table that extended out to fit three more guests, four if they didn't mind elbows and knees akimbo, set with serviceable gray pottery plates and cups. A well-washed but slightly stained linen covered the table and a jumble of crumpled napkins and extra spoons cluttered its surface.

His father sat at the place nearest the door and his mam sat nearest the kitchen. The Fenley siblings filled in the six seats between, and when everyone was home, they arranged themselves in order by age: Letty, Sam, Lucy, Laila, Laura, and Sarah. The room smelled of girls, cream sauce, and the cat named Puddles, who sat curled round his ankles.

Home.

Sam breathed it in, then finished his pud.

Time to leave. Maybe wander over to the pub and play a round of darts. Sam rose from his seat but his da pushed him down.

"Oh, no, boy." he said. "You stay right here and tell us the *whole* story, this time. It may be your money, but it's our name you think to use."

Sighing, Sam settled back against the rails of his wooden chair. Despite the money he and his father made from their emporium, Fenley's Fripperies, the family lived in Clerken-well. In a house more fitted for a tailor's family than a family as wealthy as theirs, Laura and Laila, the twins, still shared a room, and his mam employed a cook only for those days she stayed late at the store.

Sam did not begrudge his father those choices. His mam and da were happy and in love, and his sisters were—when not fighting and crying—delightful . . . ish.

This wasn't enough for Sam, though.

"I offered to buy Hunt House and its furnishings."

This set the fox among the chickens once again as they squawked about his foolish ideas and waste of money. Da said nothing, however, and eventually the rest of them fell silent.

"That mansion and every stick of furniture in it costs half of what it will cost to build a new emporium," Sam continued.

"Another Fenley's Fripperies? Why do we need more than what we already have?" Sarah asked.

A question put to him repeatedly.

Sam searched for words to convey the joy he found in visualizing, then completing a project. The freedom one felt when possessing enough money to follow a dream. The satisfaction warming his belly when something changed, right in front of him, because of his actions.

He'd never tell his sisters such a thing, however, they might think him a romantic. Instead, he gave the most logical explanation. "Our emporium cannot keep up with all the customers. Another store will accommodate more customers and wealthier ones at that."

Da sucked his teeth in thought, but Letty had figured it out quicker than most. Pain in the arse sometimes to have a genius sister.

"You mean to turn Hunt House into an emporium on Blexton Place? What will the neighbors say?" she asked.

Sam smiled wide, like a shark who'd had tea with three tasty little minnows.

"That square is on its way down, haven't you heard?" he asked cheerfully.

A developer had bought two other mansions on that stretch of road and broken them up into eight apartments, the perfect size for the families of barristers and bureaucrats.

Sam was an investor in a similar scheme. He'd doubled his money in the first year but was limited to buying smaller houses on less prestigious streets. Invitations to buy a place like Hunt House were beyond his reach without a title.

Or a titled wife.

Letty tapped her chin, bright blue eyes narrowing as she stared at Sam. No doubt calculating the odds he would succeed—or fail.

"Hunt House is close enough to St. James's that shoppers

won't care if they have to walk an extra street over, the rooms are already well set out, and the facade is plain enough we can do what we like to it without having to contend with pesky gargoyles or what have you like they put on their houses in France," Sam continued.

"Hmmm." Da made a noncommittal sound. He and Sam were equal partners in the emporium. Sam, however, had taken his share of the profits and bought the newspapers. With those profits, he'd invested in renovating great houses into smaller, more affordable dwellings for the rising numbers of middle-class folks.

"Was Phoebe there?" Letty asked. "What did she say? How did she seem?"

Sam cocked his head, unable to decipher Letty's tone. Did she miss her friend? Wish her ill?

Lady Phoebe and Letty had been friends back when they were establishing Athena's Retreat, but it hadn't been a comfortable friendship. Letty would complain about Lady Phoebe's cutting remarks and bone-deep snobbery. She believed Lady Phoebe hid her brilliant mind behind her scandalous antics in high society.

Sam got the impression Letty almost pitied Lady Phoebe, despite her exalted family ties and extraordinary beauty.

Something had passed between the Hunt women as they sat below that picture of the marquess, staring at the carcass of the deer and never at the man's face. It wasn't happiness, that was certain. No crowded table with sunlight and pudding for those folks.

"She said she would consider my offer and send word by the end of the week." Sam coughed. Here was the hardest part. "I also invited her sister Lady Karolina for a drive tomorrow afternoon."

"You what?" Letty asked.

"Asked the daughter of a marquess for a drive?" exclaimed Mam.

Sam knew he was in for another round of questioning, but his youngest sister, Sarah, saved him.

"Oi, who ate the last of the pud? I haven't even had my first piece!"

A torrent of feminine outrage followed, allowing Sam to make his escape. He went and hid in his local pub, where the fug of tobacco and beer cleared his nose of the girl smells from home. Sawdust beneath his boots, Sam stood a drink for a handful of men from the area. They played darts and insulted each other's mothers.

Had he lost his mind, considering courting the Lady Karolina?

If Sam couldn't buy a title to ease his way, he could buy the next best thing. The Marquess of Fallowshall's family name of Hunt was listed in the Domesday Book. Fallowshall's roots in Cumbria went back to the first Saxons to hit Britain's shores.

First, Sam would buy the house and the family's favor, and then he'd court the sister. He might not be a Hunt, but his children would be of their line. With Lady Karolina on his arm, Sam would possess a key to those closed doors of Mayfair. No longer would he be excluded from the most lucrative of consortiums or miss out on gossip nudging him in the direction of an even greater fortune.

With a titled wife, Sam would be unstoppable.

Lady Karolina was beautiful; fair skinned with lush

mahogany curls, neck like a swan, and damn but those Hunt eyes. She shared with her mother an air of delicacy, as though she were made of the same stuff as the porcelain she drank from. Translucent. Fragile.

A raucous laugh from the corner of the pub distracted Sam, and he gave another man his darts and wandered over to the bar, ordering a last tankard of ale before time was called.

Unlike Lady Karolina and her mother, Lady Phoebe did not appear delicate. She must have gone without a parasol during her years in America, for her skin was darker than the others' and three tiny wrinkles shaped like cups extended from the corners of her eyes.

"That's time, boys!"

The barkeep rang a bell and Sam finished his drink and walked out into the night, thinking of those tiny wrinkles and how the lady had come by them.

Lady Phoebe's eyes were not a soft purple like pansies, they were hard, like gemstones. Sam had an urge to rattle her and watch that frozen countenance melt.

He always did have a taste for danger. Still, better he keep his thoughts on Karolina. A woman like Lady Phoebe would never settle for a man grasping upward.

Instead, she'd take pleasure in kicking the man down where she thought he'd belong.

4

Respecting the nature of light we have little more than conjectures. It is considered by most philosophers as a real substance, immediately emanating from the sun, and from all luminous bodies, from which it is projected in right lines with prodigious velocity. Light, however, being imponderable, it cannot be confined and examined by itself; and therefore it is to the effects it produces on other bodies, rather than to its immediate nature, that we must direct our attention

—Mrs. Jane Marcet, *Conversations on Chemistry*

"WHAT DO YOU MEAN, LADY KAROLINA IS INDISPOSED? She was fine yesterday."

Sam Fenley stood in the front hallway of Hunt House, his voice echoing off the tiled floors and bare walls. He faced the grand staircase, which split in two, lit by a huge window on the first landing that looked out over the square.

There should be a table where Sam stood, topped by a vase spilling over with hothouse tulips.

Phoebe had sold the table, however, and the Hunt women's budget barely allowed for tea, let alone an expense like fresh flowers.

"Is this about my offer to buy Hunt House?" Sam asked. "Because it's the same whether Lady Karolina goes for a ride with me or not."

"You are sure of yourself for someone so young," Phoebe said, unsure whether she admired this quality or not. "Assuming Lady Karolina's disposition has anything to do with you."

His blue eyes darkened as clouds passed over the sun and the light in the hallway dimmed. There were tallow candles aplenty, but none of the Hunt women could stand the smell, especially not in the rooms where they might be receiving folk. Beeswax candles were too dear, however, and they compromised by using paraffin lamps.

There were none to hand now and Phoebe had to squint to read Sam's face.

"How young?" he asked.

She'd tried to read his face because his tone remained indecipherable. Had he taken offense? Phoebe didn't care.

"I beg your pardon?" She didn't. Phoebe didn't beg for anything.

"However young you think I am, Lady Phoebe, I am old enough to take your sister for a drive. Or you, for that matter."

Was Sam here to court Karolina, or was he angling to make a profit off the Hunt family's desperation?

Even more pressing was the question of why Phoebe's stomach flipped at his last words.

Or you, for that matter.

The clouds moved and Sam's smile looked like a sneer.

"Lady Karolina is unwell today," Phoebe told him. "However,

it is not serious, and she would like to reschedule your drive. Perhaps Monday afternoon would suit better."

When he stepped forward, Phoebe pulled in her stomach muscles and fought to keep from backing up. This was England and although a social-climbing capitalist like Sam Fenley pushed some boundaries, there were others he would never cross.

Still, she flinched.

Sam's gaze flickered over her face and the smirk disappeared.

Damn.

Damn him if pity softened his eyes. Too much to hope his sister Letty hadn't revealed what she knew of Phoebe's past. Back then Phoebe had been too angry to hide her bruises or make up stories to explain her long absences when her father locked her away.

"That is a shame," he said, so gently, Phoebe wanted to shake him. He glanced at the hat in his gloved hands and turned it once by the brim. "The weather is fine today, and I don't know when we will have another afternoon as warm as this one until spring."

Phoebe jerked one shoulder up rudely.

"Will you join me instead?" Sam asked.

Her gasp came out as a cough. "I'm sure I cannot."

"Come with me." His face lit with a grin, and it made him ridiculously attractive.

How annoying.

"I've gone through the trouble of borrowing an open carriage for today, I may as well get some use out of it. I will take Lady Karolina to the opera when she feels better."

Phoebe's chest was hollow enough to echo if she tapped it.

A drive along the Serpentine. How long ago had it been since she was young and carefree enough to take enjoyment from a ride in the park with a handsome young man?

Ages.

Possibly never.

"Don't be stupid," she said without bothering to hide her distress. "You cannot take *me* for a drive. I can't have speculation about where I've been and why I left in the first place."

He took another step forward, but Phoebe was too upset to react.

"What if I want to take you?" he asked, his voice ripe with a cheerful curiosity. He paused, then asked more softly, "What if it was you I wanted to sit next to all along?"

Because her chest was hollow, the beating of Phoebe's heart sounded overloud in her ears. Sam's smile was warm and golden like the sunlight that had returned and spilled down the stairway, illuminating the places on the window where cobwebs had accumulated and the blank spaces where treasures once stood.

"Go away, Mr. Fenley," Phoebe said, her throat tight with anger or sadness, she could never tell which was which. "Come back on Monday for our answer to your offer. About Hunt House," she emphasized.

"As you wish, Lady Phoebe," Sam said, his shoulders level, his chin down a fraction of an inch so he looked her in the eye. "Whatever pleases you."

He was not so uncultured as to whistle a tune when he took his leave, but he wanted to—Phoebe read it in the set of his shoulders and the spring in his gait when he turned and walked away.

"Fec—"

With a strangled yelp, Sam tripped on the threshold.

The ungainly dance that followed as his legs churned and his arms wheeled round like a windmill could have turned fatal if he hadn't stopped himself from pitching face down onto the marble floor tiles.

Instead, he grabbed his topper, which had rolled a few feet away, glared at Phoebe, glared at the floor, slapped the topper on his head, and made his way outside.

Whatever pleases you.

Phoebe sucked in the smell of dust and a hint of citrus.

"Was that the Fenley man?" Moti emerged from the library.

"Yes, that was Mr. Fenley," Phoebe replied.

"Did you walk him to the door, Bee?" Moti asked.

Phoebe turned her head aside and rolled her eyes. Her mother was no longer so superstitious it ruled her days, but some traditions stuck fast. If a guest was not accompanied to the front door, they took some of the house's luck out the door with them.

"We don't have any luck for Mr. Fenley to take with him, Moti," Phoebe said, smiling when she recalled Sam's face when he glared at the floor as if it had grabbed his ankles.

"I am sorry he is come for nothing," said Moti. "Poor Karolina."

Karolina was indeed unwell. Her courses were debilitating some months, with cramps so painful, she could not even walk. Today she lay in bed, surrounded by hot bricks wrapped in sheets and sleeping off a dose of Peterson Apothecary's Monthly Troubles Tincture.

Most remedies for women's menstrual pains were made with laudanum—a derivative of opium. An unscrupulous apothecary might include enough opium in the first dose that a woman would come to crave a second dose, then a third. Soon, she'd sleep the day away, coming out only at night when her pupils had swallowed the color of her eyes, her skin was dull and drying, and her hair greasy from inattention.

Lucy Thorne was a secret scientist with connections to Athena's Retreat who owned an apothecary, albeit in a neighborhood Karolina would never visit herself. Instead, Phoebe sent a servant to fetch the tincture, the only one she knew of that didn't contain either opium or an extract of coca.

"We must hope the Fenley man comes back for her," Moti continued. "Even if Mr. Armitage gives up his suit, there is no end of men who would take your sister for her beauty or her name and not provide for her in the way she deserves."

"Do not worry, Moti," Phoebe said. "We will play least-in-sight with Karolina, bundling her off to Prentiss Manor for a month or two. No one in their right mind would come a-courting there."

Moti worried the dry skin on her bottom lip with her teeth. "If we sell off the houses and everything in them, there are consequences. Everyone will look at us with pity and men like Armitage will see your sister as something to be bought. Mr. Fenley, on the other hand, will treat her like royalty no matter what."

Phoebe snorted. "His sister is married to Lord Greycliff. He isn't without social status."

"His is low enough. Karolina's title will mean something to him." Moti's voice thinned to silver needles of worry. "We will sell it all, yes? Down to the last scrap of carpet. There will be nothing left of your father except for his name. And when you and Karolina marry, the name goes as well."

"And you, Moti?"

"You did not have to come back to take care of me," her mother said, waving away Phoebe's concern.

Phoebe bit her tongue and the metallic zing of blood flooded her mouth.

Once, when her father had been exceptionally angry with her mother, Moti had decided to save her family. She'd woken the girls from their bed in the early hours of the morning and led them down the back staircase and out to the stables. An old turnip wagon was there, already packed with clothing and a hamper of food.

Phoebe and her sisters had not made a sound. Something light and terrifying caught hold of their throats. The youngest, Karolina, was only a babe and slept soundly in Alice's arms.

Moti had stood at the front of the wagon and stared at the reins, then over at the stable. Her mother had not thought this plan through, so Phoebe had slipped off the wagon and gone to stand next to Moti, holding her hand and leaning into her side.

"You have to hitch the horse now, Moti," she had whispered.

Tears had stood in Moti's eyes.

"I don't know how," Moti had whispered back. "I don't know how to do any of this."

Phoebe's sister Rose had volunteered to get a horse from the stables, but it was too late by then. The butler had found them and when he asked where they were going, Moti told him they were going on a picnic.

It was February.

The marquess had teased Moti that afternoon at lunch as though it was a joke. No doubt, to him, it was amusing.

He didn't even beat her for it.

"I am stronger than I was when you were a child," Moti said now. "Fallowshall, he was sick these last years. I had to"—Moti held her hands palms up as if asking permission—"to speak for myself more."

To the small child hidden deep within Phoebe, her mother's tremulous smile was like a punch to her gut. Why couldn't Moti have learned to speak for herself sooner? Speak on that child's behalf when everything went awry?

Phoebe had learned to shut that child up by encasing her in ice.

Still, she hadn't hurt herself in a long time, so she asked, "Did he mention me after I left?"

Moti said nothing. Dropping her hands at her side, she tilted her head as if listening to voices far off, then nodded slightly.

"We missed you," she said. The voices must have continued because Moti turned and walked away as if someone had called her name.

Phoebe stood alone in an empty hallway. This was what she deserved, wasn't it? She'd abandoned her friends, her morals, and her integrity when she used another scientist's work to create a weapon. The weapon had killed someone.

That this wasn't her intention did not matter.

That someone else had triggered the weapon did not matter, either.

The fact remained a man was dead.

As Sam Fenley had pointed out, anyone else would have gone to prison or been hanged. As the daughter of a marquess, Phoebe had been spared that ignominy and sent to America.

Not for her own sake, but for her father's.

The irony that Phoebe's father had imprisoned her on occasion himself did not make up for the wrongs she had committed.

Phoebe knew why her mother had refused to answer her questions.

If Phoebe's father had asked after her, it hadn't been to inquire as to whether she was coming home. It had probably been to ensure she stayed away.

"They're at it again, Fenley."

Sam had turned his wooden chair to face the courtyard window in his office, even though there was no view but a patch of dirt and the windows of the building opposite. On the top floor, Margaret Gault had established her engineering firm.

He had to twist in his seat to regard his editor, Wolfe, who leaned against the doorframe, frowning through his auburn beard. Seeing as it was after hours and the doors of the newspaper were shut, Wolfe had discarded his jacket somewhere and wore only his shirtsleeves and waistcoat. A waistcoat stained with powdered sugar from whatever pastry he'd been eating earlier.

The man was never far from a muffin, biscuit, pastry, or roll and yet was so thin, he walked sideways between the raindrops. Or so Sam's mam claimed, which is why Wolfe was a frequent guest at the Fenleys' Sunday dinners.

One day Sam would have to ask a scientist from Athena's Retreat if folks with bigger brains were the same as folks with bigger muscles—both needing extra food to fuel their energy.

"Who's at what again?"

"Those *scribblers* next door." The word dripped with Wolfe's special brand of sarcasm. Much like powdered sugar, Wolfe was known to sprinkle it generously.

Sam cast a glance out of the window and up toward a

balcony where Margaret once worked. Now that she was a married woman and a countess, she'd moved to a better address.

It hadn't quenched the scandal surrounding her decision to open a women-only firm, nor the scorn heaped on her husband, Grantham, for marrying a working woman, but it did keep her away from the unruly louts next door at the offices of *Gentlemen's Monthly* whenever the Guardians of Domesticity were planning a rally.

Had Sam loved Margaret?

He'd admired her.

But loved her? No. Not in the way Grantham loved her, as though she were vital to the beating of his heart.

Sam preferred a love like his parents'. Comfortable. Full of laughter and acceptance of one's foibles. Complementary and easy. He reserved excitement for his business dealings.

Lady Karolina appealed to him not only for her title, but also because she seemed uncomplicated and sweet. Sam was almost certain he would ask her mother's—and her sister's—permission to court her.

"Fenley. It's been a year since Margaret went and married an earl. Stop mooning about. You have bigger problems."

Sam sighed.

Rising from his chair, he dragged it over to his desk.

"What is it now, Wolfe?" Sam asked, only mildly curious. The articles in *Gentlemen's Monthly Magazine* were achingly pedantic and oftentimes simply a list of grievances. "Have they burned a woman scientist in effigy? Shut Peterson's Apothecary? What cause do we rally today?"

Wolfe ran his fingers through his beard, the two lines between his brows deepening in disapproval at Sam's tone.

Wolfe was of a serious bent.

"They have written an article about you."

What was this?

"Me?" Sam grinned. "I didn't know *Gentlemen's Monthly* wrote pieces on handsome young newspaper tycoons. Did they include an etching of me? Is it flattering?"

Wolfe's long, drawn-out sigh only served to amuse Sam. If he couldn't drive folks up a wall or two, what was the fun in living?

Ambling into the office, the editor sat himself gingerly in the chair mostly reserved for the Earl Grantham when he came to visit. It seemed sturdy enough, but occasionally furniture fell apart after holding Grantham's mass. Wolfe crossed his legs and leaned forward.

Ah. Business, then.

"No. They did a piece about the encroachment of the merchant class in areas once reserved for the aristocracy. You and your housing scheme were given as an example. The words 'trumped up' and 'exploit' and 'vultures' were thrown about."

This was the problem he'd told Grantham of a few days ago. Sam couldn't get past the invisible wall of class standing between his hunger and the men who had access to the feast.

Now *Gentlemen's Monthly* and that puppet, Lionel Armitage, were going to throw another spanner in the works.

"I suppose it would be unadvisable for my broadsheet to run a series on how the next generation of merchants are poised to create new jobs, spread the wealth, and are the most handsome men in London?" Sam asked.

Wolfe shook his head without a trace of humor in his expression. "We are currently running a series on puerperal fever epidemics and whether they are a consequence of overcrowding in lying-in wards."

Ah, yes. This was the subject on which the apothecary Lucy Thorne was advising the paper. Women scientists from Athena's Retreat were frequent contributors to *The Chronicle*. Under male pseudonyms, of course.

Folks like those Guardians were idiots.

Being a genius didn't have anything to do with your sex. It had to do with something in one's brain. Sam didn't rightly know if there was a word for it.

Great brain syndrome?

"I am not going to take space away from a serious article simply to burnish your reputation," said Wolfe, interrupting Sam's train of thought.

Sam sighed. "This is *my* newspaper, isn't it? I bought it from Grantham last year, didn't I?"

Wolfe raised one bushy brow. "Yes."

Silence.

"Then who has the last say over what we print?" Sam asked.

Wolfe sighed. "Face it, Fenley. The earl ruined this place well before you bought the paper. He never said no to those lady scientists. They have first say, I have second, and you? Somewhere behind the clerk out front."

True. Grantham had much to answer for.

"Who is Lady Phoebe Hunt?" Wolfe asked.

What was this?

Sam relaxed against the hard back of his chair and put his hands behind his head. "Friend of m'sister and those scientists. Friend of the earl as well, a while back. Why?"

Wolfe shrugged. "Noticed you personally wrote up the advert for the sale of her family's house. Saw you pulled papers from the archives from four years ago, papers full of stories about a canister weapon that went off at an Omnis' rally and killed a constable."

Genius came in all sorts. Not only scientists, but also reporters and newspaper editors. Wolfe could smell a story one hundred leagues away.

"No reason," Sam said. "She's leaving soon to go back to America. She's no one you and your team of ferrets need to be investigating."

Gah, how Sam hated it when folks raised one eyebrow at him, as though he were transparent and easy to suss. Sam could be a master of concealment if he *wanted* to.

"I smell a story," Wolfe said, a feral look in his eyes. Like holding a piece of bloody meat in front of a starving dog.

Even if Sam weren't trying to ingratiate himself with the Hunt women, he would have discouraged Wolfe from writing the story. He tried to stay far away from the sort of political intrigue that surrounded men like his brother-in-law, Greycliff, who had worked for a secret arm of the government, or Grantham with his ties to Prince Albert.

If those two had wanted anyone to know of Lady Phoebe's crimes, it would have been public knowledge long ago. Sam did not want to anger either of them by setting a hound like Wolfe on their trail.

Sam warned Wolfe away. "Lady Phoebe Hunt was a founder of Athena's Retreat. For that reason alone, we will leave her be. I know, I know"—Sam waved off Wolfe's protests—"you're going to tell me about independent reporting and integrity and such." He stood and walked to the coatrack for his heavy wool greatcoat.

"I am prepared to face the scrutiny of *Gentlemen's Monthly*, because I will overcome whatever obstacles they put in my way," said Sam as he buttoned his coat.

"Because you could out-stubborn a mule," Wolfe allowed.

"That's right," Sam agreed. "Those women scientists, though. They may be as stubborn, but until the rest of London comes around to the idea women are people, we need to protect them and what they do."

Sam put on his topper and tilted it at a rakish angle. "So, leave Lady Phoebe Hunt out of your stories. Besides, a few more weeks and she's gone for good."

5

The real truth never fails ultimately to appear; and opposing parties if wrong are sooner convinced when replied to forbearingly, than when over-whelmed.

–Michael Faraday

"DO YOU KNOW WHAT YOU ARE RISKING WITH YOUR return?" a deep voice growled.

Phoebe first discovered her love for sciences in a round-about manner. In one of the many unused rooms in Hunt House lay some great-great-granduncle's or some second cous-in's third cousin's collection of rocks and gemstones. Among the treasures to be found in the dusty heaps were two ordinary-looking stones. By happy chance, Phoebe discovered they were lodestones.

Magnets.

Even more fascinating than magnetic attraction was the phenomenon of putting like-sides of the lodestones together, whether north with north or south with south, and watching them repel each other.

"Lovely to see you as well, Mr. Kneland," Phoebe said, returning Arthur Kneland's terse greeting.

They were like-sides, Phoebe and Arthur; Violet's bodyguard turned lover turned husband. Both stubborn, both enamored of pistols, and both with a fierce, undying love for the woman who sat on the settee in between them, silent and tense.

It wasn't simply their similarities that repelled Arthur. There was also the small matter of Phoebe having shot him four years prior.

"I'm happy to see I didn't leave a gaping hole in you," she said, irritated at Arthur's tone of voice.

The task of traveling from Hunt House without drawing attention meant she was dressed like a serving girl and had left out of the servants' entrance this morning. As far as subterfuge, it was simple. The agents of Tierney & Co. had trained Phoebe to become another person in the blink of an eye.

This wasn't work, however, and when Phoebe faced down a man, she preferred to be wearing something offensively expensive.

The blue parlor of Beacon House where they sat now was one of Violet Kneland's favorite haunts. Even before Athena's Retreat became reality, Violet, Letty, and Phoebe would spend hours in this room planning their secret haven.

The walls were a simple whitewash, and the rest of the furniture coverings were a soothing mixture of pastel shades and whimsical embroidery with ancient emerald silk drapes pulled back from the windows by brass curtain hooks.

Arthur Kneland looked out of place in a room Phoebe thought of as uniquely feminine. The tall, taciturn Scot had the weathered face of a man who had lived a difficult life out under the sun and stars. Handsome in a dark and brooding way, he'd captured Violet's heart four years ago when he'd been hired to protect her.

From Phoebe, as it turned out, after she'd forced Violet into her workroom at gunpoint, both of them still dressed in beautiful gowns they'd worn to an evening of entertainment at Athena's Retreat.

You created poisonous gas canisters? My God, Phoebe. A man is dead because of them. Why? Violet had asked her.

Why?

Why had Phoebe taken a charismatic but ultimately selfish and shallow man as a lover and created a weapon that he could use against the government?

Because I will no longer sit and wait for the world to change. I will change the world, Phoebe had said over the barrel of a gun. *The corrupt old men in this country will never let us out from under their bootheels. Groups like the Omnis are tools we can use to climb out from beneath their weight.*

What hubris.

You are selfish, is what you are. Violet had shaken her finger, outrage exaggerating her beauty. *You betrayed my friendship and the trust of every other woman in the club. How can you speak of wanting a woman's voice to be heard when you broke faith with the one community who has always listened to you?*

She'd been right.

Instead of listening, Phoebe had done exactly what men did to women all the time. She'd spoken over Violet, convinced the louder voice is the voice that matters, whoever holds the gun holds the power, and rage is justification for violence.

All the while Phoebe was indulging her anger—and her ego—Arthur Kneland was intent on saving Violet. With love and compassion, not force and derision.

Then Phoebe had shot him.

Not on purpose. If Phoebe had meant to kill Arthur Kneland, or anyone, she would have succeeded.

Her aim was impeccable.

Phoebe had been stupid enough to have brandished a loaded gun. When Arthur slipped on a pile of lemon drops Violet had scattered earlier, his feet went out from under him. He'd fallen against Phoebe hard enough for her to lose control of her pistol.

She might have been forgiven by Grantham, if given a choice. He and Arthur had not gotten along when they first met. Grantham thought Arthur too old, too dangerous, and had too many scandals in his past to make an appropriate partner for someone as genuine and sweet as Violet.

Violet, on the other hand, had her own ideas about whom she should marry, and she chose Arthur, a common Scot.

A Scot with a small scar on his side, thanks to Phoebe.

"You aren't the first person to shoot me, my lady," Arthur said dryly from the corner of the room where he'd taken up residence. "I'm resilient in that way."

"Oh, for feck's sake, here we go again."

On the opposite side of the room from Arthur sat Grantham. He must have been a frequent visitor, for he sat on a low bench, the only piece of furniture large enough to hold his massive frame.

"I've been shot, I've been hung, I've been drowned, fa la la la laaaaa," Grantham sang. "Spare us the recitation of how superior a man you are and let's move on."

"Shot four times, actually," said Arthur without a shred of humility.

Violet had said nothing this entire time. She sat on the

settee, to Phoebe's right. Violet, now Mrs. Violet Kneland, had been Phoebe's best friend before Phoebe held her at gunpoint.

Even after, if truth be told.

"... when I was in Canada. There were a pack of rabid foxes chasing after me ..." Grantham droned.

"... once fought an alligator with a hand tied behind my back..." Arthur spoke over him.

Phoebe and Violet had met while Violet was still married to her first husband.

The old goat had wanted an impressionable young bride he could mold into his perfect partner. Violet, with a genius that outshone every scientist Phoebe had ever met, had proved to be unmoldable. Not by choice. If Violet could have pleased her husband, she would have. However, he'd wanted a woman who put her intellect to work on dinner parties and social maneuvering, not toward proving Avogadro's law.

Much of London once called Phoebe the most beautiful woman in the ton, but Phoebe thought Violet deserved that title.

"... rescued the baby bear from the wolf and climbed a tree to ..." Grantham bellowed.

"... twenty-four pirates armed to the teeth and me, with a broken leg, blindfolded ..." Arthur continued.

Round in the places a woman should be round, coffee-colored eyes lined with black lashes so thick, they looked painted on, with a full mouth and clear, pink, creamy skin, Violet was a pocket Venus—if Venus were color-blind and prone to blowing things up.

Violet had had a child two years ago. Such a normal occurrence for a woman of her station, yet so monumental an event, and Phoebe hadn't been there.

Motherhood had only heightened Violet's beauty.

"Is this usual?" Phoebe asked Violet, the first words she'd said to Violet since she'd sat beside her.

Violet glanced to where Arthur stood, solemnly listing every poison he'd ever ingested, then to Grantham, who was rolling his eyes and making vomiting noises.

"They are, in their own sweet way, trying to give us privacy to have this talk," Violet answered.

"No, we aren't," said Grantham. "Don't go and ascribe noble intentions to either of us, Vi. We are simply enjoying each other's company."

"Oh, yes," Kneland muttered darkly. "I enjoy watching you pathetically try to measure up to me."

Like a horn, Grantham's laugh rang brassy and low, reverberating against the walls. "I already measure *past* you, you little gnome. But if you'd like to step outside . . ."

Phoebe stared at her gloved hands and ran them down her thighs, smoothing the wrinkled material of her skirts while Violet shooed the men out of the room, closed the door, and took her seat once more.

"I missed you," Phoebe said. Softly, tentatively as if probing a wound.

"Thank you for your letters."

Phoebe's head snapped up. "You read them?"

"I received them." Violet's head tilted to the side, and she regarded Phoebe with those round eyes, warm with compassion.

Compassion. Phoebe's urge to deflect the undeserved response rose within her, but she quashed it.

She had missed Violet. She *did* love Violet. Only . . . there were times Violet's pity made Phoebe want to scream.

"I'm not hurt that you didn't read them," Phoebe said. This was true. She was surprised Kneland even let Violet know the letters had come. He had every right to hold Phoebe in contempt. "I want you to know in them, I reflect on the conversation we had the night I ruined everything."

My father terrorized every person in his life without repercussions—the opposite, in fact. If there's one lesson he taught me, it is that fear is power, and I want power. I won't be at anyone else's mercy ever again, Phoebe had said that night, holding on to her anger so she didn't burst into tears.

"What was the conclusion you came to upon reflection?" Violet asked her now.

Sucking in the tea-and-biscuit-scented air, Phoebe cleared her mind of anything extraneous as she sought an answer. The perfect answer. The one that would heal the hurt between them.

"My ultimate conclusion is fear is not power."

Violet said nothing.

"Fear is a trap." Phoebe took a sip of her tea and continued. "It trapped the women in my family. We couldn't flee nor fight. For years we were static."

Much of how Phoebe and her family related to the world was due to their inability to escape the invisible glue beneath their feet. Phoebe had courted scandal after scandal in a desperate effort to break the stasis.

Picking up a biscuit, then setting it back, Violet frowned. She was thinking.

Violet's brain whirred and clicked while she measured and probed the question.

"You wanted to make people afraid of you so you would be as powerful as your father," Violet said.

"Yes. No."

When Phoebe was sent to America, she'd met many powerful men. Some had power by dint of their intelligence. Others because of their raw strength. Many were petty bullies, possessed of no outstanding qualities other than a talent for intimidation. In fact, those who were the most feared were the most flawed.

"I understand why you did it, Phoebe." Violet sighed. "... but it wasn't until I saw what rage against your father's cruelty had done to you—turned you into someone I no longer recognized—that I truly understood why change cannot come through terror."

A lesson that took four long years in America for Phoebe to learn as well.

"You could have asked me for help," Violet said sadly. "If you came to live with me, I'd have protected you from your father."

"I know," said Phoebe. "That is why I never spoke of it plainly to you and Letty. You would have tried, and he would have killed me."

Violet winced and shook her head at the words.

Perhaps they sounded melodramatic, but they were true. Shame burned Phoebe's skin, making the cheap wool dress she wore too hot and too tight.

"I am sorry, Violet, for holding that against you when you had no control over it. I was jealous and petty and small. I hope someday you can forgive me." Phoebe owed her even more truth, so she continued. "I will never stop raging against ignorance, or injustice, or cruelty against women and children. I want a better world than the one we live in now."

"The question is, if you are to change the world"—Violet's eyes lost the soft focus she'd been employing and turned dark with humor—"what tools are needed, and might they explode?"

My God, how Phoebe had missed her. At night, cold and alone, an ocean away, Phoebe dreamed of the hours spent quipping about the potency of a gas made from male egos. How lovely if, someday, they resumed their comradery and, together with Letty, whiled away the hours drinking too much and eating just enough to give them bad ideas.

"Convince Arthur not to jail me once I finish my tea," Phoebe said. "I promise I will leave the same day that I am assured my family's finances are strong enough to keep them comfortable."

Violet's spine straightened and her smile dimmed. "You do not have to go back to America," she said. "Arthur knows my opinion and I will speak with Grantham and Greycliff. You've suffered enough, Phoebe."

"Don't worry, Violet. I am not a martyr," Phoebe assured her. "I want to go back." The truth was thick and smooth, like the taste of butter on her tongue. "I have made a life over there. One where I am not the daughter of a marquess. One where I am Phoebe Hunt; a private detective with strange eyes and excellent taste in clothing."

"... be a jackass and go tell Vi what happened ..." That was Grantham bellowing out in the hallway. Kneland's retort was too soft for them to hear, but the sound of Grantham falling to the floorboards was not.

"Excuse me for one moment, Phoebe," Violet said apologetically. "This won't take long."

Phoebe did not stay in her seat. Revealing more of herself in these past ten minutes than she had in all the years she and Violet had known each other, Phoebe was exhausted. Her apologies were important, the first step in forgiving herself for the death she'd caused, but honesty and kindness became *tiring* after a while.

Villainesses of Majestic Proportions had a limited amount of patience with being humble.

"Why are you on the floor, Grantham?" Phoebe asked once she'd followed Violet out into the hall.

A scowl carved lines into the earl's face that hadn't been there four years ago.

"I am inspecting the molding," Grantham snapped. "Why do you *think* I am on the floor?"

"You are on the floor because your arse bounces ever so sweetly when I toss you over my shoulder," Arthur said.

The insults had a practiced feel to them and no real heat. Phoebe didn't need to watch Arthur and Grantham playact to know everything here had changed since she'd left. The two men were friends now, and Violet exuded a quiet confidence, leaving Phoebe wistful.

How tedious.

Phoebe stepped over Grantham and faced Arthur head on. "Thank you for letting me visit with Violet."

He leveled a black-eyed stare at her, then nodded briefly. Not exactly an enthusiastic hug, but at least Phoebe wasn't on the floor next to Grantham.

"You will leave—"

Phoebe nodded and held up her hand, palm out, to stop him. "I will not come back. It would hurt my pride were you men to put me in prison. I would much rather be the one to imprison men instead."

She turned and studied Violet, memorizing her friend's tired brown eyes and ill-fitting dress.

"Thank you for seeing me, Violet. Thank you for letting me apologize. No, please—" Phoebe shook her head. She didn't want Violet accepting the apology simply because Phoebe had come here to make it.

"If you will excuse me," she said, straightening the cuff of her jacket and inspecting her skirts for stray spiders. "I must be home by two."

Hopefully by the time she arrived home, her detachment would return, and the burning indignity of apologizing would be over.

"I TRULY APOLOGIZE, MR. FENLEY."

Hope be damned.

Instead of apologizing, she wanted to strangle Sam Fenley. She couldn't, however, since he had just helped carry her mother from the room.

Phoebe had arrived home from the visit with Violet with a bellyache from being *nice* to people, only to realize she'd forgotten the "discussions" with their solicitor, Moti, and Sam Fenley.

"When will you want to move your family into Hunt House?" the solicitor, Mr. Nicely—of all the strange names—had asked Sam. The group was sitting in Father's office, but Moti had dissuaded anyone from sitting in her father's chair.

Staring at the empty space, Phoebe wanted to scream. If she started, though, would she be able to stop?

"My family lives in Clerkenwell and are content there," Sam replied. "My plan for Hunt House is not to use it as a residence. Instead, I see the property playing a crucial role in expanding the reach of my family business, Fenley's Fr—oh, dear!"

A horrified gasp, a rolling of the eyes, and Phoebe's mother chose that moment to faint.

Sam and Mr. Nicely jumped to their feet, calling for smelling salts, then escorting Moti out of the room to a settee next door.

Had her mother truly been so aghast at Sam's news or was she being a canny negotiator? Probably both. Phoebe took advantage of the empty room to lean over and read the contracts upside down.

When Sam and Mr. Nicely returned, they found Phoebe well prepared to negotiate on her mother's behalf.

"I must apologize," Sam said. Poor man had returned with skin a shade grayer than before. Mothers mustn't swoon as regularly in Clerkenwell as they did in Belgravia. "I should have thought about how she would receive my news."

Phoebe did not try to comfort him. His bad conscience was to her advantage as she began negotiations.

They didn't last long.

"Well, that is a . . . a sum I believe the family will agree upon." Mr. Nicely had tried to hide his surprise at the generous amount Sam offered—much higher than he or Phoebe had expected. If Sam went ahead and signed the papers in front of him, Mr. Nicely and a good many creditors would be paid in full.

Phoebe, however, gave no hint in her expression of what she thought.

Bad tactics.

Never appear too eager.

Most folks are keen to puncture someone else's joy.

"It's simply a sum reflecting Hunt House's worth." Sam's eyes twinkled, his grin shouting his contentment to the world.

Sam Fenley's contentment seemed impervious to puncture.

"I am happy to discuss details at a later date," Sam continued, "My da—my father will want to be present for part of this. The ladies may take with them their belongings . . ." He paused, then shot a glance at her father's empty chair out of the corner of his eye. "Paintings and such. Large portraits and the like."

Large portraits?

Mr. Nicely had no quarrel with this request and soon took his leave of them. Phoebe glanced at the open door, then back at Sam, but he seemed unmoved by the breach in propriety.

She supposed being a woman of thirty and unmarried made her no longer sexually appealing and thus exempt from society's strict rules for chaperoning gentlewomen. More pressing matters occupied her brain, however.

"You are turning Hunt House into a grocery?" Phoebe crossed her arms and glared at Sam.

"Not a grocery, my lady. An emporium the likes of which London has never seen."

Oh, but that would have made her father furious. She pictured him sitting behind the desk.

The more furious he became, the quieter his voice. This forced the unsuspecting object of that fury to lean forward to hear him. Phoebe's shoulders hunched. Even in death her father had the power to terrify her.

When would she be free of fear?

Phoebe coughed to clear her mouth of the rusty taste of resentment.

"What?" Sam asked, no doubt prompted by her pained expression. "Will the Hunt ancestors be turning in their graves?"

A draft from beneath the door pushed at the hem of her skirts, and Phoebe shuddered. The air was cold and stale, and the back of her neck prickled, thanks to her own morbid turn of mind and Sam's careless language.

It smelled of mausoleums and the dark.

"The Hunt ancestors sleep lightly," Phoebe said. "Be careful of what you say lest they overhear you."

Sam's brow wrinkled.

Knowing Letty and how sensible she was, Phoebe assumed the Fenley family didn't talk much about unquiet spirits or vengeful ghosts. Theirs was a life of beans and toast, counting pennies, and church on Sundays. A regular British upbringing free from violence and tragedy. Delightfully mundane.

Meanwhile, Sam walked along a row of shelves, peering up at the leather-bound volumes stamped with gold. His volumes. His shelves, as soon as the money was transferred into their bank and from there on to Father's creditors.

Sam's offer had saved them from the worst of Fallowshall's debts.

Next, Phoebe had to find someone who would buy their country seat, Prentiss Manor. Her father's family had been so certain of an unbroken line of male heirs, they had never entailed the property. That her father was the last male Hunt in existence brought Phoebe great joy. Once they sold everything, Karolina would have more choice as to whom she might marry and enough money for her and Moti to live comfortably if she chose to remain unmarried.

A quiet ending to a tumultuous tale.

"A week is perhaps not long enough for you ladies to pack for your journey north to Prentiss Manor," Sam said, speaking to the bookshelf, appearing fascinated by a handbound set of Greek tragedies.

Phoebe had already shaken each of these volumes out the

day before. Sam didn't seem like the type to sit by the fire with a pipe and Euclid, either, but if he did, he wouldn't find secrets hidden therein.

"If you need more time—"

Phoebe waved his concern away. "We do not need to pack too much. The visit will not take more than a few weeks. Once we catalog the art and furniture stored in the manor for the auctioneers, we shall return to London and try to find an auctioneer."

Nodding absently, Sam craned his neck to peer at the volumes on the highest set of shelves.

He didn't ask where Phoebe's family would stay once they returned.

Phoebe hadn't figured that out yet.

One humiliation at a time.

"I was surprised to see these were the only books in the entire house," Sam said. "Where do you keep your instruments and science periodicals? You will want to bring them with you wherever you are settling."

He glanced at her with a frown.

"Where *are* you settling after this, Lady Phoebe? Must you return to America?"

"Indeed, I must. As you said to Lord Grantham the other day," Phoebe said, trying for a light tone, "I am a villainess. I may not have been sent to trial, but I have been judged and punished, nonetheless."

Sam's brows lowered. "The constable who died?"

The constable.

He had a name, the dead constable.

Henry Witherspoon.

She'd never seen a picture of the man, only heard a few

descriptions. So, it was a featureless face whispering to her in the darkest hours of the night. A stranger she would leave a loaf of bread for on All Souls' Day.

"Yes. He was at the rally where the Omnis used the chemical weapon I created," Phoebe said.

Mr. Witherspoon had one child and a wife with a red birthmark beneath her ear extending to the center of her chin who sprinkled her sentences with pleas to God that he be willing.

Phoebe had stared at the birthmark the entire time she spoke with Mrs. Witherspoon, offering an apology the woman didn't seem to understand and an enormous amount of money, which she understood well.

It hadn't been enough to assuage Phoebe's guilt or satisfy those who knew the truth of her involvement.

Grantham and Letty's husband, Lord Greycliff, had arranged for Phoebe's banishment to America. They'd put her in the care of Tierney & Co., a private investigative firm that billed itself as accountants, only the books they balanced were more often metaphorical. They had two offices, one in London and one in Philadelphia.

At first, her role had been to ingratiate herself with whatever iteration of "society" there was in various cities and to gather information for Tierney & Co. agents. Phoebe's notoriety hadn't made the scandal sheets in America, and even if it had, her lineage more than compensated. Whether that meant fighting to stay awake during the most stultifying dinner conversations with slack-jawed fools who'd never met a lady before or drinking whiskey with men and women who spoke openly and often about the number of animals—and sometimes people—they'd killed, Phoebe never said no to an assignment.

She'd never felt so *seen* in her entire life. It had become addictive.

She had found her place.

Phoebe suspected if she told stories about her years in America, Sam Fenley would be the person who would most enjoy them.

"Grantham has promised to keep me from prison until I can be sure my mother and sister have enough funds to live on without being hounded by creditors. I'm hoping the sale of Prentiss Manor and its furnishings will go quickly. I don't want to test his—or anyone's—patience."

"And your science?"

Phoebe stared at Sam from the opposite side of her father's old desk as he continued to move, glancing at her occasionally with what seemed like idle curiosity.

What piercing eyes this man had when he wasn't beaming like an incarnation of Apollo. How annoying.

They had pulled back the curtains to let whatever sunlight might fall from the leaden sky into the room, hoping not to use precious oil or candles. Even in the murk of London's ever-present fog roiling up from the sewers and cascading from chimneys, conspiring to turn the entire city brown, Sam stood out with an inner light of his own, the center of attention with his guinea-bright hair and white teeth.

What was the point of being likable?

Sam Fenley was a man. He could have whatever he wanted simply by taking it. He didn't have to waste his time charming people or being friendly. Didn't he understand the power he held?

"My science got someone killed," Phoebe reminded him.

"When my father found out what I'd done, he took every note-book and periodical, my instruments, and anything else of mine he'd no use for—and burned it all."

Phoebe recalled her father's voice the night before she left for America, unemphatic and devoid of any emotion greater than irritation.

I do not ever want to hear your name again, girl, he'd said.

Phoebe had bitten her tongue to keep from asking if he even remembered what her name was, for she feared she wouldn't make it out of his office alive had she made the slightest sound.

She was so taken up in her memories, Phoebe hadn't noticed Sam's wanderings had taken him to her side. He leaned one arm on the desk, inches from her hip. She recalled Sam's words to her the week before.

What if I want to take you? Sam had asked her. *What if it was you I wanted to sit next to all along?*

Those words had taken up residence in the back of her head and tapped against her temples at night before bed.

If long ago, things had been different, if Phoebe hadn't been so angry, could she have loved a man like Sam Fenley; golden and smiling, whose laugh came from the belly, who was kind to children and strangers without calculating what it cost him or what he should take in return?

His blue eyes weren't innocent. He'd have seen a thing or two growing up in Clerkenwell, but he was pleasant and generous.

Sometimes the world was kind to such people.

Sometimes the world crushed them.

Phoebe admitted to herself—she would not like to see Sam Fenley crushed.

"Will you take a carriage to Cumbria?" he asked.

The words sank in, and Phoebe blushed at the direction of her thoughts. Stepping away, she turned to the window and frowned at the untrimmed hedges out front.

"We sold the carriages last week," she said, pushing her finger against the dirty glass. "The Hunt women will ride in a public train car for the first time. It will be quite the experience. I may have to dose my mother with laudanum, but I'm certain we shall survive."

Sam's gaze rested on the back of her neck, his unspoken questions picking at her nerves. She couldn't tell him about America, about her father, about the ghosts.

A flare of jealousy cramped her stomach. Unlined skin, untried heart—she'd been right the first time.

He was still a boy.

Meanwhile, Phoebe never felt anything but older than her years.

She turned and left the room without another word.

Boys could be ignored.

It was men who worried her.

"I'm not asking you to spy on her," Grantham said. "I'm asking you to be observant and—"

"You are asking me to spy on her," Sam objected.

Once again, Sam found himself opposite a desk from the Earl Grantham, but this time they were joined by Sam's brother-in-law, Lord Greycliff.

Before Letty married him and turned him into a besotted fool—besotted both by Letty and their babies—Grey had been director of a semiautonomous "information gathering" department.

Sam, on the other hand, was a businessman—an honest one at that.

This world of espionage and investigations and secret scientists was one he had no interest in joining.

"I told you the other day when we spoke at your office, people are worried about hunger." Grantham pinched the bridge of his nose. "Ask Grey if you don't believe me, but the Omnis are regrouping. Is it only coincidence Phoebe is back in England at the same time?"

The Omnis, or Omnium Democratia, were a group like the Chartists, advocating for workers and demanding the government allow for one man, one vote. They had been led by Adam Winters, a charismatic man who also happened to be Phoebe Hunt's ex-lover. The man for whom she'd designed a weapon.

"So what?" Sam asked. "Let them regroup. Universal suffrage is a worthy cause. Simply because some of them were overzealous—"

"Someone was killed," Arthur said.

"It wasn't Lady Phoebe's fault," Sam said.

Lady Phoebe didn't deserve his protection, but the way everyone spoke of her irritated him. A majestic villainess she might be, but the past few weeks had shown him Phoebe was less terrifying than he'd once thought. She had a dark sense of humor, yes, but it never became cruel. He'd observed her patience with her mother as well; a high-strung woman who looked as though she might float away at any moment, the marchioness looked to Phoebe for answers.

If pressed, Sam would admit he enjoyed Lady Phoebe's company. There was a certain thrill to engaging with her. Much like the combination of terror and exhilaration one feels when walking a ledge high above a ravine.

"Letty told me while Lady Phoebe invented the weapon, she wasn't the one who set it off," Sam reminded them. "We don't go around condemning the Manton family because they make dueling pistols."

"She designed the weapon for Adam Winters to use. She didn't design it for show," Grey pointed out.

"I never understood why Phoebe cast her lot in with him. He was all talk and no action." Grantham crossed his arms, mouth puckered as though the words tasted sour. "Phoebe was the real brains of that group."

Sam ignored Grantham and examined his brother-in-law. Grey might have gone soft in the head from love, but he'd a solid sense of right and wrong, and Sam trusted his opinion.

"Do you believe Lady Phoebe has come back to England to kill in the cause of universal suffrage for *men*?" Sam asked.

Grantham and Grey exchanged a glance and Grey stroked his chin in thought.

"Let's leave the question of motivation aside," Grantham said. "The Omnis may not even be a threat this time around. Grey, can you still call in favors with Military Intelligence?"

Grey nodded. "I'll get some men out there and ask questions as discreetly as possible. We won't bring up Phoebe's name unless we must. Hopefully, she will have left before anyone else in the government wonders why she is not in prison."

He looked over at Sam, a question in his eyes.

"I won't be party to mistreatment of the Hunt women," Sam said firmly.

"You are an idiot if you think Letty would let us mistreat her friend." Grey's face looked to be carved of marble.

An intimidating man, to say the least.

"I did question Phoebe's commitment to the cause," Grey

continued. "She carried on with Adam Winters because it would horrify her father, not because she was a republican. In fact, she thought women should be given the vote and men stay home to mind the children and increase their skills in the bedroom."

A sound halfway between a cough and a cry flew from Grantham's mouth.

Sam rolled his eyes. "Before you make a cake of yourself and announce how you don't need help with your 'skills'—"

"Well, I don't," muttered Grantham. "I happen to be a *spectacular* lover."

"For feck's sake, will you listen?" Sam interrupted him. "I promised the marchioness I would keep away crowds of strangers."

Lady Fallowshall had been trembling with anxiety when Sam had proposed an auction right there on the manor's grounds. Phoebe had held her mother's hand with surprising tenderness and asked Sam to send someone to catalog anything of great value.

"If the ladies allow, I will transport them to Prentiss Manor," Sam explained. "Once there I will recommend which pieces to sell and arrange for them to be transported back to London."

"For a price," Grantham scoffed.

Sam bristled. "For a fair price," he snapped.

"How will you explain abandoning your business interests?" Grey asked, ignoring the earl.

"If the Hunts will allow me to auction the items, I will receive a commission. This more than pays for the trip. Wolfe and the scientists can handle the paper. If I see or hear anything out of the ordinary, I will tell you. I will not, however, go creeping round and unearthing another family's secrets."

Grantham grumbled to himself, but Sam didn't care.

"I know Lady Phoebe shot Kneland, but it was an accident by all accounts. She's not going to shoot me, not if I'm the one who's going to set up her family so she can go back to America and do whatever it is she was doing there."

"If I went, too . . ." Grantham began.

Sam let his annoyance with the earl get to him and raised his eyebrows in a suggestive manner. "Oh, canny idea. You go to Cumbria with Lady Phoebe, and in the meantime, I'll stay here and see to entertaining Margaret while you're gone. You're the one told me I'm missing out on something."

Grey admonished Sam. "Don't you start a fight with Grantham. Listen. We're not asking you to search through their belongings. We cannot send an agent to Prentiss Manor—it's too isolated and there are only a handful of long-serving staff."

"I tell you once again; she is leaving for America the second she has the funds from selling the manor."

Sam did little to hide his frustration that an earl and a viscount were more likely to agree with each other than with a mushroom like him.

"The Corn Laws will be repealed with or without the influence of the Omnis," he said. "All this concern is overwrought."

"Take note of visitors and what, if anything, Lady Phoebe says about her past actions with the Omnis," said Grantham, his blue eyes hardening. "I'm sure you can agree to *that* at least."

Ridiculous.

Whatever secrets Lady Phoebe kept were her business. So long as she didn't have diagrams for a new weapon hung in the Prentiss Manor parlor, Sam doubted there would be much on this visit to surprise him.

6

⸎⸎⸎

Light is an agent capable of producing various chemical changes. It is essential to the welfare both of the animal and vegetable kingdoms; for men and plants grow pale and sickly if deprived of its salutary influence.

–Mrs. Jane Marcet

"I UNDERSTAND THE GREAT WESTERN RAILWAY WILL soon stretch to Cumbria," said Karolina.

"Hmmm. Some enterprising persons could build a railway bridge right over Hadrian's Wall. That will show those Romans," Sam replied.

Karolina gave Sam a weak smile, unable to discern if he was joking or not.

"Well, it would have been a sight easier had it gone past Liverpool, but beggars can't be choosers," Phoebe said. Indeed, beggars would have been delighted to find themselves in the Hunt women's position.

Sam Fenley had come to call—this time at the proper hour—a few days before they were to leave, and offered to accompany them north and inspect the manor as a potential investment.

Rather, he'd made a show of asking her mother if she might grant him the privilege of hosting them on a private railcar from Victoria Station to Liverpool.

Moti had agreed before Sam finished speaking.

Phoebe had her doubts, but in the end agreed as well. She suspected Sam was more interested in inspecting Karolina as a potential investment, and that was fine with her. Phoebe shared her mother's disdain for Lionel Armitage.

The slight burn in her chest at the thought was due to her change in diet since coming home. Certainly not envy.

Certainly not.

Indeed, Sam spent the first leg of the journey attempting to charm the marchioness and succeeding in charming Karolina, if her sister's pretty blushes were any indication. It made no difference to Phoebe that Sam's flirting was reserved for the other two women. With her, Sam spoke directly as though to another man.

Phoebe appreciated his businesslike manner. She was not disappointed Sam hadn't tried to make *her* blush or laugh.

After a while, the train's swaying motion lulled them. Moti and Karolina closed their eyes. Phoebe sat on a bench at the back of the railcar, staring out at the landscape. Her passion in science was electricity, but any powerful phenomenon was enough to engage her interest. The combustible engine was a triumph in engineering, and she relished the thrum of rails beneath them.

For a while, Phoebe amused herself by peering out the window and trying to calculate how many miles per hour the train might be going based on how fast they passed stationary objects, but her speculations were interrupted when Sam came and sat next to her.

"Are you enjoying your trip, Lady Phoebe?" he asked.

"My mother is enjoying the trip," she replied. She kept her face pointed toward the window but stared out of the corners of her eyes, arrested by the sight of Sam's thigh pressed up against her skirts.

Phoebe had ridden the railways in America—the cars available to paying customers, not the luxury of a car like this—and had myriad tricks up her sleeve to dissuade men who thought to use the motion of the train to "accidentally" rub up against her.

Her favorite was asking whether the man had seen the pet snake traveling in her dress pocket. The snake wasn't too poisonous, but if the gentleman could stand up and look . . . ?

This was in her second year as an agent of Tierney & Co. The first year she wasn't allowed more than five feet from her mentor agent. Luckily, her mentor promised to take good care of Phoebe's snake while she was gone.

"I am happy to provide Lady Fallowshall with these small comforts," Sam said.

Phoebe did turn her face away from the window then and rolled her eyes at his unctuous tone. Sam hadn't been able to hide his raised brow and quick gape when he came aboard the car.

"*Small* comforts? Spend much time in private railcars before today, did you, Mr. Fenley?"

The words slipped out like a blade, and she winced. Why must she be so ready to cut without thinking of how her words might wound?

Undaunted, Sam leaned over the slightest bit, bringing his entire side up against her arm. He pointed out the window and said something about not having to breathe in the soot from the engine, but Phoebe wasn't paying attention.

Her body, this bundle of skin and bones she thought had long since stopped feeling anything, was reacting to Sam's nearness.

What betrayal was this?

Perhaps something in his pomade, or the lye used in bucketing his white shirt or even his shaving soap—the chemical combination must be responsible for the tingle in her thigh, the prickly heat of her skin, and the traitorous part of her brain agreeing with her body that Sam Fenley was an attractive man.

She hadn't been awakened to sensation in a long time, and she was . . . uncomfortable with the fact it was Sam who had precipitated it.

His interest was in Karolina. As it should be. Phoebe's discomfort hardened into annoyance, and she pressed her forehead against the window, ignoring him until he went away.

The moment they disembarked from the train, Sam had hired not one, but two carriages to take them the rest of the way to Prentiss Manor. Thanks to Sam, the Hunt women were traveling on padded cushions with warming bricks at their feet, in carriages with springs intact and a set of drivers who treated their horses humanely.

There was no reason for Phoebe to keep her distance from Sam. It must have been a fluke what happened on the train.

Perhaps she'd eaten something off and she suffered gas.

By midafternoon of the last leg, they agreed to stop at an inn for luncheon, as they would not arrive at the manor until dusk.

"My editor, Wolfe, wants to write a story on the Guardians

of Domesticity since Victor Armitage is no longer in charge," Sam said while settling them in a private room and calling for tea. "It seems since his retreat from society, his nephew has taken an interest in the organization." He put his elbow on the table and leaned in to set his chin on his hand. Phoebe bit her lip when his elbow slipped in a puddle of beer and he almost banged his chin on the table.

Appearing unperturbed, Sam leaned back in his chair and surreptitiously tried to wring some of the beer from his sleeve. "Lady Karolina, do you know Lionel Armitage? I know he goes out in society a great deal."

Phoebe choked, disguising it as a cough, but Moti did not turn a hair.

"Lionel Armitage? His father, Percy, has a knighthood for some favor he did the old king, George, but no one knows what it was," Moti told him.

"I met him last summer," said Karolina. "He is a cousin twice removed through Lord Tremount. He is well read and charming."

Sam frowned at her words and the hint of approval in her tone.

"I have heard Lionel's wife died of a broken heart," Moti supplied.

Sam's smile was enough to lighten the room despite the blanket of gray smothering the Cumbrian landscape. "How awful," he said cheerfully. "He must be a monster. Tell me more."

"The rumor is she was betrothed to a man she loved, but her father forced her to marry Lionel," said Karolina. Her nose wrinkled as though she smelled something foul. "Though it is *only* a rumor. We shouldn't be gossiping about family."

Sam left the subject of Lionel Armitage easily enough but continued to ask about the minutiae of the ton. On and on, Sam brought up this lord or that gentlemen. Moti and Karolina seemed to know gossip about them.

"How have the two of you been spending your days while I've been gone?" Phoebe protested at one point. "Sifting through the rubbish bins of the great houses?"

This was something Phoebe had learned over the past four years. People think they are discreet, but they forget—trash has another story to tell.

"Why look in rubbish for gossip?" Moti asked. "All you have to do is appear bored, like this." Her mother proceeded to stare off into the distance, untouchable.

Impenetrable.

". . . and people talk so much they don't know what they say," Moti concluded.

Karolina agreed. "People like to think they are great debaters, but you cannot argue a point if you do not listen to the other side. Instead, they talk about themselves incessantly."

Sam looked surprised, as if only now figuring out Phoebe's sister had a brain.

Her late father and his cronies took it as a personal offense when the women in their lives had an educated opinion on a subject. Even worse if the opinion differed from their husband's or father's.

Sam, by contrast, appeared enthralled with the women's conversation, asking respectful questions and, when appropriate, teasing them with silly jokes and witty insights.

Their voices grew thinner, and the laughter stopped as they resumed their journey, leaving the smooth road of the turnpike on to a lane bordered on both sides with gorse and a scattering of buckthorn and crack willow. Five Scots pines poked out of the earth a mile on, like a skeleton's hand reaching from the soil.

The closer they came to the rise behind which Prentiss Manor hid, the more the three women became invisible, translucent in the eerie early-winter gloaming. The pounding of the horses' hooves against the frozen earth and loose stone grew louder as they approached a curved drive, and Phoebe watched her mother's face blur into a shadow.

No one spoke when the carriage came to a stuttered halt. Two lonely oil lamps stood in the kitchen window; no other light spilled from the house. They'd come around back to the kitchen garden full of rotting stalks and black stumps, where the last of the sprouts had been cut to store away in the root cellar.

Sam cleared his throat, his discomfort vibrating in the air, but Phoebe didn't bother putting him at ease. They were home. It took everything she had to open the carriage door and set foot on the hard-packed earth.

The driver quietly unhitched the horses and led them to a trough, then hailed the second carriage, which held the luggage and servants. The kitchen door swung open, and Karolina flinched, but it was only Cook limping out to greet them with a surly nod and a muttered promise of supper.

Moti went first toward the house, her head held high, hands hidden inside a rabbit fur muff—Phoebe assumed they were trembling. Hers were, though she'd fisted her hands and pushed them into the folds of her paletot.

None of them looked to the left, behind the garden where the doors to the icehouse stood closed and locked.

Karolina followed hard on her mother's heels, giving Cook

a wan smile as she ducked her head beneath the low stone lintel that had stood since the manor was naught but a single great room.

Sam came to Phoebe's side, and she breathed in his scent as though it were a talisman against the shades that dwelt in the rooms before them.

"How old is the manor?" he asked, his voice soft but not fearful.

Not yet.

"We don't know. Most likely it belonged to a chieftain who was displaced by the Romans when they built Hadrian's Wall. Once the Romans left, the first of my father's family took over. Whether they were the original owners or simply took advantage of the empty fort isn't recorded."

He shook his head slightly. "Imagine knowing where you come from so far back in time."

Phoebe turned and took in the sight of him. The light had seeped out of the sky, but she could still make out the color of his eyes and the curve of his chin as he lifted his head.

"Hundreds of years of history weigh heavy on a place," she said. On impulse, Phoebe reached over and grabbed Sam's hand. "Marry Karolina, if she'll have you, but please, don't make her live here."

Sam's surprised gasp sounded like a bark. "What? Are you . . . I certainly . . ."

Embarrassment fizzed through Phoebe's chest, and she dropped his hand. She faced the manor once again.

"Or do what you want," she said between gritted teeth. "You're a man. You'll do that anyway."

Cook had already gone back into the kitchen and Phoebe didn't turn around to see if Sam followed as she went inside.

If he were smart, he'd stay outside with the horses and drive back the way he came.

No good came of visiting with ghosts.

This far north, day and night lost meaning.

The early darkness of winter so close to Scotland was to be expected. What Sam hadn't foreseen was its *suddenness*.

Any light behind the Hunt women's eyes died the moment they entered their home. Only an hour after arriving, the rest of the day's light fled the entire house. Shadows that had clung to corners and behind doors grew unchecked in the dark, covering everything with shades of black and gray.

Having been divested of his greatcoat by a tiny woman whose dark black eyes gave him the shivers, Sam let himself be guided into the parlor, a scantly furnished room with two drafty windows facing each other to create a stiff breeze, and a stuffed deer head poking out from the wall above the fireplace.

He plonked himself on an itchy horsehair couch, careful to stay in the middle of the room. Until the half-moon showed itself in the sky, the only illumination came from the crooked candles obviously remade from stubs and a sickly fire twisting in the grate.

The ladies joined him soon after for a delightful taste of what was to come on this visit.

The marchioness barely spoke, and when she did, she would lapse into Lithuanian half the time so her daughters had to translate. Sometimes they didn't even bother. Lady Karolina would blush and make an excuse, and Lady Phoebe simply shook her head.

Aside from the tiny maid with scary eyes, a brooding giant

of a man with dark brown eyes and an improbably beautiful face named Jonas was the only other person who appeared. He wasn't a servant, for they were introduced, although Sam was unsure whether the names given were Jonas's surnames or a description of his profession. Sam did not understand a lick of Lithuanian. However, it did sound like Polish.

He didn't know Polish, either.

Jonas did not sit with the family. He stoked the fire and, without speaking, brought Sam a glass of something yellow. The marchioness watched Jonas as though he were going to disappear at any second, and her smiles toward him were hesitant and pleading. She spoke to him only in Lithuanian.

Jonas, for his part, treated the marchioness with equal care, as though she were made of glass, as though he had seen her broken. Lady Karolina and Lady Phoebe he treated with a bemused familiarity and ignored Sam after handing him the drink.

"I am afraid Cook did not expect us until tomorrow morning," Lady Phoebe said, translating the conversation between her mother and this Jonas person. "If it isn't too poor a fare, Jonas will bring toasted bread and cheese to go with our tea and your *viryta*."

Viryta is what he'd been given by the giant, and it was the only thing keeping Sam from running out of the house. A specialty of Lithuania, the honey liquor smelled like Christmas and was as potent as it was sweet.

"Toasted bread and cheese is my favorite meal," Sam assured the marchioness, his hearty response fueled by a healthy swallow of *viryta*. "Nothing poor about it."

The marchioness's slow blink at his declaration was an

unspoken reminder that what Sam considered "poor" and what this woman considered "poor" were oceans apart. Continents apart, even.

Deciding he'd participated enough in the niceties, Sam examined the bottom of his liquor glass, contemplating how polite it would be to get up and pour himself another drink. At his sister Letty's new home, servants seemed forever underfoot, filling glasses and cleaning up spills without a second's hesitation.

Here it seemed the family fended for themselves.

Sam leaned forward toward the fireplace, but the fire was too small, and he sat too far away to feel real warmth.

"Are you cold, Mr. Fenley?" Lady Karolina, delightful woman that she was, sat next to him and her body heat was palpable. "I shouldn't think Prentiss Manor as nice as Lord and Lady Greycliff's manor," she said, a half smile pulling her lips down like the slope of a wave.

"Who? Oh—" Sam would never get used to his sister Letty being referred to as "Lady Greycliff." Before Letty had established Athena's Retreat with Violet and Phoebe, the closest he'd ever come to the aristocracy was delivering packages to their homes.

"It's pretty countryside there," he agreed. "Lots of orchards and flowers. Sun. A great deal of sun."

Lady Karolina sighed. "Take heart, Mr. Fenley. What we lack in sun we make up for in gloom and dust."

Smelling like lilacs, the lady tilted her head and Sam admired the sight. Lady Karolina was truly a pretty woman and had a sense of humor as well. Perfect. Now all Sam had to do was be his irresistible self, and she'd fall ears over arse in love with him—worth the expense of the trip to a cold, inhospitable manor house.

"I will gladly brave the gloom and a little dust to keep company with such a delightful lady," he said, keeping his tone light but fixing his eyes on hers.

Drawing Lady Karolina into his web of charm, like a spider draws a fly.

"As long as the ghosts stay away," he teased.

The web broke.

Lady Karolina's creamy skin turned pale as chalk, and a gasp from Lady Fallowshall drew their attention.

Seated to the left of him in a straight-backed wooden chair with no cushion, the marchioness wrung her hands in distress. Next to her stood Lady Phoebe, arms crossed over her chest. The lines bracketing Lady Phoebe's mouth had been hidden in the light of day but, now revealed, made her look more her age. Twenty-nine or thirty, Sam supposed, since she was a year older than Letty.

Lady Karolina leapt from her seat and hurried over to the older woman while Lady Phoebe walked over to the cart where the collection of liquors was kept. Lady Karolina took one of her mother's arms and Jonas took the other. In a matter of moments, their good-nights were said, and the room emptied of everyone but him and Lady Phoebe.

"Please excuse my mother, Mr. Fenley," Lady Phoebe said, having poured herself a healthy glass of the *viryta*. "She will be regretful for her rudeness in the morning, but tonight she is overly tired and exhaustion has trumped her hospitality."

She fell more than sat onto the couch next to him, a glass of the honey liquor in one hand and the half-empty bottle from whence it came in the other hand.

"Thirsty, are we?" Sam asked.

"We are," she replied.

They sat for a while in an easy silence. Sam watched the fire sputter and gasp while the north wind rattled the windows.

A muted knocking sounded from somewhere outside the parlor, and Sam turned to gaze at the doorway, but no one entered. He resettled himself, back against the couch, when the knocking came again.

"Have you heard of the American author Edgar Allan Poe?" Lady Phoebe asked. She did not appear to have heard the knocking, holding the glass up to the feeble light and examining its contents.

"I have not. Is he someone you read while on your ... visit?" Sam asked.

Lady Phoebe snorted. A ladylike snort, but a snort, nonetheless.

"Visit. Is that what you want to call it?"

Ahh, frost covered her words, and although he was chilled to the bone, Sam welcomed the sensation. Unlike his frontal assault on Lady Karolina, Sam examined Lady Phoebe's profile from the corners of his eyes.

A museum. That was the only other place he'd seen such assured beauty.

Beautiful. Genius. Villain.

An inappropriate curiosity as to how her skin might taste beneath the tip of his tongue sent a wave of heat down Sam's spine.

The cold must be doing something to his brain. This curiosity would do nothing to further his ultimate goals, and if Lady Phoebe's bite was anywhere close to her bark, might even get him mortally wounded.

Still. Pity a woman blessed with looks and intelligence was so cutting and intimidating. Sam would like to hear her laugh.

Truly laugh, from the belly.

Another knock came, this time it sounded farther away. Lady Phoebe still showed no reaction.

"Poe is the author of 'The Tell-Tale Heart.' One of my favorite stories," she said.

Sam sat forward now, happily expectant. "Is it a romance? Do you know I have read all of Mrs. Foster's horrid novels. My favorite is *The Perils of Miss Cordelia Braveheart and the Castle of Doom*."

A look of disgust crossed Lady Phoebe's face.

Obviously, she knew nothing of great literature.

"'The Tell-Tale Heart' is the narrative of a nameless man who confesses to murder," she began. Her gemstone eyes sparkled in the dark.

Odd, considering there was barely light to illuminate them.

"Every night the nameless narrator would enter an old man's room and watch him while he slept. His only motivation was a fear of the old man's pale blue eye," she continued, "yet the nameless narrator insists he is not mad."

Sam clamped his lips onto the side of his glass to keep them from making a round O as he listened. In *The Perils of Miss Cordelia*, the villain kidnaps the heroine, but that's all right because he marries her in the end.

Marries, not *murders*.

"One night while the narrator is watching him, the old man wakes up and cries out," Lady Phoebe said, her eyes on some distant point. "The nameless man hears a dull pounding. It is the sound of the old man's terrified heartbeat. Worried others might hear the noise, he kills the old man and hides the pieces of the body below the floorboards in the bedroom."

"Ack." Sam cleared his throat and swallowed the last of his

Christmas drink to wet his dry mouth and settle his churning stomach. "What on earth . . . Is this the kind of story they tell in America? Pieces? Pieces of the body?"

Lady Phoebe's gaze turned to Sam, her eyes half-closed, and she tilted her head as though listening to something. Straining his ears, he heard nothing but the wind shuddering through the ancient windows.

What had made that knocking noise?

Why had it stopped?

"The neighbors heard the old man's scream and called the watch. The nameless man lets them into the old man's home and pretends nothing is out of the ordinary until a knocking sound begins." Her voice had dropped to a low purr Sam might have appreciated if he wasn't bloody terrified.

"It is the sound of the old man's heart, pounding away beneath the floorboards, louder and louder, until the nameless man is driven to confess."

Lady Phoebe set her glass on a rosewood table to the side of the couch, stood, and shook her skirts.

"Delightful tale," she said cheerfully. "I shall lend you my copy if you are interested."

"What? Is that it? *That* is the tale?" Sam asked. That didn't seem right. Where were the sword fights? The hidden treasure and tremulous embracing?

"I must apologize," she said in a distinctly *un*apologetic tone. "Due to the shortage of help, there may not be a chamber pot in your room. If you must use the necessary, there is a privy directly behind the kitchen garden, right next to the family burial ground."

What?

What?

Burial what?

"Sleep well."

With that, she left.

Sam stayed frozen after she closed the parlor door behind her. In fact, he sat in the parlor long into the night, trying to decide whether Lady Phoebe Hunt had played a brilliant joke on him or if he would still be alive when the morning came.

7

If every individual substance were formed of different materials, the study of chemistry would, indeed, be endless; but you must observe that the various bodies in nature are composed of certain elementary principles.

–Mrs. Jane Marcet

"SUNSHINE! HOW DELIGHTFUL." KAROLINA BEAMED AT the morning light, looking enchanting in her lavender day dress and paisley shawl.

Phoebe smiled at her sister's pleasure, then glanced at the end of the breakfast table where Sam Fenley sat, staring at his plate of fried cheese curds and jam.

"Mr. Fenley," Phoebe said cheerfully, "how did you sleep last night?"

"How did I sleep?" he echoed, one hand pulling down his face, which sported the slightest bit of blond stubble. "How do you imagine I slept?"

Karolina, ignorant of what had occurred the night before, frowned. An arcing wrinkle appeared over her brows, serving to remind Phoebe her sister was no longer a child. Twenty years old was more than old enough to be married and starting a family.

For her sister's sake, Phoebe had presented a test of fortitude to Sam Fenley. She reasoned if he was brave and sensible, he would appear rested and calm.

Instead, his eyes were especially wide, like a horse that had been spooked, and his clothes looked as though he'd slept in them.

"Would you prefer kippers, Mr. Fenley?" she asked sweetly. "I can have Cook bring out a plate of them."

Karolina shuddered. "You know I cannot abide kippers. I do not like my meals to stare back at me."

Kippers. Sam mouthed the word, his eyes narrowing as he fixed his gaze on Phoebe, suspicion dawning in his eyes.

Best Phoebe find something to do on the other side of the manor. It wouldn't do to laugh now.

That would ruin the entire experiment.

"KIPPERS!"

The declaration brought Phoebe up short a few hours later. Oh dear.

"Edward Poe," Sam continued to bellow. Phoebe swiveled on her heel to face him as he stormed down the long hallway connecting the library to the great room.

Sam had directed them to begin an accounting of everything of value for him to catalog and resell on their behalf. She and Karolina had each taken a wing of the house, sketching out a plan of which rooms to itemize first; what they might keep and what would be unsellable.

Hopefully, both the auction and the sale of Prentiss Manor

would go quickly. Phoebe wanted to return to America within the month but was afraid to leave before Moti and Karolina were settled.

Phoebe had watched her mother fall apart then come together over and over again through the years. If Moti were to fall apart now, Karolina would be vulnerable and there was never a guarantee that Moti would come back together.

Each time, her mother splintered into finer and finer pieces until someday she would turn to a cloud of sharpened dust.

The sunlight so exciting to Karolina had lasted throughout the day. Soon enough, the sky would fall dark, but for now a lovely carpet of lemon-colored light spread over the bare wooden floorboards of the hallway despite the dirty glass in the windows. Nothing hung from the walls except for cobwebs and peeling flakes of the whitewash over the plaster and stone walls.

Sam and Phoebe were alone.

The sunlight and bare floorboards made no difference to Sam Fenley. The sound of his feet on the floor bounced off the walls, foreshadowing the echo ringing in her ears when he tripped on—nothing! Unless a speck of dust lay before him; invisible to her eyes but large enough to bring a man down?

One second his long strides and clenched jaw made him resemble a marauder ready to sack a castle, the next, he'd pitched forward so quickly, she barely finished gasping before he broke his fall with his forearms and rolled. Without a single curse, he shot upright and headed toward her once again.

He came to a stop only inches from Phoebe, sunlight running its fingers through his hair, picking out the different shades of gold and softening the sharp line of his cheekbone.

The inconvenient appreciation of his face and figure could

not be dampened by the prodigious scowl he wore. Her eyes lowered to admire the width of his shoulders and breadth of his chest, and she surreptitiously breathed the particular scent of him; competence and soap.

"You told me that story on purpose," Sam said, hands on hips, gaze burning like a butcher readying to cut up a pig. "The question is, my lady, *why*."

That last word, *why*, was said without anger. In fact, he sounded somewhat . . . wounded?

A crushing fist of guilt grabbed hold of Phoebe's insides.

When she said nothing, an angry flush rose on his cheeks and those sky-blue eyes of his hardened. Standing in front of her was a man who had built his father's small emporium into a household word, then had gone on to buy broadsheets and mansions.

"Did you find it amusing to scare the commoner? Feeling resentful that some shopkeeper's son was going to sleep on your ancestral bed, so you found a way to keep him sitting up all night?"

Phoebe's father, her former lover Adam Winters, Grantham—they were large men in body, voice, and temper. While Sam was equally as tall, he did not loom so the shadow he cast threatened to suffocate her. His anger didn't turn her bowels to water and his frown did not make her skin cold and clammy.

Fear was not power, but fear still made her small and weak.

Phoebe wasn't afraid of Sam.

That must have been the reason she reached over and clasped one of his hands in hers. She'd left off her gloves in one of the rooms and her hands were small and pink against his large, somewhat callused palm.

"You are correct, Mr. Fenley. I did mean to scare you last night."

He deflated with a small huff, and Phoebe had to refrain from bringing his palm to her chest so he could feel her sincerity.

"Not because of your social standing. I swear," she said, feeling even worse when he raised his eyebrows in disbelief. "It was—I have a terribly inappropriate sense of humor. I am sorry."

Sam glanced at their entwined hands and said nothing.

Oh dear.

"I sincerely apologize," she promised. "I amused myself at your expense and that was . . . wrong."

Ugh.

Being noble and kind was difficult.

All these uncomfortable words; *apologize* and *sincere.*

Phoebe dropped Sam's hand, but he'd wrapped his long fingers around her wrist and did not let go.

"Why, then?" he asked solemnly.

Arrested by the sight of his fingertips over the delicate blue veins poking out from her sleeve, Phoebe's breath caught, and a wild fluttering pulsed beneath her skin. The air around them, so clammy before, was now charged as though someone had conducted an invisible current from their feet through the floorboards and into the atmosphere.

She could not tear her eyes from where they touched, and her mouth went dry.

"Lady Phoebe?" Sam whispered.

Phoebe finally met his gaze and told him the truth.

"You were already nervous, and your eyes were big, like this . . ." She widened her eyes and went slack-jawed.

Sam's mouth puckered as if he wanted to kiss her.

Or call her a nasty name.

"I told myself it was a test of your fortitude. If you slept easy after such a tale, I'd be certain you were level-headed and sensible." Phoebe sighed and forced out the rest of her confession. "Once I began, I couldn't stop. It was so . . . so . . ."

Grimacing, Sam gently loosened his grip on her wrist.

". . . so funny," Phoebe finished, exasperated at her own amusement. "How was I to keep myself in control when your voice rose higher and higher? Your ears lay back against your head and you resembled a fish on shore, gasping for water."

This morning, Sam had dressed soberly, as if for business. His coat and trousers were of a simple cut and made from wool and cotton. The wide ivory cravat around his throat had only one knot, as if to show he'd no time for anything as silly as fashion.

"I beg your pardon. Are you comparing me to a dead fish? A *kipper*, perhaps?" he snarled.

Accusingly, Phoebe pointed at Sam's face. "You're doing it again. And your eyebrows are pointy now. How am I supposed to control myself around you, Mr. Fenley, when you look as you do?"

The moment those words left her mouth, Phoebe understood how they could be construed. A wave of heat burned her face nearly to a crisp as Sam's face went blank, then practically glowed.

Oh no, oh no no no.

That smile. That insultingly bright smile of his gave even the sun pause as it lit his face further.

"No control over yourself around me, eh, Lady Phoebe?"

Horrid man.

As palpable as the heat of a candle flame, his delight washed over her. Phoebe knew him well enough now. She would *never* hear the end of this.

"Well, I have a suggestion as to what—" He quit his words abruptly and dropped her hand.

"Hallo, you two."

Karolina popped out from the great room, a sheaf of rag paper in one hand, a stick of graphite in the other. She'd covered her pretty day dress with an apron, but the white lace cap lay askew atop her head, drooping over her curls in a fetching manner.

Fresh and pretty. Young—younger than Sam, for certain. Deserving of a life with far more happiness and joy than could be found in a place like Prentiss Manor.

It was wrong for Phoebe to tease Sam. Wrong to delight in his smiles or bask in the heat of his smile.

That smile, that warmth. It should be reserved for Karolina.

Not for a woman faced with the choice of prison or exile. If in the darkest hours of night, deep beneath her blankets, Phoebe wished for someone's smiles . . . well, beggars couldn't be choosers, and Phoebe had no choices left.

There was no one to blame but herself.

"Mr. Fenley was asking me how one might amuse oneself here at the manor," Phoebe said lightly. Without taking her eyes from her sister, she gestured to where Sam stood. "I'm certain if the two of you put your heads together, you can come up with something."

Taking her leave, Phoebe walked past her sister and into the room next door, never looking back.

Fool me once, shame on you. Fool me twice, shame on you.

Sam knew this wasn't the correct quote. Wasn't it the

Neapolitans who coined the correct phrase? *Fool me once, shame on you; fool me twice, shame on me.*

Rather quick to take the blame, those southerners.

A loud thump came from the room on the other side of the wall. If Sam remembered correctly, the room had been labeled a ballroom on one old map, and armory on another. Ballroom. Armory. Not so dissimilar. The mothers of young virgins could be as frightening as a cannon pointed toward one's head.

The last time Sam heard thumps in the night was, well, last night. Every night in fact. Nightfall at Prentiss Manor was a cacophony of creaks, groans, taps, and thumps. Bizarre, since during the day, the place was silent as the grave.

The first time he'd heard noises, however, it had been a ploy by Lady Phoebe to scare the pants off him.

Sam paused and contemplated the question of him without pants and Lady Phoebe in the same room.

Thump. The sound came again, followed by a voice. Deep. Wounded.

A trick or a murder or a ghost? Or all three?

He'd been trying to find Lady Karolina since after breakfast, which was thankfully not kippers. Not coddled eggs and ham, either.

Breakfast was a travesty, is what it was, and it gave Sam the motivation to begin his master plan. Mesmerizing Lady Karolina with his excess of charm and sunny disposition, courting, then marrying her.

They seemed compatible. She enjoyed art and Shakespeare. Sam enjoyed listening to her talk about art and Shakespeare. Nothing terrifying or dangerous about Lady Karolina. A simple, pleasant, peaceful woman like her was everything Sam had been expecting in a wife.

Imagine the set of bollocks on the man who tried to court her sister, Lady Phoebe. Ha. That woman was a dragon; beautiful scales on the outside that were hard enough to break steel. Passionate fire on the inside, ready to burn anyone too stupid to spar with her.

Sam wasn't going to mess with *that* combination.

Even if he pictured Lady Phoebe in his bed, the thought of Phoebe outside the bedroom, say, standing amid the chaos of his house in Clerkenwell, was humorous. Ridiculous.

Oxymoronic, really.

Shaking his head to rid himself of such stupid daydreams, Sam examined the double doors leading to the ballroom/armory and considered his next actions.

What could be so frightening on the other side of the doors? Wasn't he a grown man? A strong, healthy grown man who had *not* pulled a dresser over in front of his bedchamber door each night to keep out ghosts. Everyone knew ghosts floated right through doors and dressers.

It might slow them, however.

Sam decided to leave the ballroom to whatever entity caused the thumps and search the ground floor for Lady Karolina when he heard the scream.

He ran halfway down the hall, then came to a halt.

Damn. That had been a mortal's scream, hadn't it?

A gentleman would have dashed into the ballroom without a second thought. Sam, being a merchant and thus in possession of common sense, had run away.

Not, perhaps, the way to impress a lady. Or a dragon.

He sighed and trudged back the way he'd run, put his hands on the doorknobs, said a small prayer to Saint Jude, the patron saint of lost causes, and threw open the doors.

Thump.

Sam's mouth twisted like a rope from a frown to a grin and then back again at the sight greeting him while his heart kept beating wildly and his eyes grew wide.

On the floor were a pile of feather bolsters and small couch pillows. Lying on the haphazard mound staring up at Sam was Jonas, looking none too pleased. Standing over Jonas, her hair pulled back into a braid of the sort milkmaids might wear, dressed in a plain India cotton day dress with no—thus the heart beating and the eyes widening—*no petticoats*, was Lady Phoebe.

Sweet Jesu, but the woman had a figure. The outline of her long legs and beautifully curved hips was clear as day. Her pantalettes showed through the thin material, and the brown striped skirt of the dress fell only to midcalf. Sam's jaw dropped when he saw how much of her stockinged leg was visible.

What was this? An orgy?

Lady Karolina stood to the side, dressed in a blue gown, *also* not wearing petticoats. Her gown had been tied high enough that her calves were showing.

Jonas, muttering something no doubt filthy in Lithuanian, wore only a linen shirt, breeches, and stockings. No shoes or waistcoats to be seen.

"What on earth are you doing, and why are you doing it without me?" Sam cried.

Lady Phoebe tucked her bottom lip over her top and released a puff of breath that failed to dislodge the thick lock of black hair plastered to her forehead by sweat.

Jesu. Thankfully, Sam was dressed and the jacket he wore was long enough to cover any reaction he had with an eyeful of Lady Phoebe, nearly naked and perspiring.

"Oh, Mr. Fenley," Lady Karolina cried, crossing her arms over her chest, her cheeks covered with cherry-colored blotches from embarrassment. "Please don't look. Please don't tell Moti. Please don't look or tell Moti."

Huh. Here was something Sam recognized. A bargaining piece. Not coin, but close enough.

Jonas levered himself up from his prone position and glared. "Is it the custom for men in London to enter a room without invitation?" he demanded.

The effect of Jonas's glower was spoiled by the hair on his head having won its battle with comb and pomade so that it now resembled more a mop. A giant mop.

Lady Phoebe did not share her sister's embarrassment. She bent her long, white neck to the side and stared at Sam with those gem-colored eyes.

"Mr. Fenley," she said, each consonant crisp and cold like the tartest of ciders. "I was demonstrating a set of skills to my sister. Would you care to help in the demonstration?"

He grinned and swallowed an evil chuckle.

"Why, what skills might they be, Lady Phoebe, which require you to present yourself in such deshabille?"

Lady Phoebe did not return the smile. Instead, she held out a hand to Jonas, then helped him to stand. He brushed off his breeches and ran his fingers through the bird's nest atop his head.

"You should have minded your own business. Now you're in for it," Jonas grumbled. With pleasantries out of the way, he left the room. Limping slightly.

No matter. Sam knew what Lady Phoebe was about.

Arthur Kneland had taught the secret scientists at Athena's Retreat how to protect themselves against dangerous men.

Letty had, in turn, demonstrated for her sisters. They had also required practice.

Sam knew exactly why Jonas limped. Sam had limped, too, after a few bouts with his sisters.

"It is my pleasure to help you ladies." Sam offered himself up to impress the Lady Karolina. Beneath the slightly damp cotton, she had a delightful figure as well.

Why, what could be more pleasant than grappling with a nearly naked sweaty woman?

Sam held out a hand toward Lady Karolina in offering, only to find himself lying on his back and gasping for air.

"Unfair," he wheezed.

Lady Phoebe did nothing to hide her pleasure, gesturing with her chin toward him.

"Do you see, Karolina? If a man tries to grab you like so . . ."

He sat, rubbing his spine. "Didn't try to grab her, milady. Offered her my hand out of good manners. This is how good manners are repaid?"

". . . you must use their weight against them."

Peering at Sam as though he were a toad, Lady Phoebe sniffed.

"I hope naught but your pride is wounded, Mr. Fenley?"

Sam got up and took a step toward Lady Phoebe, standing so close, their toes nearly touched. Her white skin had a warm peach color from her exertions and glowed in the meager daylight coming in through those few French doors that weren't boarded up. Allowing himself only the quickest of glances at the press of her breasts against her canvas stays, visible beneath the thin cloth, Sam let his gaze tangle with hers.

Lady Phoebe reached out for his arm, hoping to catch him unawares a second time and heave him over her shoulder like

Arthur Kneland was forever doing to Grantham. Why, when it was Lady Karolina he was here to impress, were the tiny cat claws of anticipation climbing up his spine as the result of Lady Phoebe's gaze upon his chest and his legs? Why was it Lady Phoebe, whose scent of porcelain and lemon, made him dizzy?

Lady Phoebe grasped his arm with her long, supple fingers and stepped in toward him, her hip butting into his stomach in preparation for another toss.

Too bad.

Sam had gotten tired of his sisters throwing him to the ground. He'd figured out a way to best them—for a while. Thus, when Lady Phoebe twisted her torso, instead of jerking back, Sam followed her movement. He embraced her from behind and, since he needed an element of surprise—and this was the only reason—his hand slipped over her stomach, coming to rest on her round, supple hip.

Rather than flipping him over her shoulder, Lady Phoebe found herself trapped in his embrace. The shock of a woman's warm body beneath him sent a shudder through Sam. The cat's claws turned sharper, and a heavy buzzing sensation gathered at the base of his spine. She was strong. Stronger than most gentlewomen, for certain. The shifting of her back muscles beneath his chest was a surprise and a heady delight.

Sam leaned down to speak into Lady Phoebe's ear, close enough when he whispered, his lips grazed her soft lobe.

"As I said, my lady. This is my pleasure."

Lady Phoebe and Sam were not alone. Lady Karolina stood only a few paces away. Nor were they in a darkened room, hidden from the world. They stood in the center of a ballroom, exposed to the daylight.

Yet . . . yet Sam, for an instant, let the world around them melt away. The thud of Lady Phoebe's heartbeat was so strong, it thumped through his own chest. A million points of contact between them merged, and if he moved even a quarter of an inch, the friction would give off a spark.

For one long, torturous, and too short a moment, he and Lady Phoebe stayed still, their hearts beating in counterpoint, their breath mingling in the humid air, an unspoken message passing between them before the spell was broken.

"Oh my!" Lady Karolina exclaimed. "Mr. Fenley, you have exposed to us a weakness we knew nothing about."

8

◄◄◄◆►►►

All *sure* in their days except the most wise.... He is the wisest philosopher who holds his theory with some doubt.

–Michael Faraday

SAM PEERED AT HIS WARPED REFLECTION IN A SPOTTED looking glass. Squinting, he tried to discern if his tie were properly knotted. Though he'd been happy when cravats went out of style, he wasn't certain he approved of the more casual ties for dinner.

"Cor, listen to me," he said to his reflection. "I sound like me da."

Huffing, he untied the length of satin, shaking his head. Talking to himself. Jumping at every gust of wind, turning around when he heard the laughter of children, sneaking past mirrors and keeping his eyes firmly on the ground in case whatever lurked in the silvered glass might stare back out at him; either Sam was acting the fool or Prentiss Manor was ensorcelled.

Of course, that wasn't true, though there were legends that

the first of the Hunts was indeed a sorcerer. There was nothing preternatural about this place itself. Rather, it was the effect the manor had on its occupants.

The wind picked up outside and icy fingers of a draft pulled at the warped window sash. Sam took his lamp and went downstairs, grateful for the bowled glass protecting the sickly flame. Every so often he passed by a window slightly open or a door swinging on its hinges propelled by an unseen breeze.

The place was a dark and scary old icebox, and frankly, Sam hated it here.

"Good evening, Mr. Fenley."

Sam nearly pissed his pants.

Lady Fallowshall had been standing so still without a light source, he hadn't seen her pressed against the wall of the corridor outside the dining room.

"Good evening, my lady." Sam managed to lower his voice to a normal register, though he'd been close to squeaking.

Fecking aristocrats and their haunted manors and eccentric ways.

He'd gone trailing after Lady Karolina this afternoon, touring the west wing of the house to help her list the valuables. For the first twenty minutes or so, he hadn't heard a word she'd said to him, deafened by the lightning that had struck him when he'd touched Lady Phoebe's skin. The sensation was like the shock he'd felt when accidentally grabbing the wire in one of the scientists' experiments with electricity.

Only, this shock was pleasurable.

"You are enjoying your visit to Prentiss Manor, Mr. Fenley?" the marchioness asked, yanking him back to the present. The dark, cold, unnerving present.

Ugh.

Sam searched for something nice to say about this morose heap of plaster and frost.

"I am surrounded with beautiful, witty women," he said instead, offering Lady Fallowshall his arm. "How can I not enjoy my visit when it is filled with such loveliness and grace?"

Her mouth dipped into a genteel smile, and a vague protectiveness filled him. Something in her manner suggested she'd a weak tether to the earth. That it would take only the slightest harm to send her sailing off into the ether.

They walked together into the dining room. Lady Karolina and Lady Phoebe had already arrived. Both stood in front of a pitiful fire. When the marchioness went to stand with her daughters, the meager firelight limned their mauve silk gowns. Sam marveled that they wore those confections without shivering. The marchioness's and Lady Karolina's dresses were au courant, with lower necklines and mourning-gray organza drapery. Lady Phoebe's was older with more of a shawl shape to the bodice and less embroidery.

"You ladies look lovely this evening," he said, accepting a glass of sherry from Lady Phoebe as he drew closer, the goose bumps on the skin between the full-length gloves and their short sleeves apparent.

"As grateful as I am that you've gone through this trouble for dinner"—Sam gestured to the elaborately set dining table, where piles of forks and spoons and unfamiliar instruments shone dully in the light of a tarnished candelabra—"I am happy to eat less formally in a smaller room."

"We can afford to give you at least one decent dinner," Lady Phoebe chided him. Lady Karolina beamed, and the marchioness blushed, nodding.

This ridiculousness, miles of porcelain and minted silver forks, shivering in the dark and who knew what sorts of cold dishes to come—this was decent?

So fiercely Sam longed for his family—for uncomplicated beef and turnips, for grumbling and swatting and even for when his sisters turned on him at once and buried him beneath their talk of creams and politics and suppositions on the secret life of library mice—that his stomach pained him.

If he were home right now, bathed in the orange glow of coal fire and paraffin and the terrible watercolors his mother had framed, what would these women be doing? Sitting in darkness with their silken gloves and the sibilant hiss of the wind finding its way in under the doors and beneath the windowsills?

This place inspired the most morbid of fantasies, and Sam was leaving. He'd been gone from London for too long. He would mention his businesses as an excuse, assure them he would sell whatever they wanted without even looking at it, and be quit of this place tomorrow by midafternoon.

Until then, Sam drank his sherry and gently teased Lady Karolina about her disdain for coffee.

"You cannot convince me that nasty brew will ever become as popular as tea," she insisted. "It smells like . . . like food."

"Perhaps that is why people drink copious cups of it in the coffeehouses," he mused. "It fills them up for less than a proper meal would."

Sam's teasing trailed off when one of the stocky servants he'd seen only glimpses of entered with a small soup tureen.

The marchioness muttered something under her breath and Lady Phoebe shushed her. Upset the meal was being served before they sat at the table, Lady Fallowshall looked over her shoulder at the bare wall above the mantel apologetically. Where a portrait or mirror might have hung, only a hole in the plaster remained.

Sam walked her to the head of the table. Before he pulled out the chair, Lady Phoebe tilted her chin and gestured at the chair to the left of the head.

Once he seated the marchioness, Lady Phoebe and Lady Karolina took their seats quickly. There was no place for him to go but the head of the table. A cold sweat broke out beneath his stiff linen dress shirt, but Sam forced himself to smile. Head of the table meant he was served first. What if he couldn't hide his disgust at one of the dishes?

These women ate fried cheese curds and jam. For breakfast. Without gagging.

The maid ladled a benign-looking lukewarm soup into their bowls, and the marchioness again raised her eyes to the blank wall.

Sam knew he shouldn't ask, but he couldn't stand it. "What—"

Oh, for the love of Christ, he needed to cultivate a poker face. Having followed his glance, Lady Phoebe silenced his question by running her finger across her throat in a gesture anyone with an older sibling knew well.

He was not supposed to ask about the obviously missing portrait that once hung there. Sam wasn't supposed to ask anything at all, it seemed, for the ladies ate their soup seemingly unconcerned with the silence.

This was the life so many coveted? This was how titled folks ate and drank?

No. Sam had dined with his sister and brother-in-law many times. Their dinner table was a place for good food and excellent conversation.

Sam took two bites of his soup and laid his spoon aside. Without a word, the door opened, and Jonas stalked in with a covered tray, followed by Cook, who carried a bowl full of boiled potatoes.

At least, in the murk of the dining room, Sam assumed they were potatoes. They could be anything.

Boiled gnomes.

Troll eggs.

The marchioness said something to Jonas in a gently scolding tone, then gestured at the seat to the left of Lady Karolina.

Jonas shook his head, his eyes set on his task of serving the dead gnomes. Potatoes, rather. Lady Phoebe gently placed her hand on her mother's arm and said something to Jonas in a soft tone unlike her usual crisp and cutting consonants.

Looking up at whatever Lady Phoebe had said to him, Jonas stared at the marchioness with an expression of affection, but again, he shook his head in the negative and left.

Without a word, Lady Phoebe leaned to the right, her shoulder pressing against her mother's shoulder. Lady Karolina watched the two of them, and Sam was put in mind of a tableau such as those he'd seen in Greycliff's home. Three goddesses, each representing a season or some such, sitting together but looking in opposite directions.

The ladies again ate in silence until Sam could take it no longer.

"One day there was a boy walking down the road when he spied a frog. The frog hopped over to him and said, 'Boy, if you kiss me, I will turn into a beautiful princess.' The boy smiled and picked up the frog, then put it in his satchel."

As they were wont to do, the Hunt women froze, the

marchioness with a piece of fowl speared on the end of her knife, Lady Karolina with a napkin halfway to her mouth.

It wasn't as funny as his story about the priest and the nun, but Sam kept going.

"After a while, the frog called out to the boy. He took the frog from its satchel and the frog said, 'Boy, if you kiss me, I will become a beautiful princess and gift you with a treasure.' The boy smiled at the frog and put it back in his satchel again."

The marchioness dropped her knife, knocking over her wineglass.

"What are you doing?" Lady Phoebe hissed at him.

"I'm telling a funny story," Sam said.

"A funny story?" she repeated.

"Yes," Sam said, his voice echoing off the empty spaces in the godforsaken room. "You know, to entertain you all. It's not naughty, if that's what worries you."

"Why does he keep putting the princess in his satchel?" Lady Karolina asked.

"Why does he—it's in the story? Don't you all . . ." Sam waved his hands in consternation while the marchioness righted her now-empty wineglass. "Don't you have *fun*? Tell funny stories? Joke? Laugh?"

"Laugh when the man traps the poor princess in a dark bag?" Lady Karolina asked, voice heavy with censure.

Sam looked to Lady Phoebe for support, but she was staring at her knife.

He gulped, rubbing his forehead as though the answer to what plagued these women might pop out with enough pressure. "It's a funny story because he *doesn't* kiss her. A talking frog is more profitable than the princess and her riches."

Holding out his palms in supplication, Sam asked, "Do you see? It's only a story."

"A story where a woman is forced to be displayed." Lady Karolina set her napkin on the table and stood. Lady Fallow-shall said something in Lithuanian, and Lady Karolina flinched but held her ground. "A story where she begs to be kissed and the man can only think of imprisoning her for profit." Despite the dark, splotches were visible on Lady Karolina's cheeks.

Poise deserting her, she resembled an outraged girl looking exactly like one of his younger sisters that time he told them the butter fairies had stopped working until they received higher wages, and no one would get buttered toast for breakfast ever again.

"I must apologize," Sam said, gazing around as if someone, anyone, might come to his rescue and right reality, which had somehow become awkwardly skewed. "I thought it was a story about a talking frog."

The marchioness rose and went to Lady Karolina's side. "They only ever see a frog," she whispered, taking her daughter's hand.

Without once looking back, they left.

"Holy..." Sam whispered, falling back into his seat. "I swear to God above, the boy never did anything bad to the frog."

Lady Phoebe had a hand over her mouth and made a noise like a pained sneeze.

Sam stared at her, then leaned forward, the better to see what she was . . . she was . . .

"You're laughing," he said in a shocked whisper. "You . . . evil, *evil* woman."

"I can't . . ." She'd a laugh like an angry goose—a honking out of proportion to her elegant bearing and exquisite face.

Sam threw his napkin across the table at her, shaking his head. "You could have said something or done . . . something. I made your sister angry, and I don't even know why."

Tears sat in Lady Phoebe's eyes, but they were the kind one gets when one is laughing one's *arse* off.

"I'm sorry, Sam, but I didn't know you would tell a story about a princess in peril." Lady Phoebe's laughter trailed off from honking to a hiccup.

Like a frog's call, in fact.

"Well, *Phoebe*. I've gone and stuck my foot in it," Sam bit out, heedless now of tears or laughter or knives or what have you. "Do you want to explain this to me?"

Phoebe's long satisfied sigh worked like a single silken finger down Sam's spine.

"Shall we take a tour of the manor while I explain?"

Sam shook his head. "Take a tour of this place at night? No, thank you."

The last echo of her laugh fell and broke into tiny shards and disappeared as Phoebe stood.

"What's wrong, Sam? Afraid of ghosts?"

Without waiting for an answer, Phoebe lit a penumbra lamp from a side table and held it up so her eyes glittered like amethysts. Sam gestured for her to lead, then followed her from the dining room.

What he should be doing was following Lady Karolina and offering an apology. Or finding Jonas and asking him to replenish the stock of *viryta* at the drinks table.

What he should *not* be doing was hanging back to admire

the way Phoebe's paper-thin evening dress showed her delight-ful figure. Nor fixing his stare on the bare swath of skin visible over the disappointingly high neckline of her gown.

"Ghosts. Not afraid of those," he muttered under his breath. "I'm more afraid of the folks living among them."

9

⫷⫸

Do not refer to your toy-books, and say you have seen that before. Answer me rather, if I ask you, have you *understood* it before?

–Michael Faraday

"THE FIRST HUNT WAS A SORCERER, OR SO THEY SAY."

Phoebe led Sam from the dining room to the great hall. Although she'd never bothered to confirm, family lore said the flagstones in here were part of the fort the Hunts had built upon when the Romans left.

Sam nodded briefly in appreciation of the fact and humored her by tapping his toe against the floor.

"In the thirteenth century, the family added a chapel, in the fourteenth century, they added a peel tower to the hall, and every other generation since then has built onto the manor until they balked at window taxes and left well enough alone," Phoebe explained.

Whitewash flaked off the plaster walls, and thick age-blackened beams poked through from the sagging ceiling. At the far end of the room, the stone was unevenly set, and scorch marks peeked out at the top molding.

"There would have been a hearth here?" Sam asked.

Phoebe nodded. "This was the center of manor life for hundreds of years, this hall. I don't know when they covered over the hearth or why. They tore down the chimney as well."

"Come," she said, and let him out the side door into a long gallery. Pieces of the floor were rotting beneath the handful of windows, cracks in the plaster around the windowsills giving evidence as to how the water damage occurred. It smelled like mold and oil.

Phoebe's lamp was the only light source, the moon having risen on the other side of the manor, and the end of the gallery could not be distinguished in the gloom.

"Oho." Sam's voice was round and golden, reaching both sides of the hall. "I knew there'd be a bunch of ancestral portraits. Look at this fellow here. Who is he?"

"Sam. That's a picture of Archangel Gabriel."

Squinting, Sam nodded slowly. "'Course. I see it now."

"He has a golden halo round his head," she said patiently. "None of my ancestors would ever have been painted as such."

"Villains, were they?" he asked with relish.

"Indeed."

When they were younger, her sisters and she had made up stories about the portraits, most of whose names were lost to history.

One great-relative they named Lord Ian the Evergassed. His diet consisted of only eggs and beans, which accounted for why there were gaps between his portrait and those of his fellows. Another portrayed the Duchess of Doom. Phoebe's older sister, Alice, had named her. The duchess lost a hair from her forehead whenever she prophesied something miserable happening to a Hunt family member.

The copper taste of betrayal kept her from sharing those secrets with Sam; a wish to preserve the handful of good memories of her childhood from the light of contemplation. What if the stories they'd made up were horrifying to outsiders? What if the little jokes and mischief she and her sisters created turned out to be morbid or damaged?

The rest of the manor squatted behind Sam and Phoebe, blanketing all sound but the shuffle of their shoes on the rotting wood and Phoebe's occasional mention of this painter or that. Men lined the hallway—from the first Baron Hunt to the fifth Earl of Brampton, to the first Marquess of Fallowshall, the Hunt men grew in peerage and power. The Hunt women, however, were mostly absent.

At the end of the gallery, the hairs on the back of Phoebe's neck rose. Here one heard nothing from the main house. This wing had been her father's domain.

He was dead, however, and Phoebe remained.

She ushered Sam into the room she and her sisters had once thought of as Father's cave. A paneled room, with high ceilings and a wall of glass doors opening to a stone terrace, here sat her father's prized possessions. Swords hung on the wall and a suit of armor leaned precariously to the left, over by the billiards table. Above the fireplace sat a hunting scene, a layer of dust obscuring the corners and dulling the gilded frame.

Best was the drinks table.

Moti and Karolina had no palate for wine and were happy to sip at the vinegar Jonas had served them tonight. In the cave, however, sat myriad bottles waiting to be emptied. If she drank enough, the ghosts would stay away.

Phoebe blew the dust from two glasses.

"Brandy?" she asked as she poured, not listening to his reply.

The aroma of dead fruit and old spices scented the air. Her father's rooms had been cold, but he'd never lifted a finger to make them more comfortable. He'd sat like a mustachioed vulture in his high-backed chair and complained of the drafts over and over. Simply the memory of his voice caused Phoebe to shudder.

Sam, having left off playing with the suit of armor once the visor slammed shut on his fingers, offered her his dinner jacket.

Manners dictated she refuse him. There was a perfectly good lap shawl hanging over the back of the settee, but Phoebe would not put anything in here against her bare skin, so she accepted.

"Come, play billiards with me," Sam said.

She swallowed the remainder of the drink and poured herself another.

"I'm afraid you'll hit me with your cue stick," she countered, walking over to the table and grimacing at his terrible aim.

"I won't hit you," he said. "I might drop the ball on your foot, though. Happens to me all the time."

She played a desultory round, but it didn't take long for Phoebe to tire of the game. She wanted to sit and drink, unbothered, until the sun rose and she could bear this place again. The floor swayed beneath her feet as she returned to the dusty bottles and poured herself yet another glass of brandy. A delightful numbness settled through her and she leaned one hip on the side of the table.

"Is every picture in this house that isn't an ancestor a portrait of your father?" Sam stared at the hunting scene hanging above her father's desk.

In it, the marquess rode astride a magnificent horse—a magnificent *imaginary* horse, for they'd never owned any animal that beautiful—with a pack of dogs running around by the horse's forelegs.

"There is an etching in our nursery of frogs dressed like little girls in the last century. Is that more to your taste?" Phoebe asked. She'd a headache from the brandy, and she reexamined the bottles, hoping to find some *viryta*.

Sam's thumbs hooked into the top of his trousers, tie askew, the brocaded black satin waistcoat shining dully in the low light. The ever-present darkness coddled his cheeks and the divot at the center of his chin, trailing down the hollow at the side of his neck and disappearing into his collar.

Phoebe made her unsteady way to stand next to him, leaning on her billiards cue for support.

"Other than those frogs, yes. Every portrait in this manor is of my father or one of his ancestors." A short puff of air, almost a chuckle, escaped her and she lost her balance.

"Why is the portrait in the dining room missing?" Sam asked.

Phoebe ignored him and gestured to the painting in front of them. "This is one of Papa's favorite themes. Himself, high above the rest of the world, surrounded by bitches set to do his bidding."

The cue slipped on a bare patch in the rug, and Phoebe grabbed for Sam's shoulder.

"You're drunk," he accused her.

"Do you blame me?"

Sam looked around him, no doubt seeing the gold leaf on the picture frames, the thick leather bindings of the folios stacked on the shelf, the ivory inlay on the doors of an ebony cabinet.

He couldn't see the stain in the carpet where a drink had

been thrown, nor the imprint of a shuddering body in the corner. Certainly, he'd never notice the two ghostly girls peering through the windows, shaking their heads in displeasure. Stupid man, blind to anything that mattered.

Sam caught her at her waist, but when Phoebe opened her mouth to scold him using some adjective like *commoner* or *grubby*, the floor tipped beneath her.

He was simply holding her up.

"Let me go," she said, pushing against his hard stomach.

"I will if you would head toward a chair or a bench or something other than the side of the table."

How dare Sam worry a fall could hurt her.

For the sake of hospitality, Phoebe allowed him to lead her toward a chair but stopped at the sight of an abandoned pipe on the table next to it.

"Get me out of here," she said. "Take me out of here, please."

He'd managed to force open the door at the far end of the billiard room and hustled the two of them out into the faint moonlight. Now the warmth of doing a good deed had faded and he was cold. Sam stared at his jacket and contemplated chivalry and whether he—being of the merchant class—was obliged to indulge in it.

Phoebe, having emptied half a bottle of brandy, did not appear cold at all, which meant Sam might be fine if he asked for his jacket back. Or she might slit his throat. Or both.

Phoebe wasn't looking at him, she was staring out at the icehouse in the barren fields. Lord knew what they grew here in Cumbria.

Cabbages, probably.

Cold and green and bland.

Because Sam was stewing over how cold he was—and how supper had been abruptly finished and he was hungry—because of that, it took him a second when Phoebe turned to him and laid her head on his chest to remember he should under no circumstances do anything as intimate or maudlin as hold her close and rest his chin on her head.

"Would you take me to bed if I asked?" Phoebe's question took him aback. She'd asked in the same tone with which she might venture a hypothesis. Detached. Slightly curious.

Sam would've been insulted if he didn't have the same urge; simply to touch another warm person, laugh, find release, and fall into a deep, untroubled slumber.

"I suppose you think I'm that sort," he said, trying to place her scent in the panoply of perfumes he'd sampled for Fenley's Fripperies over the years.

Not tuberose. Cowcumber? Sage?

Phoebe pulled her head back and her eyes slowly focused on his face.

"Do you prefer men?" she asked without rancor.

"I like women just fine," he answered. "No, I mean you think I'm the sort who'd tup a woman at the snap of her fingers."

Now Phoebe's head tilted as though he'd spoken another language.

"*All* men are that sort, Sam Fenley." She sounded put out, as though he'd disappointed her. "Pretend I'm a barmaid at whatever pub it is you frequent in Clerkenwell," she said, her words sticky with drink. "If I were some Masie or Rosie, you'd take me up against the wall without a second thought."

Sam sighed.

From the moment he stepped foot in the manor, it was obvious Phoebe's father still ruled here. Sam had seen his fair share of bully boys and sadists while growing up in London, and while he empathized with the Hunt women, he struggled with this dichotomy of privation amid privilege.

Rather than contemplate the misery clinging to the surfaces here like dust, Sam decided to put Phoebe in her place.

"If you were a barmaid at my pub," he said, tipping Phoebe's face up, thumb beneath her chin, "I would tell you how pretty you looked tonight. How I've never felt anything as soft as your skin."

He stroked her cheek as he spoke, thinking to call her bluff.

By God, but her skin *was* soft—glowing in the silver cast of a crescent moon, begging to be warmed.

The sensation of skin against skin had the same effect tonight as it had earlier in the day. Tiny trails of sparks went off down his spine.

Leaning over, Sam whispered in her ear. "Well before I'd even considered where or when I'd take you to bed—and it would be a bed—before I'd made you come, not once but twice, before I'd spread you out like a feast and set to pleasing every sweet pink part of you . . ."

Phoebe swayed and Sam tightened his grip on her, cursing himself. He wasn't telling her a story now, he was describing a dream they'd both had as her hand came up and curled round the back of his neck, and he nudged his hips closer to her, letting his cock rest against her stomach.

"Before that, I would know your name. Your whole name. How many uncles you have and what ale you like to drink and your favorite color."

Sam stepped away then, still holding her in case she fell over, but enough that she could read his expression as he continued.

"Because I'd want you to have time for a second thought, and a third, and however many it took. Because I'm *that* sort."

"I've offended you," she said.

"You have," he agreed cheerfully.

A lock of hair had come loose from her chignon, thicker than it appeared when done up. She pushed it impatiently out of her face and pouted.

"Does that mean you won't be pleasing my sweet pink parts?"

He pulled his jacket tighter around Phoebe's shoulders, then turned her around and pushed her gently back toward the manor.

"Not tonight."

He must have sounded convincing enough, for she walked away without argument—and without bidding him good night.

10

⫷◆⫸

To confess the truth . . . I am not disposed to form a very favourable idea of chemistry, nor do I expect to derive much entertainment from it.

—Mrs. Jane Marcet

THE NEXT MORNING THE SUN HUNG MIDWAY TO THE top of the world, bare and unflinching in a gray-colored sky.

Stupid sun.

The gravel of the stone drive looping around the manor house sounded like gunfire when Phoebe walked over the tiny stones. Around back near the stable, Jonas and Sam stood facing each other. Karolina had come to get her, saying the two men were outside arguing, but now that she'd been assaulted by sunlight, Phoebe's head hurt too much to intervene in whatever pissing contest was taking place between Jonas and Sam.

"Well, then, if the horses are lame, why not send a boy to the nearest village to fetch another set of them." Sam did not speak louder than he had to, but he bit off the ends of his words in a manner that irritated Phoebe's nerves.

The same nerves already overburdened by the suspicion she had propositioned Sam last night. The fact that she woke fully clothed in her own bed meant if she had, in fact, propositioned Sam Fenley, he had turned her down.

She would have remembered if he'd tupped her. Her headache wouldn't be so bad, for one.

"There is no boy to send," said Jonas.

Phoebe pressed two fingers against the throbbing between her eyebrows. It didn't help, but perhaps the men would take the hint and shut up.

"No boy? Then send a man. Send yourself. Send out a woman if you must," Sam said.

"I'll go," Phoebe said.

The men ignored her.

"We do not have a man to send. We do not have a woman to send. This is not London, where crowds of paupers roam to do your bidding." Jonas folded his arms and stared at a spot over Sam's left shoulder.

"Crowds of paupers? Who do you think I am?" Sam asked.

"Go yourself, Mr. Fenley," Phoebe suggested, inserting herself between the two men. "It's a six-hour walk to the nearest coaching inn. You could get a post from there."

A plume of steam extended from Sam's nose as he examined the boots he wore. Boots designed to travel short distances on paved streets, not hours-long treks on dirt paths.

"Or, you can stay one more day and ride out with the stable master when he comes back with the other horses," Jonas said slowly, as if speaking to a petulant child.

Deciding the matter settled, Jonas turned on his heel and headed back toward the stables. Phoebe would have to speak with him, later. They hadn't had much time together since she arrived, and she needed to know if Jonas would stay with her mother or return home to Lithuania.

"Will I . . ." Sam looked up and watched Jonas's back with a thin-lipped frown. "Will I have to eat beet soup again?"

They'd had beet soup and jellied beef for lunch. Karolina had apologized for her outburst the night before, and Moti hadn't even bothered to come down, asking for lunch to be brought up to her while she continued her counting of bed linens and candelabras.

"I will ask Cook to make something else," Phoebe said.

"Are you going to throw yourself at me again?" A twitch at the side of his mouth betrayed Sam, but Phoebe's face warmed anyway. She was grateful, though, he'd taken whatever she'd done last night with good humor.

That wasn't the case when she'd used men as means of drowning out her awareness. There were worse things than a headache. Unlike drinking, if Phoebe picked the wrong man to use, the pain lasted long after the act.

Not with Sam, though.

Phoebe vaguely remembered Sam pushing her in the door and back to her own room.

"I don't know," she said now. Touching a finger to the side of her chin, she posed, as if in thought. "Are you going to attend dinner half dressed again? It's hard to resist you when you're practically naked."

Relaxed, his mouth fell back into its usual shape and his smile started at the corners of his eyes.

My goodness, this man was beautiful in the clear light of day.

"I wasn't naked, I was wearing a *tie*. I will have you know the haberdashers in London insist the cravat is on its way out of fashion. Out of fashion, Lady Phoebe, is not acceptable for a man such as myself."

Nothing cutting came to mind. Nothing unpleasant or off-putting at all.

Despite her best intentions, Phoebe nodded in approval.

"A man such as yourself," she said, then looped her arm in his, walking back toward the manor. "By this, do you mean the man who is fast becoming the face of a new generation of merchants stepping out from behind the counter to become as well known as the goods they carry?"

His mouth opened, then closed.

"I am appalled you choose to read rags like *Gentlemen's Monthly*," he said. "*The Capital's Chronicle* is much more informative."

Phoebe pulled him to the left, and they rounded the stone path leading to the back garden, such as it was.

"My father was a subscriber to *Gentlemen's Monthly*. It was the only reading material lying around the house other than the books he kept for show in his office."

This was the truth, although it had been Moti who'd brought the article to Phoebe's attention, worried Lionel Armitage had Sam in his sights.

"Was the author of the piece more offended by the temerity of a merchant in the public eye or the fact that I bought a rival broadsheet?" Sam wondered aloud.

He shielded his eyes and gazed across the landscape. From here you could barely make out Tobias Hill, beyond which lay portions of Hadrian's Wall.

"You are . . ." Oh dear. It had been forever and a day since Phoebe had complimented someone without an ulterior motive. Perhaps the Cumbrian air had a dulling effect on her brain, or the cold did something to her circulatory system to make her maudlin.

"You are an impressive man," she said, fighting a blush. "The article had a condescending tone, but even Armitage could not hide the amount of success you've had in such a short time."

As Phoebe feared, Sam came to a halt, his eyebrows arching to form a caterpillar-like rainbow across his forehead. The familiar glint of mischief sparkled in his eyes.

Yes. The cold *must* have confused her brain, for Phoebe continued. "I heard you, when you complained to Grantham; the obstacles in your rise are because you lack a title."

The caterpillar broke apart when Sam furrowed his brow. Phoebe spoke quickly so the prickly sensation of being *kind* would be over with soon.

"Perhaps, the lack is your patience with yourself, Sam," she said. "Most men would run over anyone in their way of a fortune. Instead, you are gracious and decent, and you've remained loyal to your family and your friends. I . . ."

Ugh. This was painful to her nerves, like the scratching of silver forks against porcelain plates.

Sam wasn't making it easier, staring at her as though she'd grown two heads.

"As an uninterested and impartial observer, I would advise you to stop and look back at all you've accomplished."

Why, oh why had Phoebe opened her mouth? 'Twas the opening in a floodgate through which words rushed out in an unpunctuated stream. "Ask yourself, if it were any other man that had done this, would you think he needed anything as superfluous as a title to help him along?"

Phoebe stared straight ahead at the vestiges of a shrubbery maze, waiting for a joke. When Sam said nothing, she glanced at him from the side. He wore a thoughtful frown and his jaw moved back and forth as though he spoke to himself.

A comfortable silence descended on them. They continued to walk along a small stone path that led to a narrow bridge spanning a nearly frozen stream. Black water rushed over stumps and half-rotted reeds, traveling west along the lines of the estate borders until it emptied into a small pond a mile away.

"If I wear a cravat," Sam asked finally, "will you be able to refrain from throwing yourself at me?"

While grateful he hadn't made a joke at her compliments, Phoebe wouldn't blush again if that was his aim. "I suppose I will try," she said with a sigh.

"That's all women can do when faced with my presence. It becomes a strain, I tell you, to walk down the street and have women overcome with desire as I—shite—"

Phoebe gasped in alarm, then covered her mouth. Somehow Sam had stepped off the side of the bridge and stood, knee-deep in the black water.

"This is a dangerously deficient bridge. Anyone who crosses might fall off the side," he exclaimed, looking around as though an invisible hand had pushed him off.

"How on earth did you manage to fall off a bridge that's only two feet from the ground?" Phoebe offered Sam her hand.

Sam huffed and ignored it, dragging his soaked boots up the slight rise to meet her at the other side.

"I know an engineer who could fix this hazard," he said, crossing his arms while water pooled at his feet on the slate stones making up the rest of the path.

"Did you love Margaret Gault?"

Oh, whyever had she asked?

As though the answer were written across the bald sun, Sam looked upward, then back at Phoebe.

"You truly are obsessed with me, aren't you?"

A laugh flew up from her belly before she could stifle it, and Sam's suspiciously white teeth flashed in his warm grin.

"Your laugh is like the honking of a goose," he said.

Phoebe brought both her hands over her mouth.

"You are doomed, Phoebe. Now I've heard you laugh, I will never be happy until I hear it again. It is like the tinkling of a mirliton or the delicate baying of a donkey."

His insults only made her laugh harder. So pleased with himself was he, rather than stalk off to the manor to change his boots, he walked backward, compelling her to follow him, listing off more comparisons while she continued to laugh.

Like an elephant's sneeze, an orangutan's belch, the bellow of a bull in heat; he threw the similes at her one by one, his smile growing wider each time, pleased with his own cleverness, even more pleased with her amusement.

Finally, a gust of wind flipped Phoebe's bonnet up and a sprig of ribboned asters fell off. They chased the unraveling strips of peach and purple silk, both laughing, bumping shoulders like hoydens. Like friends.

Sam caught the ribbons at last and held them out to her. Phoebe ignored them, staring at Sam's open expression, and drank in his genuine amusement.

"Stay," she said, then bit her lip while her heart pounded in her chest from running. From running, not from fear he would laugh at her rather than with her. Fear he would know she meant it.

"Well, if you insist."

Phoebe smiled.

"I'm going to spend the afternoon with your sister," he said. "Do you know, does she read novels?"

Oh, that stung. Once again this merchant's son had punctured her pride with his decency. Well, this was what they wanted, wasn't it? A man to take care of her mother and sister, relieving the guilt Phoebe felt at having made a mess and the shame of her punishment.

Phoebe's feelings didn't matter.

What mattered was that this man who lived in light and fell up, down, and over whatever object he encountered at least four times a day was going to stay and share his warmth with them for a little longer.

As they walked back to the manor, Sam bemoaned the state of his boots, and enumerated the methods by which Phoebe was to salvage them. She had enough self-discipline to keep from laughing (Phoebe should take a boot in each hand, hold them up above her head, and run in circles until the boots dried; Phoebe should tie the boots to a pole and swing them around; Phoebe should write an ode to his boots before they were ruined) but nothing pierced the bubble of happiness resting in her chest against her ribs.

"*Still Life with Apple and Knife*," Karolina supplied.

Sam diligently wrote the name of the painting onto a page of rag paper. The soft paper made from a mix of cotton and flax fibers, often reused from old rags, was a dark brown with tiny flecks of red throughout. Sam was grateful he had a pencil to hand, for the rag paper was poorly made and ink would soak through and spread, making his list illegible.

God forbid he'd have to go through this torture again.

"The artist is . . . hmmm." Karolina turned the painting over to examine the back. "I cannot find a signature. We will have to investigate further. Next is *Still Life with Cheese*."

He stifled a groan, but Karolina heard him anyway.

"Do you not care for art, Mr. Fenley?" she asked, her tone conveying disapproval.

They stood side by side in the great hall. The sun from yesterday had taken its leave and today's sky remained a morose gray, casting the manor's rooms in a veil of gloom. Sam suspected there wasn't enough money for both coal and candles. He and Karolina struggled in the murk to identify the pictures hanging on the east wall.

Sam had already explained that the frames would bring more money than the paintings, but Lady Fallowshall insisted the paintings be sold at auction as well. She and Jonas were on the other side of the room, investigating the art on the west wall.

Their heads were bent toward each other, Jonas dwarfing the marchioness, so the ribbons of her cap came only to Jonas's shoulder. They were not related by blood, for neither resembled the other. Nor were they lovers, at least not that Sam could tell. Was Jonas a butler, a secretary, or a headsman?

He was everywhere underfoot and nowhere to be found when furniture needed moving.

No one had offered information about Jonas's relationship to these women.

One more secret in a house sick with them.

"...great painters. We are their stewards until they are sold," Karolina was saying.

Sam hadn't been listening, but he'd drifted off too many times in the past hour to say *I beg your pardon* one more time. Instead, he nodded and made a humming sound that could be construed as positive.

"Does that mean you *don't* think we should celebrate the work of great painters?" Karolina asked, outraged.

Or it could be construed as negative, Sam supposed.

Karolina raised her voice with that last question, and within seconds, Jonas had crossed the room to stand behind Karolina, arms dangling at his sides like Arthur Kneland often did—he said he liked to have his hands free to grab a knife.

"No, no," Sam said quickly, smiling at Karolina while keeping an eye on Jonas. "All I meant was . . . is it me, or are there an unusually large number of still life paintings?"

Karolina stared at him with a gaze like his younger sister's. That look which expressed a certain pity and questioned a man's intelligence.

If he had a tuppence for every time a woman gave him that look, Sam wouldn't have to find a title. He'd be too busy swimming in a river of coin.

Her gaze, however, was mirrored by the giant hovering over her. They had the same way of lifting their eyebrows, bending their necks, narrowing . . . oh.

Sam figured now was not the time to ask if he was correct in guessing Jonas and Karolina shared a father.

"What do you mean?" Lady Fallowshall joined them, her lilac silk dress smothered beneath a tatted lace shawl, its pointed ends sweeping the floor, past even the hems of her skirts.

"Well." Sam hesitated, then shrugged. He was past caring if his tastes and manners were that of a crass merchant looking to ingratiate himself with the aristocracy to better his station in the world.

That was exactly who he was if you substituted *crass* with *good-looking*.

Sam glanced at the list in his hand. "We've got *Still Life with Apple and Knife, Still Life with Cheese, Still Life with Fruit and*

Dead Pigeon, Still Life with Persimmon, and *Still Life with Dead Chicken and Sheaf of Wheat*."

The three of them remained silent, staring at him as though he were on display in a menagerie.

"What, exactly, is the great skill in painting things that are *still*?" Sam asked. "Why is it fruit? Apples, persimmons, pears, grapes—why not pudding and cream or, if it must be fruit, fruit cake?"

Silence met his query.

In for a penny, in for a pound, he supposed.

"If I was to pay good coin for a picture of something, it should be something worth looking at, something I've never seen. I simply buy an apple and a pear and I've got my own *live* still life. See?"

Blinks all around.

Much to Sam's surprise, it was Jonas who came to his rescue.

"The man is correct. Why paint food when you can paint battles?" Jonas asked.

The marchioness waved her hand, dismissing his opinion. "Faugh. Paintings full of smoke and dirt and blood. Who finds pleasure in this?"

"I do." Jonas and Sam spoke in unison. They stared at each other in surprise, then shifted places slightly so they were opposite the ladies.

"The point of a still life is to showcase the artist's talent in perspective," Karolina explained slowly, as though to a child. "Look at the shine on the apple, the way it curves, and the realistic path of its shadow."

Jonas shook his head and spoke in the same pedantic manner. "Apples are *boring*, Lina. Battles are interesting."

Karolina's lips pinched into a plum-colored butterfly.

"Name one thing interesting about battles that doesn't have to do with killing people."

"Swords," Sam offered. "Swords are interesting."

"Swords have much to do with killing people," the marchioness pointed out.

Sam and Jonas regarded each other.

"Uniforms? Uniforms are more interesting to look at than apples," Jonas supplied.

Sam crossed his arms and nodded in agreement. "Fascinating. Buttons and medals and whatnot."

"That is the most ridiculous statement I have ever heard!" Karolina exclaimed. "If you want to enjoy weapons, look again at the knife in the still life with the apple. You can make out where the blacksmith—"

"Terrible weapon. You would lose a fight with *that* knife," Jonas opined, sniffing in derision.

Karolina's brows lowered. "I'll tell you exactly what I would do with that knife, why . . ."

Sam peeked over at Lady Fallowshall's reaction to this squabble. To his great delight, she smiled behind her hand, watching Jonas and Karolina tease and laugh at each other.

Agreeing to stay at the manor wasn't simply Sam's reaction to Phoebe's plea. He'd done so out of some bizarre intuition the Hunt family needed him here. They would be trapped in this place forever, simply fading from people's memories and then from existence if he hadn't been an anchor tying them to the real world.

The strange sensation of feeling necessary sat in his chest through the rest of the afternoon. It lent an odd solidity to his legs and clarity to his sight.

Was this what Sam had needed to keep himself upright? To

stay in one place and strengthen its structure rather than forever rushing forward in search of bigger and better?

He'd replayed his conversation with Phoebe over and over in his head for the past two days, trying to decipher her aim. Why had she said such complimentary things? Was it to lull him into complacency before gutting him with some well-placed insult?

Or was it because she meant it?

11

I ... think I have got hold of a good thing, but can't say; it may be a weed instead of a fish that, after all my labour, I may at last pull up.

—Michael Faraday

"THIS WAS A TERRIBLE DECISION," SAM DECLARED IN THE wake of an abominable luncheon of undercooked dumplings and overcooked carrots.

None of the women surrounding Sam had the grace to look the least bit ashamed. They'd lured him into their trap with the promise of post-luncheon tea and he'd fallen for it.

"There are some who look down upon *slapkopf* because it is a game the peasants play in Bavaria," said the marchioness as she examined her cards. "I find it more pleasant than quadrille or skat, myself."

"Yes, it is a good game, except—"

"*Slapkopf*," Karolina cried. Startled, Sam jumped, then ducked too late to avoid her open-handed smack in the back of his head. "I win," she crowed merrily, sweeping the cards toward her.

Rubbing the back of his head—Karolina was stronger than

she appeared—Sam clenched his teeth and ignored Phoebe, who sat with her cards covering her mouth.

Laughing at him again, no doubt. He'd been slapped in the back of his head so often in the past hour, it was a wonder his eyes remained in his head.

"How . . . why did you get to call *slapkopf*?" Sam asked. "I thought you had to have won at least three rounds."

Karolina launched into a detailed explanation that made no sense about acorns and leaves and what have you, while the marchioness recounted the points and Phoebe interjected a caustic observation every two seconds.

Except.

They weren't caustic anymore.

"Now, if Phoebe had won twice in a row, you could have called *slapkopf.*"

He scratched his head. "Are you certain the game is called slap*kopf*? I can't imagine the Bavarians smacking each other in the back of the head at the card table. Seems to me it would lead to more than a few duels."

Karolina shook her head. "No, Mr. Fenley. This is how it is played; I am certain. My sisters and I have played it all our lives. Now, it is Moti's turn to deal."

The food had not gotten hotter or more appetizing, nor was the manor less cold and haunted, but things had changed since the afternoon Sam questioned the purpose of still life portraits and found himself in agreement with Jonas. He had been given tacit permission to leave off the honorifics when he spoke with Phoebe and Karolina, though he never took the liberty of using their pet names.

Add that to the many times since then he'd fallen over some stray piece of furniture and made them laugh. Plus, even Lady

Fallowshall found the ridiculous compliments he came up with amusing.

By simply paying attention to their moods and being himself, Sam had been judged and found acceptable.

It should annoy him that these *noblewomen*, especially a villainess of majestic proportions, cared one way or another what he said or did.

Instead, it occupied far too much of his brain space.

Sam was under no delusions that he was as intelligent as his sister or the rest of her scientist friends. A good two-thirds of what they said went in one of his ears, buzzed around his skull like a dying wasp behind a curtain, then flew back out the other ear. Yesterday at breakfast (lukewarm gruel, lukewarm eggs, fried curd cakes with jam) he'd asked Phoebe whether she had continued her studies during her travels.

'Twas as if he'd found a key, unlocking a secret stash of charm and excitement that had been hidden for years. Phoebe went into excruciating detail about electrolysis, someone named Faraday, and a cascade of terms he assumed had to do with whatever branch of science it was that interested her. Might have been physics. Might have been chemistry. Might have been chemophysics.

Sam wasn't certain that was a scientific discipline, but it should be.

More surprising was that Karolina had followed along with the explanation and then asked a question about volcanic piles or something. Phoebe's face had lit like a candle as she answered.

If you asked him, volcanic piles sounded uncomfortable, but no one asked him. They did laugh at him, though, when he fell up a flight of stairs.

Twice.

He didn't mind. Their laughter was clean and real, like a cup of fresh water after drinking brackish water.

That night after supper (cold potato soup, gristly beef roast, more boiled gnome eggs) Karolina and her mother invited him to play cards again, but Sam wasn't falling for it.

"The back of my head will be flat if I play with you ladies," he complained, only half joking. "I am a man of some stature, and if you keep slapping me in the head, it might diminish my masculine charms."

When Sam waggled his eyebrows with the last remark, Karolina and her mother laughed delightedly, as they should.

Phoebe rolled her eyes.

Jonas, who had come in to feed the measly fire, snorted like a bull at Sam's words. Or at least Sam assumed it was his words to which Jonas objected.

"You play cards because the English cannot play chess."

All of them turned to stare at Jonas when he made the declaration.

Karolina peered over at Sam, who hovered at the doorway, thinking to escape back to his room. "Do you play chess, Mr. Fenley?"

Did he play chess?

Well, he had mastered the subtle art of manipulating the public at the early age of ten. He had convinced princes to buy baubles, earls to buy tin soldiers, and dukes to buy key rings. He had outmaneuvered his competitors when he figured out that those enormous mansions in London were too expensive for the coin-poor aristocrats, and quietly invested in buying them up and then breaking them down.

If that wasn't chess, what was it?

"Of course," Sam said. What he left unsaid was, *I can also ice-skate and climb mountains. Theoretically.*

"Oh, wonderful," said Karolina. "I love chess."

Feck.

"I will play you," Jonas said.

Even Phoebe raised her brows at this.

A sly grin twisted the edges of Jonas's lips. Revenge perhaps for Sam having seen him sprawled on the floor like a rag doll a few days earlier. If Sam said no, he would disappoint Karolina. If he said yes, he'd have to sit opposite Jonas for an extended period.

Lose-lose.

"What a splendid idea," Sam declared.

From Phoebe's expression, the smile Sam dredged up and pasted on his face was in no way convincing, but Karolina clapped her hands in approval. He tried not to drag his feet over to where Jonas pulled out a second table, then opened a small drawer to reveal a polished rosewood and ivory chess set.

Funny, now that Sam wasn't playing cards, the ladies switched to a nonlethal game of skat while they watched the men. Their palms must be too sore from smacking him on the head all afternoon.

"We won't bet money," Jonas said. "*This* time." His fingers were thrice the size of the tiny pawns, but he set the board deftly, quietly humming a tune.

Then came the slaughter.

"Well," said Karolina when it was done, her voice overly sweet as though she spoke to a dying man. "Well, that was an interesting strategy, Mr. Fenley. Was there a reason you chose the Spanish opening?"

Sam opened his mouth, trying desperately to conjure a brilliant lie, but gave up and shrugged instead.

Spanish opening. Was that a chess term for *failing spectacularly*?

"Perhaps you played too many hands of *slapkopf* today?" the marchioness asked.

"Oh dear," said Karolina sympathetically. "You fell over that bench this morning as well."

Phoebe's mouth twisted as a smile fought for dominance with her usual pout of superiority. "I suspect you may be fighting the effects of continuous brain injuries, Mr. Fenley," she said.

"There is nothing wrong with my head," Sam retorted.

"Then we should play again," said Jonas.

"I don't think . . . Oh, look you've set the board up again," Sam said. "Lovely."

Horrific, more like. The second game was even more embarrassing.

"Do you have many headaches?" Karolina asked Sam afterward.

Sam glared at Jonas. Wonderful. Now the Hunt women were wondering if he were damaged.

"You play too much," said Jonas.

What was this supposed to mean?

"Playing is the point of the game, my dear sir," Sam said.

Shadows gathered around the other man. He frowned as though Sam had insulted him.

"Not here," Jonas chided him. "Here, the point of the game is to win."

The words hung heavy in the cold of the room, and Sam knew Jonas was not speaking of chess.

For a man who hoarded his words like coins, Jonas was a skilled teacher. Without saying anything more about Sam's abysmal performance, he set out each piece, then demonstrated its moves. Slowly, Jonas repeated their earlier game, moving the pieces on both sides of the board, humming the entire time, in such a way that Sam saw what he'd done wrong.

In the next game, Sam moved his pieces, and Jonas would move them back and show Sam alternate ways to move, never saying much other than "Back, over, try again."

Every so often Sam would glance over to see Phoebe staring back at him and Jonas, a speculative expression on her face.

Speculative.

Not angry or dismissive, the two most familiar expressions Phoebe wore when she encountered the outside world.

But not with Sam. Not anymore.

They finished with an abrupt "Good enough" from Jonas. He stood up from the table and nodded at Sam. "Again, tomorrow night," he said, then left the room without a backward glance.

Sam stared at the board, humming along to the same tune Jonas had favored, and replayed the last four moves. Easy to see how this game could become addictive.

"You are an admirer of Beethoven?"

When Phoebe sat opposite him, Sam started. The fire was mostly embers. Karolina and the marchioness had gone to bed without him noticing.

"Who is Beethoven?" he asked, flicking the pawns back into line.

"The piece you were humming," she answered, moving her pawns so they were off-center.

How appropriate.

"Who is Jonas?"

There were still a few candles lit, but the curtains had been closed in the parlor to keep the worst of the draft away, and shadows lunged along the sideboards and turned in slow circles on the ceiling.

Phoebe lifted one brow and pursed her lips, but rather than a rebuff, she let out a thin sigh.

"He is a . . . relative, of sorts."

In the dark, Phoebe's eyes were the black of a night's sky—a sky that would be purple in the light of a star, but no stars twinkled back at him. Her long fingers kept troubling the chess pieces, picking them up and moving them round, the only sign of her restless nature.

"Of the sort born on the other side of the blanket?" he asked, using polite society's term for a bastard.

"You might say that, if you were rude enough," she allowed.

"Not much of a talker," Sam said.

"He had a stutter. My father used to mock him terribly for it."

A draft had found its way past the thick brocaded curtains billowing against the wall.

"Will you tell me?" Sam asked. "Will you tell me why you are all horribly, horribly sad? Why your half brother serves us dinner, why your mother keeps opening windows, and you talk to empty picture hooks?"

Phoebe's face closed and she sat still, staring at the queen held loosely in her palm. "What does it matter?" she asked finally. "We aristocrats with our eccentricities are the last of a dying way of life. Soon the world will belong to men like you, unburdened by history. There is no point to talking about what we cannot change."

"Men like me?" he asked quietly. "What about women like you? Your mother might be muted by her upbringing, but you are from a new generation, too. You and those secret scientists will run the world someday."

With a cynical laugh, she stood. "Women like me will never run the world. We are a man's worst nightmare."

Sam's head jerked in response. "What nonsense is this? Beautiful. Brilliant. You are a man's dream, Lady Hunt."

Not his dream, though. The last thing Sam wanted to dream about was the fire and ice that made up Phoebe Hunt. He liked sweet dreams of cakes and pies. He wanted to dream of Karolina.

Or he would, if he could fall asleep in this damned mausoleum.

"I don't care what men dream, Mr. Fenley," Phoebe said. "That is my fatal flaw. I do not care. How I look, how I smell, whether supper is on the table, or how your day has been. I do not care."

Liar.

Phoebe cared. She cared too much, and it hurt, so she numbed herself to everything, the bad and the good.

He didn't say this, though. She would only deny it.

Besides, Sam wasn't certain if she were armed.

Phoebe opened her hand and let the queen fall to the chessboard. "Good night, Mr. Fenley."

"G'night, Phoebe," Sam said, but she had already walked away.

"Moti?"

Phoebe stopped at the entrance to the nursery and had to hold on to the doorframe when the scent hit her.

The barren nursery still smelled like girl sweat and paper, fear and love, cold porridge and old biscuits hidden beneath pillows for midnight snacks.

The room had been cleared of the cribs that once stood side by side, covered with moth-eaten netting and home to a motley assortment of rag dolls and puppies. They'd a nurse, once upon a time. Phoebe remembered her whiskers, which tickled their eyelids when she kissed them good night, and the crooked fingers that sewed tiny versions of what she loved best. Babies and dogs.

Only a handful of books lay scattered on the bottom shelf of a dusty bookcase where once there had been piles of cloth-covered volumes, a precious few in Lithuanian. A clothes stand stood empty, and the golden curtains stained with whatever liquids one encounters in a nursery had been removed from the newly cleaned windows.

This room had been their refuge, the safest place in the manor, since the men never climbed past the first set of stairs. Terrible storms would roll across the countryside to smash up against the Pennines to the south, but the thunderous winds and lashing rain were a far-off countermeasure to the silly songs and haunting stories Phoebe and her sisters told one another in the flickering candlelight.

Phoebe rubbed her eyes as the past superimposed itself upon the present and the room was simultaneously full of color and bare of any sign of life.

"Moti?" she whispered.

"Here."

The first step pained her, but Phoebe walked across the empty room to where her mother sat on the floor, back against the bare wall, heedless of the dust and grime. Without curtains, the windows let in the peculiar light of this part of the country, blue and gray with a hint of green, which, when it hit the yellowing walls, muted even the brightest hues.

Beneath one of the windows stood a wooden bucket. A small puddle of something brackish had spilled and smelled of vinegar.

Phoebe inhaled sharply and knelt at her mother's side even though she would ruin her skirts.

"Moti, were you cleaning the windows yourself?" she asked.

Moti looked at her hands, red and wrinkled, and grimaced. "No one will come here to clean. Not even Jonas. They are too afraid."

Phoebe did not reach out to touch her mother. When Moti considered wandering away from the world, she did not want to be touched.

"Leave it, then. Let the windows stay dirty," Phoebe said.

A broom leaned against the wall inside a circle of clean floorboards.

"Are you tired?" Phoebe asked. "You go lie down and I will finish—"

"Look in the closet," Moti interrupted.

Phoebe froze. Her mother's beautiful eyes shone clear, and she spoke in English. This was a good sign. Still, there could be anything in that closet. Or nothing.

A consequence of living with a parent who crossed the boundaries of sanity was the temptation to follow them. To leave behind a world becoming more difficult to navigate with each passing year and spend your days with ghosts.

To give up.

To let go.

One of the reasons Phoebe used to cut herself was that the

pain pinned her to the present. When she split her skin with the edge of her blade, thoughts of past or future were wiped away by the sight of her private abomination, the only way she knew how to stay in the present without resorting to madness.

For many years, Moti spent days and sometimes weeks in the company of the unseen and the dead. Precipitated by a visit from the marquess, her mother would pull into a tiny ball of a being, her retreat marked with sudden outbursts of creativity; painting murals on the walls or dyeing yards of muslin and draping a room with the cloth in a blinding maze of still-dripping material.

Phoebe's oldest sister, Alice, showed signs of joining her mother in her journeys when she turned seventeen. A nervous girl, Alice developed a fear of sleeping during adolescence. At night Alice would walk the halls of the manor, tallow candle in hand, holding conversations with invisible beings, staving off the inevitable surrender to exhaustion.

Their father decided Alice suffered a condition of the womb.

The doctors of the day agreed, opening asylums for women who displayed symptoms of "female hysteria." The patients were mostly wives sent by their husbands. Women who were prone to saying *no* or *stop* or disagreeing with the man of the house one too many times.

"What she needs is a babe or two," the marquess once opined at the breakfast table while holding a broadsheet in front of his face. "Women who don't breed go mad."

Indeed, the common wisdom among the medical profession was hysteria might be a disease of the mind, but its effects had a direct impact on a woman's reproductive system. In other words, women who said no to sex with their husbands were diseased. Conveniently the reverse was true as well.

Women who wanted too much sex or enjoyed sex were also suffering female hysteria, and daughters or sisters who were guilty of intercourse outside of marriage with men or women were committed to these asylums until they were "cured" and vowed never to commit such an unnatural act again.

Though he never looked up over the paper that day, her father knew they hadn't nodded in agreement. He'd lowered his arms slowly, eyes flicking across their faces like tiny slaps; the sight of so many daughters offending him, as though he'd forgotten they were there. Breathing in the tiniest hint of disagreement, his nostrils quivered.

"Isn't that so, wife?" he asked. "That a woman's behavior can make her barren. Or unable to produce a boy child."

Caught in the currents of danger Phoebe stared at her father as one might a cobra rising from the basket. Her mother sat to his right, head bowed, silent, thankfully. Surrounded by the women of his family, her father might be eating alone for all he took notice of them until he settled on whom he would single out for condemnation. Mostly it was Moti. That day it was Alice, who'd come late to breakfast, then wandered off, crying silently.

Phoebe had loaded marmalade onto her toast, hoping it would help her swallow past the tension in her throat.

"My lord, I wish you would reconsider." Her mother's voice had rung out in the anxious silence. "Can we not give Alice a season first? She is from a distinguished family. To have a beautiful dress and dance at a ball, every girl should do such things."

"Out of the question." He hadn't bothered to extrapolate, just buttered his toast.

Phoebe had known what would happen next. Still, she prayed silently, *Don't argue, Moti. Please.*

"My lord, I do not understand."

The smack of her father's palm against the breakfast table had shocked a small gasp from them all. As his head swiveled and his glare fell upon her mother, Phoebe and her sisters began at once to fade, melting into the furniture, ghosting their way to the door. The odor reminiscent of burning refuse; the scent of fear and a harbinger of danger crawled down the back of Phoebe's throat. Numb limbs carried her to safety, so she never saw what happened next. Imprinted on her brain was the jumble of pronouncements that still echoed through the years.

"Perhaps we harvest the funds for a season from the money tree out back?" His voice, so calm.

"There are many ways to economize, my lord . . ."

". . . tried to bring you happiness and all I hear are complaints and demands . . ." Now he adopted a wounded air. It twisted Phoebe's insides into a tight ball that took days to unravel again.

The more her mother's voice rose, the quieter her father's replies.

"You've no concept of the cost of a season, do you? Are you truly so selfish you would rob the bread from your children's mouths to pay for whatever new gowns you will insist on for yourself and the girl?"

Crouched outside the dining room like a coward with the rest of her sisters, Phoebe listened to her father pull apart her mother's arguments as a child might pull the wings off a fly. The truth was her father was ashamed of his wife with her heavy accent and odd ways. His trips to London were for his pleasure; this made obvious by the way he looked upon his return to Prentiss Manor. Well-fed, newly dressed, smelling of cigars and expensive cologne.

Daughters could be bargained away like cows or horses without having to pay for them to be displayed.

"How can you take pleasure in disagreeing with me when your defiance poisons your womb?" he'd asked, calmly.

Until the rage came.

Yet, women were the ones suffering hysteria?

"Do you not grieve for the children you have killed?" he demanded.

Phoebe shook with anger at each accusation. The worst of the fighting ended with this—what her father saw as her mother's ultimate betrayal. Her inability to give him a living son.

The words were indistinct, but her mother's pain came through clearly.

". . . hope this time . . . everything the doctor told me . . ."

"I have told you repeatedly your disobedience is the cause. You are a most unnatural creature."

Waving goodbye to their sister, bundled into a carriage on the first leg of a long journey to Lithuania two months later, they'd hoped marriage and motherhood would keep Alice in the present and out of the clutches of ghosts.

Phoebe and her sisters had shed a tear or two, but Moti had cried for days after Alice left. Phoebe reckoned they were selfish tears. She thought her mother cried because the rest of her children showed no signs of a similar madness and she felt somehow ill-done by them. She wanted company.

"There is nothing bad in there, Bee," her mother said, startling Phoebe from the quagmire of memories lapping at her toes. Every time she entered this room, Phoebe catapulted somewhere back in time and lost herself in reminiscences.

Never were they happy times her mind chose to revisit.

Phoebe rose and crossed to the closet, one hand on the doorknob.

"Moti," she said, not opening the door, "if you hadn't come here and been married to Father, what would you have done?"

"What would I have done?" Moti echoed, one eyebrow rising in an expression of confusion. "I would have married someone else and had babies. It is what women must do."

Phoebe pulled a breath in through her nose and held it, staring at the tarnished brass beneath her fingers.

"Yes, I know, but if you hadn't come here, would you have had fewer children, or gotten a painting instructor, or learned to ride, or . . ."

Moti waved her delicate hand in the air, dismissing the questions.

"Why do you ask such questions? Ever since you were a child. Why? Why?" She'd been staring out the window, but Moti now turned her gaze toward Phoebe.

Expecting the question to have been rhetorical, Phoebe said nothing, but Moti wanted an answer.

"Tell me, Bee. You are a scientist. You ask questions to which none of us have answers. Why?" Moti asked.

"Because I have no faith," Phoebe replied.

Moti moved her mouth as though she were tasting the truth of this admission.

Phoebe continued. "I have no trust in benevolent beings, no desire to leave anything to so ridiculous a concept as fate. Because the earth must be solid beneath my feet."

Her mother tilted her head, the northern light intent on siphoning her outrageous beauty. Phoebe was struck not by how young her mother appeared but how little the terrible events of her life had left a mark on her skin or hair. Her scars were on the inside.

"What do you do when there is no answer?" her mother asked quietly. "You cannot expect to go through life always in control. The world will shake you up and down no matter what."

Tightening her hand on the doorknob, Phoebe pretended to consider Moti's words. What her mother didn't know was that Phoebe had figured out long ago how to sidestep a shaking world; camouflage weakness with sarcasm and drown desire for affection in a healthy dose of rage and despair.

"Open the door, Bee."

Inside the closet were narrow shelves that once held the nursery's bed linens. Only three shelves were occupied now. Two books, *Chemical Manipulation, Being Instructions to Students in Chemistry* and *Experimental Researches in Chemistry and Physics*, squatted on the second-to-bottom shelf. *Chemical Manipulation* was partly singed, but *Experimental Researches* looked untouched.

"Those books, they were the books you loved, yes?" Moti asked.

Phoebe couldn't answer, her throat had closed. On the shelf above the two textbooks stood a handful of blackened glass flasks, two wooden stands she had built herself to replicate Faraday's experiments on electromagnetism, and a handful of warped Faraday discs she had spent two years' worth of pin money to obtain.

"I thought he'd burned it all," she whispered finally.

Moti shrugged in that way she had of distilling their father's monstrous deeds into matters of small importance.

"What he burned can be replaced."

Phoebe closed her eyes and pressed her lips tightly together. She would not gainsay her mother, not after a gesture such as this. They both knew it for a lie, but only Moti believed the lie could transform into the truth.

Before she discovered the existence of women scientists, before she even thought of herself as a scientist, Michael Faraday had been Phoebe's idol.

Historically, scientists had believed there were different kinds of electricity. That stuffy old Italian, Luigi Galvini, posited the force moving within a living being was "animal" electricity, separate from "static" electricity.

Faraday knew only one electricity exists, and different phenomena were caused by increasing the intensity and quantity of the same electricity.

Only one power.

While Faraday might have believed wholeheartedly in his religion, his work proved to Phoebe that religions were a way to keep the populace complacent. The church's answer to *why* offered no room for competing theories, no margin for error, and ensured women were forever yoked to a purposeless life.

There was no all-knowing Father, capricious and vengeful, who fueled the world. Nor myriad spirits of water and trees, no miracles, and no ghosts.

Only electricity.

A flow of power without a gender or race.

The same power charging the sun charged her body. Her mother's body. The world's bodies.

Once Phoebe understood this, she understood why women scientists threatened men. Why the world was ambivalent toward scientists in general.

Science proved men and women were made of the same

stuff. That the same life force flowed through colonizers and the people they oppressed. That a king was a king because he said so, not because anything holy that ran in his veins set him apart from his subjects.

Science is a truth hard to swallow.

12

Faraday's First Law of Electrolysis: The mass of a substance deposited or liberated at an electrode is directly proportional to the charge.

"SO, THE *M* STANDS FOR MASS. YOU SEE, THE MASS OF elements is directly proportional to the charge, which we represent with *Q*."

Sam stared at Phoebe's mouth, willing the noises she made to turn into words he recognized.

$$m \propto Q \rightarrow m/Q = Z$$

She'd written the equation on the same paper where Lady Fallowshall had marked points from their card games. For some bizarre reason, Phoebe assumed writing it down would help him follow her explanation.

"That means there are a lot of them, right?" he asked.

Phoebe, having opened her mouth to continue her elucidation, now froze, giving him a view of the inside of her mouth, stunned into silence by the depth of his ignorance.

"A lot of masses. That Fermat believes is elemental," Sam said. "The *m* there."

One perfectly shaped eyebrow rose, wrinkling her forehead.

"Your sister was a finalist for the Rosewood Prize. Would have won if she were not a woman," Phoebe said slowly.

"Yes." Sam nodded. This was true. "Letty's a genius."

"At the supper table, does she discuss her work?" Phoebe asked.

"Oh, yes. She enjoys the math where you use letters instead of numbers. Taught m'sisters some of it. Now the younger ones are chatting about theories of color and prisms. Why blue is blue and whatnot." Sam cleared his throat.

Why was she looking at him as though he'd sprouted horns? He'd tripped over, then broken a chair on his way into the parlor this evening after dinner. Karolina had quoted some dead Greek bloke at him, and he'd asked if it were Shakespeare. He had been staying at the manor for almost three weeks.

Hadn't Phoebe already noticed he wasn't the sharpest knife in the shop?

Karolina had. She'd taken to slowing down when she spoke with him and pointing out hazards when they walked together. Like grass.

And the floor.

The paper containing the equation lay on the chessboard. The chessboard where Jonas had trounced Sam's arse.

Less bloody this time but still a massacre.

Karolina and her mother had gone to bed already, Karolina stopping to pat him gently on the shoulder and praise his progress, Phoebe hiding her laugh behind a cough.

Now they were alone in the parlor, a drafty room with high ceilings and hard chairs. A single fireplace lent flickering light but little heat to the room, and Phoebe had covered her out-of-date dinner dress with a tattered black knit shawl that looked older than her. Sam, knowing his place, had not unbent enough to replace his dinner jacket with a sweater, but he did wear two undershirts and an extra pair of socks.

The chessboard sat somewhat to the side of the fireplace, not close enough for a stray lick of heat to touch the players. If Sam played black and sat facing the back of the room, his neck was exposed. If he played white and faced the door, a window on the other side of the room could be seen out of the corner of his eye, and the curtains there would move on their own sometimes.

This was the third after-dinner chess game he and Jonas had fought. Once Sam's demise became apparent, the Hunt women usually turned their attention to subjects less embarrassing.

Plumbing, for one. The manor needed updating to fetch a good price. With much hesitation the marchioness had finally agreed to Phoebe's suggestion they add water pipes before the official sale.

Ha. As though anything could improve this house. Last night Sam heard children giggling in the corridor outside his room. He hadn't looked because there was no such thing as ghosts. Also, if there were such things as ghosts, it would be downright unfair for them to be in the guise of children.

He shivered at the thought, and Phoebe, who had taken Jonas's seat opposite him, let out a *pfft* of disappointment.

"How is it you are surrounded by scientists and yet claim to understand none of it?" she asked, the acid in her tone scratching at Sam's ears.

Sitting back from the chessboard, he examined her face.

Phoebe Hunt was a beautiful woman. Beautiful and angry.

Damn him if that wasn't an enticing combination.

"It is my theory a man's brain can only hold a certain amount of information," he said cheerfully, knowing full well it irritated her when he refused to take himself seriously.

When Phoebe became irritated, her irises darkened from amethyst to mauve. It woke Sam's pulse. This, in turn, made Sam grumpy. He wasn't supposed to be lusting after this villainess. He was supposed to be lusting after her sister.

Phoebe's attention shifted to the chessboard. Her long, slim fingers moved the pieces into different configurations, the black bishops on the attack. The white queen in danger.

"You should pay attention," said Phoebe. "My sister is intelligent and has an interest in science as well as for her books."

"Well, I have an interest in neither," he said, with the smallest snap in his *t*'s. What was the matter with his brain tonight? It took all his willpower not to stare at the bridge of her nose or the long column of her neck.

"Why did you say nice things about me the other day? Before you pushed me into the stream?" Sam asked.

Not that the compliments made him examine Phoebe more closely during meals or when they cataloged books together in the dim candlelight of the dusty library. They didn't make her seem softer around the edges. Accessible.

So damn beautiful.

"Beautiful? You are a blockhead," Phoebe snapped.

Sam's mouth made an O as if he hadn't meant to say those last three words out loud. His gaze darted side to side as if someone else had called her beautiful and was hiding behind his chair.

"Asking you an innocent question makes me a blockhead?" he asked.

"No," she said. "Well, yes. Yes it does."

He wasn't a blockhead. Sam Fenley was a good man. However, Phoebe wanted to fight. She needed to feel something after Moti surprised her with the rescued books this morning.

No.

She needed to feel something other than the guilt and grief her mother's gesture laid upon her. Phoebe's fingers tightened around the ivory carving in her hand, breathing with relief at the pain where its sharp edges cut into her skin.

Not pleasure. Simply relief.

Phoebe had no taste for pain in bedsport. Although she never wanted to be responsible for another person's death, if a man were to hurt her physically ever again, she would fight back with all the weapons at her disposal. Right now, for example, she had a knife in her pocket.

Why had Sam called her beautiful?

"Phoebe . . ." Sam said from far away. Her eyes followed his lips again as they formed her name.

Phoebe had watched him, tonight, watching her. The line of his shoulders, the arc of his arm, the way he smiled, like cups of sunlight he spilled heedlessly about him.

"Phoebe?"

Why had she let him come here and melt the edges of everything?

"Phoebe! What are you doing?"

Taking hold of her hand, Sam pried her fingers open. The points of the queen's crown had punctured her skin and the blood looked black in the dim light.

"It's nothing. It doesn't . . ."

Her center of gravity plummeted from below her ribs to her core when he put the tips of her first two fingers in his mouth and gently sucked.

Idiocy.

Sheer idiocy to allow it, but when had Phoebe ever made the safe choice?

Sam pulled her up from the chair as she was standing, and she fell flush against him. Both moved toward each other, and in the end, she didn't know who kissed whom first; it didn't matter because finally Sam's mouth was on hers and it was everything she'd wanted.

Holding her throbbing hand over her head, Sam walked her back until her shoulder blades hit the wall, never stopping the kiss, pressing the evidence of his arousal right where her body craved friction, and a raw, red ache of lust pulsed through her.

If Phoebe knew anything about Sam Fenley, it was that he could be sweet and gentle.

Not here, though.

Not now.

Sam kissed her as though he needed the air from her lungs to breathe. As if he could crawl inside her skin if he kissed her hard enough, deep enough. If she could, she'd figure out how to stop wanting him, but she suckled his tongue, and he tasted like caramel and tea and beeswax candles and sunlit corners and everything she'd mocked yet secretly desired.

Sam set a hand next to her head, holding up the wall, holding himself back. Like soft strokes, his warm breath slid up and down the slope of her neck.

All Phoebe knew was the pounding of blood at her temples, in her chest, between her thighs. When he bit lightly on her earlobe, his silken hair brushed her chin, and she wanted that silk across her breasts and down her belly.

"Say the word, and I will take you upstairs and take such

good care of you." The last four words were a crooning plea that touched Phoebe over the whole of her body.

"Say a different word and I will put this out of my mind," he breathed. "As ever, it is your choice."

As ever?

When had anything ever been Phoebe's choice?

The tiny sparks of relief after cutting herself with the ivory chess piece were nothing, were drops of mist compared to the ocean of pleasure this man gave her. Every inch of her skin had shrunk so tight her bones might burst through at any moment, and the hardest part of him surged against her as his hips rolled ever so slightly. Just the once.

Phoebe wanted and because she wanted, she hated herself.

"Oh, it is I who am to blame if we continue? You have no say in the matter?" she whispered, arching her neck to allow him access.

Sam laughed, the warm air tickling her skin. "If I could walk away from you, I would be in Sussex by now."

The kisses stopped, his lips hovering above the curve where her neck met her shoulder while he waited for her to surrender.

It was this notion of surrender that sent a wave of fear through her, frost smothering the fire of desire. Phoebe pulled Sam's hands away from her face, ready to hurt him, ready to rend herself as well when he let out a gasp. His palm was streaked with her blood.

"Your hand," he muttered, and reached for her, but Phoebe was already gone, pushing herself past him and through the door, ignoring the whispers behind the curtains, the scratching at the windowpanes, and the unfilled need at the center of her.

13

⋘◆⋙

Q: But can the mere contact of two metals, without any intervening fluid, produce electricity?

A: Yes, if they are afterwards separated. It is an established fact, that when two metals are put in contact, and afterwards separated, that which has the strongest attraction for oxygen exhibits signs of positive, the other of negative electricity.

–Mrs. Jane Mercet

PHOEBE MUST HAVE KNOWN SAM WOULD FIND HER AT some point today. What happened between them last night left its imprint on them both.

Like a godforsaken bee to a flower, Sam couldn't leave her alone after that kiss.

That kiss.

"It's three hundred years old," Phoebe said without turning around.

Her voice didn't carry more than a foot inside the gray stones of Prentiss Manor's chapel. Something about the way the ceiling sloped or the slabs of rock that formed the back wall cut her voice in half.

It was the carved rood screen stretching across the front of the chapel. An empty pedestal at the top once held the rood itself, a crucifix showing Christ in the throes of agony. Such a piece would be priceless if carved by a master carver.

Whoever carved the rood screen had pagan sympathies. In between the curlicues and fleurs-de-lis, there lurked exotic animals such as monkeys and tigers. Strange birds had found their way into the carving as well. One had an enormous bill larger than its body. Did such a bird even exist in nature?

Sam sauntered closer; the sound of footsteps was sucked into the stone. The only noise he heard was her breath. Stopping a foot behind Phoebe, the scent of her soap roused the pulse in his wrist.

"Your hand . . ." Sam stumbled for words.

Phoebe held her hand up without turning around. Two small gray plasters covered her thumb and forefinger.

"It's fine," she said, her words falling flat instead of clipped.

What kind of a chapel turned voices to lead?

Oh, yes, the kind of chapel one found in a haunted bloody manse in Cumbria. That's what.

"I wanted to apologize for the liberties I took last night."

There. That sounded like something a gentleman would say after kissing a woman whom he was *not* supposed to kiss for many, many reasons.

Sam preened when Phoebe turned around on one heel and regarded him seriously. He did have a way with words, didn't he? She looked impressed.

Should he keep talking?

"Think nothing of it, Mr. Fenley," Phoebe said, a faint air of—was that pity in her voice? "Perhaps in your experience such fumbling is construed as kissing. I can assure you; I took no . . . offense."

Sam knew his jaw had dropped, for the gelid air of the chapel hit the back of his throat, but it took a moment to shut his mouth and compose himself.

"Oh. Well. I'm happy to hear that. We'll forget it, then," he said.

Obviously, Phoebe was lying.

Sam had kissed her with passion and *expertise*. No doubt her icy demeanor was the result of a sleepless night spent tossing and turning with unrequited lust.

That mystery solved, Sam crossed his arms behind his back and joined Phoebe in staring at the rood screen.

"It has held up well. The craftsmanship is . . ." Sam blinked.

At first, he'd assumed the rood screen depicted Noah's ark, albeit with animals one never encountered in the Bible. Surely giant lizards and snakes with two heads were not among Noah's original manifest.

Upon closer inspection, Sam discerned a few human figures in there as well, male and female, some of them . . .

"Holy Mother of—" Sam exclaimed. He forgot the awkwardness between them as he craned his neck and squinted. "Is that woman touching—?"

His head jerked back, and he stared at Phoebe in outrage. "How long have you known about this screen?"

Shrugging, she lifted an eyebrow as though amused by Sam's reaction. "It's three hundred years old. Most everyone who has been in this chapel for hours on end has had time to look at this screen."

"Look here—" Sam could not contain his fascination. "This little man is holding his—my goodness, that *can't* be to scale."

Wicked woman! Now she was laughing at him. Not aloud, but she'd sucked the side of her mouth in and the three wrinkles in the shape of cups at the corners of her eyes straightened when she swallowed her amusement.

Gah. This was no laughing matter.

"How could your family have let this stand?" he asked. "This isn't suitable for children."

The more he looked, the more Sam found little imps and witches and whatnot cavorting in the most carnal manner. "Then again," he said mostly to himself, "I might have spent more time at church if we studied this instead of scripture."

"How puerile," Phoebe drawled. "Is that what it takes to save a man's soul? Naked breasts and outsized penises?"

When Sam squeaked with surprise at her words, Phoebe melted.

Her laugh was no less discordant in the chapel than it had been outdoors the other day, but it cheered Sam immensely. This manor was a place that turned the world upside down. When Phoebe laughed, however, everything around him righted.

A wan shaft of sunlight speared the stained glass and illuminated the slight cloud left by her breath. Was her nose as cold as his? Should he offer her a jacket? His arms?

"It was carved when the chapel was expanded in 1521," Phoebe explained. "Do you have suggestions as to how we might describe it in the auction catalog?"

Sam knew a hundred ways to describe this, none of them fit for public reading. Taking a step or two back, the more egregious figures faded back into the cacophony of curlicues and larger carvings. To the left, above the pulpit, was a small loft. The railings there were carved in the same manner as the rood screen.

"What's up there?" Sam asked. The light from the stained glass fell onto the altar and transept where they stood, but the rest of the chapel was murky and shadowed. "That isn't the choir loft, is it?"

Phoebe's laughter faded. "That is the women's loft."

"Women's loft?" Sam echoed.

"It was the practice here for women and men to sit separately during services," she explained.

Sam wasn't a regular churchgoer like his mam and da, but he'd never heard of such a thing.

"I suppose it was something the men did back then," he said, uncertain if he were teasing or truly offended. "Hiding the women away so they wouldn't be distracted."

Phoebe didn't respond. She walked toward the pulpit, ducked below the stairs, and pulled open a small wooden door.

"Do you want to see?" she asked, looking back at him.

Why *wouldn't* he want to go up into the unlit loft of an unheated stone chapel? Why, there was certain to be treasure up there. Mice. Rats, perhaps. Possibly a ghost.

What fun!

Sometimes Sam wondered if his thoughts were so loud, other people heard them, for Phoebe stopped two stairs above him, turned, and said in a low voice, "Do not be afraid. The ghosts won't come up here."

"Well, that's a relief," he said cheerfully.

Phoebe continued up the stairs and Sam followed. "As I am not prepared to meet a ghost and fear I will come up short in their presence."

Ha. Haha.

Phoebe said nothing. She didn't even chuckle.

Pushing open another thick oak door, she led him into the loft. There were a scant handful of benches up here, six at the most, one of them on its side. No pillows or moldering cushions like in the pew benches below. A squat wooden shelf sat against the back wall, thick with dust, no sign of the missals he supposed once lay there for the ladies' use.

Phoebe walked to the edge of the loft and set her hand on the railing of the carved gate. Sam, a little sick from standing in so narrow a space high above the pews, did not venture over to Phoebe's side. He was content to stand against the wall and keep watch for mice.

Not ghosts, though supposedly there were no ghosts here.

Should he whistle?

It would dispel the heavy aura of disharmony and misery thick in the air of the unused rooms in the manse.

Then again, what if it attracted the ghosts?.

"What are you doing now?" he asked her. His voice thunked to the floor, bounced off, and echoed on the flagstones below.

Phoebe had crouched at the opposite end of the loft. Pushing aside the empty bookshelf, she ran her fingers over the wall.

"If this has something to do with summoning ghosts . . ." he warned, "I will jump off this loft and be grateful when I fall unconscious."

Phoebe shoved her shoulder against the wall. "There is another part to this loft."

Sam glanced around to be sure nothing white or gray hovered in the air, then made his way over to squint through the gloom.

"How do you know?" he asked.

Phoebe rapped on the wall. "You can see when you walk in that this floor goes to the back of the chapel. There is obviously a hidey-hole on this side of the wall. Listen."

She rapped again and it sounded different this time. Hollow.

"I would explore when I was a little girl, but my father had the chapel padlocked after Karolina was born. I tried but was unable to pick the lock."

Aha. Perhaps there *was* treasure here! That would make this trip worth his time.

"What is in there? Gold?" he mused aloud. "Chalices with jewels in them and such? Silver candle holders?"

"Priests."

Phoebe pushed one more time and a rectangle-shaped piece of the wall fell inward.

"Priests?" he cried. "You said there would be no ghosts."

"Not dead priests," she said matter-of-factly as she pulled the piece of wood out of the hole, then stuck her head inside. "Live priests. It's a priest hole. I thought . . ."

Her next words were muffled when Phoebe stretched out on the ground, turned on her side, and wiggled her torso inside the hole.

Of all the . . .

Scientists!

Sam should have known Phoebe's brain would need something to ponder. No scientist he'd met at Athena's Retreat would have been satisfied, either, without some sort of discovery.

Or explosion.

Please don't let there be anything explosive in there.

Nothing burst into flames, as luck would have it—then again Sam had found little luck since coming to this place.

None, actually.

None whatsoever.

So, when the sound of a door opening and scratching the stone floor came from below the loft, he didn't even bother to panic.

All he knew was that when he got back to London, he would never again have anything to do with noble families. Or scientists. Or women.

No more women. Ever.

"I thought I saw Mr. Fenley come in here." That was Karolina.

"There is no reason to come into this chapel. Your father had it closed off when you were a baby. Unless . . ." *That* was the marchioness.

"I'd forgotten about the chapel altogether. You know, Moti, when I was little, I thought I heard . . . oh. Ummm, what strange carvings there are on this . . . Ohhhhh. Oh!"

Sam grabbed Phoebe's skirt and yanked.

"Your mother and sister are out there," he whispered.

"I am never, *ever* getting married." That was Karolina.

"They aren't that big in real life." *That* was the marchioness.

This could not be happening.

Sam crawled to the railing that hid the occupants of the loft from those in the chapel proper and looked down.

Karolina and her mother stood in the nave, peering up at the carved rood screen, one with skepticism, one with great interest.

"What . . ." Karolina asked, "what exactly must one do to accommodate something of that size?"

"We may be viewing it from the wrong side. It might be if we . . ."

The women bent sideways at the waist.

"Oh, that makes it worse. Is he putting it—"

Behind him, Phoebe twitched.

Sam knelt next to Phoebe's boots, the only part of her that remained outside the priest's hole. "Phoebe. Your mother and Karolina are there. We must leave," he breathed.

"I can't."

"What if they decide to look up here?"

"I'm *stuck*," Phoebe wailed softly.

"What?"

"I can't get out. I tried, but I am stuck."

Sam clamped both of his hands over his mouth. No. No, he would not laugh. This was a serious situation and he needed to find a way out of it.

"Sam," Phoebe whispered, her legs scissoring, exposing a sliver of her calf and poorly mended stockings above the tops of her ankle-length boots.

Agh.

Sam let go of his mouth only to slap his hands over his eyes. Phoebe would murder him if she knew he was ogling her legs.

"You have to help," she whispered. "There are splinters all over. They've tangled in my hair and when I tried to get loose, they caught on the skirts of my dress. Reach in and unhook me."

"We need to clean from top to bottom in here. It smells like mouse droppings and it's colder inside than outside." Karolina's voice was faint, but Sam heard her well enough.

"I agree. We will ask Jonas," the marchioness said.

"Yes, better him than . . . Oh, Moti. Look at this. How does he walk with such an enormous—"

Sweet Jesu.

Sam stared into the priest's hole where Phoebe was lying on

her right side. He saw nothing past the rise of her hip. The hole was three feet wide, enough room for two if they snuggled close.

"Sam, simply reach in and . . ."

"I can't reach my arm in," Sam said, trying to stick his head in the hole without hitting the top of it. "I'll have to lie beside you."

"No. Don't come so far in. You're blocking the light, and you won't be able to see what you are doing." Her low whisper could not hide the slight nervousness beneath her words.

Sam ignored her. He'd have them out of there in ten seconds. Lying on his side, he scooched his body into the tight passageway until he was flush up against her like two spoons in a cutlery case.

"I can do it by feel if I get close enough," he whispered.

"You are too close," Phoebe complained. "I am pressed up against you and can barely move to take a breath."

Sam's leg twisted beneath him. If the squinty-eyed, prodigiously endowed little goblins cavorting on the rood screens below could see him, they would piss themselves with laughter as he tried to reach his arm up and over the angry woman who writhed next to him.

"Stop moving for one moment." Sam was lucky his voice remained even. Each time Phoebe twisted her hips, her bottom rubbed against his cock.

The horror and hilarity of their situation was not nearly enough to distract him from his growing erection and the way her hips stilled at its presence. She was indeed captured where her topknot had caught on a crooked nail. The maid must have been good at her job. An army of hairpins kept Phoebe's hair in place so that no matter how hard she tried to pull away, her hair stubbornly refused to unravel, and only a few curls at her temples were allowed to escape.

If he were to reach up, it would take but a moment to free her.

Except, with her hair caught up, her bared neck was less than an inch away from his mouth. Sam smelled herbs; sage, tansy, and . . . He put his nose a hairbreadth from her skin and inhaled. Purely for professional reasons. If he bottled this scent for the emporium, it would make him a fortune.

"Lemon and rosemary," he said. "Is that what you use to rinse your hair?"

He couldn't see her expression, but he'd wager a pound Phoebe had just rolled her eyes.

"First," she said in the crisp manner of a schoolteacher, "a gentleman does not ask after something so personal as a lady's intimate toilette. Secondly, you do not need to be so close to free me. Third, your hands are nowhere near where they need to be, oh, oh, Sam!"

His hands were indeed far south of where she remained firmly caught.

"Shhh," he whispered. "You must be quiet, or your mother will find us for certain."

"Are they still there?" she asked.

The two of them froze, straining to hear if the women were still below or had, heaven forfend, decided to look in the loft.

Sam heard nothing. Then again, given the way his luck had been going, the marchioness and her daughter could well be standing staring at their feet. This might have wilted his enthusiasm for being this close to one of the most magnetic women he'd ever encountered—might have—except Phoebe chose that moment to sigh.

Not in an annoyed I'd-like-you-to-leave-now-before-I-shoot-you manner. In a way that signaled exhaustion.

If Sam had hated every moment spent in this place, how must Phoebe feel? That she and the women in her family endured abuse was clear. That they still walked on tenterhooks, still jumped at every shadow. How must it feel to be so tied down by memory, you never even looked for an escape?

That sigh undid something tight within him. He knew this woman now. Knew she would never flat-out say she needed help. That she was overwhelmed and tired and so sad.

Phoebe Hunt would have to be safe to use those words.

Sam Fenley wanted to give her safety.

She sighed again and his high-minded sympathy drowned in a crashing wave of lust as the action pushed her bottom tight up against him.

Madness. Utter madness, but what a powerful madness this was. Like pressing up against a fire, anticipating the burn, hoping to be left in a pile of ashes afterward.

The knobs of the bones in her neck shone like pearls in the faint light. Closing his mouth over one, he sucked, and she squirmed in response.

"I knew you would taste delicious," he whispered. "Some folks might think you were made of porcelain, but you are made of spun sugar."

"I am made of vinegar," she whispered back. "Something must be wrong with you."

After a moment she spoke again. "Perhaps you should taste once more to be sure?"

This woman would be the death of him.

Still, if Phoebe offered, Sam was not the man to turn her down.

He smoothed a hand down the line of her waist and the rise of her hip, then cupped her bottom and she stilled.

"If you lean back a little more, I can make you feel good, Phoebe."

He put his mouth to her skin again and let the taste of her flood his tongue. An addictive mix of salt and soap and woman.

"I'm certain I won't . . . uhhh." Phoebe's words slurred into a moan, and Sam's cock jumped at the sound.

"You deserve a tiny bit of pleasure, my lady," he crooned softly. "I will be gentle and quiet and"—his mouth wandered from her neck to her shoulder—"attentive to whatever you might desire."

"We shouldn't but I . . ." Her voice was full of a delicious tension, and he rewarded her by pushing more insistently into her bottom as he swept his palm to the juncture between her legs, and her hiss of pleasure sent the last of the blood from his brain directly to his cock.

In the dark, her desire rose from her body like morning mist on the river. His nose was full of it, and it drugged him in the best way possible.

"What would you like, Phoebe? A small release? A tiny favor, between friends?" Sam's voice was velvet and silk, sliding down her spine and pooling around the center of her pleasure.

A small release.

Between friends?

"Yes," she said to herself. She must have said it aloud as well because his hand closed over her calf where the hem of her dress had twisted itself. Before he could slide her pantalettes up her legs, Phoebe took hold of his wrist and brought his hand beneath her skirts, pressing his fingers to the slit in her drawers.

Sam stilled in surprise.

Would he take a disgust of her that she knew where best to please her? Phoebe held her breath.

Before she changed her mind, Sam combed through the soft curls between her legs. His hot palm pushed against her quim, and she dampened under his touch.

"I want to touch you, as well," she complained.

Devil that he was, Sam flicked the tiny bud at her center, and she muffled a cry. Lightning raced from her quim to her nipples. They hadn't done much more than press against each other and already Phoebe hovered on the edge of completion.

At the sound she made, his hips strained against her, his thick shaft pushed at her bottom, and his other hand twisted in her hair.

Craning her head around, she relished the slight pain at her scalp where her hair was caught between the splinter and his fingers. The kiss was clumsy and off-center but Sam's mouth was hot and wet, and he thrust his cock against her backside slowly at the same time he used the heel of his hand to make her writhe.

That they were both trapped made it even more exciting. Neither of them had the upper hand in this space. If they moved too much, one of them would get hurt. If they made noise, they would be discovered.

There would be no explaining this away.

"Please," she hissed into his mouth. "Now," she begged, then suckled his tongue.

Sam did not tease her. He gave her what she wanted and slipped his long, thick finger into the center of her while he pressed hard, tight circles with his palm. Her legs trembled from the tension and a deep growl issued from him, like the satisfied purr of a tiger, quiet enough that it was all vibration, leaving Phoebe shaking with desire.

All it took was another press of his hand and the clumsy knock of teeth against teeth for the winds to race across their bodies, thunder pound in their ears, fire burn and twist inside them until the storm broke and Phoebe cried out her relief into his mouth.

Sam let loose a curse and held her still against him as she rode the wave of pleasure.

"Oh Gods. Don't move," he begged her.

How could she? Her muscles were limp, melted from the heat between them.

They lay together in a tangled silence until their breathing returned to somewhere near normal. His hand slipped from between her legs and pulled at her skirts. She drew in a breath to speak, gasping instead when he gently set his teeth to the side of her neck.

Damn him. She would dream about that sensation.

Releasing her, he traced her ear with his lips and whispered.

"I don't believe . . ." After only a moment's discomfort he succeeded in untangling her hair from whatever was holding it.

He continued, "I don't believe I have ever been this aroused. I may well leave this loft and dedicate myself to the little men on that rood screen below us."

"There is no reason I cannot help you finish," she whispered.

"Only the embarrassment of a stain on my breeches I could not explain away if we were caught," he said, voice strumming with mirth.

Caught.

The warmth from her climax left Phoebe like blood draining from a wound, only to be replaced with guilt and shame.

The one time she engaged in an illicit tryst without an intention to hurt herself, Phoebe had created an opportunity to hurt someone else. Karolina should have the right to choose a husband, and if she'd become fond of Sam, Phoebe would be guilty of killing that fondness.

"Get out, then," Phoebe said abruptly.

Sam, who had been sniffing at her hair again, froze. "I've said something—"

"We went too far."

Did Phoebe have to explain this to him?

No.

Sam silently disentangled her with a brusque manner that left Phoebe cold and confused. If it were that easy to free her, why hadn't he done it first thing? Had she signaled acquiescence to him so readily?

Her own fault, that.

"You stay here," Sam said when he finished. "Count to one hundred, then come out, so we won't be seen together." His voice was flat and sounded far away.

"Sam—"

Before she finished saying his name, Sam was gone.

14

So, then, the sensation I feel on touching a cold body,
is in proportion to the rapidity with which my hand
yields its heat to that body?

—Mrs. Jane Marcet

SAM SLEPT POORLY AND WOKE READY TO LEAVE THIS
place far behind.

When he came to breakfast, Karolina and the marchioness
acknowledged him but kept chattering like magpies about
something in Lithuanian.

Probably goblin penises.

"We are almost finished cataloging anything of worth, Mr.
Fenley," Lady Fallowshall said proudly as he took a seat.

Good.

Time to get them the hell out of this place. The dark was its
own beast here. Sam was sick of it wrapping around everything
one touched and riding on his heels. It left no room for laughter
nor love, for that matter.

"I will take one last look at the music room," he said. "If we
finish this morning we'll set out this afternoon. I've been too
long away from the emporium."

The women agreed and sent Jonas into town to reserve a train car back to London. Funny, there were plenty of horses today and not when Sam first wanted to leave.

"Did you sleep well, Mr. Fenley?" asked Karolina.

What was Sam supposed to answer?

No. I had a raging cockstand all night, thanks to your sister. Ever since I've arrived, I've had nightmares of being buried alive, a man clad in black laughing all the while. I have never pitied anyone as I pity the three of you, and I miss my family so much, it feels as though I've lost a limb.

"I slept fine, thank you for asking, my lady."

When the cook brought in a platter of fried cheese curd again, Sam made his excuses and walked toward the music room.

"When I get home, I am going to kiss my mam's feet and eat all the rashers I can get my hands on," he said as he passed by a portrait hanging slightly askew in the hallway. The potato-nosed man with a lugubrious expression and a hideous peruke stared back at him without comment.

Thank goodness.

The music room was pretty compared to most of the manor. Two sets of French doors in the outside wall looked out over a short lawn and a staircase leading down a slight hill.

"Right, well, I'll start at the far end of the room, then," he said to himself. There was no reason to be afraid. Full daylight fell through the windows, and he'd seen no sign of anything eerie or strange in this room, but the sound of his own voice in the preternatural quiet soothed him. "I'll bet there's a standup harpsichord beneath those cloths," he continued.

Carrying a ledger, Sam would write the name of the object and a price range with the pencil first, then transfer it to sturdier parchment and ink later tonight.

"Good morning," Phoebe said quietly as she entered the room. She was wearing a simple blue woolen day dress reminiscent of the previous decades. No doubt it was part of her adolescent wardrobe. The shoulders and neck of the dress were made from a cotton print of stripes and forget-me-nots, buckled at the waist with a plain leather belt.

This was the first time Sam had seen her out of mourning colors. Had the year of mourning completed or was Phoebe finished pretending she cared?

"Moti tells me we will be leaving late this afternoon," she said. "I was going to help you, but it seems I must pack."

She didn't look directly at Sam. Instead, she wandered past the swaddled instruments, stared out the doors, and regarded the Cumbrian sky.

What happened yesterday weighted the air, but neither of them was ready to speak of it.

Trying to think of something innocuous to say, Sam examined a stack of paintings. While he could tell in an instant if a table linen or snuffbox would sell for more or less than it was worth, the argument he and Jonas had had with the Hunt women proved he was rubbish with anything to do with art.

The first canvas was framed simply with gilt and wood and depicted—wonder of wonders—a still life. A silver bowl sat atop a golden tablecloth, and resting against the bowl's pedestal were a few winter apples and next to that, a dead rabbit with its entrails removed.

Gah.

"Always the dead animal," he said aloud. "For heaven's sake, could they not paint a live rabbit? Or one that hasn't been eviscerated?"

Phoebe's reply was lost when he sneezed, the dust circulating around the room now that he'd removed the drop cloths. Sam pushed the still life to the side—probably worth more than anything else in the whole room—and squinted at the painting lying beneath it. Unframed, part of the canvas had come loose from the glue, and he set it upright carefully, wiping it off with a cloth.

There were two girls dressed in pinafores, each a different pastel color, but their sashes were the same shade of blue. They stood to the side of a beautiful woman, barely a woman, really, seated on a stool, dressed in a deep green gown with an embroidered shawl about her shoulders and a small cap covering her head. A man loomed behind them, dull gray eyes staring out from dark sockets, the nose identifying him as the late marquess.

"Who are they?" Sam called out.

Phoebe's footsteps were brisk until she came around the corner of a covered harp and saw the portrait.

"Why are there portraits in the music room?" she asked of no one in particular. She came closer, breath slightly faster as though she'd run from the other side of the room instead of walked.

"This is your mother and father, but these girls don't look like you or Lady Karolina."

They looked like opium eaters; the artist having painted them with pupils so dilated, one could hardly see the color of their irises. He peered closer and saw even the marchioness's eyes were devoid of their extraordinary color. In contrast, Phoebe's father's eyes were clear and hard. Dangerous.

"Those are my four older sisters," she said, her voice level, pleasant even.

There were only two girls in the picture.

Perhaps he'd misheard. "Those are your sisters," he acknowledged. "The ones you told me about. Alice is now married to a count, and Mari is the widow in Paris."

Two girls in the picture, not four.

Next to him, Phoebe trembled gently, but enough so a buzz of the strength it took to hold her emotions in traveled through her feet and to the floorboards beneath them.

Sam waited.

"The twins. My father had them painted out." Phoebe pointed to the space in front of the sitting woman. "They were there, at her feet."

Half of one of the remaining girls' black slippers was obscured by a single dash of ivory paint that might have been an overlooked ruffle from a skirt.

The air thickened and the sun fled, allowing the gloom to settle close. Sam had known two of the marchioness's children had died but assumed they'd died as infants. Why had they been forgotten in such a cruel way?

"If I made a joke right now . . ." he said softly.

"I would kill you," Phoebe finished for him. She'd lost color in her face and her eyes had melted into pansies. Bruised pansies, pansies stepped on too many times to count.

Sam took one of her limp hands in his. Her hands were so cold, he felt it through her gloves.

"Will you tell me about them?"

Whatever Phoebe said next would be ugly and haunting. He took both Phoebe's hands, breathed warm air on them, then chafed them, ready to listen. A gift, listening. An agreement to share the burden of whatever dark and dismal images her words might create. This was all Sam had to give her.

Phoebe closed her eyes and breathed out a long, weary sigh,

then rested her head upon Sam's chest. As if a tiger had come to sit in his lap, Sam stood frozen, caught between terror and tenderness. He let go of one of her hands and put his arm around her waist, pulling her gently against him, and waited to see if she would kill him after all. A cap trimmed in lace and a silk ribbon the same color as the forget-me-nots on her dress covered her thick ebony hair. "Will you . . ." Phoebe pulled herself a step back and gazed into his face, her own expression shuttered and locked tight. "You have already done so much for us, Sam. Will you do me this last favor and have Jonas come and take this pile of paintings out to the carriage shed? He will know what to do with them."

She spoke as though she barely knew him, as though he hadn't tried to find a way beneath her skin last night and touched the deepest parts of her.

"All of this is to be sold away?" he asked. "The secrets never to be told—"

Phoebe's lips tightened and her eyes flashed.

Dangerous woman. He wanted to sink his teeth into her shoulder and hear her scream his name while she came.

"What do you know, Sam Fenley, about secrets?" Phoebe drew herself up and looked down at him although she was three inches shorter.

"I know enough to lance a festering wound," he snapped back. "The girls that are missing from the portrait are the ones who died." Sam paused and took a deep breath. "Did he kill them?"

All color left Phoebe's skin so it resembled polished stone. The purple of her irises stood out starkly against the gray of her skin. She looked otherworldly.

"No," she said, shaking her head, brows drawn in confusion. "No, he wasn't even here."

Sam waited.

Phoebe turned back to the picture and wrapped her arms around her torso, setting her palms beneath her armpits.

"When the influenza came, rustic as we were, we knew fresh air could be unhealthy. My mother shut the house up tight as a drum against foul humors, but it did no good and we fell ill."

This was a small relief. Sam hated to think of Phoebe growing up knowing her father was a murderer.

"Poor Rose and Agne, they died side by side in their bed. Alice, Mari, and I recovered, though a secret, shameful part of me was jealous of the twins. They had each other's loving company for their entire lives and never would be parted nor subjected to the continuation of life at Prentiss Manor."

My God, to be envious of death? Sam wanted to hold Phoebe in his arms again, but she was barely aware of him now.

"My father did not come to Prentiss Manor often, and for that my mother was glad. Each time he left she was pregnant. Each time he came home, she had produced a disappointment."

"Girls," Sam said softly.

"Worse." Phoebe sank to her knees in front of the picture, heedless of the dusty parquet. Leaning close, she traced the lost piece of lace with a finger. "Rose and Agne died, but what you don't know is that we had brothers."

She turned to regard him with a blank and frozen expression when he gasped.

"There were boys born before and after Alice. The last boy, Karolina's twin, was named Markus. All were stillborn."

"I'm so—"

"When Jonas came to live with us, he was meant as a rebuke to my mother. He is my father's natural child from an affair. A living reminder of how my mother kept failing him," she said quietly. "It is a testament to Moti that she loves Jonas as she does."

Jonas, the enigmatic giant who drifted along the hallways like a silent specter. Had he remained here in hopes his natural father would name him the heir?

"She used to paint," Phoebe said. "The doctor told my father that Moti should not have more children after Karolina. Father was furious. He took away Moti's brushes and her paintings. That is why the walls are covered with portraits of men and dead animals."

Phoebe stood, brushing her skirts. She left the painting and walked to the French doors, then pressed her forehead against the glass.

"You can't see it from here."

Sam went to her side but kept a few feet's distance between them, reflecting on the way Phoebe's mother spoke to Jonas, as though he were still a boy.

"What can't I see?" he asked.

"The icehouse."

Dread. Sheer freezing dread clamped Sam's spine straight and shook him to his toes.

"Agne and Rose survived together and died together. It went quickly during one of the worst winter storms anyone could remember."

Sam immediately thought of the two high voices laughing out in the corridor at night. The tail end of whispers coming from empty rooms.

"It took most of the day for the servants to clear a path from the manor to the icehouse."

Unbidden and unwelcomed, the image came to Sam of two little girls, curled up together, skin blue and lips purple, alone in the dark. Sweet Jesus, of course there were ghosts here.

"When the snow thawed, the ground was still frozen. They had to light fires, wait until they went out, then dig as far as had melted. The girls stayed in the icehouse for two months. My mother . . ."

The suggestion of frailty about the marchioness, her anxiety about strangers in her house, her habit of standing utterly still; all this made sense now that Phoebe was telling Sam the story.

"Lithuania was converted to Christianity, but certain beliefs still remain."

Phoebe turned her body toward Sam, keeping her face to the glass. The tiniest film of frost sat in the corners of the windowpanes, but she showed no sign of suffering from the cold.

"When someone dies, a *vėlė*, a soul, comes from the head of the corpse and goes to live with the ancestors in a place full of windows and gates. But the girls, their bodies lay without touching the earth, and my mother became convinced that rather than *vėlės*, their souls had been twisted by early death and improper burial, and they returned as ghosts."

"Not only your mother," Sam pointed out.

"No." Phoebe's smile was a cup for the tears standing in her eyes. "She had the entire household convinced. She would leave open windows and doors so the ghosts could find their way out, but they wouldn't go. Every mishap, every raindrop, every bad dream was the result of the twins not being laid to a true rest."

She shook her head and sucked in her cheeks. "I believe this is at the root of my fascination with science. It is absolute. It is eternal. It is consistent and there is nothing in science that depends on a God, on a person, on any living thing."

This made sense. Sam's sister Letty said something similar about mathematics. You could not tell lies when you used math to tell a story.

"Is that why the food is bad?" he said, the realization making him ashamed of his criticisms. "Cook stopped using the icehouse?"

Eyes wide, Phoebe's smile twisted like a rope, up and down, until a hoarse croak issued from her throat.

A laugh.

"No. The food is bad because Cook is a terrible cook."

"Oh. My apologies, I wasn't making a joke on purpose," Sam promised, setting a hand over his heart. "It would be difficult to store food there when . . ."

Phoebe had stopped paying attention, though. She'd flung open the doors and walked outside, heedless of the wind that blew her skirts and yanked her hair.

Against the backdrop of the unending sky, she stood like a barren tree, a monument made of straight lines; endurance and vulnerability.

"Why did he have them painted out?" Sam asked finally, coming to stand in front of her. She'd lost weight since he first saw her weeks ago in his office, and the hollows of her cheeks gave her an ethereal look—like one of the ghosts. He wasn't sure why, but the look in her eyes scared him. As if she saw past this world and into the next. He needed Phoebe to stay here, with him.

"Moti went mad," Phoebe said, her lips barely moving, eyes still unfocused. "When my father came back, he found us in disarray. His solution was to pretend the twins never existed."

Sam's head reared back. "What? What do you mean?"

"He erased them. He burned their belongings like he burned my scientific papers and Moti's paints. He threw them away." Phoebe's voice went thin and high, and nausea squeezed Sam's stomach.

"So, when your mother mourned those girls . . ."

"He would become angry and say, 'What girls? Who are these Agne and Rose? You cannot mourn people that never existed.'"

Setting his hands on Phoebe's shoulders, Sam lowered his head and looked her in the eyes.

"You know your father was the mad one, don't you? That what he did amounts to torture. You know he was in the wrong."

Her eyes flicked to Sam, then back to wherever she'd been the past few minutes.

"Yes," she said dully.

But she had been a child. How could she have known a father would be so cruel? What did they go through, these women, at the power of a man so twisted?

Tilting his head toward the sky, Sam took in a deep breath, trying to find the right words, to find any words, to convince Phoebe she was safe. That the world was not a terrible place.

"No," she whispered. "He was wrong, yes, but Moti—why couldn't she appease him? Why not lie and say she didn't remember, either?"

Phoebe wasn't looking at him, she was looking at whatever memories had sucked the weight from her bones and the sense from their heads.

"Every time she said their names, he grew angrier and angrier." She shook her head slightly.

A profound and terrible rage woke at the lack of inflection in those words. At what that monster had done to these women.

"Perhaps . . ." Sam hesitated. He had no conception of what living with such a person might be like, but he'd observed Phoebe's mother, the way she looked at her daughters. "Perhaps she wouldn't go along with it because she worried if she did, your sisters truly would be erased. Perhaps it was worth whatever punishment your father doled out to keep their memory in at least one person's mind."

Her regard weighed him down, but Sam locked his knees against the weight.

"It may be why she treats Jonas with affection, no matter why your father brought him here in the first place. I think . . ."

Sam wasn't certain Phoebe even heard him, but he said the last part aloud. Because he needed to remember the good in the world, or this house would have done its job and crushed him.

"Your mother is a truly strong woman to love the way she does," he confessed.

"Everything is ready."

Sam had been so focused on Phoebe, he hadn't heard Jonas approaching from around the side of the house.

Here was another person who had suffered at Fallowshall's hands. Would Jonas remain after the rest of the family had fled? What was to become of him?

Her half brother's appearance brought Phoebe back to the present, and she said something to him in Lithuanian, causing him to blanch and head back into the music room.

"He will burn it so Moti never has to see it," Phoebe said.

"I need help." Jonas stuck his head out the door and nodded to Sam.

Sam did not want to leave Phoebe's side, but she waved him away.

"Help Jonas, please," she said, her skin so white, it looked smudged against the watery sky.

"It's not . . ." What could he say?

What he wanted was to wrap his arms around her and warm

her now that he understood why she lived encased in ice. Sam had seen people do terrible things in the streets around his home in Clerkenwell, but nothing so evil as what Phoebe's father did.

Sam's admiration for the marchioness and her daughters grew tenfold. To have survived such a man, such a home, and continued to thrive was nothing short of a miracle. If Sam could, he'd shoot the marquess without a second's thought.

Phoebe's anger had resulted in the creation of a chemical bomb.

A bomb was exactly what Sam wanted to level at the world when he heard Phoebe's story. Phoebe wasn't a villainess. She was an avenger whose anger had been misdirected because the man who hurt her was beyond her reach. Sam drew closer but Phoebe held up a hand, palm facing him, to stop him.

"You shall not pity me, nor my family, Sam Fenley," she said, turning her palm down, then pointing her finger at him.

"Never," he promised. This was the truth. Never pity. Only admiration.

"Now," Jonas said in a deep bass voice. "Before the mistress comes."

Without saying anything else, Phoebe turned away and walked on the gravel path that looped the house.

JONAS AND SAM CARRIED THE ENTIRE STACK OF PAINT-ings out into the carriage shed and threw them in a pile. Neither of them had bothered to check if the paintings were of family or not. Sam couldn't stomach looking at another one, and Jonas, mouth set in a grim line, didn't show interest in what the canvases held, either.

"Where will you go?" Sam asked the other man once they'd piled high every canvas found in the music room.

Crossing his arms, Jonas peered up at the sky as though the answer lay there. He wore a loose-sleeved linen shirt and a brown canvas waistcoat, but no jacket. His boots, however, were of fine leather and his clothes were clean and well-fitting.

"I may follow Lady Fallowshall to London," Jonas answered eventually. "When all is finished here."

Sam waited a beat "Why . . . why did you not fight it?" Sam asked.

Jonas cocked his head in question.

"The sale of Prentiss Manor?" Sam said. "If you prove your parentage, you might—"

Eyes wide, Jonas stared at Sam as though he'd turned bright pink. "Fight for this house? This house is built of misery and pain."

"Cor," Sam said, impressed. "That's poetry right there."

"If that is all it takes to impress you," Jonas said, wiping his hands on his dusty canvas trousers, "it says much of why you are bad with chess." He left the barn without looking back, head shaking in disapproval.

"I am not bad with chess," Sam shouted after him. Something scurried across the loft overhead and gave him a start. Hoping no one would disturb the paintings before Jonas added them to a bonfire, Sam walked quickly out of the stables. Who knows what might fall on his head if he—

Feck.

A crooked board in the plank floor had crept up on him and Sam fell forward, throwing his hands out in front of him, then turning to the side to avoid a face full of horse dung. He lay on his back, waiting for his breath to return and ready to shout the filthiest of curses when Karolina's head came into view.

"Oh, Mr. Fenley," she said sadly, shaking her head. "You've fallen. Again."

Damn.

"Let me help you . . ."

"Please, my lady." Sam ignored Karolina's hand and sat up by himself, hoping there was no dung clinging to the back of his shirt. "I am perfectly fine."

Hands clasped, palm to palm, in front of her chest, Karolina regarded him with round eyes, frowning, her expression the same as one might see on a surgeon about to amputate.

"Won't you consider seeing a doctor when we arrive back in London?" she asked sweetly. "It cannot be good for you to suffer so many falls. Perhaps . . . might you need spectacles?"

"I need *something*," he said wryly, rubbing the back of his head.

Karolina bit her bottom lip, stifling a smile. Not a *my, aren't you charming* smile.

More like a *yes, indeed you do* smile.

Taking a seat on the slanted bench set against the wall of the carriage shed, Karolina placed her hands in her lap. She wore a dark gray woolen pelisse with a matching winter cap, the brim of which was naked of decoration as becoming a daughter in mourning. Her hands were tucked into a white rabbit-fur muff, and from the hems of her skirts and petticoats, two tiny sets of cream leather boot–shod toes peeked out.

Karolina looked lovely and Sam ought to have said so. Instead, all he could think as he carefully stood and brushed off his trousers, was what Phoebe might have said had she been here now. How the blue wool of Phoebe's dress made her skin pale, and whether Phoebe had a warm pelisse and muff as well.

"My mother is of the opinion twenty is past time for a woman to be married," Karolina announced.

Sam's stomach plummeted faster than if he'd swallowed a brick. "Is that so?" he asked rhetorically, voice cracking.

Dear God. Was Karolina proposing to him?

Karolina shrugged. "You might think Moti would concern herself more with Phoebe, considering she is thirty and still unmarried, but..."

A crack echoed in Karolina's voice and broke her last word in half. Sam stilled. Karolina's smile stayed fixed, her eyes downcast and shoulders bent forward.

"... but Phoebe is the exception to every rule?" he guessed.

Her eyes flicked up at him, then back down again.

"I'm not jealous," she said. "Only... sometimes it is a unbalanced equation."

Gingerly, Sam sat on the bench, but a good two feet away from Karolina. Not because he worried they would cause talk by sitting close. He worried if their weight wasn't balanced, he'd fall over again.

"The fewer rules Phoebe follows, the more I am expected to obey."

A flock of swallows murmured above them, weaving a parabola across the pale gray sky. They listened to the echo of Karolina's complaint and watched the black dots forming, falling, then re-forming wave after wave above the horizon.

"My sisters feel the same way about me," Sam confessed. "I am a man, and I do not face the same pressures. I am given freedom and responsibility simply by virtue of my sex, while they must fight for every opportunity to do what they love or say what they believe."

Karolina nodded. "Even Jonas has more privilege than me."

He'd no argument to this.

"I don't want to be married right now, Mr. Fenley," she said, her eyes fixed on him. "I'm sorry if you expected—"

He held up his hand, palm facing her. Sam shook his head. "I was under no expectations, my lady. You have no reason to apologize."

"Moti thinks highly of you," she told him. "She will worry Phoebe did something to drive you away. Or you were repulsed by the state of Prentiss Manor."

Well, Prentiss Manor *was* repulsive. It wasn't the reason Sam was relieved by Karolina's declaration, but if he never saw the outside of this cursed house again, it would be too soon.

Before he could assure Karolina of this, however, she continued. "I know the truth."

Had she discovered he'd set a chest of drawers in front of his door the past few nights?

"The truth is you do not want to marry me, either."

"Oh, my lady. That's not so," he insisted. The entire reason he'd come here was to charm Karolina. Wasn't it?

Wasn't it?

"You possess a multitude of admirable qualities," Sam said. "Your beauty, your grace, you—"

"The truth is you are fascinated with my sister."

His mouth snapped shut with a click, and Sam nearly bit off his tongue. How had Karolina known? Had he given himself away somehow?

She stood and shook out her skirts. "As formidable as she

may seem, the more I come to know her, the more I understand how fragile she is beneath her thin coat of ice."

"Fragile?" Sam echoed.

"Yes." Karolina returned both hands to inside her muff, her jaw jutting forward, giving her a look of determination. "Fragile. I know she wants to protect me from the cruelty of the world. Well, I want to protect her."

So did Sam's younger sisters. They might squabble from sunup to sundown, but their loyalty to one another was unquestioning.

"I admire your sentiment," he said.

"Good." Karolina sent him a sweet smile. "Because I have a pistol."

Sam watched the young woman walk away and shook his head. While he doubted Karolina would shoot him with her pistol, he made a silent wish that the next time he had the stupid idea to try and charm an aristocratic gentlewoman, Karolina might hit him over the head with it and knock some sense into him.

IN THE END, IT WASN'T UNTIL THE NEXT MORNING THEY piled into the carriages. Cook had said her goodbyes in the form of curiously salty scones. Only Jonas stood outside when they left, one hand raised in farewell, motionless as they drove out of sight.

No one spoke the entire journey to Liverpool, nor did they speak much on the train, the marchioness drawn into herself and Karolina pretending to read a book of poetry.

Phoebe sat opposite Sam and stared straight through him.

Neat trick, that.

Not at all lowering.

When the train pulled into the London station, Phoebe rose and went to her mother's side. Lady Fallowshall had insisted on keeping the windows shut, and the air was close and humid. Sam wanted to open the door and let in the air, no matter how much it smelled of ash and sulfur.

"Mr. Fenley," Karolina called from the back of the car. "Can you help me with my hatbox?"

Sam got up and shuffled toward where she stood, when a familiar face passed by on the station platform outside of the window—his brother-in-law.

What the hell was Greycliff doing here?

Sam turned back toward the open door and caught sight of the Earl Grantham's enormous shoulders blocking the exit to the train car, a grim expression on the man's face.

"Grantham?" Phoebe had also gotten up. She held her mother's hand, her bonnet sitting slightly skewed. "What is this?" she asked.

Grantham looked to the marchioness, then to Sam, and sighed. "Phoebe, you need to come with Greycliff and me, please."

What the hell?

Sam pushed past the earl and made it to the platform without tripping. Greycliff walked toward him and held up a hand halfway, shaking his head before Sam opened his mouth.

"There's been another bombing, Sam," Greycliff said. "Three people are dead, and Phoebe is a suspect."

15

The force of the temptation which urges us to seek for such evidence and appearances as are in favour of our desires, and to disregard those which oppose them, is wonderfully great. In this respect we are all, more or less, active promoters of error.

–Michael Faraday

FOUR YEARS AGO, PHOEBE LET RAGE CONTROL HER. NOT until she'd gone so far—too far for her friends to forgive her—did she realize that by fighting back at her father with the same weapons he used, she had become him.

All she'd wanted was to live loud enough that no one could erase her.

Phoebe couldn't find the energy to say this to Grantham. The earl was so large, his body took up the entire aisle of the train car and then some. Inside the car, the shock of Grantham's announcement—a bomb had gone off amid a crowd of police called in to break up a pro-Chartist rally and *she* was suspected of setting it—was still reverberating in Phoebe's ears.

"You can accompany us to Athena's Retreat while we sort this out. Everything will be over quickly," said Grantham. The last sentence was for Karolina, who was trying to calm Moti, whose voice rose until the icy edge of hysteria coated her words.

"*Kur mes einame?*" Moti asked. "Where are we going?"

Grantham thought Phoebe might have done it. She could tell by the way he looked everywhere but directly at her.

Sam climbed back onto the train.

"Right, I've talked to Grey. This is how things are going to go." Sam pushed past Grantham and came to stand in front of Phoebe, blocking her view of the exit. "Lord Grantham will take Lady Karolina and your mother back to Hunt House."

Sam, on the other hand, did not look at her with suspicion. Instead, he regarded her with ambivalence.

Phoebe's stomach churned while Sam loaded Grantham with boxes and extra coats and hampers. Before her mother finished tying her bonnet ribbon, Sam had thrown Phoebe's coat over her shoulders.

"Lady Phoebe, you and I will exit the back of the train and meet Greycliff at the other end of the station for safety's sake." Not even a *hint* of surprise in his voice. No outward sign of shock that Grantham had accused her of setting a bomb, no censure—it was as if Sam had already known what Grantham would say.

Had Sam known? This entire time at Prentiss Manor, the kisses, the card games, the tumbling over furniture, had it been an act the entire time?

The floor of the train car beneath her feet disappeared, and Phoebe stumbled like a drunkard—like a stupid child— toward the back door, away from her mother and sister. Grantham's voice was low and soothing even though Moti had not stopped asking questions in Lithuanian and not waiting for an answer before asking another one.

"*Kas vyksta?*"

"*Ką tu darai?*"

"Faster, now, before they figure out what we've done." Sam's words hit her like tiny pellets, but Phoebe couldn't absorb them.

There were too many people at the station, and the train heaved and growled like a living thing, smoke from the engine combined with soot from the rails and the dirt from the fog outside.

Not until he pulled her from the platform and onto a set of wooden steps that led away from the station exit and toward the blackened steel tracks did Phoebe understand.

They were running away.

"What . . . where are we going?" she whispered, although no one would hear her over the din surrounding them.

"I don't know." Craning his neck toward the sky, Sam moved his arm from her elbow to grasp her hand in his. "But we have two minutes before Grey realizes we're not coming around front. You'll have to get rid of your bonnet so we can hide in the crowd."

Sam hadn't known.

It hadn't been a trap.

A surge of relief washed through Phoebe, followed by satisfaction. For the first time since she left America, her lungs expanded all the way.

No one had been more surprised than Phoebe at how quickly she'd taken to the role of private agent for Tierney & Co. Folks paid a tidy sum for a Tierney agent's services. Unlike their colleagues in London who were called upon for discreet services for the Crown, the American agents were most often called upon by the wealthy.

Railroad barons, financiers, men with both "new" money and "old"—they knew a Tierney agent could be counted on for intelligence and discretion. Receiving letters threatening to expose a mistress unless a payment was made? Tierney's agents would find out who sent it. Suspect arson in a train fire? Sabotage in a shoe factory?

Assignments deemed too refined for whatever sheriffs might have jurisdiction or require intricate plotting beyond the scope of private police forces, such as the railway police—this work came to Tierney's agents.

"We should not take a direct route," Phoebe said quietly, steering Sam to a narrow alley. "No matter where we are going, it makes sense to double back and see what manner of search Greycliff and Grantham mean to employ."

"I see . . ." Sam trotted along at Phoebe's side. His bemused gaze tickled her cheek, but she kept walking, not too fast and not too slow.

"If they have help, it will be good to know if they're on horseback or a single conveyance. We'll want to take the smaller streets but be sure not to go down alleys that come out into a courtyard, in case we are cut off." Within moments, she had copied the gait and mannerisms of the people around them.

"Ahh, well . . ."

Phoebe tensed when Sam took her elbow but allowed him the liberty when she looked at the people passing them by on the street. In this section of town, they passed as a barrister and his wife hurrying home for an afternoon meal.

"Give me your topper," she said.

Without questioning, Sam handed her his felted top hat and Phoebe slapped it against a dirty brick wall two or three times.

"Oi," he protested. "That's a new hat."

Phoebe brushed off the worst of the brick dust and gave it back to him. Now Sam looked more like a harried barrister and less like a man of wealth. She let her shawl slip from her shoulders, leaving it on the railing of a stoop. Surreptitiously she pulled the silken flowers off her bonnet crown. When they rounded a corner, she ducked into a doorway and turned her pelisse inside out.

The benefit of having the best seamstresses in her younger days. The inside of the coat was as well made as the outside, and no one would notice the seams unless they were looking closely, but the color of the inside lining was less noticeable.

"What were you *doing* in America these past few years?" Sam queried, leaning in so the brim of his hat poked her now-ribbonless bonnet askew.

"Impressed, are we?" she asked.

"We are." Sam took her arm as a barrister might do for his wife, and they left the station and its occupants far behind.

"Believe me when I say it truly was a punishment at first," Phoebe confided, then pulled Sam into a niche between buildings, searching the crowd for familiar faces. "Americans do not stray far from their reputations as loud and unmannered."

From oil barons to farmhands, the people Phoebe met in America had been loud. They'd also seemed more colorful, happier, freer than folks back here in England.

"Why do you think that is?" Sam asked.

She pulled her gaze away from the crowds and stared at him. The niche was small and he stood partly behind her, half his body pressed up against hers. He appeared to be searching the crowd as well, but a pulse in his neck had sped, and the way he grasped her elbow spoke to her of an equal awareness on his part that if they turned a few inches toward each other, they would be in a full embrace.

Dropping her eyes, Phoebe tried to freeze from the inside out, blocking the heat that threatened to fog her head or cause her to make stupid choices.

"I think that on a small island where the goal of exploration is conquest, people grow complacent."

The way mountains sliced open the blue skies, the sheer expanse of forests where few humans had ever tread, the simple size of the place—all that gave people room to breathe, to fill their lungs, to demand better.

"You admire them, the Americans," Sam said.

"Hmmm." Phoebe nodded in affirmation. "If only they could make a bloody cup of tea."

16

❖

I could trust a fact, and always cross-examined an assertion.

–Michael Faraday

THE FARTHER THEY GOT FROM THE STATION, THE LESS Phoebe resembled the daughter of a marquess.

"We are heading toward Clerkenwell," Phoebe said, checking over her shoulder. "Do you have someplace in mind?"

Sam held out a hand to help her over the hole in the walkway, but Phoebe had already hopped ahead as a woman might do if she were annoyed with her husband.

Huffing a laugh, Sam picked up the pace to keep at her side.

"Don't laugh," she reprimanded. "I can blend in so no one recognizes Lady Phoebe Hunt, but you must help."

"How shall I do that?" Sam asked, not in the least upset that Phoebe had given him an order.

"Just stop . . ." Stop what? Being so bright and beautiful? Sam Fenley exuded charisma the way Faraday cages gave off lightning.

"Look at you," Sam said, oblivious to Phoebe's musings as

he dodged the crowds doing their shopping for supper. "Looking straight ahead rather than down your nose, moving aside so a man might have the right of way. No one would know it was you from far away."

Phoebe bit her lip to contain her pleased smile. "I told you. I'm good at this."

"You are better than good," he replied.

She tripped over the compliment. How did Sam do it? Phoebe got a headache thinking of something nice to say, yet this man who, from the outside, had less than her, was able to hand compliments out freely.

As though it felt good to be kind.

As though being kind did not mean being weak.

Before they turned another corner, Sam yanked Phoebe backward and steered her to the street running perpendicular to them.

"If we go too far west, we risk the chance of running into someone who knows me."

Three twisted lanes over, Sam stopped short in front of a warped oaken door. Above the entry hung a painted sign in the shape of a rooster.

"The *Hairy Cock*?"

"Paint's peeling. Welcome to the *Hearty* Cock, milady."

"Don't call me that, even in jest." Phoebe held on to the handle and peered over Sam's shoulder. "Who am I?"

This had to be the worst of situations they could find themselves in. The former head of a semiautonomous government agency and a friend of Prince Albert—both noblemen—were looking for her right now, convinced she had something to do with another killing.

Unconvinced, obviously, that she had changed enough or worked hard enough to erase the mistakes she'd made.

Still, despite the danger and the possible ramifications this would have on his welfare, and possibly his life, Sam Fenley continued to be so. Goddamned. Cheerful.

If she wasn't falling in love with him, Phoebe might kill him.

Wait.

What?

"We'll be fine," Sam assured her, chucking her under the chin. It was a measure of Phoebe's shock that she refrained from elbowing him in the gut for that.

"You are a shop girl from a bookstore on Brompton Street and I am me, because even this far over to Farringdon someone might know me."

Phoebe nodded; unsteady on her feet.

"Shop girl," she croaked. "Bookstore."

"Aye." Sam's smile faltered. "Are you unwell?"

Yes. Yes, she was unwell. That must be it. Perhaps she'd contracted a tropical disease that ate away at her brain.

"Do I look unwell?" Phoebe asked. How could one tell if a person's brain was being eaten away?

"You look as though you've bitten something sour. Or been given beet soup."

Perhaps this was the reason Phoebe had such a ridiculous notion. She had eaten something sour.

"Yes," she said. "Yes. I have eaten something sour and that is why I look this way. There is no other possible reason for me to look this way. Is there?"

Sam bit the corner of his lip, concern creasing the skin above his nose.

"Let's go inside and have a sit-down," he suggested.

Wonderful idea. She would sit, her stomach would eventually empty, and the outlandish idea she might lo—all outlandish ideas would disappear.

Sam brought Phoebe into the pub and settled her in a corner by a cheerful fire. There were one or two other couples in the great room, and a group of older women in the snug; a back room for women to drink without fear of uninvited attention.

Only after he'd brought back their drinks did Sam continue.

"Phoebe, a shop girl wouldn't clean the rim of her glass with a handkerchief."

A familiar spark of irritation lit her eyes.

"A shop girl from a bookstore on Brompton Street *would* know to do such a thing," Phoebe said. "She wouldn't wipe her chair or the table before she sat, and as you can see, I refrained from such."

"True." The exhilaration from their escape still bubbled in his veins. "Don't recognize anyone here, but it doesn't mean they don't recognize me. Here's the story. We wait here until Fenley's Fripperies is closed. There will still be a few people working, but I'll send them home with pay and tell them . . . dunno, tell them it's a saint's day. They won't correct me, because who speaks against a day off with pay?"

Phoebe sipped at her lemonade and squelched a grimace. "Do you know some argue holy days off should be paid because it isn't the worker's fault they aren't working on holy days, it's the owner's decision to close the factory."

"Bosh," Sam said. He sipped his ale and swallowed a curse. This tasted like warm piss. He wondered if the barman had given him the weak stuff because it would look bad for him to complain in front of a girl he was courting.

"Hmmmm. I seem to recall your broadsheet railing against the exploitation of workers," Phoebe said. "What's good for the goose is good for the gander, no?"

Sam scoffed. "'Tisn't the same at all. I pay my workers well, see to it they have the means to send their children to day school, and make sure no women are unsafe in their job."

"The landowners who benefit from the Corn Laws claim they use the profits to feed and house their tenants, send their children to Sunday schools, and keep them from having to leave their families and slave away in the dirty, dangerous city," she countered.

Sam opened his mouth to argue, then closed it. Phoebe was right. The landowners who exploited their workers did use such excuses.

He'd never considered giving pay on holy days. No one did. However, simply because no one did it, didn't mean it was a bad idea. Sam chewed on this thought while Phoebe sipped at her ale.

Behind the wooden screen that separated the snug from the rest of the pub, women laughed; one of them too hard. A racking cough bounced off the walls and ceiling, followed by sympathetic murmurs. The coal fire crackled, and three old men in a corner debated the outcome of a bare-knuckle fight in a desultory manner, mellowed by ale and age.

Sam regarded Phoebe across the table. "Tell me. What *do* you believe in? In one breath you speak of ghosts and curses. In the next you talk about workers' rights. Before we leave here, you will have made some snide remark about commoners and their willingness to sit in dirty chairs and drink from dirty glasses."

She pursed her lips as though in thought, but mischief sparkled in her eyes.

"I am a woman of many facets, Mr. Fenley." She paused. "And it isn't only the nobility who objects to drinking from dirty glasses. I would venture to say even the merchant class might object to filthy—"

"All right. Note taken."

"I . . ." Despite the clouds, the sky had been enormous in Cumbria, stretching overhead like the silk of a parasol, shades of gray and blue, sometimes green, or purple even. So vast and clean. Inside the pub, though, the windows were rarely given a cleaning; the soot and fog from outside left its trace on the sagging glass and everyone inside.

Phoebe might also appear small and dirty in this setting, but the Cumbrian sky had found its way into her pores and caused her skin to glow like the inside of a mussel's shell. She would taste like enamel and salt if he set his tongue to her skin.

"I believed in him, at first."

Sam blinked at the confession. "Believed who?"

"Adam Winters. My former . . . the former head of Omnium Democratia," she clarified. "You may laugh at the stupidity of a socialite aristocrat falling for a rough-and-tumble radical, but I believed in their mission."

How odd.

"You're a republican at heart? Yet you call me a mercenary for turning mansions into flats?"

"Adam said in his speeches universal suffrage should include women." Phoebe's slightly abashed expression hardened.

"As soon as he stepped in front of a crowd, it was as if some unseen chemical reaction occurred. When he spoke, any suspicion that he didn't believe what he was saying disappeared. Everything Adam told us sounded . . . achievable. And right and fair."

While the Chartists believed each man deserved a vote regardless of whether they owned property and rallied to end rotten boroughs, Sam remembered Greycliff saying the Omnis, led by Adam Winters, went even further than the Chartists. Granting women suffrage was radical in the extreme.

"I was angry at my father, convinced of my own intelligence—" Phoebe broke off with a bitter laugh. "I didn't understand how much privilege I possessed, despite my father's treatment. I wanted to be considered equal to a man, even if he was a bad and faithless man. That this bad and faithless man lied and never considered me an equal, never genuinely believed in my science or in me? Well. I learned an important lesson about trust from him. I should be grateful."

"*I* should like to beat Adam Winters to a pulp," Sam said, surprising himself with the vehemence in his voice.

A blush turned her skin the color of a sunrise, reaching from her temples to the neckline of her dress. The dress was too fine for her to pass as anything other than a gentlewoman, but Phoebe had kept her inside-out pelisse around her shoulders and somehow managed to look a little less regal than usual.

She said nothing but rolled her eyes up and to the side. Sam considered teasing her even more but was distracted by her flush and how it set off her fine eyes.

If she had been a shop girl . . .

The tiny seed of an idea, a terrible idea, a truly awful idea, went and planted itself in his head. The idea that if Phoebe had been a shop girl, they would not have to hide. Sam could walk down the street with her, laugh with her, court her.

He might even come to . . .

No. Oh, no. That seed was a rotten seed giving root to a rotten idea. Sam wanted comfort and peace. Quiet and simplicity. Not a hurricane in human form.

Hoping to change the direction of his thoughts, Sam finished his ale in two gulps and hurried off to the bar to order more. Because Phoebe was not a shop girl and Sam never would be courting her, he took the opportunity to warn the barkeep against giving him another half-pint of donkey piss.

Outside the fog turned to mist and then to a desultory rain. By unspoken agreement, he and Phoebe stopped teasing and fell into an easy silence.

Listening to the hum of precipitation on the roof and the occasional rusty laughs from behind the wooden screen, they nursed their drinks along with their secrets.

17

It is the great beauty of our science, chemistry, that advancement in it, whether in a degree great or small, instead of exhausting the subjects of research, opens the doors to further and more abundant knowledge, overflowing with beauty and utility.

–Michael Faraday

"IS THIS PINK? THEY COME IN PINK AS WELL?"

Phoebe held a silken scarf to the faint moonlight shining through the front windows on the third floor of Fenley's Fripperies. How had she not known Letty's family owned a veritable paradise?

Still silly from her ale, she'd walked slowly with Sam along Clerkenwell Road, careful to avoid Farringdon, where Sam could be recognized. She'd folded herself into the tiniest space between two buildings across the road from the emporium and waited while Sam went inside. Ten minutes later, a group of young men and a few boys burst out through the doors and walked in the opposite direction, laughing and slapping at one another and lampposts in that way boys had of having to hit things in order to imprint them in their brains.

Another ten minutes went by until Sam peered out from the alley running along the side of the emporium and waved her over, locking the door behind them. He told Phoebe he'd played the generous drunk and invited his employees to close early, go out, and put themselves in the same state.

Phoebe had never thought to imagine what the inside of such a shop might be like. The surprise had been a good one.

Now Sam took the scarf from her hands and refolded it.

"Pink is far too gauche a color," he said, distracted. "It's blush."

"I'll take three."

"You'll take none, or my mam will know someone's been here after hours," Sam said. "When this is over, you can walk through the front door like any other customer—"

"Pfft." Phoebe snatched the scarf back and flung it over her shoulders. "Any other customer. As if the daughter of a marquess walks into this place every day."

"Well, the wife of a viscount does," he retorted. "Listen to me, Phoebe. We are supposed to be hiding in the store, not raiding it."

"Semantics," she murmured.

The walls were covered with mirrors that threw the cacophony of colored scarves, shawls, dresses, and bonnets around and around like the ever-changing colors in Sir David Brewster's kaleidoscope.

"Watch your step," Sam said over his shoulder as he led her up a set of unpainted wooden stairs past the third floor— "offices," he explained—to the fourth floor where a crooked doorway stood partway open.

Unlike the display rooms on the first three floors, the space on the fourth floor was an organized clutter. Boxes and crates of varying sizes were stacked higgledy-piggledy, but the floor was spotless and windows were clean and hung with bright yellow curtains.

Lavender and orange peels scented the air, no doubt from the barrels in the corner, one of which was opened to reveal mounds of dried rosebuds. Phoebe made her way to the far wall, the familiar scent of sachets ladies used to scent their linen drawers pulling her closer.

"Usually, we hold most of these in the cellar," Sam explained, peering at the stenciled letters on the top of a rectangular carton. "We were looking into having water in the building and moved the lightest of the boxes—who went and ordered these coverlets when we already . . ."

When he pried open the box, an explosion of gold, orange, and red silk fell out. Phoebe drew in a breath of wonder and sank to her knees, heedless of the bare wooden boards.

"These are beautiful." The raw silk coverlet's embroidery showed crimson and green vines, blue birds, and purple fruit.

What must it be like to grow up surrounded by beautiful colors and smells, mirrors and crystals, and half of London walking through the store; folks from all corners of the world talking and laughing together?

"They're pretty, I suppose," he said, "but we've too many of them. Someone must have doubled the order by mistake. Going to have to lower the price and—"

Phoebe peered at Sam from where she sat in a puddle of sunrise, having pulled the rest of the coverlets from their box and wrapped herself in them, luxuriating in their brightness.

"What?" she asked.

They'd lit only one lamp and the oil was running low. Moonlight came through the opening in the curtains, but not enough to illuminate their expressions. Phoebe knew Sam was regarding her and not the coverlets.

"Was I not supposed to touch them?"

Sam crouched down until he was on his knees, level with her. Nothing was said, but her pulse sped and heat crept along her chest and pooled low in her belly. Slowly enough that Phoebe could pull away if she wished, he pressed his thumb to her lower lip, then traced a line to the corner of her mouth. The sensation set off crackles of anticipation beneath her skin, and her pulse grew stronger, making her squirm.

"I wanted it to be a bed," he whispered in a voice deep and rough with longing, blanketing her in a caress.

"If I said no?" she whispered back, and Sam held his hands in the air, continuing to stare at her mouth.

"I will never touch you unless you want it, Phoebe."

It hurt to breathe a little bit, having to force the air past the trapped bird inside her chest where her heart once lived.

"Will you still touch me even if I *shouldn't* want it?" she asked.

Sam sat back on his heels, eyes meeting hers. "I don't want to marry your sister . . ."

Phoebe frowned.

". . . and Lady Karolina doesn't want to marry me," Sam said. "She told me before we left Cumbria."

Oh. Well.

The more Phoebe got to know her younger sister, the more she enjoyed the woman Karolina had become. Moti's warnings about Lionel Armitage had influenced Phoebe to see Karolina as a victim, a girl to be protected. Shame on her for not recognizing Karolina was brave and resourceful and perhaps did not need marriage to Sam as a shield.

A dizzy relief spun her head until the memory of who she'd been and what she'd done stopped the spinning.

"I shouldn't want you for a million reasons besides my sister," Phoebe said. A cracked laugh escaped in a puff of air. "I shouldn't want you because you *won't* hurt me, because I don't deserve your care, because there is nothing kind I cannot kill."

Within seconds she was on her back and Sam's mouth covered hers. The kiss was long and hot with teeth and tongue, harder and harder he ate at her mouth. She held on to his shoulders to keep from dissolving from lust and longing.

He pulled away and she gulped the air; a gorgeous ache like a clenching fist blossomed between her thighs.

"You . . ." he said, and that smile of his, the one that lit him from within, as if he'd bitten the sun like a persimmon—it changed his face from merely handsome to something approaching true beauty ". . . have a tendency toward the melodramatic."

Of all the . . .

One golden blond brow rose slightly and Sam lowered his head toward hers. "I can't wait to hear you describe my sexual prowess in such dramatic terms."

Like the bubbles in champagne, a stream of giggles buoyed up.

The giggles grew into laughter, a cleansing laughter from her belly, and shook her whole body.

Obviously used to women bursting into hysterics beneath him, Sam sipped the laughter from her skin, lips moving across her shoulders to her temple.

"By God, you are—" she began.

"Irresistible," he supplied, biting the tender lobe of her ear.

Phoebe shuddered. How lovely.

"Yes, but also you are—"

"Superbly well-endowed."

Oh, for goodness' sakes. Setting her hands to either side of his head, Phoebe pushed him a few inches away, then covered his mouth with her thumb.

"Do you know how high you've set my expectations, Sam Fenley?" she asked. "You had better meet them tonight." Better he believed she lusted for him than know she . . .

"I will exceed them, my lady. Come here." Sam pulled her out of her nest of coverlets and draped them about her arms and shoulders, then took her hand and guided her to the corner of the room behind the barrels of dried flowers. There, leaning against the wall, were rolls of dark green and aubergine velvet and brocade. With brusque practiced movements, Sam unrolled the fabric into a pile at her feet.

"I shall return in one moment. Feel free to divest yourself of any encumbrances," he said. "Clothes, for example."

He walked to the other side of the room and rummaged through a carton.

"I really *really* wanted this to be in a bed," he said once he returned, humor threading through his low growl of desire, a tin of condoms in his hand.

Phoebe let him take the coverlets and lay them into a crazy quilt of colors. She'd no time to tease that it had better be his arse on the bottom or that a bed would make no difference to what she planned to do to him before he stood to face her, and his mouth was back on hers.

His entire body kissed hers, his hands traveling up the back of her legs to her bottom while his tongue slipped over the front of her teeth and the roof of her mouth, hips rubbing up against her ever so slightly. A frisson of friction, just a hint of what was to come, made her knees weaken and she grabbed his waistcoat tight, answering his desire with her own.

Her skirts bloomed into a bell shape at her feet when his nimble fingers found the tapes. Off came his waistcoat and long-tailed linen shirt with nary a protest from him. Alone in the enormous building, they might have been in the farthest corner of Cumbria or the Outer Hebrides for what they sensed of the outside world.

Sam's groan of pleasure when Phoebe ran her fingertips down his breastbone was the sound of honey dripping down her shoulders and resting in the cup above her clavicle. He pulled his mouth from hers and let his hands slip into her coiffure, holding her tight.

She matched his hungry stare with her own. The thin cotton of her chemise felt like bark against her nipples, and the rough coils of the hair on his legs rubbed her through the slit in her pantalettes.

When had he taken off his pants?

Quick as a whip, he turned her to face the wall and pressed one large palm against her stomach while unlacing her corset with the other hand. In a matter of seconds, the corset and her chemise were on the ground as well. His cock was hard and hot through the fine lawn of her pantalettes.

What in the name of God was she thinking?

Phoebe faced him, prepared to say something, anything, to regain her composure, but he was naked, and all she wanted was to run her tongue along the planes and lines of him.

Sam kept his eyes locked on her as she pushed her palms into his skin and dragged them down, down over the muscles of his chest, the stacked boxes of his abdomen, and then to the center of him.

One hand slipped below to cup his balls, and she wrapped her other hand around the hot length of him. His cock twitched at her touch, and a tiny flame of lust awoke at her own center.

When Phoebe delicately stroked him, brushing her thumb over the slick seed at his tip, the summer sky in his eyes darkened into a storm.

Sam fought a groan until the tendons in his neck stood out. It didn't matter. Phoebe knew he wanted her as badly as she wanted him. The air grew redolent with the scent of dried roses mixed with their warm, wet breath, leaving her dizzy.

Never had Phoebe knelt before a man.

Oh, she knew what she was doing when she dropped to her knees and let the plum-shaped head of him rest on her tongue before sucking it into her mouth.

Knew he would bend his head back against the surge of bliss, clench her skull loosely in his hands to keep himself from falling as she took as much as she could of his cock until the tip of him hit the back of her throat.

Knew the guttural words of praise he whispered, the encouragement, the way he called her his Phoebe-girl was from gratitude and desperation, not derision.

Knew when he shouted her name at his release as she swallowed the proof of his desire that his entire body would shake for long, aching moments even after he came.

Until Sam Fenley, Phoebe had insisted this act be mutual. That her lovers pleasure her at the same time she gave them relief.

Only with Sam had she performed this act alone.

His pleasure had been her only aim, not once wondering what she looked like or if he would look down upon her afterward. If he would thrust too hard, if he would pat her on the head like a pet, or if he would simply turn over and fall asleep.

An act of submission on the face of it; it had been, in fact, an act of courage on her part.

18

Electricity is often called wonderful, beautiful; but it is so only in common with the other forces of nature. The beauty of electricity, or of any other force, is not that the power is mysterious and unexpected, touching every sense at unawares in turn, but that it is under *law.*

–Michael Faraday

THAT WAS THE MOST CARNAL FELLATIO SAM HAD EVER received.

A lady, this lady, kneeling before him and swallowing the length of him, her cheeks red with exertion, her hair falling out of her pins and down her shoulders as she urged him on with her tongue and her fingers.

Her bloody fingers. Pulling at his sac and teasing the base of his cock with swift, then slow movements.

He didn't say this.

He didn't say any of this.

Instead, the pleasure she'd given him fled when she raised herself from her knees and stepped away, arms crossed, words brittle with ice, and fear lurking in her eyes.

"Well." Only Phoebe could turn a one-syllable word into a paragraph of disdain. "I hope I gave your barmaid Rosie some competition."

Ahh, the villainess had returned.

Undeterred, Sam pulled her right back into his arms and kissed her as if it were their last kiss. It might be, if he didn't take care of Phoebe the way no one ever had. The way only he could.

She tasted like salt and ale, and Sam lost himself in the pure pleasure of exploring Phoebe's mouth with his tongue. Dear Christ, but he wanted this woman.

When he was certain he'd convinced her of his appreciation, he broke the kiss, holding her flush against him.

"I don't know anyone named Rosie," he said softly, letting his lips touch only the rim of her ear, "and the only barmaid I've ever called by her first name is Harriet Blystone. She's married to Dougie Blystone, who owns the pub down the road from us."

Her shoulders dropped the tiniest bit and a single muscle twitched in her jaw.

"Harriet wields a bar clout like a whip. Once, she dragged young Pete Whetstone home by the ear and deposited him on his mother's doorstep."

Phoebe could only dream of intimidating Sam as well as Harriet Blystone had.

He absorbed the infinitesimal tremors of the laugh she tried hard to swallow.

This woman needed light and laughter—enough to uncover the dark places, enough so he could go there with her when she needed him.

Stuttering shadows curved around them as the oil ran dry in the small lamp he'd lit; difficult to see the details of Phoebe's face, the dimness smoothed the tiny lines across her skin, evidence of a life lived outdoors, outside the gilded cages of the British aristocracy.

Sam didn't need to see those details to know when she let desire take precedence over her prickly self-defenses. Although he was already hard again, he focused only on kisses. Gentle kisses taught him the shape of her lips, tiny nips so he could taste her, sucking her lip into his mouth and running his tongue back and forth, delighting in her responses; quiet whimpers and her fingers digging into his shoulder and his arse.

Once she'd melted and her body became pliant, Sam found the place right above her shoulder on the side of her neck where, if he covered his teeth with his lips and nibbled, she would rub against him. His hands cupped her bottom and he let out a grunt of pleasure when she wrapped one leg around his hips.

Even as he slipped his hands around her waist, up the back of her neck to hold her head still for his kisses, he was planning two moves ahead.

Before she broke his hold, he'd laid them both down on the nest of colored silk and velvet. Noting the stiffness in her spine, Sam decided now was the time to pay homage to her breasts.

"Look at how pretty you are here," he whispered, fondling her carefully, rolling her nipples. "Like plums and cream. I want to fill my mouth with you."

He did as he'd said and let his tongue trace the outline of her dusky rose areola, round and round until she relaxed beneath him and her fingers spasmed. Only then did he take one nipple between his teeth and gently bite, then cover her with his mouth and suck.

The tiniest of tremors and dampening of the cloth against

his thigh told him Phoebe had experienced a small release when he'd done that.

Something to tuck away for future use.

Still aroused, still touching him—still consenting—Phoebe reached between them and guided his cock to her quim, pushing aside the material of her pantalettes. Sam levered himself up and over her to give her access to his cock. A dreamy smile lit her face.

"Where did you hide that tin?" she asked, her eyes closed, her two front teeth biting down at the corner of her bottom lip.

Jealous, Sam set his thumb to her mouth and pulled her lip away. If anyone was going to sink into Phoebe's flesh, it would be him.

"Do not worry, my lady. I will ask for your aid when we are ready."

He covered her quim with his hand and gently stroked her damp folds.

She gasped and her eyes opened reluctantly.

"Are we not ready now?"

"Impatient, my Phoebe-girl? First, I have to taste—"

"*No.*"

Phoebe's hand moved from his cock to his chest, holding him in place.

Had he been too rough? Perhaps he hadn't explained enough what he wanted to do to her and how it would feel. Galling as it may be, there was a good chance Phoebe's previous lovers may not have used their mouths on her.

Witless fools, if this was so.

"You can tell me to stop if you don't find it pleasant." Sam pressed his thumb against the tiny pearl at the top of her quim, and she squirmed in pleasure. "I promise, when I kiss your qu—"

The squirming stopped. Phoebe's dreamy expression turned pained, though she kept a smile on her face. "Darling . . ."

This was not good.

"Enough talk. Let's get on with this, shall we?"

Sam threw away his plans and recalculated. Perhaps this act was too intimate for her? He wanted to give her that pleasure, but Sam heeded her discomfort and gave her a reassuring smile.

"As you wish," he said, leaning down and kissing her slowly, then pushing himself back onto his arms. "Let's get to the part where you scream my name over and over."

Phoebe's smile broadened into something more natural. "Or vice versa."

He laughed, relieved all was well again. "Yes, please."

The wind picked up outside and the clouds began to move faster. The moonlight flickered in their wake and Sam watched her eyes follow him as he sat back on his knees, then pulled the tin of condoms from his pocket. He showed her a condom, the ribbon trailing down his finger.

"Why don't you help me, Phoebe-girl? Tie this on while I take off the last of your clothes."

"No." Again the false smile flickered on Phoebe's face.

No?

"Just . . ." Her smiled turned into a grimace. "For Christ's sake, Sam. You must be the only man in Britain that won't just get the job done."

Sam was lost.

Job?

Was his touch a chore to be endured?

He moved his hand from her core to pat her thigh and leave her with a few more kisses, because he had to stop.

Job.

"No," she blurted out. "Don't look. Don't . . ."

His hand stilled.

A surge of rage built even before he moved his thumb against the raised ridge of skin running across her thigh beneath the thin fabric.

A scar.

An unholy light glowed in Sam's eyes, but Phoebe wasn't afraid. Only ashamed.

"He . . ." Sam's voice came from deep within him, nearly a roar. "Your father did this?"

Phoebe sat while he gripped her thigh, but not tight enough to hurt.

"No, he didn't," she said softly. No use trying to close her legs or pretend everyone was normal. When he'd understood that the skin beneath his hand was scarred, she had allowed Sam to pull her pantalettes to the side, and in the murky moonlight, the wavy lines shone a dull pewter against the alabaster of her skin.

"Who?" Barely articulated, it was more of a growl.

"I did this. *I* did it, Sam."

Incomprehension created worry lines that hadn't been there before on his smooth forehead and between his eyes. Somewhere deep inside her, her protective reservoir of exasperation and disdain awaited.

Some other day she might have tapped the source and told him to let go her leg, not everyone was as unblemished as he and his happy little family; that he was a child. A golden boy to whom life had been unfairly kind.

Except.

He dropped his head and smoothed the material to cover her back up, then moved away to sit beside her, not letting his skin touch hers.

Phoebe's stomach dropped.

The scars revolted him. He was disgusted with her. She'd lived up to every drop of contempt he'd ever had for aristocratic women.

Wetting her dry mouth, Phoebe tried to find it in her to tell him she didn't care. She didn't care if he left and never saw her again. She didn't—

"You do not owe me an explanation," he said, looking over at her. "You owe men nothing, Phoebe Hunt. If you can, however, I would like to understand a little better why you might do this. Was it an accident? Did someone force you?"

Phoebe pushed her legs together and stared at her stockinged feet.

"Did you . . . Were your other lovers more worldly perhaps and had seen this before?" he asked.

Sam's eyes rested on the side of her face, but Phoebe kept her gaze fixed on her feet until he slipped his hand over hers and curled his fingers.

The words spilled out. Like water. Like blood.

"My other lovers were a sight more eager than you, Sam Fenley," she said. "They never bothered to undress me fully before we completed the act."

"The act of making love?"

"The act of sex," she corrected.

"Fecking idiots is what they were."

Phoebe agreed but said nothing. She was an idiot, too, she supposed. Before Sam stumbled around with more questions, she told him. Curtly. As calmly as she could.

"I cut myself with a razor."

His neck bent and she knew he was staring at her legs. It was stupid at this point to try and hide her shame.

Phoebe untied the tapes to her drawers and slipped out of them. They were both naked except for her stockings.

The lines stood out like a legend to a map of her adolescence. A small mountain there when her father had hit Moti hard enough to loosen a tooth. A thin river here when she hadn't slept for two days and needed something to break through the fog. A cut there when the fear and pain were too much to bear. A cut here when there was no fear or pain or anything at all, and Phoebe worried she might have become a ghost without knowing it.

Sam curled his fingers round her hand tighter and tighter as Phoebe traced the scars and explained how she had a special razor with a pristine blade. That it was the sight of the blade parting flesh that calmed her almost as much as the sweet sting after.

Then the words went dry, and they sat some more.

"Where do you cut yourself now?" he asked. Phoebe sneaked a glance at him studying her feet. She leaned over and untied the ribbons of her garter and rolled down the stockings. Nothing to see there.

"I don't. It stopped helping after a while," she said, flexing her toes and shivering. Sam reached over and pulled one of the orange silk coverlets over her shoulders.

For a time, simply existing hurt. Phoebe lied when she insisted she didn't care what other people did to her or thought about her. The truth was she cared so deeply, she was constantly in pain. The only relief from the pain was cutting herself. It made no sense and Phoebe doubted she would ever be able to explain it thoroughly.

"Are you familiar with Michael Faraday's experiments with electricity?" she asked.

Sam's mouth thinned into a straight line. "Are you going to tell me more math made out of letters?"

He'd wanted her to smile, but those muscles were numb.

"Faraday made a number of observations around electrical charges," she said. The scientific words came easier than explanations having to do with emotions or the strange urges that lived inside her. "He conjectured the excess charge on a conductor stays only on the surface. It never passes through the conductor and has no impact on anything inside of it."

Another time she might have teased Sam as he repeated her words, his mouth moving but issuing no sound. Instead, Phoebe struggled to make him understand.

"Faraday covered the walls of a room with metal and struck it with electrical charges. Although the effect was spectacular, like lightning crackling across a plain, he proved none of that charge could make its way into the room."

"I think . . ." Sam chewed on the inside of his cheek. "The tumult and terrors in your life were the lightning. Wild and frightening."

Phoebe nodded, then stared down at her toes. "None of it touched me. Nothing hurt. When I was a small child, this was a good thing. When I got older, the numbness scared me. All that lightning across my skin never finding its way inside. I needed to feel something, even if it was a terrible something. At first, a blade was the only way I knew to pierce my armor."

"Then you found other ways to provoke pain," he said. Not a question.

"Yes."

No point in enumerating the variety of ways in which a

young aristocratic woman could hurt herself, or others, trotting her self-loathing out for the ton to see. Phoebe wasn't the only woman in a ballroom to disappear midway through the night and come back more relaxed. Sex, brandy, opium, gambling—the options were endless and most of the time affordable.

"I can't," he said, scooping her into a cocoon of silk and laying her down on the piles of velvet, careful not to touch her between the legs. He wasn't aroused, but he raised his body over hers as a lover might.

"I don't expect you to now," Phoebe told him. "You must be disg—"

Sam set his finger on her lips. "I can't hurt you."

Phoebe said nothing, not understanding why he was still atop her, then.

"If you like, when you are naughty, I can spank you. Lightly."

Her jaw dropped as Sam slid his finger from her lips, down her chin, down to the center of her chest where the coverlet edges rested. With the same finger, he gently nudged the coverlet away, uncovering her breasts.

The cold made her nipples hard. It was the cold, wasn't it? It couldn't be that Phoebe was aroused after making a cake of herself.

"I cannot go further than that, Phoebe. If you need pain to bring you pleasure—"

Was it desire lingering in Sam's darkened eyes? Would he still want her?

"I don't," she assured him, gasping when he found the line of her collarbone with the tip of his tongue. "I don't want you to hurt me. I want . . ."

Slightly fearful, slightly shamed, beginning to understand

this didn't portend the absence of pleasure, Phoebe let hope wriggle free. The memories would never fade, but she put them to the side when Sam whispered of his anticipation against the skin beneath her breasts.

If any man could pull joy from pain, it was Sam Fenley.

Phoebe pulled him up by his hair, shivering when he hissed his pain/pleasure of her touch. He set his bottom teeth to the base of her neck and scraped gently upward, leaving peppery sparks behind until he met her lips with his.

The kisses were forthright. Carnal. He took control and matched his tongue's thrusts with the movement of his hips, his cock rubbing against her belly. This wasn't what she wanted, though.

"I want you to please my pretty pink parts," she said. "Like you would if I were Rosie."

Sam, the gentleman that he was, readily obliged. From her mouth to her nipples to the backs of her knees until he settled himself between her legs, he suckled and nipped, bit and tongued the sweet pink parts of her, and everything in between.

"So pretty," he whispered as he spread her with his thumbs then licked her with the flat of his tongue.

The silken texture of his hair brushed against the scars inside her thighs like a feather. Phoebe did not think she could watch and still enjoy the act but Sam, being Sam, turned everything upside down, then back to rights again.

He increased the pressure of his kisses and set one of her legs over his shoulder, stopping only to tell her how good she tasted and how pleased he would be when she came on his tongue.

Phoebe's eyes closed and her head fell back. She almost left her body, except Sam would not let her.

He growled against her quim, then set his mouth over the pearl at the center of her and flicked it with his tongue until she shook, grabbing handfuls of silk in her fists and crying out.

"Please, Sam. Please make me come."

So, he did.

She barely heard his self-congratulatory nonsense over the sound of her womb clenching deep within her and the blood running riotous through her veins. Phoebe rolled into a ball, trying to cup the pleasure and keep it close as she throbbed in release for long seconds afterward.

"Are you well, Phoebe-girl?" Sam asked.

"I am . . . it keeps going and it's lovely," she said.

He laughed, that goddamned golden laugh of his, and helped her along to a second climax with his hand. By the time the pleasure began to taper off, Phoebe found herself rolled atop Sam's hard body, the ribbons of his condom tickling the inside of her thighs.

"You are in control, my lady," he said, holding her head still for a long, hot kiss, then releasing her and setting his hands behind his head. Everything about him glowed; his body drawing every ray of light to be found in the milky moonlit room, his smile its own small sun and his eyes taking in the sight of Phoebe sitting naked but for the gold silk coverlet she'd draped over her shoulders.

"That cape you wear puts me in mind of a queen," he told her, his hands restless and petting the tops of her thighs, the sides of her hips.

"Not a princess?" Phoebe asked. Her own fingers traced the path of fine blond hair from between his nipples, down his flat stomach to the thatch surrounding the base of his cock that twitched in anticipation.

"Not a princess," he promised.

No matter how intense the pleasure he'd given her, Phoebe was still happy the murk covered most of her scars. Not that Sam would see them.

His storm-blue eyes had turned black in the night, and they would not look away from her face. For the first time, Phoebe held herself naked above a lover. Slowly she pushed her hips down, fitting his shaft to her center and wincing slightly at how tightly he fit.

"Go slow, Phoebe-girl," he said. "I want this night to last a good long time so you never forget how strong you are and the pleasure you deserve."

The question of what she looked like through Sam's eyes distracted her from the pleasure. She was older than him by almost five years. Did she look old to him? Did the scars on the inside of her thighs brush against his skin?

As though he read her mind—terrifying thought, that— Sam lifted his arms and cradled her breasts in his hands as she moved slowly back and forth, causing him to gasp.

"By God, you are a beautiful woman," he said, only awe and wonder in his voice. "The way you look above me; regal but so *soft*."

He slipped his palms to her sides and pulled her down for a kiss. Their bodies fused together, and Phoebe gasped when Sam thrust his hips to meet her gentle glide.

"Is that a happy sound or an unhappy sound, Phoebe?" he asked.

"Happy. Even happier if you do it againnnnn," she moaned.

Clever man, Sam slipped his hand between the two of them and added to her pleasure.

"Trust me. Trust me to make it good."

Nothing about Sam resembled a supplicant. Swaddled by a dark different than the place they'd come from—a dark mixed with the smell of dried roses, the sounds of skin over velvet, the sensation of safety—Phoebe allowed herself to let down her guard. To trust him.

"Do you know how smooth, like silk, you feel when I run my hand down your back and over your arse?" he whispered, caressing her bottom and pulling her ever tighter against him.

Instead of growing numb, her senses heightened. The slightest of breezes licked her shoulder blades and she shivered with joy. Phoebe grew dizzy with anticipation when Sam moved his mouth to her breast, holding her flush against him, hips grinding against hips.

"By God, you are sweet and wet. I want to put my mouth on you again," he crooned, as if confiding a secret.

A long red thread of tension wrapped itself from her core to her spine to her nipples and out the top of her. Words broke apart in Phoebe's head and all she knew was the red thread, the pounding of her heart, the hammering of the pulse at the center of her, and Sam, the source of this pleasure.

Blindfold her and she would find him by smell. By touch. Her body knew this man although this was the first time they were fully naked together.

Phoebe's climax took her by surprise. One moment she was climbing, the next she was flying through a shower of sparks. Unable to look away, she held Sam's gaze while she came apart. He took her face in one hand and shouted when he came, thrusting into her again and again.

How glorious. How beautiful.

Joy and contentment welled up in her and came out in a tiny

burst of laughter. Sam, being Sam, smiled so widely, his face must have hurt.

Until Phoebe burst into tears.

Sam rolled them onto their sides without saying a word and held her close, running his fingers over her scalp and through her hair in a steady rhythm. He stopped only once to remove the condom, then pulled a coverlet over them both.

"I—I don't know—" No words could explain why she cried. She didn't even know herself.

"S'all right," he whispered, brushing her cheek with the side of his thumb. "My sisters do the same when they are overwhelmed."

He offered her a corner from one of the bolts of cloth next to their heads, and Phoebe blew her nose.

"You think your talents at lovemaking have overwhelmed me, I suppose," she said after she'd blown her nose and dried the tears on her cheeks.

"No, Phoebe-girl," he said. "I know my talents have overwhelmed you, but I don't think this is why you are crying."

Phoebe-girl. She should hate that name. Sam had her in bed, but he addressed her like a child?

She tried to work up a rage at this, but instead she snuggled her head on his chest, listening to the beat of his heart. Because it didn't sound like he was talking down to her.

It sounded like affection.

19

❖

Q: But, pray, Mrs. B., what is the cause of the chemical attraction of bodies for each other? It appears to me more extraordinary or unnatural, if I may use the expression, than the attraction of cohesion, which unites particles of a similar nature.

–Mrs. Jane Marcet

NOISES FROM THE STREET DRIFTED THROUGH A cracked window.

To Sam, the call of the coffee sellers and newsboys were the herald of the dawn, not the sun. Not in London, at least, where soot and grime coupled with damp air created a brown fog through which no heavenly light could penetrate.

He dropped a kiss on Phoebe's forehead and ignored the sharp pain in his chest at the sight of her; naked, vulnerable, still flushed from the pleasure he'd given her.

Phoebe had woken the instant he left the covers. She'd said nothing, sitting but holding the coverlet over her chest. Her hair had escaped from the confines of hairpins and cap, her thick black locks spilling down her back, a few wisps still clinging to her face. A red S-shaped wrinkle resembling a vine stood out on one cheek.

"Good morning," he'd said, infusing cheer into his voice, unsure of how Phoebe might respond, but knowing anything less would wound her.

Although she'd been mortified by her tears last night, he'd known what they meant. He had sisters. Tears were shed for happiness and joy almost as much as they were for frustration and sadness.

Sam had told her the tears were an honor and his pleasure to provoke. She'd rolled away and covered herself with the orange silk while he went to fetch a pail of water and some clean clouts. When he'd returned, she threatened him with delightful tortures if he ever mentioned her tears again.

Which meant he would have to mention them many times.

Now he walked, naked, to the far side of the room and pulled a sheet from where it had been covering a stack of unused wicker tables, then wrapped it around his waist.

Sam took his time while walking, assuming Phoebe was staring at his body. She'd said nothing, but Sam knew her eyes were upon him, like he knew she would avert her gaze should he swiftly turn.

Phoebe had been denied so many pleasures, small and large, she no longer believed she deserved them.

He brought back more water along with a few small apples he'd found in one of the desks and a tin of biscuits.

"I have an idea," he told Phoebe an hour later after they folded the coverlets and then dressed.

"We don't have time," Phoebe said. "At least not time to enjoy it properly."

Happiness. Was that the right word?

Unadulterated *happiness* lifted Sam from his perch at the window and back over to where Phoebe dabbed a cloth soaked in rosewater beneath her armpits. Her full arse shimmied against his thighs when he came up behind her and kissed the nape of her neck.

"That's not what I'm talking about. Or, it wasn't before you made me think of it."

How was it her skin tasted like spring? An aftereffect of what they'd done, he supposed. Went and mixed up his senses. The floor had turned to clouds, and everything smelled like whatever soap it was she used in her hair.

Huge brass warning bells were ringing, but Sam was ready to dance to their tune, not run away. The time for sensibility and caution lay behind him. Phoebe had changed in the night from untouchable to human. Sam had never, ever imagined passion as a spectrum, but the two of them had plumbed its depths.

Bliss.

That was the word he'd been looking for earlier. Not happiness.

Bliss.

"If you're finished panting like a hound in heat, do you mind helping with these corset strings?"

Sam obliged. "Do you know, when you look as though you've been sucking on a lemon, it gets me hot and bothered and thinking of sucking—Oowf."

Phoebe had twirled round and pinched his lips closed.

"Do you know when you talk about getting hot and bothered it gets me bothered. Just bothered."

Sam didn't believe a word of it. A shadow of pink bloomed

high on her cheeks and her eyes remained dark and interested. He allowed Phoebe her delusions and pulled his mouth back quick, bit her fingers lightly but suggestively, then turned her around and finished lacing her corset. She had been brave last night, and Sam wished to honor that.

"This corset is five years out of date," he said when she leaned over—very nice—and picked up her dress. "Later you should stop and see Madame LaTour on the second floor for a fitting. There are new sorts of busks that are far more flexible."

Without pause Phoebe stepped into her dress and tugged it over her arms, and he began the sad task of buttoning her while she weighed her next words.

Sam knew that's what she was doing. Being one of those genius scientists and all, her brain was of the extremely large sort that hummed when it worked this hard.

Phoebe's manner of calculation differed from his sister Letty's. Whereas Letty would dive into her equations as if lost among them, tying one mathematical phrase to another, Phoebe examined the world from far away, like a hawk. Taking in variables, gathering evidence, then forming conclusions.

Kept her separated from what might influence her decision. Like now.

"Reverting to your shopkeeping ways already, Sam?" The muscles in her neck tensed and she lifted her chin. "You're not going to make a good impression with the noble ladies you wish to court if your conversations consist of you trying to sell them undergarments."

"Oh, I don't know," Sam said. "Seems whatever I've been doing up until now is working well enough."

"Hmmph." Phoebe made a sound of disagreement, but said nothing more.

She would put up a fight; Sam knew it in his bones, but it would be a good fight.

A fair fight.

A fight worth getting hurt in when all was said and done.

Phoebe had lived up until now equating love with pain.

Sam was going to help her unlearn that equation.

Naked.

It didn't matter that Phoebe was fully dressed and wrapped in a new pelisse, this one ready-made (*oh, the horror*) as she drifted anonymously—she hoped—through the busy morning crowds.

Clothed or not, Sam Fenley had seen her naked.

Vulnerable.

He'd seen her scars.

Seen her tears.

She really may have to kill him now.

"Smells like snow," he said.

"Watch your step now."

"Here, walk on the inside so your skirts won't get dirtied."

As he followed close on her heels along the cobbled streets, past buildings so old, they looked likely to topple over, Phoebe had to set her hand against the collar of her pelisse to be sure she was covered, so exposed he'd made her feel.

"The Fancy Footmen is around the corner," Sam said, then reached for her arm. Phoebe stopped abruptly and backed into the entrance to a stucco building full of holes in the facade.

"Stop," she said, biting the word almost in half.

Sam tucked his hands into the pockets of his greatcoat. Only two lapels for him and buttons carved of wood rather than brass, but the heavy indigo wool was of high quality and the coat fit his broad shoulders to perfection. A top hat so dark a blue, it appeared black sat atop his golden hair and his cheeks were red from the cold.

He was beautiful.

He was certain to mock her frailties and dismiss her fears. Wasn't he?

"Stop talking to you?" Sam asked. A cloud passed overhead and the faintest of wrinkles remained behind when he furrowed his brow. "Stop with the plan? Stop looking at you? What? Tell me what I can do so you won't knife me in the back simply because I survived the act of making love to you with your integrity—and my bollocks—left intact."

This man was going to give her an apoplexy.

How could he stand to be with her in the light of day knowing she'd done something so grotesque to her body? How could he be so bloody charming and irrationally kind?

"Phoebe." Sam looked both ways down the street, then crowded her against the doorway. The knocker pushed her bonnet forward and the brim tipped. She could see only the red wool of his scarf popping out of his greatcoat.

"I can honestly say making love to you was life-altering, and as with all life-altering events . . ."

"Oh, for the love of God." She rolled her eyes.

". . . I will never cease speaking of it. However"—he held his hand up when she spluttered her objection—"*however*, at your request, I will stay silent on the subject until we can speak privately again. Ideally in a bed."

"I'm not . . ."

The words stuck in her throat when two women walked

past. One was stout and wore a ridiculous bonnet with a stuffed raven hanging to one side and the other, dressed much more sensibly, looked over at Phoebe and winked.

Winked.

Her humiliation was complete.

Oblivious to his surroundings, Sam continued speaking as if passersby had not winked at her.

"Now, we're going stop in for a glass of gin at the Fancy while I slip some coin to your fella behind the bar, got it?"

This was the plan they'd come up with this morning once Phoebe had dressed and tried to recover her composure after last night.

They'd overheard in the pub yesterday that the bomb had gone off near Kennington Common. An anonymous letter had been sent to *The London Times* with a warning that more violence would follow if the Corn Laws were not repealed.

Phoebe believed if the bomb truly was set by former Omnis, there would be talk of it in the "regulars." The pubs and bars where the Omnis used to drink.

Her plan was for Sam to buy information from the barkeep and use whatever he picked up to ingratiate himself among the patrons. Phoebe had donned a dress left behind by one of Sam's sisters at the emporium, where the seamstress they employed had been prepared to shorten the hem and add trimmings. Phoebe planned to settle in at a table and listen for familiar phrases or stray bits of information, watching the crowd for familiar faces.

At first, Sam had outright refused.

"I would never take a lady to one of these places—"

Phoebe had cut him off. "I have worked hard to become invisible by choice."

"What if there are Omnis in the pubs? What if they recognize you?" Sam had asked.

"Would anyone who knew Lady Phoebe Hunt believe she was in a gin hall, with a merchant, wearing ready-made clothing and drinking from dirty glasses?"

"But what if—"

"Sam. I invented a weapon that caused a man, a father, to die. I was going to sell it to the highest bidder, not out of political ideology or desperation. Out of anger. Anger at a man who can't hurt me anymore."

Sam had fallen silent, one hand rubbing at the down covering his chin, staring at her with eyes so pretty, they masked the brain inside his head.

"Watch," she told him. Phoebe closed her eyes and pictured what sort of woman might sit quietly in a gin hall. Must have worked all day. Most likely there were children at home in a one-room flat who needed tending and a man nearby who needed soothing. For half an hour, this woman would clutch at this time alone harder than she held her gin cup.

From the look on Sam's face when she opened her eyes, she'd succeeded in deepening her wrinkles, dulling her eyes, and letting her mouth fall into the lines of a woman who rarely laughed.

It was startling, then, when he set his palm to her cheek, the robin's-egg blue of his eyes darkening to indigo.

"You are a wonder, Phoebe Hunt," he said, brushing his thumb along the line of her jaw. "For a woman who claims not to care for anyone outside the aristocracy, you have a remarkable talent for observing the humanity of other people."

Phoebe said nothing, neither acknowledging his words nor disputing them. Remarkable her observations might be, what she wore on her face was not a mask. She'd never had a room full of hungry children awaiting her, true. That desire, however, to hide from those dependent on her, the bone-deep exhaustion from a caste that couldn't be described but to which women belong—that was real.

"I wouldn't recognize you looking like this," he said. Admiration had drained from his voice and sympathy replaced it.

Goddamn Sam Fenley and his overly large heart. Why was it him who could truly *see* her?

Phoebe pulled away from his touch. "Let me do what I'm good at, Sam. We don't have time to waste."

He'd deferred to her after that, but only in the planning.

The rest of the day, Sam treated her as if she were breakable. As if he could see the woman beneath the armor, the one who cried when she came, the one who had gone and lost all sense when it came to him.

They spent the day traveling from gin hall to pub to crowded inn; stopping every few hours at coffeehouses, where Sam tried to sober up between visits.

By the time a strip of pale gray had appeared in the east, Phoebe was unsteady with exhaustion.

"What do you think, then?" Sam asked. "Had enough for one night?"

They'd left the last pub, nothing more than one room fitted with shelves that ran round the wall at chest height. Attached to the shelves were cups an angry old woman in a ragged blue cap would fill for a ha'penny.

Both had sobered right quick. Even Sam couldn't stomach drinking from cups that hadn't been washed.

"I'm too tired to think," Phoebe replied.

"It's too far to walk back to the shop and still get a few hours' sleep," Sam said. "There is a doss near my house. We can buy a few hours there."

Phoebe tried to hide her shudder.

Doss houses were scattered throughout poorer parts of the city. Many men and women did not earn enough coin to rent a room monthly. Forced by circumstances—some earned, most not—they would work odd jobs or, for the women, work as prostitutes, to make enough money for a warm meal, a few cups of gin, and a place to sleep for the night.

Those who had the most coin slept in the doss's beds, four or five beds to a room, mattresses almost guaranteed to have bedbugs and lice. The men and women who ran the doss houses were creative in their ways to pack even more people into their houses. For only a pence, you could buy a seat on a bench with a rope hung between two walls, and when sleep over-took you, lean over the rope rather than sprawl on the hard wood of a floor. If Sam suggested it, there must be no other choice. They couldn't risk sleeping outside. Their pockets would be picked, or a constable would wake them with the call to *move on now*.

"Did you ever sleep doss in America?" Sam asked.

Phoebe thought back to her travels. "Not often. Doss houses are different over there, with most of them used by laborers. They're separated by sex, too."

"'S there a different name for those ones that have only women?"

"Not unless it's a brothel," she said.

Sam tripped over a rotted board in the walkway.

"You didn't . . ."

The lobes of his ears turned cherry red. Phoebe let him sweat for a moment before answering.

"I did not. I stayed mostly in rooming houses or decent hotels. Sometimes when I went out to the Iowa Territory, I slept outside, beneath the stars. The landscape of the American west is . . ."

There were no words, truly, for the sight of the unbroken horizon; a sky so clear, it might have been a glass dome over the whole. The sound of wind when it careened through a canyon, the astoundingly loud roar a river made when its water turned white and brown, smashing against boulders that looked to be strewn by a giant's hand.

Sam said nothing as Phoebe attempted to describe the scent of scrub brush and warmed sandstone, the ungainly majesty of a herd of bison, the weightlessness of living in a place where no one knew your past.

"What happens when you're lonely?" he asked. "What about at night when you've a mind to set yourself in the parlor and play a hand of cards—*not* slapkopf—and have a coze with your family?"

"Sam," she replied, too tired to pretend irony. "Even in England I have never, ever had a 'coze' with my family."

A yawn escaped him then. He hid it behind a broad palm and strong fingers. Walking in the early-morning haze of river fumes and chimney smoke, he glowed with his healthy skin and guinea-bright hair.

On their way to the doss, they stopped at a bakery opening its window. Phoebe accepted a fresh baked roll from Sam and let the taste melt on her tongue like the most delicious of meals as they walked along the wooden walkways and cobbled streets.

"Grantham was right to worry," Phoebe said. "Nearly

everyone in those pubs was talking about how the Omnis are back and working with the anti–Corn Laws lobby."

Sam tossed his roll in the air and caught it neatly. He'd been surreptitiously spitting his gin back in the cup for the last few hours and didn't seem much worse for wear.

How annoying. It must be lovely to be young and fresh. Phoebe felt like a crone in comparison.

"Not all of them. Sounds like only a few of the hotheads are still around. Did you recognize the names? The ones I heard most were Aled Brew and Cai Llewelyn.

"I never interacted with most of the Omnis. They were hardworking men and women from Limehouse, Wapping, and Whitechapel. They weren't violent per se; they were simply . . ."

Sam took a bite of his roll and made a sound of appreciation, but he kept his gaze on Phoebe.

She did not have to explain herself to him. She could continue walking and leave the subject behind.

"I told you; Adam had magnetism."

He rolled his eyes. "Aye, the kind of magnetism that would overcome an intelligent woman's better sense."

Was he jealous?

The thought prickled beneath her skin, and Phoebe wished they were anywhere else but Farringdon in the early hours of the morning—perhaps a cozy cottage somewhere in the Lake District, or even better, out beneath the wide-open sky of the western territories. Difficult to dissemble in the blistering light of an all-seeing sun and the visceral embrace of the night in places where no other human had yet trod.

"The kind of magnetism people use as their excuse for violence."

"Did you?" Sam asked.

This was a fair question, wasn't it? She'd developed a weapon ostensibly to sell and get her the money to make a new life away from her father, but also because she was in pain, she wanted to inflict that pain on others as well.

"Once upon a time I did," she confessed.

More people appeared on the street. In a few minutes, the bells would ring from St. Bart's to let folks without timepieces know the morning hour. The coffee sellers had already packed their carts with their scalding potion and would trundle off to wherever the corner was that they'd staked their claim.

"What changed?"

A girl, no more than five or six, walked toward them, clad in a rough, homespun frock, holey stockings, and a thin shawl. She carried a basket full of wilted violets tied into tiny bouquets with dirty ribbon. An older girl, most likely thirteen or fourteen, walked with her, her own basket full of shriveled oranges.

If Phoebe bought out their baskets, she would bring too much attention to her and Sam. Besides, it wouldn't change anything for them at all. They would turn around and go back for more dead flowers and sour oranges because that was the fate of poor girls in London.

"Tierney's spent three months training me before I was sent out to the Iowa Territory. They thought I'd have less a chance of seeing someone I knew than if I were in a shared territory like Oregon," she explained, watching as the girls walked together, each with their eyes on the ground, bumping into each other in a familial fashion.

The instant Phoebe set foot in America, the people's expectations and desires hummed through the crowds, in the cries of the sailors, and the bellows of the carriage drivers. It was intoxicating.

Iowa Territory had been a huge shock. There everything not native—from towns to farming to the people themselves—were brought by White settlers from the east hoping to reinvent themselves. Starting anew meant purging the land of its Indigenous peoples, however. Each day brought the juxtaposition of settlers who treated the Indigenous like vermin but treated the people in their tiny communities like family.

"Almost a year after I came to the territory, there was a public hanging."

Phoebe stopped talking when the girls drew abreast of them. Sam winked and tossed each of them a pence, pocketing an orange and presenting Phoebe a wilted posy.

"There was a great deal of disagreement as to the guilt of the man, with some saying he'd been made a scapegoat by the farmers," she said. Distracted by memories, she thanked Sam and tucked the posy into the bodice of her pelisse.

"He'd been blamed for stealing livestock, but his family claimed he'd been home during the times the livestock was taken. Like here, there had been alcohol served, and a crowd gathered to watch. Unlike here, the alcohol was a type specific to the region. They called it firewater, and if you drank too much, you were certain to go blind."

"Cor," said Sam with a note of admiration in his voice.

"Everyone was drinking, and then one of the man's relatives began a fight with one of the farmers. Soon they'd both drawn others into the argument and it turned . . ."

Phoebe had seen a prairie fire once; a sight that was both terrifying and arresting. The violence that followed in the wake of the men's argument that day was like the prairie fire. It swept the entire crowd and burned as hot.

"I'd held myself in remove when the Omnis demonstrated, and had never seen anything like the sight of armed and angry men screaming hateful words and ready hurt, or even to kill."

Phoebe hadn't been frightened for herself. A dark, wounded part of her lived forever in a rage. She almost wanted to wade into the fight with a similar urge to the one she used to get before cutting herself.

"The crowd forgot why they were fighting and engaged in destruction for no reason." The smell of smoke and sounds of shots fired had filled the streets. Profanity of both the horrific and the mundane had echoed against the buildings, followed by the sound of glass breaking as stores were looted.

"The next morning those men slept, sated after the violence while the women swept the glass from the broken windows, put paper over the windows, and carried on what needed to be done. The children had to pick their way through piles of broken furniture and glass, skip over the puddles of blood."

Not one single man helped to clean the mess they made.

Only the smallest part of Phoebe walked the streets of London with Sam Fenley. The rest of her was back in that town, the next morning. The smell of violence had made her gag.

"Before I left for America, Violet told me this would happen, but I didn't listen because I was angry," she whispered, more to herself than Sam. "It's true, though. Whenever men beget violence on other men, no matter how noble the cause may be, it is women and children who endure most of the damage. It is their livelihoods which are burned in riots, women's bodies raped in war, children whose innocence is lost, littered along the road like ashes when the fires go out."

Sam pulled Phoebe out of the way of a coffee seller's cart and steered her into a row of mews behind a block of well-kept houses.

"Oh, it is excellent to have a giant's strength, but tyrannous to use it like a giant," he said.

Glory be, Sam Fenley was quoting Shakespeare.

"My father is physically strong," Sam said. He stopped and stood facing her, taking both Phoebe's hands into his, eyes searching her face. "But my mother's will puts his muscles to shame. You are right. Women and children are victims in the aftermath of violence men visit upon each other when in conflict."

"I didn't understand that using violence as a means to an end made me into my father," Phoebe said quietly. "I took away a woman's husband and a child's father."

The truth of that sat like a coal in her chest every day. A little boy laughing, a woman holding on to her man's elbow as they crossed the street—small gestures of love would set that coal to burning and fill her belly with shame.

"You are not your father, Phoebe," Sam said. "You would never be that cruel."

How did he not understand? She could be crueler than he could imagine. Every time her father had belittled her, every time his palm struck her skin, he had transferred his self-loathing and fear onto her. Like a fungus.

Phoebe wouldn't infect Sam with this same disease.

Although her heart cried out against it, Phoebe pulled upon the last reserves of her strength, lengthened her spine, and looked down her nose at Sam. How familiar the cold felt as she numbed herself. She could say anything, do anything, and it wouldn't touch the secret soft part of her.

"You are a fool, Sam Fenley. I suppose living in a hatbox with as many siblings as your jolly pa and sweet little mam could breed has led you to believe in such fantasies."

Sam nodded thoughtfully. "Might be."

"Well, why don't you leave me alone and go back home, Mr. Fenley?" she said. "Tell your family happy endings are a lie."

Instead of appearing affronted, Sam simply nodded again. "Or tell them yourself. One of them is standing behind you."

20

⟞⟨⟨⟨◈⟩⟩⟩⟞

Shall we educate ourselves in what is known, and then casting away all we have acquired, turn to our ignorance for aid to guide us among the unknown?
—Michael Faraday

SAM HAD TO CREDIT PHOEBE. SHE TOOK THE REVELA-tion with one hundred times more sangfroid than he had a few weeks ago when she'd popped up behind his back as he was calling her names.

Without blinking—uncanny, that—Phoebe turned to face the girl who'd been sneaking around the corner of the building behind them and hoping to come upon them unnoticed.

"Hmmmm." Phoebe let out a sound halfway between a feline growl and a disappointed sigh.

How did women do things like that?

"This must be one of your pack, Mr. Fenley. Introduce me."

Back to Mr. Fenley, were they?

"Certainly, dear. Here is one of my many, many sisters. Sarah Fenley . . ."

The purring had ended in a cough. Phoebe shot him an outraged glare. "What did you call me?"

Sam bit his upper lip to keep from smiling. Wait until she met the rest of his sisters: Laila, Lucy, and Laura. No matter what seven kinds of chaos they would leave in their wake, no matter what insults or tears or long monologues about the inherent uselessness of the male sex—Sam's sisters loved him unconditionally and he loved them back without reserve. Everyone should have a family like his. Especially Phoebe.

Sarah ignored him, concentrating on the woman standing in front of them.

"Are you wearing one of our Pretty Pelisses by Poppy? From the second floor of Fenley's?" Sarah asked. "It hangs nicely, but you'll want it taken up an inch. Do stop by the third-floor tailors when you have a moment. We give a discount for clothing purchased at the store."

"I . . . thank you?" Phoebe said, staring, eyes wide, at Sam.

Perversely, he decided not to intervene.

Sarah shook her head sadly.

"You let her leave the store without a matching bonnet." She cocked her head a fraction, eyes narrowing in thought, then reached out and straightened the collar of the pelisse.

Phoebe's expression grew more panicked.

"Greycliff and his friend Earl Grantham have been looking for the both of you," Sarah said, still walking in a circle around Phoebe, measuring the skirt by eye, no doubt, and thinking of various ways to tailor it. "They didn't tell me anything, but you know how I am. I listened at the door. It has to do with the bombing in Kennington Common."

"How did you know we were back here?" Sam asked.

Sarah snorted. "You sent the stock boys home with a penny each. The talk was all over town by this morning. Then, Olivia

Scattering's sister's beau saw you *drinking* during the *day* at the Hearty Cock."

"What was Olivia's sister's beau doing at the Hearty Cock in the first place, I'd like to know," said Sam.

Sarah rolled her eyes. "He's a *man*. I figured out where you two might hide, and Greycliff will figure it out as well. He's not as thick as some."

Sam frowned. "Are you referring to me?"

The sibling love lasted for only a short time before it devolved into squabbles.

"It was a pleasure to meet you," Phoebe said. "Unfortunately, I must be going."

Having had a moment to adjust, Phoebe had pulled herself back together. She presented a cool facade, the untouchable aristocrat.

Sam knew better. He knew the woman who lurked behind the pinched mouth and narrowed eyes, and he wanted her back in his arms as soon as possible.

"Nice try, Phoebe-girl, but you cannot get rid of me that easily," he said to himself.

"Going where?" Sarah asked.

Phoebe did not bother to answer. Let the girl think her rude. It was time to leave before Sam got any bad ideas.

"Mr. Fenley. Thank you for your help in this matter." Phoebe did not look directly at Sam as she spoke, instead staring down at her wrist as she unbuttoned and rebuttoned her glove. "I do not want your family to be adversely affected by this situation. I will return home to my mother and sister and . . ."

"Did you do it?" Sarah asked.

Phoebe considered the young woman. The woman, girl, had the same small frame as Letty, except her hair was a plain bark color, rather than the distinctive cornsilk blond–bright golden locks of her brother and sister. She had sky-blue eyes that darkened with curiosity.

Sam's eyes darkened with desire.

The two of them were beautiful but in a different way than her sisters and Moti. The Fenleys seemed to come most alive when there was a question to be considered, a puzzle to be solved.

Was this perhaps Sam's attraction to her? Was Phoebe merely an equation waiting to be worked out?

"Of course she didn't do it," Sam snapped. The angry note in his voice scared her a bit.

"Well, all right," Sarah said, taking a step back and holding up a hand. "No need for you to fly in the boughs. If she's one of yours, Sam, she's one of us."

One of . . . What the devil?

It took all Phoebe's self-control to keep her jaw from dropping at that declaration. Good thing she had hold of herself, for she might have made a most unladylike noise when Sam came beside her and wrapped his arm about her shoulders.

In a public place! His arm!

Moti would faint dead at this.

"I knew I could count on you. Now, where shall we hide her until we sort this mess out?"

Deaf to her protests, the two swooped around her like pigeons, clucking and cooing, and carried her on their noisy wings down the row of mews, and then another.

Phoebe understood the bonds between siblings. She and her sisters had spent their girlhoods on the lookout, protecting one another from their mother's confusion and their father's loathing.

This, the laughter and secret phrases, the teasing, and the insights; this was family of a different kind.

Family without fear.

Sam nodded at Phoebe as they approached the tiny alley that wound behind a row of houses. Only a handful had the money to keep horses, but there were enough stables that the alley smelled of manure and hay, a comforting smell covering the stench of the street from the front of the buildings.

America smelled just as bad, but only parts of it.

Her knuckles ached, and Phoebe tried to unclench her fists, but a strange fancy that if she relaxed her body the slightest bit, she would lose her composure kept her jaw tense and fingers curled.

"Told Mam I was going to Mrs. Eason's house to bring her some tea and scones since she's poorly," Sarah whispered as they lurked behind a stable, watching the back garden of the Fenleys' house to make sure no one was in the privy when they snuck across to the house. "Greycliff doesn't know where you are yet, but if he puts Letty on your tracks, it won't take long to find you."

Sarah's pert nose wrinkled as they navigated around a dung heap. "Lucy is home, but writing speeches in her room and doesn't know anything. Laura and Laila know, though. We thought to hide you in the last place they'd look—right under their noses."

In his element—participating in a half-baked scheme— Sam's smile was so bright, he lit the entire alley.

"Do you know, it is almost worth the nonsense I have to put up with to have such brilliant sisters," he said.

"You are a pain in the arse, Sam," Sarah said cheerfully while they crept into the Fenleys' back garden. "But we still love you."

Clouds of cinnamon-and-yeast-scented air enveloped them as they tiptoed into the Fenleys' kitchen. Sarah explained that the cook came only three times a week; they could hide in the kitchen for the nonce. The smells of sweet bread were from something their mother "slapped together." Phoebe's stomach growled at the news, and the young woman clucked like a hen.

"When was the last time you had a meal, Lady Phoebe?" Sarah asked, reaching on her toes to pull out a thick ceramic mug and plate. "Shame on you, Sam, for not feeding your . . ." Silence fell like the sharp blade of a guillotine at Sarah's pause, and Phoebe could not look away from Sam's twinkling eyes.

It had hurt.

It had hurt to hear him call her by a pet name as a tease.

Phoebe was practiced at numbing herself to the injuries a man's words could inflict, but Sam Fenley rendered her skill useless. Each second in his presence robbed her of another half inch of armor.

Love, she was learning, was a knife. It cut away her defenses, so she was bare to the world, a mass of nerves and sinew.

Her first impulse was to take that knife and slash deeper than Sam ever could, to hurt everyone around her. Her second impulse was to use the knife on herself, cut deeper than anyone else would dare.

"I don't care if you call her Your Majesty. Letty and Greycliff are on their way here, so youse better hide quick. Don't tell Laura where you hide because she can't tell a lie." This came from a pretty blond woman who had craned her neck around the doorway, the lashes of her big blue eyes so long, the ones at the corner had tangled; her hands were on her hips.

"What? Laila, what do you know?" Sarah asked. Laila's head disappeared for a second, then she tiptoed into the kitchen while Sam continued to rummage through an icebox and Sarah sliced pieces from a loaf of brown bread.

Not until Sam walked over and took Phoebe's hands did she realize she'd been shaking. His palms were warm, she almost pressed them to her cheek. Almost.

"Hide them in your room, Sarah," Laila said. "No one in their right mind would enter that room unless they prefer to be blinded."

Sarah's thick brown eyebrows drew together. "It's called art, Laila Fenley. No one understands, not one of you." She dropped her knife, spun on her heel, and stomped off, her petticoats flipping up as she exited.

"*No one* understands," said Sam without an ounce of sympathy.

"It's called *art*," Laila explained, placing cheese and pickles between the slices of bread that Sarah had already buttered.

"Philistines," said Sam as he poured hot water over a basket of tea leaves set in a squat clay pot.

Sam carried a tray with the food and hot tea. Phoebe followed on his heels with Laila behind them. Sam led Phoebe into Sarah's room while Laila scurried off to collect bed linens and a ewer for washing up.

Blinding for certain, but Phoebe would also use the words *startling* and *beautiful*.

The chamber smelled of turpentine and oil paint, not so strongly as to be unpleasant, and against the walls were propped painting after painting. They were unapologetic in their use of color, but what fascinated Phoebe the most was they depicted real life in the streets of Clerkenwell.

"These are . . ." Phoebe stopped to stare at one picture that portrayed a little violet seller like the one she and Sam had encountered earlier this morning. Sarah had made no attempt to romanticize the misery of such a life. Instead, the little girl's face was pinched with worry, her stockings were obviously mended at the knees more than once, and the posies in her basket were as wilted and pathetic in the painting as they had been in real life.

"What?" Sarah stood behind the door, one foot raised to scratch the other ankle, a look of sullen resignation pulling her mouth into a pout.

"Incredible."

Sam, who'd been moving the easels and painting supplies to one corner, stopped his work and stared at Phoebe.

"This work is of the quality one sees in the National Gallery," Phoebe continued. "I'm sorry to say I don't believe a young woman's work will ever hang there, but if it did, it should be work like this."

Sarah's mouth opened and closed, then opened again, her brows pulling down as she frowned.

"You are making that up," she said, but Phoebe was already shaking her head.

"This is as far from romanticism as one can get," Phoebe pointed out, then stooped and held her finger above the brushstrokes. "Your choice of colors is untraditional but bold, your brushstrokes can be choppy, and you need to practice more, perhaps with a tutor." She straightened and looked at Sam. "I've spent hours at the gallery and been given lessons in art since a child. Your sister is magnificently talented."

Sam glanced at Sarah, then back at Phoebe. "You aren't doing a good job at being a villainess right now."

Shrugging, Phoebe examined two more paintings, both of a greengrocer in Covent Garden. "I can be a villain and still speak the truth."

"You aren't telling me anything I don't know," said Sarah, her arms straight at her sides, fists clenched.

"Good." Phoebe nodded in appreciation at the display of ferocity and self-confidence. "Those who don't understand art you can ignore. It is the men who know what you're doing and find it threatening you must watch out for. They will malign your talent and dilute your passion if you let them."

The two women stared at each other, a volley of unspoken frustrations bounced between them, and Sarah nodded slowly. She had already encountered such men, it appeared.

"I am happy you have come to stay with us, Lady Phoebe," Sarah said quietly.

"I am honored, Miss Sarah," Phoebe said in return.

"If this mutual-appreciation society could conclude the opening ceremonies," Sam interjected, "we should figure out how to hide if Letty decides to peruse Sarah's paintings."

"She never would," said Sarah darkly. Nonetheless, the three of them moved the easels, and behind them, Sam hung a cloth dirtied with paint spatters onto two hooks.

"I will tell them I am experimenting with backdrops," Sarah said when they'd finished. By this time Phoebe had eaten two cheese-and-pickle sandwiches.

"These are delicious." She held a third sandwich and marveled at it. "How did I never know how delicious bread and cheese could be?"

"Because most likely you've never been hungry before,"

Sam said. His tone was light and easy, as if he'd put no thought into the words, but they slapped Phoebe awake as though he'd tossed a handful of pebbles at her.

"I have been hungry many times in my life," she contradicted him. "I think it is I've never been fed this generously."

Sarah frowned, but Sam understood. Phoebe was again naked before him, her envy of this family, its uncomplicated, messy love exposed in her words and in her gaze.

"If you would like anything else, I will bring it to you," Sarah offered.

Smiling to hide a flush of shame, Phoebe gestured to the tray. "I can't fit anything else in my stomach. I might burst."

A furtive knock at the door silenced them. After a second, the door opened, and Laila stood in the doorway, handing linens over to Sam.

"Letty and Grey are here to take Laura to the doctor's with Mam. Sarah, you go down, you're good at distraction. I've told them I've a headache so I can hide away without breaking down. Lucy is already haranguing Grey over the anti-Corn legislation. We can only hope they'll be too distracted—or irritated—to wonder over anything out of the ordinary."

Sarah followed Laila out of the room. Stopping at the exit, she turned and regarded Phoebe.

"Thank you, Lady Hunt. Even if you didn't mean it."

"Oh, I wouldn't lie, child," Phoebe said. She'd tried for her usual hauteur, but the familiar aristocratic chill had deserted her. "Why lie when the truth is so painful?"

The truth was, no matter Sarah's talents, she would never become known for her art. Thus was the world, and even the loving Fenleys would have to accept this.

21

The object of chemistry is to obtain a knowledge of
the intimate nature of bodies, and of their mutual
action on each other. You find therefore ... that this
is no narrow or confined science, which compre-
hends every thing material within our sphere.

—Mrs. Jane Marcet

"WELL. MY SISTERS SHOULD KEEP LETTY AND GREY OUT
of the way for a while and, oh, look—a bed."

Sam hadn't expected Phoebe to tear off her clothes and
jump on the mattress, but a man can dream.

"Mr. Fenley," she began.

He'd shaken her formidable defenses, and because Phoebe
had grown up amid war, her defenses were as vital as her lungs,
as her heart.

Easy to ruin everything with one bad joke, one missed clue.
If he made a misstep, it would kill anything between them and
might sour Phoebe on taking a chance with any man.

They stood facing each other behind the sheet he'd slung

across the room. To their right was a small dormer window, well glazed, no hint of the cold that turned the skies outside to the color of wet paper and smoke.

What a delightful change from her haunted manor.

Sam considered giving way to Phoebe's prodding and letting his temper flare—he'd remind her what they'd done was much more than sex, but it would send her only further into retreat.

He could be patient in pursuit of a goal.

"As I said . . ." Sam gestured to the other side of the sheet. "There's a bed here. I haven't slept in two days. Unless you have an urge to *converse* . . ." He waggled his eyebrows and leered.

"Shut up," she said without inflection. Phoebe's eyes went to the bed now, her jaw moving back and forth, perhaps biting down a yawn.

"We'll spar later, Phoebe," he allowed. "When we wake, we'll figure out what happens next."

The bed was not big enough for them both. It said much about how tired Phoebe truly was that she turned her back without comment. Sam removed her pelisse and unbuttoned her dress, then loosened her corset. Her only objection when he took a pillow and blanket from the bed and lay down on the floor was that he'd left her with a pillow in a case with blue flowers when she preferred his, with yellow flowers.

They traded pillows and Sam lay on his back, staring at the humps of plaster on the ceiling, inhaling the scent of linseed oil and rosewater.

"Sam."

"Yes, my lady."

"When Letty heard I was back in Britain, did she . . . did she ask after me?"

Sam rolled over onto his side and stared at the bed where Phoebe lay like a queen on a bier, her face too pale, wrists nothing but skin and bone.

He wanted to feed this woman. He wanted to take a bite of her as well.

"She asked how you seemed, yes."

A slight hum in the air told Sam that Phoebe was thinking. Quiet and sleek, not like the nearly audible whirring and sparking of Violet Kneland's brain, nor the measured certainty of Margaret when she took on a project.

Having spent years in the company of women scientists, Sam recognized they worked their problems in a different manner. Some of the scientists, like Lady Potts, moved their lips as they worked. Others, like Letty, sat motionless, eyes vague and fingers still. Sam imagined Phoebe's brain worked like a clothes press, taking an unruly equation and smoothing it out until not a wrinkle remained.

"Did you miss her?" he asked, more out of a desire to keep her talking than true curiosity.

"She knew," Phoebe said.

It took him a moment to place her words into a context. They were tired, too tired to make good decisions. Sam would have to rely on his sisters for help.

"She knew . . . what your father did to you?" he clarified.

Phoebe's fingers twitched.

Ah, well. He would have wound up under her anyway. Sam stood, scooped Phoebe in his arms, sat back on the bed, and plopped her on top of him.

Delightful.

"Sam," she hissed, outraged. "We are not going to engage in . . . in . . ."

"Lovemaking," he supplied while pushing her hair from her face.

"*That*, in your sister's bed," she finished.

"You smell like marble."

Sam was many things, but a man who tupped a woman in his sister's bed was not one of them.

One of his sisters was lecturing someone. Letty would be in the kitchen with his mam and the babes. You couldn't hear anything in the kitchen from Sarah's room. You couldn't even smell the nice smells, either, because of the mix of turpentine, linseed oil, and paint in here.

"I listen better when I'm not on the floor," he said. "Don't worry, I am going to keep my hands above your clothing."

Phoebe made a *hmm*ing sound of disbelief, but after a moment she continued.

"I tried to make light of it, but Letty looked at me in such a way I thought she might pity me."

Sam imagined this would send Phoebe off into a fit.

"Didn't like to be pitied?" he asked, stroking her cheek. What he wanted to do was put his thumb in her mouth and watch her suck it between her plum-colored lips, but he refrained from doing anything more than he did now.

Gods be damned, but he'd turned into a *saint* while freezing his bollocks off in Cumbria. The one probably having much to do with the other.

"I didn't know why," Phoebe said. "You see, I had imagined this house, this family, the emporium . . . differently. I thought she was delusional to prefer her life to mine."

Oh, but the irony in her voice. Phoebe Hunt was many things, but dishonest about herself, she was not.

"Because living in a haunted house with a madman and a mother who would rather be anywhere else—that is so wonderful a life you cannot imagine anyone else's coming close?" he asked, chuckling.

Once she accepted Sam would not be fondling her (yet) Phoebe relented and stretched herself like a cat, then nestled herself against him. The bed was too narrow for them to lie side by side, but exactly right for him to hold her above him and cuddle her.

Cuddle. Phoebe Hunt.

More than a few people's brains would struggle with *that* equation.

"Although it was . . . uncomfortable to live with my father, he was the last in a line stretching back to the defeat of the Roman Empire. A marquess. When he criticized the temerity of the lower classes to want to educate their children, the ridiculousness of letting uneducated rabble have the vote, I knew he was wrong. Yet . . ."

Sam understood.

This entire escapade had begun with Sam's desire to expand, gain influence, and add to his fortune, but Da's reservations still tapped away in the back of his head.

Why not be content with what is in front of you?

More isn't always better.

Mind your place.

Don't make a fuss.

Some of this was no doubt due to a scandal Letty had weathered years ago and the effect it had on his other sisters' marriage chances. Only now that Letty had been married a few years—married to a viscount, no less—and had babies were the boys coming to call for his sisters again.

"He was your father. There was no one telling you not to believe him," Sam said.

"No matter how hard I tried, I could not stop repeating some of the things he said," Phoebe confessed. "Not stop wondering if perhaps he had it right and everything I believed was nonsense."

Sam squeezed Phoebe tight. This brought her delightful body much closer than he'd meant, but it seemed necessary. Right. That he comfort her with his arms and his slight, soft kisses on the forehead as well as his words.

"I said unkind things to Letty," Phoebe whispered.

Sam waited.

Phoebe raised her head and looked at him.

"I was cutting and dismissive," she told him.

He nodded and set one arm behind his head, looking back at her without hurting his neck.

"Aren't you going to say something?" Those purple eyes narrowed, and a thrill went up his spine.

"Phoebe. I have been in your company for almost a month now," Sam said, displaying a heroic amount of patience with this new Phoebe. This tentative Phoebe.

She wouldn't last long. As soon as the bliss of lovemaking wore off, her special suit of armor would be back.

"You create your place in the world by carving out space. If you were a man, you'd most likely have done it with a knife. Seeing as you're a girl . . ."

"Woman," she growled, and poked at his chest.

"Woman," he repeated dutifully. "You did it with your words. Does that sound right?"

Phoebe dropped her head back down on his chest. "I admired your sister more than she knew. More than I could unbend enough to tell her. I regret that."

When Sam chuckled, Phoebe turned her face; her lips met the skin at his collar where he'd left off his cravat.

Evil woman. How was he to resist her?

"Well, I suppose you could tell her yourself, now you're back?"

Phoebe yawned and he reciprocated. What he wouldn't give for them to be lying side by side.

"Would she listen to me?" Phoebe asked.

"Oh, certainly," Sam assured her. "Imagine the novelty of hearing a villainess of majestic proportions say she is sorry."

"Sam, we can't—

Another yawn cut off whatever Phoebe was going to say. Sam reached over and pulled the blanket off the floor, then covered them both.

"Go ahead and argue with me for as long as you like," he said, "but let me shut my eyes for a few seconds first."

Her response was a small snore, but Sam lay awake for a while longer, examining the ceiling and cataloging the ways this woman could break his heart.

"You look beautiful, Letty."

Letty Fenley gaped at the compliment.

A hot knot of shame pulsed in Phoebe's chest. She didn't remember the last time she'd complimented her friend without attaching a barb in the years before she left.

"Motherhood suits you," she continued.

The child at Letty's breast moved beneath the blanket Letty

wore over her shoulder to cover her naked chest from anyone who might walk into the kitchen on their way to the privy.

As Phoebe had done.

Having drunk half a pot of tea, she'd dozed for only a few minutes when she woke having to visit the necessary.

She had carefully pushed herself off Sam, but he slept soundly and didn't move. Tiptoeing across the room, Phoebe had listened with one ear at the door. Casting a last glance to be certain Sam still slept, Phoebe's heart skipped a beat, a stutter powerful enough to knock her off-balance, and she leaned against the wall to stay upright.

Good God, Sam Fenley smiled in his sleep. An unadulterated, childlike grin made him look years younger and desperately beautiful. It hurt to look on him. Pain was a familiar sensation, however; Phoebe grabbed hold of it and squeezed.

Painful to look on him not because he was too good to be true. Sam was canny with a brilliant mind for business, but he was also a terrible liar, like his sister. He had never pretended to be anything other than himself: a compassionate, genuine soul in a tenuous relationship with gravity.

He wasn't too good to be true—he was too good to be hers.

So, although she tiptoed down the stairs, Phoebe didn't think twice about opening the door to the kitchen, for in her experience, the only people one would find there would be servants.

Or her former friend Letty Fenley, now Lady Leticia Greycliff.

"Phoebe," Letty said now, her mouth still agape with shock but her astonishing brain already working, as evidenced by the glance she cast at the ceiling, then back at Phoebe.

"You must—" Whatever Letty meant to say was cut short by the wail of a child. Phoebe gasped when Letty moved a cradle at her side with one foot, both hands being occupied with holding the baby at her breast.

"Two of them?" Phoebe said. "Sam never said. My goodness, where did you put them in that little body of yours?"

Letty's foot moved faster as the baby's cries intensified. "Oh, Phoebe, don't even ask. It will put you off children forever, just . . ."

Gently, she pulled the blanket back and put her finger in the suckling baby's mouth in a hooklike motion. Pulling her chemise up to cover herself, she set the child over her shoulder and patted. An enormous burp issued from the one baby as the other one thrust its arms in the air and screamed.

"Hold Wilhelm while I feed Millicent, please," Letty said, holding out the child toward Phoebe.

The scent of cinnamon mixed with the smell of sweat and milk. A terrible longing rushed through Phoebe's body, thickening her blood, blurring her vision. Not longing for a child. Longing for what Letty and Sam had experienced; a mother who baked for them, a safe home, a security with themselves and the world like that which allowed Letty to hand her baby or Sam his trust over to a woman who could hurt them badly.

She took the baby from Letty's hands and stared down at him, rocking back and forth on her feet as she'd seen women do with their infants.

"You named them after Milly and Willy?" Phoebe asked.

Millicent and Wilhelmina were the oldest members of Athena's Retreat. The last time Phoebe was in England, they'd been experimenting with pyroglycerin and nearly blown the building to bits.

They were also steadfastly in love and had made a life together in a society unwilling to acknowledge that love.

The wailing ceased when the second baby, Millicent, began sucking furiously, her arms still waving, her feet churning like an eggbeater.

"Well, Will is a boy, so we had to compromise, but yes." Letty tried to hook her foot onto a small stool, and Phoebe nudged it closer. Letty put her feet up and sighed.

Will's eyes were gray, like his father's, and sported one patch of cornsilk-colored hair at the top of his head. He was in fact a beautiful baby. Phoebe held him close to her nose and inhaled. A pain similar to the one that took her breath away watching Sam while he slept twisted her lungs.

Letty pulled the blanket back over Millie. Her lovely blond hair sat in a soft bun and the curls at her temple were damp with sweat. The brittle edges she'd honed during her years as a social outcast had softened, premature wrinkles at the corner of her mouth were smoothed, and her gaunt cheeks were rounded.

"Greycliff will be back soon. He took Laura and Mam to a doctor's appointment in the carriage. He accompanied them more to avoid Lucy's speechifying than because he thought they needed escort."

Phoebe settled herself in a chair opposite the kitchen table from Letty and rested the baby against her chest, sniffing every now and then. He smelled like peach tarts.

"You are happy? I didn't think you even liked Greycliff."

Letty smiled. "He was besotted, so I took pity on him."

"You Fenleys have the same humor," Phoebe said.

The baby beneath the blanket detached herself with a loud smacking noise and began mewling imperiously. Letty switched sides.

"About Sam . . ."

Phoebe shook her head. "I won't hurt him, I promise."

Letty sighed. "There are different sorts of hurt, Phoebe."

The baby in her arms stirred and Phoebe rocked in her seat, staring down at the huge eyes set in the tiny face.

"You mean the hurt of having been betrayed by your friend who stole a member's work, used it to create a weapon, and planned on selling that weapon to the highest bidder?" Phoebe asked, keeping her eyes on Will.

"That is nothing compared to the hurt of knowing your friend was in pain and not being allowed to help her," Letty replied.

Ridiculous.

"What could you have done?" Phoebe gently traced the line of Will's nose from top to end while he gazed at her with guileless eyes. "Single-handedly dismantled a patriarchal aristocracy so I wouldn't have anyone to rage against?"

Letty sniffed. "That is the dream, isn't it?"

When Phoebe chuckled in surprise, Will's mouth puckered into a rosebud.

"Instead of asking for help," Letty continued, "you kept your anger leashed and pretended not to care about anyone or anything—"

"I don't," Phoebe snapped. "I don't care about anyone, and you have no call to be sympathetic. You are like Sam with your ridiculous optimism and foolish trust in a person's better nature."

Damn.

"Sorry," said Phoebe. "I'm sorry, Letty."

A door opened, and the sound of laughter filtered back to the kitchen. Letty pulled the blanket from her shoulder and dislodged Millie with the same efficiency she had Will.

"She looks drunk," Phoebe said, momentarily distracted by the baby's gaping mouth and lolling head.

"I've a mind to give up mathematics and study biology instead," Letty confessed as she set the baby over her shoulder and patted her back. "Already, I've a set of observations about infant behavior that would provide years of study. Do you know, most male physicians are stupid?"

"I'm going with Grey," Phoebe said.

Letty must have anticipated this, for she showed no surprise and kept rubbing the baby's back while Phoebe took one last sniff at Will's head for courage.

"I didn't set off that bomb." Phoebe had intended to say it with confidence, but it sounded like a plea in her ears.

Millie's opinion came in the form of a wet belch.

"Are you going with Grey because you don't want to hurt Sam or because you want to prove yourself innocent of setting off the bomb?" Letty asked, settling Millie back in the cradle.

"Look after Karolina and my mother, please. Tell Sam . . ."

The door to the kitchen opened and Letty's husband, Lord Greycliff, stood in the doorway, a quick jerk of his squared chin the only sign of his surprise at seeing his wife and Phoebe sitting at a kitchen table like two housemaids.

"I told you so," Letty said to Grey.

The viscount rolled one shoulder up in acknowledgment. "Yes, I know. You were right. You are always right, my miniature little wife."

"Yet you continue to doubt me, my enormous melon-headed husband." Letty sighed at his obduracy.

Her friend might have been smaller than her husband, but the force of Letty's personality lit her like a flame, and Grey leaned toward her like a moth enamored of an unobtainable light.

"The two of you need to stop the sweet talk," said Phoebe dryly. "You're making me blush."

"Do you have anything to collect?" Grey asked Phoebe politely. "If not, we should go now. If you and Sam hadn't run off together, this might have been over by now."

"Yes, much shorter distance to Newgate than to Clerkenwell," Phoebe said dryly.

The viscount rolled his eyes. "Not Newgate, Phoebe. Sam left before I explained that we are not convinced of your involvement with the bomb, but there are reporters sniffing around. You might be recognized. While Grantham and I know you will keep your word and leave, not everyone in the government is inclined to feel the same way."

This could have been sorted by now.

Then again, Phoebe would never have spent the night with Sam.

She rose slowly and settled Will in the cradle next to his sister.

"Will I see you again before I leave?" she asked Letty, keeping her gaze fixed on the baby. "I would like to, if that's possible."

Letty patted Phoebe's arm. "Yes, dear. Besides, it isn't as though they are taking you to some underground torture chamber. Only, beware the basement if you are afraid of ants."

Phoebe put her hand over Letty's and looked her in the eye. "Do you believe me? That I didn't have anything to do with the bomb?"

Millie yawned and a wet spluttering sound issued from her

diaper. A second later, Will imitated his sister, his spluttering even louder. Letty sighed and looked to Grey, but he held his hands in the air, walking backward out of the door.

"Oh dear. So sorry, Phoebe and I must be on our way," he said, not even pretending to be sympathetic.

Letty's pink lips twisted into a tight line Phoebe found foreboding. She wouldn't want to be Greycliff later today.

"Take good care of her, my lord," said Letty, reaching down and lifting the blanket off the babies, wrinkling her nose as the scent of soured milk filled the air. "She has friends, none of whom you want to anger."

The statement fell like a stone in front of her, and Phoebe tripped over it. *Friends*. Somehow, after all she'd done, Letty—and hopefully Violet—considered themselves her friends.

Amazing.

The couple continued to bicker as Phoebe excused herself to the privy. When she returned, Laura and her mother had joined Letty in the kitchen. Upon hearing Phoebe was one of the founders of Athena's Retreat, Mrs. Fenley filled a basket for her with the rest of the cheese and bread.

"Tell your sisters I said goodbye," Phoebe told Letty as Greycliff assisted her into the carriage.

Letty waved as Grey climbed in behind Phoebe and shut the carriage door.

"I have no problem conveying your farewells to my sisters," Letty called as the carriage rolled away, then shouted something about not wanting to be there when Sam found out.

Well.

Sam couldn't have expected Phoebe to remain with him. He had a fortune to make while Phoebe had an ocean to cross and an atonement to carry out.

22

The man who is certain he is right is almost sure to be wrong.

–Michael Faraday

"VIOLET HAS MISSED YOU. SO HAS LETTY, FOR THAT MAT-ter, but not as much as Violet."

Phoebe kept her gaze fixed on the tiny crack in the curtains of Grey's carriage as it squeezed its way through the bedlam of Clerkenwell's streets. The roads here were narrow, never having meant to hold the conveyances of the aristocracy. Some of them were little more than jumped-up lanes meant for live-stock to walk, nose to tail.

The bones of London were there to see if you scraped away the dirt and pulled down the occasional cathedral. A nation's capital, to be certain, but predominantly a trading city. A place for bargains and wagers. Risks and terrible loss.

"What am I supposed to say, Greycliff?" Phoebe asked. His resentment smelled like peppercorns, and she rubbed her nose with a handkerchief.

"I should think you would evince some regret."

They'd known each other forever, she and Greycliff.

When she was fifteen, Phoebe and Greycliff had stood awkwardly side by side at a garden party once, silently agreeing not to mingle. Stationed next to a platter of tarts, Phoebe had eaten steadily while Grey watched from the corner of his eye, until she turned green and went to vomit beneath some early-blooming shrubbery. He'd directed partygoers away from the site of her ignominy until she'd finished.

That night Phoebe had cut herself so badly, she believed she might die.

They'd known each other for years, but he didn't *know* her.

"I will evince anything you'd like, my lord. It doesn't matter how I feel." Phoebe tried to keep the petulance from her voice. "You have made up your mind, and nothing I do short of shaving my head and prancing around in sackcloth will appease you."

Grey frowned. "Well. Sackcloths might be pushing it too far."

"My point, Greycliff, is—" Phoebe's explanation stopped halfway. The carriage curtains had blown open, giving her the smallest glimpse of a wagon trundling alongside the carriage. A wagon holding two familiar figures.

"Halt the carriage or I will shoot!"

The carriage stuttered to a full stop. Grey and Phoebe stuck their heads out of the windows, then popped their heads back in and stared at each other. Phoebe's lower lip trembled.

"Don't laugh," he warned her.

"Is that Lucy or Laila?" Phoebe asked.

Grey stuck half his body out of the window, then sat back down and pinched the bridge of his nose.

"I suppose I should count myself lucky that none of them are Letty," he muttered, mostly to himself.

There, sitting in a wagon with "Fenley's Fripperies" painted onto the side, were two women wearing scarves tied around their noses and mouths.

Pink scarves Phoebe wagered had cost a pretty penny.

Standing in the road was Sam.

Also, with a scarf tied around his nose and mouth.

Brandishing a pistol.

"Where did he find a pistol?" she asked, mostly to herself.

"Hullo." Sam climbed on the lip of the carriage below the door and stuck his head in through the curtains.

"You are the worst highwayman in England," Phoebe said.

She didn't need him to remove the scarf to know Sam's smile was ear to ear.

"I could have a pistol in the carriage. I could have shot you." Grey did not sound the slightest bit worried.

He sounded constipated.

"Well, you didn't, so here I am," Sam announced. "Myself and my two cutthroat compatriots."

Sam spoke giddily, and Phoebe smiled with him against her will. How could a man be this happy and not drunk?

Surely it wasn't healthy.

"This is a robbery," he said.

"No, it's not," said Grey glumly.

"Yes. I'm stealing this pretty lady." Sam motioned with his pistol toward the street. "Now, there is a grumpy tanner in the wagon behind us and if we don't get this robbery over quickly, he and I will come to fisticuffs."

"Good," said Grey.

"Sam, this isn't a good idea," said Phoebe.

Sam looked straight into her eyes, and Phoebe knew she needed to get the hell out of London and away from this man.

She was lost.

"*I* think it's a good idea. *Lucy* thinks it's a good idea—"

"Lucy is a goddamned menace," Grey interjected.

"I didn't do it," Phoebe said. "If you take me away, it makes me look guilty, Sam."

He pulled down the scarf, his brows tilted in hurt surprise. "That wasn't my intent. You left before we could plan together. This was the best I could do."

Phoebe waved her hands toward him, warding him off. "Your intent doesn't matter. It is our actions, not our intentions, by which we are judged. Go home, Sam. Take care of your sisters and leave me alone to fix this. Please."

The tanner Sam had worried about, screamed at the carriage horses.

"'S this a fecking robbery or a godsdamned tea party?" the man hollered.

Sam didn't move.

"Phoebe," he said softly, but Phoebe did not want to hear him say her name anymore. She did not want to see his smiles or warm in the heat of his regard.

The truth lay bare before her.

She could live with falling in love.

She could not live if she were loved in return and then was found wanting.

The tanner continued his diatribe and someone—Lucy or Laila—told him to shut up. That they were committing a crime in the name of love. More than a few people trying to get past the carriage and wagon had opinions on the subject of crime and love, but their words smushed together beneath the pounding in Phoebe's head when Sam slipped down and walked away.

The carriage jerked forward, and they slowly made their way past the crowd.

"He's a good man," said Grey.

Phoebe nodded, staring at the top of the carriage where a scorch mark had puckered the material.

"He is the best of men," she agreed.

They did not speak again until they arrived in the cramped mews behind Athena's Retreat.

Grey waved away the footman and handed Phoebe out himself.

"Grantham and Kneland will follow up on the names you gave us," he said. "Once we have enough evidence for the Home Office, you are free to go."

Phoebe lifted her shoulder to indicate she'd heard his words.

Grey stepped in front of her before they entered the back door to the Retreat.

"I know," he said, then coughed and stared at the darkening sky. As usual the weather in London hadn't sorted itself and hovered between freezing rain and clammy smog. "I know," he repeated, "what a father can do to a child. How much of what we're told as children can hinder—or even harm—the people we become as adults and the people we love."

Phoebe cocked her head. She hadn't been here in England when Letty brought this frozen prince to his knees. Obviously, falling in love with Letty Fenley had changed Grey. For the better.

Grey cleared his throat, peering intently at the pile of clouds above them. "Don't let him. Your father." Grey stopped.

Whatever irritant had lodged itself in Grey's throat now wedged itself into a lump in the back of Phoebe's throat as well.

"He's dead, Phoebe. You are alive and . . . don't let him take away your future the way he took away your childhood."

Phoebe swallowed, concentrating on breathing around the object in her throat.

Grey did not need a reply. Turning, he then led the way into the building, holding himself straight, though inside his trouser pockets, his hands were clenched into fists.

Phoebe let him lead her through the kitchens into a hallway that split in two, up a back staircase and down a long corridor on the right. She could have walked it blindfolded, so many times had she come to call on Lady Violet Greycliff, ostensibly for tea and gossip, but in truth they walked down these same corridors to the hidden laboratories of Athena's Retreat.

Grantham used to say the halls rang with the low hum of brilliance. Certainly, there were geniuses among the scientists here.

"I take it I am not allowed to leave the guest wing?" Phoebe asked. In the corridor hung a beautiful series of etchings of the British coast of the North Sea in simple gilded frames. Another time Phoebe would have stopped to examine them. The sea fascinated her after having grown up surrounded by miles of walls.

Greycliff shrugged. "I'd say the decision was Kneland's, but it's Violet's."

"Then let me speak with Violet," Phoebe said.

He paused before a door. "As you wish." Before Phoebe could question him further, he turned and walked back the way he had come without another word.

Not very chatty, Greycliff.

Not like his brother-in-law, Sam.

Phoebe drew in a breath and swallowed. Swallowed her

exhaustion, swallowed her fear, and tried to swallow her temper. Someone waited on the other side.

A friend, hopefully.

Once ready, she opened the door.

Each of the guest rooms at the Retreat had an outer sitting room, often with a fireplace, settee, and bookshelves, and an inner bedroom with a water closet attached.

This sitting room was painted a bright yellow, since there were no windows. A gold and ivory striped silk settee sat in the center, and a low marble table in front of it held an enormous vase filled with hothouse carnations and roses. Violet sat in the middle of the settee glaring from across the room. Next to a shelf full of bound copies of journals and pamphlets stood her husband, the object of the glare.

"I am pleased to see you again, Violet," Phoebe said calmly, "I'm sorry it had to be under these circumstances."

"Yes, well." Violet sniffed, then faced Phoebe and patted the settee next to her. "Once this foolishness has been sorted, we will have a proper visit."

"People have died," Kneland said. "That isn't foolishness."

No. No, it wasn't.

"I am ready to leave," Phoebe said to Violet.

Kneland shook his head. "Not until we can prove you weren't responsible."

Phoebe ignored him and sat next to Violet. She breathed in the comforting smell of tea and sugar with a hint of lemon. The smell of a place she once called home.

"I am ready to go back to America," she explained. Twisting in her seat to include Kneland in the conversation, Phoebe continued. "Please hurry your investigation. For certain, I could have found the proof faster, but I will not cause more conflict between . . ." Phoebe faltered then, unable to say the words *between friends*.

"Arthur will work quickly," Violet assured her. "The sooner they find the true bombers, the better for everyone."

She peered closely at Phoebe's dress. "Why do you have baby spit-up on your shoulder?"

Phoebe looked down and shuddered. "Eugh. I held one of Letty's babies. It must have happened then."

Baby spit-up was the least of the stains on this dress. She'd been wearing it for three days straight.

"Not to worry, the stain will come right out," Violet assured her. "My theory is a baby's gut is too immature to digest the milk it takes in. That stain is simply regurgitated breast milk."

When Phoebe retched slightly, Violet patted her shoulder. "The more interesting question is why and how this changes once solid food is introduced."

Against her better judgment, Phoebe found herself discussing the possible chemical reactions that might happen in a baby's belly. Soon enough, Kneland had left with some murmured words about "distracted" and "remember to eat." Two hours later a maid came by with tea and a plate of sandwiches.

Although Phoebe had no interest in the role acid played within the human digestive system, she kept asking Violet questions. She didn't want to remain at Athena's Retreat, but goodness, it was lovely to remember for a while how things had once been.

"Oh, for the love of all that is holy, if you are here to botch another robbery, you can turn around right now." Grey's mouth pinched into a surly twist.

Sam, because he was a fine fellow, resolved not to roll his

eyes at his brother-in-law's expression. He supposed a viscount with a past as a secret agent being held up in public by two girls and a shopkeeper's son might be a smidge embarrassed. Still, that was three days ago. A better man would be past it by now.

"I'm not going to rob you. I wasn't robbing you before." Sam considered his words. "I was attempting a *kidnapping*."

Grey snorted. "You did a piss poor job of it."

Fine fellow or not, Sam lost some of his patience with the man. "I would have done an excellent job of it if my victim hadn't told me to go away."

They stood in a small receiving room on the first floor of Athena's Retreat. Sam had been here plenty of times before when he came to see Letty before she'd married, or when he stopped by with his hedgehog, Fermat, to visit Mala Hill. A cheerful pink-and-red-striped paper covered the walls along with paintings of different types of spiders displayed in lovely gilt frames. A tiny fire jumped in the grate, lending light but not much warmth.

Grantham and Kneland were sitting at a small cards table next to the fire, a few papers spread out between them. Kneland wore a pair of spectacles that did nothing to lessen the intensity of his gaze.

That man was scary.

"I'll admit that plan was ill thought out. I should have known Phoebe was with you by choice. She's too good to have been caught unawares," Sam said, not bothering to hide the pride in his voice. "The time for scheming is over. I've a plan."

"Lord save us from your plans, Fenley," Grantham said from his seat by the fire.

"My *plans* have made me a fortune," Sam retorted. "I've a brain, even if I lack a title before my name."

Grantham said nothing in the loudest way possible one could say nothing. He crossed his arms, rolled his eyes, and shook his head as though Sam were a precocious child.

"Sam . . ." Grey began.

Ugh.

That tone of voice. The tone that said because Sam was not highborn, his plans—his ideas, his dreams, and his aspirations—were too big. Too unreasonable. Too impatient.

This is how life was for Phoebe or Letty or Sarah. They had massive brains and outstanding talent but were considered merely a step above children in their abilities by the men who held the power. Even if their genius was acknowledged, their personhood was never in question—they were women and thus less than.

Similarly, Sam had many times stood before a group of titled men while they looked through him, as though the place in which he was born determined the boundary at which he was expected to stop and be grateful; to keep his ambitions small and frustrations to himself.

"Let her go," Sam said, cutting off whatever pap Grey had been poised to spew. Something about waiting for men in charge to take care of things.

Well.

Sam was a man in charge as well, even if he wasn't a lord.

"If you don't think she did it, I will find a place to hide her until the auction is complete."

Kneland and Grantham looked over at each other. Neither said a word.

"Why keep her cooped up here?" Sam asked them. "What of her family? Her mother must be—"

"Listen!" Grey snapped.

Sam shut his mouth. Grey's manner had shifted from annoyed brother-in-law to former government agent in an instant.

"Phoebe's mother is the sole descendant of the House Gediminas," Grey said.

Sam shook his head to convey his ignorance.

"The Grand Duke Gediminas and his children ruled Lithuania for three hundred years of prosperity. They brought peace with Poland and are credited with bringing Christianity as well."

The tiniest pebble of foreboding roiled in Sam's stomach. This was to do with Phoebe's family—with that terrible manor house in the north.

Grantham picked up the story, no hint of condescension in his voice. "When Napoleon set his sights on the region, his emissaries approached the last living member of the House Gediminas. It was a girl, Aldona, who was fourteen at the time and lived a cloistered life. She was surrounded by a group of men whose families had been loyal villeins. They housed her, fed her, and advised her."

A fourteen-year-old girl.

The portrait Sam had seen in the music room was of a woman far too young to have had so many children. He pictured Phoebe's mother standing stock-still in the hallway at Prentiss Manor before dinner that night.

Small.

Lost.

Fragile.

"The Lithuanians welcomed the French without a fight and

promised to support Napoleon if he kept Russia at bay," Kneland said, his gravelly voice carrying easily across the room. "Aldona's advisors, however, they went a step further."

"It . . . whatever they did, it wasn't enough," Sam said, remembering his history. "Russia took over in the end."

Kneland nodded. "In hindsight it was a bad deal, but the Lithuanians wanted to remain independent so badly, they blinded themselves to the French army's flaws."

That made sense. Hope could make anyone see things that weren't there.

"In return for their allegiance," Grey explained, "Napoleon promised to restore the House Gediminas by setting Aldona, and her husband, on the throne."

Good God.

Sam was sick to his stomach where the pebble of foreboding had grown into a boulder.

"Napoleon sent her here at fourteen to wed the marquess?" Sam asked.

Grey nodded, sympathy melting the ice in his gaze.

Sam thought of his sisters at the age of fourteen. Too young. Too bloody young.

"Why would Fallowshall agree to help Napoleon?" he asked. "How could any man with his history betray England?"

Walking down the hall of ancestors at Prentiss Manor was a walk past the history of their nation. This had to have weighed heavily on the marquess.

"As you've witnessed, Prentiss Manor is not a rich estate," Grey said.

Again, Sam thought back to the painting of the beautiful young woman and her girls; both the living, and the dead. A fourteen-year-old innocent wedded to a strange adult, having to bear his children, alone in that haunted house. What might that do to a woman's soul?

Sam would never know the helplessness of being a woman trapped in a marriage. Oh, there were ways for women to leave, but they required funds or extended family and a willingness to brave ostracism.

Poor Lady Fallowshall never had that.

"Wait," Sam said. "Why was she sent to marry an English noble and not a French one? And the marquess? Why wasn't he charged with treason?"

Grey scratched the underside of his chin where a hint of shadow had appeared. "He didn't commit treason because Napoleon was defeated before they went back to Lithuania," he said. "Instead, Fallowshall claimed he met his bride the last time he visited the country. He immediately fell in love with her and rescued her from the evil machinations of the French and the Polish. The truth is he had an affair with Aldona's married chaperone, Maria, and left the country after finding out his lover had become pregnant."

Jonas.

"Reports were that Maria's husband was livid. The official word is she died of a fall," said Grey. "The child disappeared when he was six."

The entire scenario—the child bride, the narcissistic marquess, the bastard son—it made Sam sick.

Phoebe's mother had expected to be a princess in return for marrying a sadist. The sadist had expected a throne in return for taking a bride not of his own choosing.

"You never told me this," Sam said. "Awfully important information."

Grey shrugged. "We didn't think you needed to know."

Sam gritted his teeth and swallowed a curse. Obviously, information was currency, and his brother-in-law wouldn't toss it about to just anyone.

"Even if you had told me, that was before we were born," Sam said. "The war is over, Napoleon is dead, as is Phoebe's father. None of this matters."

Grey disagreed. "It matters to the Home Office," he said. "It matters to the head of Military Intelligence who fought the French on the peninsula."

"What if Russia leaves?" Kneland asked, his raptor's eyes hard and black, searching for the weakest part of a man. "The Hunt women are still the last descendants of that house."

"So what?" Sam asked the question even though he already knew the answer.

"So, it's a powerful incentive to start a revolution," Grey said, then yawned. "If you can recruit a group of men who would do anything to upset a monarchy, then arm them with weapons that cannot be defended against, it might be enough to convince the Lithuanians to rally behind a long-lost princess."

"Phoebe's sister Alice is married to an influential nobleman," Kneland pointed out.

"Don't be daft. Those women were abased and abused by the marquess," Sam retorted. "The last thing they want is to raise an army against the Russian empire."

Grantham frowned faintly as though he couldn't comprehend Sam's remarks, a hint of pity in his eyes. "You don't understand what you are taking on if you defend Phoebe."

"I am not 'taking on' anything," Sam countered. "Phoebe is a person, not a problem."

Grantham stood and walked to the mantel, poking at the fire.

"Yes, Fenley. I know she is a person. I've known her for years and am aware her father was a tyrant." Grantham's mouth pulled down on one side and he glanced at Kneland, then set the poker against the wall. "It doesn't excuse her from accountability for her actions. She was not supposed to return without permission. It makes her look guilty."

Kneland stood as well and moved the poker to its tray. "There are hundreds of thousands of women who have similar if not worse backgrounds. None of them set off bombs that killed constables."

Sam threw his hands up in disgust. "No, they don't all make bombs, but they do continue the cycle of violence that begat them and mistreat their children, their husbands, themselves. It isn't an excuse; it is a motivation. And she didn't set off the bomb that killed the constable, she invented it."

Stepping forward, Grey put himself between Sam and Grantham. "Do you know for certain, Sam, that Phoebe had nothing to do with the violence at Kennington Common? Were you with her the entire visit to Prentiss Manor?"

"Indeed, as was her mother, the marchioness, and her sister Lady Karolina," Sam retorted. "The four of us were boarding a train to Liverpool that morning."

"Doesn't mean anything," Kneland said. "She could have planted it the night before and set a timer. Lady Grantham taught me that trick. Or had one of the Omnis set it for her. That's what happened the last time."

Letty had told Sam about the demonstration where the bomb went off after Phoebe had been shipped to America.

Phoebe had claimed the weapon was not perfected when Adam Winters told one of his men to use it at the demonstration. Letty had been unsympathetic to the claim Winters hadn't trusted Phoebe's intelligence and had his men set the bomb off. Incorrectly, as it happened, causing death where it was meant to cause mayhem.

"This isn't like the last time," Sam insisted. "She isn't the same person, and this isn't the same set of circumstances."

He rubbed a hand over his face. "I have told you what we learned in the pubs the other day. It sounds as though a splinter group of Omnis, mainly Welsh, have regrouped to protest the Corn Laws."

Grantham stretched his leg out and moved the poker tray a foot to the left. "Why don't you leave the investigating to those of us who know what we are doing and go back home?"

"Have you always been this obnoxious, or is it something to do with your marital state?" Sam asked, practically seething with rage.

Kneland sniffed. "Yes, he's always been this obnoxious."

Grantham scoffed. "It is not obnoxious to state the obvious—"

"Yes, it is," said Kneland.

"It can be," Grey agreed.

"Makes you want to punch him in the face," Kneland continued.

"If you could reach that high, I'd let you take a swing." Grantham's face flushed with affection. "As it is, I have to hold you off with one of my massive arms . . ."

Grantham reached out and set his palm on Kneland's forehead as though pushing away a child, even though Kneland was only an inch or two shorter than the earl. Quick as a wink,

Kneland trapped Grantham's hand and twisted the earl's arm behind his back.

"Could the two of you please stop touching one another, for the love of Christ," Grey complained.

Sam sighed.

Men.

"When we asked you to go to Prentiss Manor and report back your observations . . ." An enormous yawn interrupted Grey's words and the viscount blushed, covering his mouth. "'Pologies. No one sleeps when there is colic in the house," he said.

A prickly shiver tapped at Sam's neck. He set his palm there, expecting a breeze, but the curtains were closed, and no draft swept through the room.

The door to the parlor stood partly open.

Sam had closed it when he'd come inside.

He ignored whatever Grey was saying and ran to the doorway. Sticking his head out, he looked down both sides of the hallway. No one was there.

Except.

She didn't wear perfume, Phoebe. She could have drifted through the world smelling of dried lavender and money, but she didn't.

Phoebe Hunt smelled . . . peppery. Plus a note of sage. Tart. Salty.

Sam inhaled, trying to detect something beneath the familiar cleaning scents of beeswax and vinegar.

"What are you doing?" Grey asked, having followed him into the hallway.

"Phoebe was here," Sam said.

He tasted her on the back of his tongue.

"She's upstairs in one of the guest rooms, yes," Grey allowed, "but you heard what she said, Sam. She doesn't want you to rescue her."

Sam sucked on his lower lip, then sighed. "Not the problem, Greycliff. The problem"—he spun on his heel slowly like a weather vane pointing in the direction of a storm—"the problem is she was *here*. She *heard* you say I was investigating her family."

Grey had the grace to appear embarrassed. He washed his face with a hand, pulling his mouth down into a frown. "Now she thinks we were gossiping about her family?"

"No, you idiot." Sam slapped his palm over his eyes. "Now she thinks I only took the time to get to know her at Prentiss Manor to report back to you. That I took advantage of the lot of them."

"You did go there to take advantage of them." Grey's tone of aggrievement plucked at Sam's nerves like the sound of knives scraping across a piece of porcelain. "You went to look good for the marchioness so she'd let you marry Phoebe's sister."

"Yes, that is why I went," Sam agreed. "It isn't why I *stayed*."

He sighed, wondering how long it would take for him to convince Phoebe of the truth and if it would involve harm to his person.

Most likely.

Nothing for it, though.

"Sam, whatever it is you are thinking, I need you to wipe it from your brain. Right. Now." Grey said, reaching over to set a hand on Sam's shoulder, perhaps to restrain him. "You and Phoebe are the mismatch of the century, and none of this will come out the way you expect it."

True.

Courting Phoebe was a terrible idea. She was so infamous that doors would slam in his face rather than swing wide open. She wouldn't want Sam's courtship anyway. She'd come back only to help her mother and her sister and would return to the wilds of America to . . . do whatever it was she did over there.

Holding up coaches. Sharpshooting contests with rugged men in silly hats. Finding gold in the riverbeds. Being extraordinary.

Phoebe Hunt summoned a love that broke your heart, made you doubt everything that came before, and could get you killed. A love his sister read novels about. A love that inspired men to paint. To write poetry. To abandon long-held dreams and make one's way through the rest of life unsure of anything other than that one single love.

This was not the love Sam had ever wanted for himself, but the world kept spinning on its axis (supposedly—no scientist had yet been able to convince him the world was round) no matter what Sam's wishes might be. The world had spun Phoebe into Sam's path, and he would hold on to her now.

"What are you expecting, Sam?" Grey asked gently. "Phoebe will remain in England for you? Even if we came to an agreement with the Home Office, can you imagine her baking a lemon loaf in your kitchen in Clerkenwell? Tidying the scarf display in your new emporium? You can't keep her. It will only hurt you both."

"*Keep* her?" Sam was aghast. "She's a phenomenon, not a hedgehog. I don't expect to keep her. I simply want to say goodbye before she sets sail to conquer a continent."

23

These electricities seem to me to be a kind of chemical spirit, which animates the particles of bodies, and draws them together.

–Mrs. Jane Marcet

"OH, LOOK. A BED."

Phoebe bit her lip and stared hard at the ceiling, but she couldn't help it.

She laughed.

Sam had knocked on the door to her room in the Retreat's guest wing a minute ago, his face drooping—like a child whose favorite toy had been smashed.

With her tiny capitulation, he glowed.

That damned glow.

"Yes. A bed," Phoebe echoed. "It's comfortable, actually."

How proud she was of herself. Standing upright, breathing, smiling at the same man who had crushed her heart beneath his heel only a few minutes ago.

That's what you get for eavesdropping, she supposed. Usually her anger kept her warm, but this wasn't simply anger.

Phoebe grasped for the heat of her rage but couldn't break past the cold. The room, her hands, her lips—so cold.

They stood inside the bedroom facing each other. Phoebe shivered as the draft from beneath the windowpane swirled round her ankles.

"Did Grantham finish telling you the family secrets you hadn't yet uncovered for them?" she asked, embarrassed by the slightest of tremors in her voice. It was difficult to speak naturally when your body had suddenly turned to glass.

Expecting him to placate her with excuses or to distract her in the same manner he used to keep people from looking past his charm to see the real man beneath, Phoebe turned away from him and walked toward the window. She twitched shut the heavy linen curtains, hoping to stop the draft.

Sam followed, standing behind her. When she didn't say anything, he hooked her smallest finger with his.

They touched only there, but somehow Phoebe felt his embrace.

Didn't he know she was fragile?

Didn't he think she would break?

"I would have gone even if Grey never said anything to me."

"Yes, I know. All the better to woo my sister."

The way Sam drew breath was different from any other man she knew. As if in the next moment he would need all the air in his lungs to laugh, long and hard.

As if he lived with purpose.

"If you will remember, my attempt to woo Karolina was over before it began."

"Stop."

Ignoring her, Sam moved closer, not touching, but close enough that Phoebe could feel the outline of him.

Of the many discoveries by Michael Faraday that interested Phoebe, the most compelling was electromagnetic induction.

Electromagnetic induction proved when magnets circle each other around a conductor, they don't just create an attraction, they create an electrical current. An unseen force strong enough to run a motor; perhaps someday to light a household—a city even.

When she and Sam circled each other, they created an electrical force. Unseen and devastatingly compelling.

"I made Karolina and your mother cry when I told them the story of the frog because it reminded them of how powerless princesses truly are in most fairy tales," Sam said quietly.

"Powerless in real life as well," Phoebe said.

"If you had confided in me, I would've told them my story about the nun and the blacksmith instead."

Genuine sorrow gentled the teasing. Unhooking her finger from his, she stepped away, then turned to face him.

This room was painted the same color as the inside of a mussel shell and was spacious enough to include a bed, a dresser, two night tables, and a writing desk. A stained oak door to the left led to a bathing chamber and the heavy linen curtains were dyed a deep indigo.

Phoebe and Sam stood inches from the foot of the bed.

It had too many pillows and a garish purple velvet bedcover. Whoever picked the furnishings for this room was enamored of that dressmaker, Madame Mensonge, for the entire space was riddled with pinks and purples, mirrors, and crystals hanging from this light or that candelabra.

As if the Retreat was in the habit of hosting Parisian courtesans rather than a group of outcast scientists.

"We could end things here," she said. "In that bed. One last time."

Sam's eyes flicked toward the bed, then back at Phoebe.

"One last time," he repeated without inflection.

"Once Grantham finds out who set off the explosion, I am leaving. It shouldn't take long. Whatever information you gave them won't make any difference."

Shaking his head, Sam let go a loud sigh. "I never spied on your family, Phoebe. Greycliff asked me to keep an eye out for anything strange or incriminating—"

"Shut up, Sam."

He fell silent, regarding her as though she were feral. Somewhat dangerous. His lips and jaw moved a few times, his thick gold brows pulling together to make a V of concern on his forehead.

Testing out words, hoping for the right ones.

"I'm not going to hurt myself," Phoebe lied without pause.

Sam's shoulders dropped down from his ears, and he relaxed his jaw.

"I am supposed to meet Violet and Letty for supper tonight," she said, licking the top of her teeth, her mouth gone dry. "Until then, no one will look for me."

His eyes darted to the bed and back to her.

"This isn't a good idea, Phoebe." He was disciplined enough not to sound disappointed. "My plan was to get you out of here—"

"And into a bed," she interjected.

"Yes, well. I'm no monk." Sam flapped his hands at the bed as though fighting it away. "Eventually, into a bed. In the immediate future, out of this room."

From an early age Phoebe learned to ease the pain inflicted by others with pain she inflicted on herself. Eminently more satisfying.

With no blade, Phoebe needed a different weapon with which to wound.

She walked toward Sam, who had the natural intelligence to know himself cornered. There was no place for him to run. Reaching out her ungloved hand she ran it, palm down, from his sternum to his belly. They stood close enough that her skirts brushed his toes. She let her hand rest on his slowly hardening cock between his legs.

Anything could be used as a weapon.

"Take me to bed, Sam," she whispered, aware of the memories this sentence stirred in them both.

Good.

All the better to split her skin.

"Take me to bed and tell me what I like."

Sam breathed in as though she'd slapped him, and his fingers curled into fists, as though he could fight her—fight *for* her, even.

His hesitation was born from consideration, not distaste. That Sam wanted her was evidenced by the familiar darkening of his eyes, the cadence of his breath, and the lengthening of his cock beneath her hand.

That she wanted him in return might have been as obvious to him. Perhaps her own eyes darkened, her breath became heavy, or he could smell the desire blooming between her legs.

Tugging at his cravat without finesse, Phoebe scratched his throat in her haste. Sam grabbed her wrist, gently enough that he would leave no marks, firmly enough that she could not move her hand. He put his mouth close to hers and she tasted the tea he'd had some time before.

Before she lashed him with words so sharp, he wouldn't know he bled until moments later, Sam touched his mouth to hers, then caught her bottom lip in his teeth.

Anticipation clenched her quim, and Phoebe nearly toppled against him as her legs turned liquid. He further reduced her spine to yarn by biting down and at the same time clasping her arse firmly in his hand and holding her hips against his cock.

Phoebe wanted to climb him, rub herself along his lean frame like a cat in heat, and press herself tightly to him, melting into his skin and against his bones.

"I do know what you want." He spoke against her lips, sending a vibration through her body.

Electricity.

"Then give it to—"

"You want me to be the blade you press against your skin."

The prickling heat of a numb limb coming back to life crept over Phoebe's skin. Was she so transparent? What did that make Sam? Omniscient? Or was Phoebe predictable?

He wouldn't let her out of his arms. Instead, Sam ran his fingers through her upswept hair and pulled the tiniest bit. Sparks of almost pain peppered her scalp and quickened her pulse.

"I will tell you now, I will be a soft place for you to land. I will never hurt you intentionally. I will never let you hurt yourself by using me."

What was there to say to this?

"You already did hurt me," she said, setting her forehead to his chest. "You come into our lives with your laughter and your bloody jokes and want to pull the curtains down, and what you don't know is how much it *hurts* to know what life could have been like. What I was supposed to want. What I will never have."

Phoebe would admit she used ice to fashion her knives, cold to freeze people so they stayed away. Sam—and it had taken her overlong to figure this out—Sam used warmth. He used his smile and that bright blue gaze of his to turn down the intensity so he could back away to safety.

"Do you know, Sam," Phoebe said carefully, "you do not always have to be cheerful or kind."

Sam's body stilled and his eyes narrowed before he rearranged his features to pretend confusion, but Phoebe knew he understood her.

"People will still care for you if you are grumpy or selfish sometimes."

His head jerked back as though Phoebe had slapped him.

"You are compelling for the whole of you, not only the part that makes me laugh."

There. Now she'd done it. If he was going to strip her bare and see her scars, Phoebe wanted him naked as well. This satisfied her urge to wound, but the pain was from the lancing of a boil, the cracking of a shell.

"All of me, Phoebe-girl?" Sam whispered, taking her chin in his hand and tilting her head up for examination. "You will not run away if I grow angry? If I lose patience? You will not be afraid and compare me to your father?"

"Do not"—Phoebe's breath caught on the tightness in her throat—"do not deflect, Samuel Fenley. There is no comparison between my father and a man who is genuine and honest. You could be miserable and insulting, but I know, and you know, it wouldn't last forever. There is dark as well as light in you. Be yourself with me."

A plea. The need in her voice, the craving in her chest embarrassed her.

The room tilted when he picked her up, wrapping her legs around his waist as though she were light as a feather. As though the weight of her was nothing in comparison to his need for her.

"I will try," he said. Sam set his forehead against hers and she fell into his eyes. "You might change your mind, once you see the whole of me."

"I promise I won't," Phoebe said.

"I will hold you to that." This time, when his smile returned, it was fierce and wicked. "But first, I am going to make you scream, Phoebe-girl."

Not a promise, but a warning, and like the slap of a palm against the skin of a drum, the pulse between her legs thrummed in expectancy.

The soft golden features of this beautiful man hardened as he stripped each item of clothing from her body while backing her up to the bed without saying a word; the tinkling of tiny buttons hitting the floor, a counterpoint to the sound of her skirts falling to the ground, followed by her petticoats, her corset, and her chemise.

Setting a hand on her stomach, he guided her so she lay on the purple bedcover still wearing her pantalettes with her legs partly splayed. Standing above her, he touched his eyes to the places he most coveted while he undressed himself. Not rushing, but fast enough he was naked before her within seconds, his body outlined by the wan sunlight falling through the window behind him.

"Touch yourself," he demanded.

Phoebe gasped, her hand covering her quim.

What was this?

Who was this man to tell her what to do?

Who was she to do as he told her?

"Show me," Sam demanded.

Phoebe decided she was simply humoring him when she touched herself, opening her legs for him. He said nothing but nodded approval, then took himself in hand with long, hard strokes.

This was wrong.

The world had turned light and soft and blurry around the edges.

Compelling.

Beautiful.

The damned man couldn't help himself, as he covered her body with his own and pushed one long finger into her, then crooked it, rubbing against a place deep within her, and when she came, hard and wet, he smiled.

Smiled in satisfaction, yes, but dear God, when Sam Fenley smiled, the entire world lit up around her.

"Condoms," she whispered, running her fingers through his soft hair. He didn't answer at first, busy pushing her body up the bed until her head rested on the pillow, dipping his tongue in and out of her mouth, palming her breasts, nipping at her chin and neck as though she tasted sweet.

Where were her thorns? Where was her armor?

"Not yet," he said, eventually, then suckled her nipple and left a trail of tiny red marks down her stomach and over her thighs.

"When?" she gasped.

He set one of her legs over his shoulder and answered before he put his mouth to the center of her.

"After you call my name."

He'd read that in the American west, wildfires would spring up spontaneously in their dry season. Infernos would appear from nowhere and burn everything in their path. Rather than leaving a dead and blistered landscape, they cleared the forest floors of debris, leaving new trees space to grow.

Phoebe Hunt's passion was a wildfire.

After he'd brought her to climax with his mouth, she'd found his cravat and tied one of his hands to the bedpost. Certain he wouldn't "have the upper hand," she'd gone rummaging in her valise for a tin of condoms.

Forbidden from helping, Sam watched with pleasure as Phoebe used her mouth again to make him hard, harder than was comfortable before she relented and tied the condom around the base of his cock.

They both knew he could pull his hand away from the bedpost at any time.

It didn't dampen either of their pleasure, though. She came over him then slid down, inch by torturous inch, until he was deep within her.

Pretending Phoebe had no effect on him despite the beads of sweat sliding down his temple, Sam toyed idly with her nipple, pinching and rolling it between the fingers of his free hand while she rocked her hips.

"Well, hello again, my queen," he said, lifting his hips and meeting her thrusts with shallow ones of his own.

Phoebe gasped and he stopped, uncertain if she'd enjoyed it, until she leaned over and sucked his areola into her mouth, then bit lightly.

"Do that again," she demanded.

This wasn't the same as their night in the emporium. Phoebe had regained her equilibrium. She didn't pull the cover around her to hide the largest of her scars, didn't close her eyes when her head dropped, and she watched the place where his cock pushed into her quim.

So brave, his Phoebe-girl.

Because she was brave, because she was a queen, Sam pulled his hand loose from the cravat and grabbed her by the waist, rolling them both to the center of the bed, stopping when he rested over her.

The purple velvet coverlet beneath them was a shade lighter than the color of Phoebe's irises. With one long, smooth thrust, Sam seated himself deep within her, so deep, a haloed depression appeared around her body where she sank into the mattress.

"Say my name," he demanded, nudging his hips even tighter against hers, relishing the hiss of her breath and the pinch of her fingers digging into his arms.

"Fenley."

Oh, he could spar for hours with this woman, on this bed.

Sam reached down and pushed Phoebe's legs so her heels rested on the blanket, her knees bent to give him more room.

"Say my name." His thrusts were gentle, shallow, and he canted himself to brush against the sweetest part of her.

"Uhhhh, Fenley-boy," she groaned, a smile sharper than the edge of a leatherworker's knife flashing below him.

He swallowed a laugh and thrust a little harder, a little

faster; she had to hold on tighter to his arms, lifting one leg and wrapping it around his back.

By God, he was going to explode. At the base of his spine spun a buzzing sensation, and Sam forgot the challenge, forgot his name even, as the climax approached.

"Sammmm."

A jolt of pleasure shot from his spine out of Sam's body and into Phoebe's when she purred his name. They gasped in unison as they shook, and Sam nearly fainted from the force of his climax.

This woman. This queen.

Phoebe Hunt was a gift from the universe, and he was never, ever going to let her go.

24

It is right that we should stand by and act on our principles; but not right to hold them in obstinate blindness, or retain them when proved to be erroneous.

—Michael Faraday

"HOW *DOES* ONE TAKE OVER A TERRITORY IN AMERICA? I know women don't have the vote, but can they hold political office? I should like to be the governor of somewhere without having to be in the army first."

Ten years ago, Phoebe, Letty, and Violet met in a parlor, having individually escaped the crowds of a grand ball. Seconds after introductions, they were engaged in a heated discussion of chemistry. The three of them once spent entire afternoons drinking brandy, eating tarts, and examining serious questions such as how best to prove Avogadro's law and whether shortbread was a biscuit or a bread, and if it was a biscuit, why did they call it *shortbread*?

Heady, intellectually demanding questions such as these occupied them for hours.

Much had changed since those days.

Letty Fenley had become Lady Letitia Greycliff. Lady Violet Greycliff had become Mrs. Violet Kneland.

Phoebe had become an outcast.

They sat now, the three of them, in a not-completely-irreputable pub near the London docks. Though sawdust littered the floor, a cheerful fire burned in a clean hearth and the walls were the particular shade of brown defining the combination of London's air and the fug of clay pipers. A barmaid who had no patience for nonsense wiped the tables with vigor and exchanged good-natured insults with a group of dockworkers who played a desultory game of dice.

Letty wore her customary plain coat and sensible boots. Her bonnet was a deep indigo–colored velvet but had no adornments other than a blue satin ribbon around the crown. Violet, in contrast, wore an explosion of colors. A chartreuse dress over brown boots, covered with an aubergine paletot and topped with a pink bonnet.

Phoebe said nothing. She had tried for years to get Violet to dress differently, and it never took. Despite Violet's protestations, Phoebe remained convinced her friend was color-blind. This had to be the reason she paired orange with purple. The alternative was simply too upsetting.

They nursed pints of warm ale while Violet listed the various changes that had occurred at Athena's Retreat since Phoebe left.

The positive changes included housing giant ants in the basement of Beacon House, the replacement of their former doorman, Henry Winthram, with a matron who forged her own knives, and Violet's decision to turn part of Beacon House into a small nursery for her daughter, Mirren, and any other children too young for day school whose mothers had projects ongoing at Athena's Retreat.

The negative changes included allowing Lady Potts to continue her tarantula-breeding program—escape-proof cages, her *arse*—and using the funds from Flavia Smythe-Harrow's nightmarish bird hats as stipends to women scientists who could not otherwise afford to take time away from their families and household duties.

Negative because Flavia's bird hats were so horrifyingly ugly, they hurt Phoebe's eyes and terrified her the tiniest bit.

After a while, the conversation turned to children. Violet had a two-year-old daughter, Mirren, and Letty had her twins. Phoebe made all the right noises and nodded at the right times, but Violet and Letty had wandered off into some other country where the language was foreign and Phoebe was lost to them.

"Yes, well, it doesn't stop Arthur from wanting to make another one. Why, last night—oh, Phoebe, all this talk and I haven't told you the most important news. Grey had me study the residue from the Kennington Common bomb."

Violet Kneland had the face of an angel, round and soft, with expressive eyes and long black lashes. She had the heart of an angel as well. Violet's brain, however, her brain was a steam engine; powerful, intimidating, relentless. Phoebe loved her but hadn't always been kind to her.

Phoebe supposed her own heart was that of a devil.

"I explained how the weapon you built was a two-chambered canister," Violet said.

The different chemicals in each chamber mixed only when thrown hard enough against a surface that the wall between both chambers collapsed. Once the wall collapsed, the chemicals mixed to form the gas.

It was a clumsy delivery method, but Phoebe had been rushed by Adam Winters during the last stages of design and testing. That weapon had killed the constable.

"This Kennington Common bomb was explosive," Violet continued, "and left no traces of aluminum—with which you prefer to work but not many others can afford."

Phoebe kept her eyes on her pint glass as though the bubbles therein were of great importance, as though she couldn't care less what Letty and Violet believed.

"Yes. I remember Grey said while some bystanders reported a cloud of gas, most described a cloud of smoke smelling of sulfur," Letty chimed in. She sniffed the warm ale appreciatively but didn't drink.

"Mmm." Violet made a noise of agreement. "Obviously, this weapon included gunpowder. You would never have used something so crude."

True. Phoebe may have stolen the idea for her weapon from other scientists' work, but at least she'd put some art into it.

"Arthur and Grantham have gone in search of the Welshmen," Violet said gently. "Once the men confess, this will be finished."

Phoebe said nothing.

She was no longer suspect, but only because Letty and Violet vouched for her.

It stung.

Even though she deserved their mistrust—it still stung.

"When you left for America," Violet said as she ran her fingertip around the lip of her pint glass, "you were angry."

Phoebe took a sip of her ale and wished it were whiskey. "I am still angry, Violet."

Her reticule sat on her lap; within it lay a ticket to New York, issued by the Cunard Line for one of their new steamships. It cost her a pretty penny—twenty pounds!—but she would arrive in America by the beginning of January. Three weeks and she could pick up where she left off.

Alone.

"Are you?" Violet asked. "You do not seem angry. You seem content."

Letty's eyes narrowed. "You do seem awfully sanguine for someone on the run, Phoebe. You know, I saw Laila this morning. She said Sam never came home last night."

An image of Sam when she left without waking him, his ever-present smile making him look angelic, popped into Phoebe's head.

Violet shifted in her seat to stare at Letty. "What does Sam not coming home have to do with . . ."

Letty smirked. Violet's eyes went wide, and she whipped her head back to face Phoebe.

"Oh my." Her eyebrows poked almost to her hairline. "Is this true, Phoebe? You and Sam?"

Once upon a time Phoebe would have allowed Violet's pleasure to fizz through her own veins, but the ticket had been purchased and the steamship lay docked only half a mile away.

She opened her mouth to say something dismissive. Something cutting.

Nothing emerged.

"Are you . . . do you love him, Phoebe?" Violet asked.

Again, Phoebe searched for a put-down, a searing remark that would set everyone back in their place on the outside and leave her alone. Where it was safe. Where she could be untouched and untouchable.

"Are you serious?" Phoebe let go a chiming laugh. "Love? Love is for idiots and children."

"Ooooh," said Violet. She looked at Letty. "She loves him."

"I am leaving for America tomorrow," Phoebe said quickly. "Grantham has agreed to loan a generous sum to my mother until the auction is finished."

"But . . ."

"My reason for returning to England was to ensure my family had enough funds to be secure after my father's death, not to try and clear my name. I am guilty of the crime," Phoebe said over Violet's objection. "My punishment is not complete."

"Still, you could . . ." Letty interjected.

Phoebe shook her head; the bitterness of the ale dried her tongue and her words sounded stiff and mean.

"Even if the two of you are convinced of my innocence this time, what happens next time?" she asked. "Political violence has become inevitable. Will I be hauled in and interrogated every time a bomb goes off?"

Violet tried again. "Now, Grantham and Grey know it wasn't you—"

"I did a terrible thing, Violet."

Her friends' agreement was implicit in their silence.

"I don't believe in sin," Phoebe said, "but neither do I believe in divine grace. No one can or should forgive me other than myself."

The study of science had taught Phoebe the universe was subject to the laws of physics, not the whims of a cruel and arbitrary old man on a throne of clouds. The electrical force that fueled a bolt of lightning or the beating of her heart couldn't grant forgiveness. There were no legions of angels awaiting her in the next life to mete out justice.

Only one life was available to them. No amount of prayer nor proselytizing would change Phoebe's fate.

Acceptance, then action.

"Why can't you forgive yourself here?" Letty asked. Her eyes, like Sam's, were slightly unfocused as she waited for Phoebe to answer, a calculation of some sort running in the brain behind them. "You are the same person with the same flaws no matter where you find yourself."

Phoebe wished she knew what gave Letty such insight. There was far more to Letty, to Violet, to most people than their surfaces, as pretty or as polished as they may be.

Violet gulped her ale, creating a wave of white foam, some of which stuck to her top lip.

"I could stay," Phoebe agreed. "Swallow my rage and be a *better person*."

Letty used her handkerchief to wipe some of the ale Violet had spilled. "You are the only person I know who can say 'better person' and make it sound like 'leaking pustule.'"

Taking another sip, then wiping the foam from her mouth, Violet agreed. "It is a singular talent of yours."

Phoebe preened, then continued. "Or I go somewhere that doesn't remind me of who I am and where I've come from. Someplace young and wild enough, anyone can start over."

"Arthur says the Americans are brash and overloud. They make friends easily and take too many risks." Violet relayed this in a tone of voice that conveyed more admiration than apprehension. "Also, they make terrible tea."

That, at least, Phoebe could confirm.

Really, how difficult was it to boil water?

"Start over? What about your science?" Letty asked. "Won't you stay for Athena's Retreat?"

Karolina had asked Phoebe the same question before they left Prentiss Manor. Phoebe gave her friends the same answer she'd given her sister.

"Because I am not in the laboratory or writing papers every few months doesn't make me less of a scientist. The greatest gift studying science has left me with is the willingness to question everything and the good sense to admit when I am wrong and have made a mistake so I can learn how to rectify the mistake."

That and a good deal more, Phoebe had said to Karolina before they bundled themselves into the carriage for the long journey home. She'd encouraged Karolina to read widely about the world, to remain open to wonder, quick to absorb information, and slow to judge.

In turn, Karolina had said something to the effect of Phoebe sounding like an old man issuing proclamations from on high. Phoebe, being older and wiser, responded by sticking out her tongue.

"I suppose it is enough you are well educated in science. I agree, you don't have to blow things up to appreciate how they work," Letty said, glancing at Violet, for whom those last words seemed to be meant.

"Hmmm. Theorizing has its place, but *experimental* science advances civilization," Violet said, the ends of her words curving softly now that she'd finished the last of her ale.

"Civilization is dependent on blowing up other people's chicken coops?" Letty asked with a heavy dose of sarcasm.

Oh dear.

"Civilization is made of husbands who were eager participants . . ."

"Ahem." Phoebe interrupted before Letty and Violet went

further. She couldn't picture Greycliff a party to an explosive science experiment, but in the end, most men are boys and boys love it when things blow up.

"Did you know there are several women agents for Tierney and Company in America?" Phoebe asked.

Violet, looking sheepish, grabbed hold of Phoebe's distraction. "Are they scientists as well?"

Phoebe smiled. "They are scientists and flimflam artists, poets and blacksmiths. They are a motley mix, and I know you would love them."

"Are they . . . are they like us?" Letty asked. "Friends?"

Friends.

"They are as different from you as night is to day in many ways," Phoebe allowed. "They are the same in every other respect."

Violet leaned forward, her eyes glassy from finishing her ale quickly. "Are they outlaws, Phoebe? How exciting."

Phoebe could not remain in London, or Britain for that matter, even if the Home Office begged her to remain. Something had happened to her in that overwhelming landscape beneath the ambivalent American sun.

She had grown.

Grown too independent to submit to the rigid confines of British class hierarchy. Grown too confident to go back into hiding behind the walls of Athena's Retreat.

"The Tierneys are opening a branch in the city of Chicago," Phoebe said. "They hope to form an all-woman detective division. Before I left for England, I asked to be assigned to that division. Permanently."

Simply saying the words sent a rush of anticipation through her veins.

Chicago was a place big enough to hold her. For a little while, at least.

Violet frowned down at the tabletop, then over at Phoebe. "You will not be coming home again, will you?"

"No," Phoebe said. "I may still be hemmed in by my skirts, but I am not hemmed in by my title when I am there," Phoebe said softly. "I am any woman and every woman, and America is large enough for me to find a place to fit and to begin anew, and to help. Just . . . to help. Not to harm. Not any longer."

The women fell silent at Phoebe's declaration, remembering, perhaps, whom Phoebe had harmed. Who had harmed her in return.

"Tell Sam, when you see him," Phoebe said to Letty, "tell him he deserves better than this country will give him."

Letty frowned. "He deserves to be loved."

"He deserves to be respected, to be honored, and for the rest of London to get out of his way while he turns this city on its ears," Phoebe countered. "Tell him I asked that he help Moti and Karolina if they need him, and I will never, ever forget him."

If some nights Phoebe would dream of another life, one where she remained here with Sam and her family, well . . . dreams would vanish in the light of day.

Sam was going to change everything by becoming rich, powerful, and *kind*. The first mogul to live in Farringdon and let his sisters tell him what to do, a captain of industry who bought wrinkled oranges from little girls.

Sam belonged here and Phoebe, no matter what she did, would never truly be welcome ever again.

"We will miss you, Phoebe," said Violet softly.

"I will miss you, too."

25

One has more happiness in oneself, in endeavoring
to follow the things that make for peace.
—Michael Faraday

SOME PEOPLE THOUGHT SAM HAD AN ENORMOUS EGO.
As though that were a bad thing. He supposed if he'd used his
massive self-confidence for evil, or let it make him blind to the
suffering of others, it would be a detriment.

The way he saw it, his ego kept him afloat when other men
might be drowning.

When he woke, the day had passed and it was dark. He
knew Phoebe had been gone for a while, because the other side
of the bed was cold.

She'd left without waking him.

Without even a letter.

He'd been so tired from spending nights in gin halls and days
rousting Welshmen, a few bouts of lusty lovemaking were all it
took to send him into a sleep so deep, Phoebe could slip away.

Another man might have taken this as a sign Sam should do
as Phoebe had told him. Let her go. Live a good life. Find a safe
love.

His ego, however, had piped up loud and clear.

Sam Fenley was going to make Phoebe Hunt admit she loved him.

Because she did.

Phoebe had seen to the heart of him, seen the man behind the jokes and smiles. Every time she'd examined him, she'd come away with indisputable findings; he did deflect with humor, he did need to step back and appreciate his successes. She couldn't have come up with these theories if she didn't care for him, worry about him . . . love him.

And Sam loved Phoebe in return. Loved her in a way that had permeated his bones. This was a love he'd never wanted to find. He'd been permanently altered; loving this woman ran through his veins, his fingers, his mouth, his words, and his dreams from now until the day he died.

He hadn't set out to look for this love; this love had found him. Sam and Phoebe were two lodestones and an invisible force guaranteed they would come together.

Always.

Sam set out for Hunt House readying his reasons for Phoebe to marry him. While their obvious compatibility in bed and similar taste for cheese-and-pickle sandwiches topped the list, he prepared plenty more arguments.

He could make her laugh.

She could make him be serious.

He was young and energetic.

She was older and wiser.

He would be honest with her.

She would return the favor.

Most important, they would champion each other. Sam knew Phoebe would approve of his breaking down social barriers erected by the titled class. Why, she'd pick up a club and help him demolish them. In return, Sam would use his broadsheets to protect and even advance her reputation until Phoebe could be free from the cloud of suspicion and return to the ladies at Athena's Retreat.

He hailed a hack and made the short trip to Hunt House, where he encountered two of the three Hunt women. After only fifteen minutes, Sam added *patience of a saint* to the list of his desirable traits.

"What if she is face-to-face with lions?" The marchioness paced the length of the parlor in Hunt House where Sam had first met her. Color had returned to her skin and despite the brown tint to the light from outside, the lady looked more alive than he'd ever seen her.

Would she grow in substance the farther away she moved from Prentiss Manor?

"What of those bison she showed us in the folio of animal prints? They are too large to be tamed. They will eat her, I'm certain of it."

"Lions are not found in the American west, my lady," Sam assured her. He sat on one of the needleworked chairs and watched the marchioness march past Karolina, who scurried about with more tea and handed her mother a newly ironed handkerchief.

"Nor do highwaymen outnumber citizens, and Americans do, indeed, use napkins at table." About that last part Sam wasn't sure, but he needed the marchioness to leave off her crying and tell him where her daughter had gone.

"I told you, Moti," Karolina said. She sat, finally, having refreshed the tea. In a day dress of lilac, she resembled a flower, her long neck a stamen and the ribbons of her cap fluttering like butterflies in the breeze left by her mother's pacing. "Also, bison do not have teeth."

Sam opened his mouth to refute this assertion, but shut it again when Karolina glared at him. Gads, but she had a way of looking at a man that was nearly as frightening as her sister's.

The marchioness stopped abruptly and pointed at Sam. "You have come to propose to Karolina?"

Oh dear.

"He has come because he is madly in love with Phoebe," Karolina announced before Sam said a word.

Well. That was . . . straight to the point.

"No, Karolina," the marchioness remonstrated gently. "Mr. Fenley is to save you from that horrible Mr. Armitage."

Karolina cocked her head and examined Sam as though he were a specimen. It would unnerve him if he weren't used to women scientists doing the same.

"*Did* you truly wish to marry me, Mr. Fenley?" Karolina asked. "You didn't do a good job of attracting my interest."

Again, Sam blessed his ego. It protected him from the offense another man might take at such an uncomplimentary statement.

"I thought we agreed, my interest lay with Lady Phoebe," he said through gritted teeth, still smiling, however. "If my interest lay with you, I can assure you I would have swept you off your feet—"

"By falling into me and knocking me over?" Karolina asked sweetly.

"You cannot marry her, Mr. Fenley," said the marchioness sharply, her thin fingers pulling at the lace of her handkerchief. She'd gone to the windows and twitched the floor-length curtains, peering down at the street below.

Now, this was getting confusing.

"I cannot marry . . . ?"

"Phoebe," the marchioness clarified, letting the curtains drop and coming to sit next to Karolina on the settee. "You cannot marry her. She is leaving England for a new life. A better life. This island is not large enough to hold her. She said . . ." Lady Fallowshall smiled and a knot formed in Sam's chest. What this woman had endured, what she had lived through, and still she was capable of love. Amazing.

". . . Bee said she wished to live beneath a sky so big, she remembers why she is on this earth. I think this means she wants to be louder than she ever could be in London. Loud enough to reach the sky."

The marchioness wasn't sad about Phoebe's departure. She was proud.

Sam understood.

This had kept him from contemplating a future with Phoebe, even when he recognized that she'd gone and stolen his heart. Even when Sam had seen in Phoebe's eyes that she'd gone and given him her heart in return.

Here was another hurdle he'd have to scale, but Sam had spent his life convincing women to take a chance on whatever he was offering. He'd enough money to buy whatever Phoebe needed to be happy. Another Athena's Retreat, if that was what she wished. He'd raze Prentiss Manor to the ground and start over again with her.

"I can make sure she is happy here, my lady. I will make it my life's mission," he promised.

The marchioness did not look convinced.

Karolina, still gazing at him with sympathy, set down her teacup in its saucer and shook her head sadly.

"Best of luck, Mr. Fenley. I have relished this time coming to know my sister better. From what I have learned, though, I doubt you will dissuade her."

Some of the hope bled out of him.

"Whatever Phoebe's answer," she continued, "I hope you know you are one of the few people who have ever made her laugh."

"The lady laughs because he falls all the time."

Delightful.

Jonas was here as well. *Everyone* was here except the one person Sam wished to see.

Dressed in fashionable trousers and a cutaway coat, Jonas wore a funereal black waistcoat and a cravat tied in a simple knot. He'd obviously not lost his custom of lurking, for he'd come into the room silently. Hopefully, the man would unlearn the ways of Prentiss Manor after a while spent in London and tromp around like an elephant—the way everyone else did.

Jonas went and stood behind the marchioness, setting his hands on the back of the settee and smiling down at her when she looked at him.

"You think to convince her without injury?" Jonas asked, breaking his gaze with the marchioness and fixing Sam with a glower. "Without injury to Phoebe," he clarified. "You will definitely be injured."

"Yes," Sam declared. "No injuries. No worries. Please, just tell me where I can find her."

AN HOUR LATER, SAM STOOD ON A RICKETY DOCK AND stared at *The Queen of the Seas*. An impressive ship. If one enjoyed a protruding front.

Which Sam usually did.

"I said, Lady Phoebe Hunt!" he shouted to an agitated little porter hanging over the ship's rail ten feet above him.

"You're feeling a what now?" the porter called back.

For feck's sake.

Holding a leather wallet, Sam carefully extracted a few paper notes and held them out toward the ship.

"I will give you two pounds if you find . . . Oh, well, that worked, didn't it?"

Sure enough, as soon as the notes were flashed, the porter had scurried off out of sight. Now Sam had to find the words to woo the most recalcitrant woman he'd ever met. After his sisters, that is.

"Sam Fenley. What are you doing down there?"

Ah. Even at a distance, annoyance carved lines on her face. Beautiful woman.

His woman.

"My darling!"

That was sure to get a rise from her. Nothing he loved more than seeing this woman turn to fire rather than ice.

"I am telling you, Sam Fenley," Phoebe shouted, "if you don't stop calling me that, I will shoot you. I will."

He didn't doubt it. Rather than deterring him, it urged him on.

"You *are* my darling, Phoebe Hunt," he called back.

Sam had racked his brains searching for the perfect words to convince Phoebe to stay in London. Luckily, he was a devoted reader of Mrs. Foster's novels. Why, she was the inventor of the grand gesture. Every man he knew who'd wooed and won a scientist from Athena's Retreat had done something out of a Foster novel.

Sam had never dreamed he'd be in such straits. He'd

assumed he would knock the woman of his dreams off her feet (not literally . . . well, perhaps literally) and his obscenely good looks and piles of money would do the rest.

Whatever happened next, he was *not* going to jump into the Thames.

Grantham had already done that as a grand gesture to Margaret and besides, Sam had worn his new coat, and the river water was filthy. No, for Phoebe Hunt only an argument that satisfied her brain would do. Flailing about in the river would simply earn him pity.

Perhaps even mockery.

Gulping in the fetid Thames-scented air, Sam sent a quick prayer heavenward that his voice would hold out. That Phoebe would not only hear but *listen* to what he had to say to her.

He cupped his hands around his mouth and shouted, "You've spent so many years without a man saying these words—these important, essential words any young girl needs to hear; you *are* my darling. Not only that, but you are also *brilliant*."

Phoebe rocked back on her heels, one hand going to her chest. A fierce wave of joy rushed through Sam's veins. This would work. She would believe him.

He continued. "You are funny, you are captivating, you have incredible powers of observation and so many talents."

"I don't believe you. I don't," she insisted.

"You already know you are beautiful," Sam called, walking ever closer to the edge of the dock.

"What you don't know is how incredibly kind you are to your mother and sister. How your face lights up when you talk about volcanic piles . . ."

"Voltaic piles," she called down to him.

". . . and how I explode with joy when you come apart beneath me."

By now nearly every stevedore and sailor had stopped what they were doing to listen. Sam did not care. This was his one chance. He wasn't going to let it go.

"I love you, Phoebe Hunt!"

"Don't say that!" she shouted into the wind.

"Don't say it unless I mean it?" he called.

On the deck above him, Phoebe said nothing, but she pulled a handkerchief from her reticule and frowned at it, seemingly furious.

"I don't know whether you could love me, love any man after what happened to you. If you could see your way to return my affection . . ."

Oh, dear God, she was lifting the handkerchief to her face. He'd made her cry. She would kill him for that. Gulls overhead screeched encouragements, or were they warnings? The sounds of the crew making ready to cast off buzzed around him and the earth shook beneath his feet.

Sam flung one last plea into the air between them.

"If you have the courage to love me, Phoebe, I will spend the rest of my life making certain you never regret it."

These, then, were his parting words to her.

A challenge.

Phoebe shook her head and said nothing. The horn blew from the captain's perch, and the anchors rose on either side of the ship.

Sam didn't move, not even to blink.

Please.

Please.

With excruciating languidness, Phoebe raised her hand, palm outward, and held it in the air for a long moment until Sam raised his hand as well.

Then, without batting an eye, Phoebe jumped off the side of the ship.

26

All this is a dream. Still examine it by a few experiments. Nothing is too wonderful to be true, if it be consistent with the laws of nature; and in such things as these, experiment is the best test of such consistency.

—Michael Faraday

"JESUS, MARY, AND JOSEPH!"

The blasphemy ejaculated by the dockworker next to him summed up Sam's thoughts perfectly. Then he was done thinking. He took two steps back and made a running start to jump off the dock.

Or at least, he tried to.

Instead of leaping into the Thames, Sam choked on the dock, his collar in the firm grip of someone behind him.

"Think with your brain, not with that embarrassment between your legs, for Christ's sake, man."

Sam twisted in the grip and turned to confront the Earl Grantham. Or Grantham's chest, for the earl would not let Sam go.

Mother of . . . how did Grantham manage to show up when one least expected him?

"I need to help Phoebe!" Sam cried.

She could be dead.

She could have hit her head on the side of the steamer when she jumped from the bow of the ship.

She could have broken her limbs upon hitting the water.

She could have drowned from shock at the cold.

"Phoebe can take care of herself," Grantham admonished.

"She shouldn't have to!" Sam wrenched free of the earl's grip and pushed him in the chest with the flat of his hand. "For once in her life, Phoebe has someone who will take care of *her*."

He turned away from Grantham and ran to the edge of the dock, examining the water below them for a sign of Phoebe.

"Me, by the way," he called looking back over his shoulder. "I'm going to take care of—whooa!"

Feck, but the Thames was disgusting.

That was the second thought that roiled through Sam's head after falling off the dock. The first was Grantham would tease him mercilessly for this. Thank goodness Grey had taught him to swim last year at his country estate. The viscount had spouted some nonsense or other about Sam being prone to accidents near water.

Ha.

He tried to keep his mouth shut when his head broke the surface of the river, but the greasy brown water got in through his nose and ears. *Faugh.*

"You are a walking disaster, Fenley," Grantham cried from above. "I should let you drown!"

Sam ignored the earl, twisting in the freezing water, trying to find the spot where Phoebe had jumped, but there was nothing but ships and his own head bobbing in the water. Panic sank its talons into his spine.

He couldn't lose her.

Not now.

Their love would be huge and unwieldy and require he strip himself as bare as she had when she admitted to her scars. Sam wanted that love more than anything.

Anything.

"Phoebe!" he screamed, fighting to be heard above the sounds of the docks and cries of the sailors aboard the steamship that a passenger had fallen overboard. "Phoebe!"

Nothing.

Grantham shouted that he was getting help, but Sam knew what he had to do. Taking a deep breath, he dove back under, straining his eyes to see in the brown-green murk of the river. The pillars of the dock behind him were coated with green slime and barnacles. The black hull of the steamship was sparkling in comparison. Nothing thrashed in the water. All was silent.

Lungs betraying him, Sam kicked and swam upward, losing a shoe in the process. When he emerged, shaking the water from his eyes, sound slapped at his ears.

"Phoebe," he gasped, wiping his eyes and spitting a nasty taste out of his mouth along with his summons. "Phoebe?"

"You look ridiculous."

If she had told him he was the most beautiful man on earth, he couldn't have been happier. Holding the pilings on the opposite side of the dock, wet, dirty, and with a clump of seaweed pasted to the left side of her head, Phoebe Hunt had never looked so beautiful as she did right then.

"I love you," he said while the waves slapped arcs of dirty brown foam around like fireworks. "I love you," he said again. In case something happened. In case he forgot how to swim or the numbness in his fingers caused him to let go his grip.

"You shouldn't be allowed anywhere near water," Phoebe informed him, her teeth chattering so the scold sounded more pathetic than Sam supposed she'd planned.

"I love you," he told her. The cold was slowing his brain, but if he told Phoebe enough times he loved her, she would finally believe.

Sam pushed himself away from the piling he held and swam over to where Phoebe was losing her grip on the slick, algae-covered wooden posts.

"I love you," he reminded her as he set his arms around her and held her body close to his. "I swear, if you stay and marry me, you will wake every day knowing this is true. I will never stop trying to make you happy. *Please* don't drown or freeze to death before I can convince you of this properly."

The rancid odor of dead fish and refuse saturated the air. Not the most romantic setting for a declaration of love. Then again, nothing about her and Sam had ever been conventional.

Luckily, Phoebe had left her heavy winter paletot in her cabin. Even so, her waterlogged woolen petticoats and stout leather boots weighed her down like stones in her pockets.

Would they die?

Dear God, she hoped not. How uninspiring a demise—drowned in the Thames. Bodies in the Thames were as common as those ducks floating by.

"Just hold on and don't let me go," Sam said. He'd swum to the rotted pole she'd been holding and wrapped one strong arm around her, lending her his warmth. Phoebe curled her fingers into her palms and put her arms around his neck, while currents tugged at her pantalettes and rough waves slapped the back of her head.

Just hold on.

The darkness in Phoebe, the part birthed in that lonely manor in the north, had made its presence known just as she stepped off the side of the ship; a ghost whispering poison into her ear as her toes grew numb and she struggled to shore. With that one step Phoebe had committed to staying with Sam, but what would happen when he finally saw how stupid, how horrible, how deformed, and defaced, and how unworthy she was of love?

I love you.

"Why, Sam?" she asked, her words slurring as her lips numbed from the cold. "I've made so many mistakes. Hurt so many people."

Sam knew what Phoebe was asking, even though she couldn't say the word. "I cannot think of a single reason not to love you," Sam replied, putting his mouth to her temple.

All the years she'd been on earth, she'd been told she took up too much space for a woman; her words weren't important, or someone would have heard her screaming all these years. Damaged and sharp, she ripped jagged pieces through the world, tipping out of balance between anger and exhilaration.

"I can think of a few." Her stuttered reply was cut into pieces by her chattering teeth.

Pushing its way to the surface was the reason she carried with her always; a stillborn hope she swaddled and held carefully to her breast in case it someday came alive.

Phoebe was broken; for if her *father* could not love her, why would any man?

She had never inspired the tiniest vestige of love in her papa. Her entire childhood, Phoebe believed the fault to be one-sided. Hers. That whatever woman she was becoming, could become, aspired to—it wasn't enough and never would be enough for anyone to love.

"Why did you jump off that ship, Phoebe?" Sam asked, his gaze holding her tight, seemingly oblivious to the chaos and consternation they'd caused on the docks above them. "Why would you do something as"—he paused—"something so . . ."

"Romantic?" Phoebe finished his sentence.

I love you.

"You are a terrible kidnapper," she told him. "You turn your nose up at the law of gravity and brawl with staircases. You refuse to take life seriously and make me laugh at the most inappropriate of times."

If she hadn't been holding on to him, the power of Sam's smile might have sent her reeling back among the waves. Dear God, that smile.

"When you put it like that, you might as well climb back up into your steamer," he said gently.

"No, Sam," Phoebe said. "No, you promised to wake with me every day, and I jumped off that ship because I know you keep your promises. No matter how dark the world might look, I believe you when you say those words."

I love you.

This love with Samuel Fenley was loud. It made no sense, broke the rules, and burned bright as a star in the western sky. Senseless or not, Phoebe held tightly to the miracle that had tripped and fallen into her life. That ghost whispering its poison was no match for a man like Sam Fenley. His love was a current that fed the starving parts of her. Like electricity, love was powerful without need of gender or liturgy—all were equal while in its grasp.

"We are almost saved, Phoebe-girl," Sam said, his blue eyes glinting like jewels set against the brown of the water and gray of the sky.

A splashing of oars from half a dozen boats of all sizes drowned out her reply. In the smallest boat, Grantham stood at the bow, unevenly counterbalanced by the slender oarsman behind him scrambling in the prow sitting high off the water's surface.

Grantham bellowed, gulls screeched, stevedores shouted, and the steamship blew its ghastly loud horn.

So it was that Phoebe waited until they were pulled aboard a partly rotting skiff by two burly fishermen before she spoke. Kneeling on the watery deck, she put a hand to Sam's cheek so that he could look nowhere but at her.

"I jumped off that ship because I love you, Sam Fenley," Phoebe said. "I want to wake beside you every morning and hear you say those words for the rest of our lives. I am never going to be easy . . ."

Sam threw his head back and laughed, then pulled her into his arms and onto his lap.

How undignified.

How wonderful.

". . . and you are never going to stay upright, but together"— Phoebe sighed and pressed her forehead against his—"together we are electric."

As the words flew from her tongue like sparks, the air around them lit with a sun only they could feel.

Epilogue

⫷⫷⫸⫸

But still try, for who knows what is possible?
 —Michael Faraday

St. John's Church
Two Weeks Later

"YOU MUST AGREE, THE ORIGINAL GRAND GESTURE OF jumping into the Thames was mine," Grantham announced. "Now everyone is doing it. That Mrs. Foster ought to write a book about me. I'm what they call a romantic hero."

Sam considered borrowing a pistol and shooting Grantham in the foot.

"Will you shut up?" said a voice that sounded like a blade against a whetstone. "We're not here to listen to an encyclopedic recitation of every stupid thing you've ever done, you great *eijit*."

If he shot Grantham in the foot, Sam would have to shoot Arthur Kneland in the foot as well. If he shot Arthur anywhere else, Grantham would complain that Arthur had a bigger wound in a more important appendage.

The two of them stood behind Sam at the altar of St. John's church in Clerkenwell. Recently spruced up by a friend of his father's, William Griffin, it had been the site of Letty and Greycliff's wedding as well.

Less grand than St. George's or St. Bart's, for certain. Perfect for the Fenley family and their friends.

"You're jealous because you didn't rescue anyone," said Grantham. "I did. It was magnificen—put away that knife or I'll throw your tiny Scottish arse out the window."

"You touch my arse—"

One of the great mysteries of life was how a woman as lovely as Violet could be comfortably married to a man who exuded danger the way Kneland did. Another great mystery was how Kneland had not used his famed skills as a counter-assassin to mortally wound, or at least permanently mute, the Earl Grantham.

". . . still firm and supple, as opposed to yours, sagging with age . . ."

". . . way to stick it down your throat, catch hold of your bowels, and pull them back out through your mouth . . ."

Jonas, the object of myriad women's attention now that he'd shaved and put on a suit from this century, stood opposite Sam and frowned. Every time he moved, Sam's sisters turned their heads to watch him.

". . . shove that blade so far up . . ."

". . . a head that big and yet so empty . . ."

From the pew a few feet in front of him, Sam's mam cleared her throat loudly and glared at the men behind him.

"Now you've done it," Kneland whispered to Grantham. "I'll bet you fifty pence Mrs. Fenley won't let you have a piece of her lemon cake at the breakfast afterward."

"Fifty pence? Are you a pauper now?" Grantham countered. "I'll bet you a pound she gives me an extra slice."

When would this torture end?

"Shut up or I will give your children hedgehogs and puppies for Christmas every year they are under your roofs," Sam threatened.

The men immediately fell silent. To Sam's great relief, the doors of the vestry finally opened.

Five years earlier, the Queen had been married in a white dress. Since then, British brides wore white with a plethora of skirts and lace and flowered headbands.

Not Phoebe Hunt.

She wore gold, Sam's bride. The same color as the coverlets upon which they'd slept that night at the emporium. The same material, too—her dress had been hastily sewn by a trio of bemused seamstresses he'd located in Hockney, as no one had ever given them bedclothes as material before. They were geniuses, these women, and shot through the gold silk were the green and purple embroidered flowers Phoebe had admired.

Phoebe's hand sat on Greycliff's arm, and Letty beamed at them both with love in her eyes. They walked steadily to the sound of the church's organ playing Beethoven's Piano Concerto No. 3. Appearing buoyed by the impossibly beautiful notes, Phoebe, with admirable grace, settled in her place opposite Sam in front of the vicar.

Gone were the days when the banns would've been read for three weeks straight. For almost a decade, a civil marriage license could be had within a week.

Thus, it hadn't taken long for his mam and Violet to organize a wedding and a wedding breakfast with little notice.

Thank goodness, for Sam thought he might go out of his mind with anticipation of his wedding night.

Finally, the vicar began the ceremony.

Sam looked down into eyes the color of pansies, untrodden and fresh, sparkling with the dewdrops of unshed tears.

"I love you," he whispered.

Because Phoebe needed to hear those words once more and perhaps again later and certainly each morning until the end of her days.

"I love you."

Sam had told her this multiple times a day since Grantham had hauled them from the freezing waters of the Thames two weeks ago, repeating it like a catechism. Like prayer. Phoebe swore she would remain by his side, he didn't have to say it on the hour, but Sam did it anyway.

It might take years for her to tire of those syllables ringing in the air like bells. Like trumpets.

I love you.

She had said it aloud only twice. Once when they lay gasping, clinging to each other in the bottom of a rotting skiff.

The second time was a week ago.

Moti understood their haste to wed but still insisted the formalities be followed. This meant Phoebe must spend every night after dinner in her childhood bedroom at Hunt House.

Luckily, Sam had a key.

It took him three days to work up the courage to sneak into the house and visit her.

"Look," she'd whispered when he'd poked his head into her room. "A bed."

At first, having to be quiet enough not to alert the servants made the act more piquant. Afterward, they'd lain together and stared at the faded blue linen canopy; plain compared to the riots of colors during their last trysts.

Sam had played with her hands, then kissed the indent between her knuckles, and Phoebe had closed her eyes and said a prayer to Saint Faraday and the universal current that their nights might end like this.

"One more week," Sam had whispered.

One more week until the wedding, he meant.

"Violet, Moti, and your mother have been terrible bullies," Phoebe had complained, only half jesting. "I cannot sit for one minute to breathe without being asked the most inane of questions. Do I prefer violets to lillies of the valley. Should we have two kinds of muffins or three at the wedding breakfast."

She'd shuddered, but Sam showed no sympathy and chuckled at her distress.

"I thought after your enthusiasm over the emporium, you would be thrilled to pick out anything you desire for your trousseau and new household," he said.

At first, Phoebe had been giddy at the chance to walk through the emporium and see the wonders it contained; powder made of rice and arsenic to whiten the skin, hairpins with paste jewels affixed to the ends, funny-looking teapots from the East, and more gloves than there were people in London to wear them.

After a day or two, however, the reality of what would happen after the wedding, that Sam would return to the emporium to oversee the staff or go to the newspaper and decide what news to print while Phoebe performed the duties of a newly married gentlewomen—this sat on her shoulders like a shawl made of bricks.

"Your sisters are a delight, and I have enjoyed myself," she said. This, at least, was the truth. Phoebe did enjoy the Fenley sisters' company.

She faced a life that she never thought she would have again. A family. A man who loved and respected her. A coordinated effort by everyone she knew to bring her back into society without scandal.

Phoebe should be ecstatic. Instead she felt suffocated.

"I have been thinking about Hunt House," Sam whispered.

Phoebe had no head for business, but she was already so bored, she seized at the chance to put her brain to some use other than picking out chemises.

"What are you planning?" she asked.

"Would you like to live here?"

Sam might as well have doused her with a ewer of cold water. Phoebe bolted upright, clasping the coverlet to her chest with both hands.

"I cannot think of anything I want *less* than to live in this house ever again," she said.

Worry pricked in the back of her brain. Yes, she loved Sam, but how well did she know him? What other terrible ideas might he have about their future?

Sam did not react to her concern, resting the back of his head on one arm in a languid manner.

"Shall we find some room in the house in Clerkenwell, then? Mam and Da love having family around."

There must be a correlation between exuberant orgasms and terrible ideas.

"We cannot live in your *parents*' house," Phoebe said, "Are we to share a room with Sarah? Whatever are you on about, Fenley?"

She examined Sam closely. He had tripped twice yesterday when coming to call. Once down a half flight of stairs.

A brain injury could take days to present itself.

"Well," he said, rolling onto his side and smiling up at her, "if we aren't going to live in your house and we aren't going to live in my house, we shall have to compromise and find a third place. One that suits both of us."

Phoebe settled down and nestled close to Sam's side. "That will keep me busy for a while," she admitted. "Looking for a house will occupy me for weeks."

"Mmmm." Sam nuzzled her temple and a shiver slid down Phoebe's spine. "Especially if we wish to build a home near to Lake Michigan."

"What?" she spluttered, again sitting up, not bothering with the coverlet this time, her shock was so great.

What?

Phoebe's heartbeat quickened when Sam let loose that special grin of his. He remained on his side as though he hadn't said something explosive.

And wonderful.

"I think it best, Phoebe-girl. Your mother told me this island wasn't big enough to hold you. You belong beneath a sky that goes on forever, not in a place where you will constantly be butting your head against the ceiling. I love that you agreed to follow me, but I want to follow *you*."

That was the second time she'd said "I love you" to Sam Fenley.

". . . take Samuel Duncan Fenley to be your lawfully wedded husband."

The wedding would be over after Phoebe repeated the vows,

the breakfast would be eaten, and their new life would begin with a torrent of blessings from their family and friends.

"Will thou love him, comfort, honor, and keep him in sickness and in health . . ."

They would board the steamship first thing tomorrow morning. As Letty reminded her, they would still be the same people, but they would make a new start. In a new world.

". . . keep thee only unto him for as long as you both shall live?"

"I will," Phoebe answered.

The vicar cleared his throat to signal the end of the ceremony, but Sam wasn't going to wait. To the cheers of the scientists, gasps of the aristocrats, consternation of Jonas, and delight of all that knew them, Sam reached over and pulled Phoebe to him.

"Yes, you will, Phoebe-girl," he crowed, then kissed her.

Phoebe kissed him right back, knowing when the two of them touched, they both glowed.

Love is an invisible current like electricity. It has the power to pull the world out from beneath your feet, to light you up, or to propel you forward into the unknown.

Their love gave off a spark, and a spark is all it takes to set the world on fire.

AUTHOR'S NOTE

Tierney & Co. is fictional. However, it is based on an American institution. The Pinkerton detective agency wasn't founded until 1850. This private detective agency provided both investigative and security services throughout the American states and territories. The first woman detective ever recorded, Kate Warne, was hired in 1856 and went on to become one of Pinkerton's best agents. One of her many assignments may have saved Abraham Lincoln from an assassination attempt.

Mrs. Jane Marcet's *Conversations on Chemistry* was a textbook written by Jane Marcet in 1805 especially for girls to learn the science of chemistry. In *Conversations*, her lessons take the form of questions from a student and answers from a teacher. This is still regarded as an accomplished yet extremely accessible teaching tool. The young bookbinder, Michael Faraday, credits his interest in science to binding and reading this book.

Self-harm is not an illness or a disorder. Instead, it is a behavior, formally known as nonsuicidal self-injury (NSSI)—a means of coping that is associated with illnesses such as PTSD and depression. Girls are more prone to NSSI than boys, and most self-harming behavior begins around age eleven and continues through college age.

While statistics vary widely, most studies I have seen from

sources as varied as the NIH, the Canadian Institute for Health Information, and *The Lancet* suggest that self-harm has risen in the first twenty-eight to thirty months after the pandemic; again, more among girls than boys, especially those in middle school. It is far more common than attempts at suicide, but it is not the same and does not garner the same amount of attention or prevention programs.

If you or someone you care about is self-harming and in crisis, there are several hotlines in the US, including: 988 Suicide and Crisis Hotline, Boys Town National Hotline (1-800-448-3000), The Trevor Project for support of LGBTQ+ youth (1-866-488-7386), and the National Sexual Assault Hotline (1-800-656-HOPE). In Canada there is Talk Suicide Canada, where kids or teens can call Kids Help Phone: 1-800-668-6868. There is also the International Association for Suicide Prevention at https://findahelpline.com/i/iasp, which lists the crisis hotlines by country.

More information for yourself or to share can be found with nonprofit organizations in the US, including: To Write Love on Her Arms, Adolescent Self-Injury Foundation, National Alliance on Mental Illness, and Self-Injury Outreach and Support.

ACKNOWLEDGMENTS

Thank you to my husband, to whom I will have been married for over twenty-five years when this book comes out. Every hero I write about in my novels contains one or more of his characteristics. He taught me to care for myself as well as others, which, for me, was life-changing. Marriage is a constant conversation and the true body of a love story. Saying "I love you" the three hundredth time while a child is puking/coughing/crying/peeing nearby means something different and greater than saying "I love you" the first time. I'm so glad we get to say those words three hundred times more. Hopefully with less mucus and urine in the picture. Thanks to my kids, too. You guys are the best, especially now that you are house-trained.

Thank you to my ever-patient agent, Ann Leslie Tuttle, to my editor, Sarah Blumenstock, to Liz Sellers for her input, to Stephanie Felty for being a badass, and to Anika Bates, whom I hopefully haven't traumatized. Thank you to Rita Frangie Batour, my uber-talented cover designer, cover illustrator Kelly Wagner, interior designer George Towne, proofreader Will Tyler, and cold reader Abby Graves. I am deeply grateful to have such art adorning my story. Thank you to Vanessa Townsend for her help. Thank you to the delightful and amazing romance book convention organizers who give me a place to meet readers and fangirl over my favorite authors, and the ladies of HEA Events and Erica Holland for making me feel special at ApollyCon. Thank you to the romancestagram community, especially everyone who has helped with spreading the word about the scientists, helping with cover reveals and sending me DMs that make me tear up. Thank you to the incredible booksellers I have met over the past two years—I so appreciate you. Thank you #2021berkletes for your love and support; thank you, Libby, Ali, and Mazey and the Saratoga Heist crew. Many thanks for the support from the Park Ave Moms, Highland Hotties, Mom and Doug, and a special shout-out to Jess Buss for kicking my ass. Finally, thank you, readers, for everything. For buying my books, for taking them out from the library, for coming and talking to me at signings, and for inspiring me to keep writing romance and smashing the patriarchy.

Don't miss

THE LOVE REMEDY

On sale now from Berkley Romance!

London, 1843

"'OW MUCH FOR PULLING A TOOF?"

Any other day, Lucinda Peterson's answer would have been however much the man standing before her could afford.

Since its founding, Peterson's Apothecary held a reputation for charging fair prices for real cures. If a customer had no money, Lucy and her siblings would often accept goods or services in trade.

Today, however, was not any other day.

Today was officially the worst day of Lucy's life.

Yes, there had been other worst days, but that was before today. Today was *absolutely* the worst.

"Half shilling," Lucy said, steel in her voice as she crossed her arms, exuding determination. She would hold strong today. She would think of the money the shop desperately needed and the bills piling up and the fact that she truly, really, absolutely needed new undergarments.

"'Alf shilling?" the man wailed. "'Ow'm I supposed to buy food for me we'uns?"

With a dramatic sigh, he slumped against the large wooden

counter that ran the length of the apothecary. The counter, a mammoth construction made of imported walnut, was the dividing line between Lucy's two worlds.

Until she was seven, Lucy existed with everyone else on the public side. Over there, the shop was crowded with customers who spoke in myriad accents and dialects as they waited in line for a consultation held in hushed voices at the end of the counter. Not all patients were concerned with privacy, however, and lively discussions went on between folks in line on the severity of their symptoms, the veracity of the diagnosis, and the general merits of cures suggested.

Laughter, tears, and the occasional spontaneous bout of poetry happened on the public side of the counter. Seven-year-old Lucy would sweep the floor and dust the shelves as the voices flowed over and around her, waiting for the day when she could cross the dividing line and begin her apprenticeship on the other side.

All four walls of the apothecary were lined with the tools of her trade. Some shelves held rows of glass jars containing medicinal roots such as ginger and turmeric. Other shelves held tin canisters full of ground powders, tiny tin scoops tied to the handles with coarse black yarn. A series of drawers covered the back half of the shop, each of them labeled in a painstaking round running hand by Lucy's grandfather. There hadn't been any dried crocodile dung in stock for eighty years or so, but the label remained, a source of amusement and conjecture for those waiting in line.

The shop had stood since the beginning of the last century, and even on this, her absolute worst day, Lucy gave in. She wasn't going to be the Peterson that broke tradition and turned a patient away.

Even though today was Lucy's worst day ever, that didn't mean it should be terrible for everyone.

"For anyone else a tooth is thruppence," Lucy said as she pulled on her brown linen treatment coat. "So I'm not accused of taking food from the mouths of your we'uns." She paused to pull a jar of eucalyptus oil out from a drawer and set it on the counter. "I suppose I can charge you tuppence and throw in a boiled sweet for each of them."

Satisfied with the bargain, the man climbed into her treatment chair in the back room, holding on to the padded armrests and squeezing his eyes shut in anticipation. Lucy spilled a few drops of the oil on a handkerchief and tied it over her nose.

While the scent of eucalyptus was strong enough to bring tears to her eyes, the smell from the man's rotted tooth was even stronger. She numbed his gums with oil of clove as she examined the rotting tooth and explained to him what she was going to do.

His discomfort was so great, the man waved away her warnings, and so, with a practiced grip, Lucy used her pincers to pull out the offending tooth.

Both wept, him from the pain, she from the stench, as Lucy explained how to best keep the rest of his teeth from suffering the same fate.

"You're an angel, miss," the man exclaimed. At least, Lucy hoped he said *angel*. His cheek was beginning to swell.

She sent him off with the promised sweets as well as a tin of tooth powder and, seeing there were no customers in the shop, she locked the front door and closed the green curtains over the street-facing windows to indicate the shop was closed.

Lucy's younger sister, Juliet, was out seeing those patients who were not well enough to visit the shop, and her brother,

David, could be anywhere in the capital city. Some days he was up with the sun, dusting the shelves and charming the clientele into doubling or even tripling their purchases. Other days, he was nowhere to be found. Days like today.

Worst days.

Lucy sighed a long, drawn-out sigh that she was embarrassed to hear exuded a low note of self-pity along with despair. Exhaustion weighed down her legs and pulled at her elbows while she cleaned the treatment chair and wrote the details of the man's procedure in her record book. She'd not slept well last night. Nor the night before. In fact, Lucy hadn't had an uninterrupted night's sleep for nine years.

Standing with a quill in her hand, she gazed at the etching hanging on the far wall of the back room, sandwiched between a tall, thin chest of drawers and a coatrack covered in bonnets and caps left behind by forgetful patients. Made in exchange for a treatment long forgotten, the artist had captured her mother and father posed side by side in a rare moment of rest.

Constantly moving, and yet always with time for a smile for whoever was in pain or in need of a sympathetic ear, her mother had been a woman of great faith in God and even greater faith in her husband.

"We work all day so we can make merry afterward," her father would tell Lucy when she complained about the long hours. Indeed, evenings in the Peterson household were redolent with the sound of music and comradery, her father loving nothing more than an impromptu concert with his children, no matter their mistakes on the instruments he'd chosen for them.

The etching was an amateurish work, yet it managed to convey the genuine delight on her father's face when he found himself in the company of his wife.

It had been nine years since her parents died of cholera, a loathsome disease most likely brought home by British soldiers serving with the East India Company. When the first few patients came to the apothecary with symptoms, the Petersons had sent their children to stay with a cousin in the countryside to wait out the disease. Lucy and Juliet had protested, both having trained for such scenarios, but their father held firm.

Her parents' deaths had come as less of a shock to Lucy than her father's will. Everything was left to her; the apothecary and the building in which it stood, as well as the proprietary formulas of her father and her grandfather's tonics and salves.

She had been eighteen years old.

"What were you thinking back then, Da?" she asked the etching now, the smell of vinegar and eucalyptus stinging the back of her throat. "Why would you put this on my shoulders?"

Her father stared out from the picture with his round cheeks and patchy whiskers, eyes crinkled in such a way that Lucy fancied he heard her laments and would give her words of advice if he could speak.

What would they be?

A yawn so large it cracked her jaw made Lucy break off her musings and remove her apron.

Exhaustion had played a huge role in her string of bad decisions the past four months. Ultimately, however, the fault lay with her. Lucy's guilt had been squeezing the breath from her lungs for weeks.

On the counter, slightly dented from having been crushed in her fist, then thrown to the ground and stepped on, then heaved against the wall, sat a grimy little tin. Affixed to the top was a label with the all-too-familiar initials RSA. Rider and Son Apothecary.

Rider and *Son*. The latter being the primary reason for this very worst of days.

The longer she stared at the tin, the less Lucy felt the strain of responsibility for running Peterson's Apothecary and keeping her siblings housed and fed. Beneath the initials were printed the words "Rider's Lozenges." The ever-present exhaustion that had weighed her down moments ago began to dissipate at the sight of the smaller print beneath, which read "exclusive." The more she stared, the more her guilt subsided beneath a wave of anger that coursed through her blood. "Exclusive patented formula for the relief of putrid throats."

Exclusive patented formula.

The anger simmered and simmered the longer she stared until it reached a boil and turned to rage.

Grabbing her paletot from the coatrack and a random bonnet that may or may not have matched, Lucy stormed out of the shop, slamming the door behind her with a vengeance that was less impressive when she had to turn around the next second to lock it.

Exclusive patent.

The words burned in her brain, and she clenched her hands into fists.

One warm summer afternoon four months ago, Lucy had been so tired, she'd stopped to sit on a park bench and had closed her eyes. Only for a minute or two, but long enough for a young gentleman passing by to notice and be concerned enough for her safety to inquire as to her well-being.

While the brief rest had been involuntary, remaining on the bench and striking up a conversation with the handsome stranger was her choice, and a terrible one at that. Lucy had allowed Duncan Rider to walk her home; not questioning the coincidence that the son of her father's rival had been the one to find her vulnerable and offer his protection was down to her own stupidity.

Now, as Lucy barreled down the rotting walkways of Calthorpe Street, she barely registered the admiring glances from the gentlemen walking in the opposite direction or the sudden appearance of the wan November sun as it poked through the gray clouds of autumn.

Instead, her head was filled with memories so excruciating they jabbed at her chest like heated needles, rousing feelings of shame alongside her resentment.

Such as the next time she'd seen Duncan, when he appeared during a busy day at the apothecary with a pretty nosegay of violets. He'd smelled like barley water and soap, a combination so simple and appealing, it had scrambled her brains and left her giddy as a goose.

Or the memory of how their kisses had unfolded in the back rooms of the apothecary, turning from delightfully sweet to something much more carnal. How kisses had proceeded to touches, and from there even more, and how she'd believed it a harbinger of what would come once they married.

A shout ripped Lucy's attention back to the present, and she jerked back from the road, missing the broad side of a carriage by inches. The driver called out curses at her over his shoulder, but they bounced off her and scattered across the muddied street as Lucy turned the corner onto Gray's Inn Road.

Halfway through a row of weathered stone buildings, almost invisible unless one knew what to look for, a discreet brass plaque to the left of a blackened oak door read:

TIERNEY & CO., BOOKKEEPING SERVICES

Lucy took a deep breath, pulling the dirty brown beginnings of a London fog into her lungs and expelling it along with the remorse and shame that accompanied her memory of Duncan holding her handwritten formula for a new kind of throat lozenge she'd worked two years to perfect.

"I'll just test it out for you, shall I?" he'd said, eyes roaming the page. Duncan and his father had long searched for a throat lozenge remedy that tasted as good as it worked. Might Duncan be tempted to impress his father with her lozenge? His lips curled up on one side as he read, and Lucy recalled the slight shadow of foreboding moving across the candlelight in the back storeroom where they carried out their affair.

"I don't know," she'd hedged.

Too late. He'd folded the formula and distracted her with kisses.

"I've more space and materials at my disposal. I know you think this is ready to sell, but isn't it better that we take the time to make sure?"

It might have been exhaustion that weakened Lucy just enough that she took advantage of an offer to help shoulder some of her burdens. However, the decision to let Duncan Rider walk out of Peterson's Apothecary with a formula that was worth a fortune was due not to her sleepless nights, but to a weakness in her character that allowed her to believe a man when he told her he loved her.

Now, four months later, somehow Duncan had again betrayed her.

Having already lost the lozenge formula to Duncan's avaricious grasp, Lucy had been horrified to find a second formula missing. She'd come up with a salve for treating babies' croup, a remedy even more profitable than the lozenges. What parent wouldn't pay through the nose to calm a croupy baby?

Lucy was certain that Duncan must have found out about her work and stolen both the formula and the ingredient list for the salve.

This time, Lucy would not dissolve into tears and swear never to love again. This time, she was going eviscerate her rival and get her formula back.

Then she would swear never to love again.

"AND THAT IS WHY I WOULD LIKE YOU TO KILL HIM. OR, perhaps not so drastic. Maybe torture him first. At the very least, leave him in great discomfort. I have plenty of ideas how you might do this and am happy to present them in writing along with anatomically correct diagrams."

Jonathan Thorne blinked at the incongruity of the blood-thirsty demand and the composed nature of the woman who issued it.

He almost blinked again at the sight of her face when she leaned forward and into the light but stopped himself at the last second.

None of that now.

Never again.

He'd been in the back room when he heard her come in off the street, asking for Henry Winthram, the tenor of her husky voice sounding sadly familiar.

The sound of a woman almost drained of hope.

"Miss Peterson, I appreciate your, erm, enthusiasm?" Winthram said now.

Henry Winthram was the newest and youngest agent at Tierney's and, with his raw talents, he'd also brought along a decade's worth of experience handling a mind-boggling array of poisons, explosives, insecticides, and *scientists*.

Winthram brought the woman into the small receiving room.

"Tierney and Company are in the business of helping clients solve burdensome problems," Winthram explained.

"It would relieve me of a great burden if you would take care of Duncan Rider," the woman said quickly.

"I'm not a gun for hire, miss," Winthram informed her, sounding offended.

"Of course you're not. I'm sorry, Winthram. I don't want him murdered," the woman apologized. "I do tend toward hyperbole when I'm angry."

"You don't say." Winthram's head turned when the floorboards squeaked as Thorne came into the room from the hall, where he'd been lurking.

"Allow me to introduce you to one of the senior agents," the young man said without bothering to hide his relief. "Mr. Jonathan Thorne, I'm pleased to present to you to Miss Peterson, the owner of Peterson's Apothecary."

For close to thirty years, the brass plaque affixed beside the front door of Tierney & Co. had advertised a bookkeeping service, but in fact, the five agents working here, Thorne and Winthram among them, did little to no accounting.

The books they balanced were more metaphorical.

Whenever the government had a domestic situation that could not be resolved through official channels and might lead to some embarrassment of the extended royal family or members of the government, Tierney's received a visit from a bland, middle-aged functionary who pushed an envelope across the desk and then disappeared. Shortly thereafter, a certain dignitary might find himself transferred back home after his superiors received information about said dignitary's unsavory predilections. A palace servant might suddenly leave their post the day after a cache of love letters were returned to one of the queen's ladies-in-waiting.

On occasion, Tierney's would agree to take on discreet services for an ordinary citizen who had been wronged. A widow would suddenly receive her late husband's back wages, or a poor family's home be spared a tax rise.

The request by an apothecary owner for the assassination of a rival apothecary was certainly out of the ordinary, but the fact that the apothecary owner was a woman—an almost preternaturally beautiful woman—might have made the request the most unusual in Tierney's history. Except, since Henry Winthram began working here, extraordinary women had been showing up in droves.

Thorne nodded at Winthram and steeled himself to impassiveness before he walked to the ladder-back chair where Miss Peterson had just risen to her feet and presented her hand in greeting.

There were some ladies of the most elite circles of British society who used to come and watch Thorne when he was a famous prizefighter. They would scream for blood and shout for pain alongside the common rabble from behind the safety of long cloaks and heavy veils. Afterward they would remove their veils and ogle him as though regarding an animal let loose from a menagerie. Thorne hadn't cared. When he was drinking, he hadn't accounted himself much better than an animal.

Over time, the tally of his fights wrote themselves on his face: ears that puffed to the side like lopsided mushrooms, a poorly sewn cut high on his left cheek that left him with a permanent sneer, a bent nose. All these conspired to change his appearance so much that his own mother had difficulty recognizing him and the ladies no longer simpered at him. Instead, they would hold their gaze in such a way that took in the whole of him without having to examine his face too closely.

A technique Thorne employed now as he bowed over Miss Peterson's hand, his eyes taking in her plain day dress of a faded India cotton print with a shawl collar up to her neck, her sturdy but well-worn boots, serviceable gloves, and ten-years-out-of-date straw bonnet, none of which could have provided much warmth on such a windy day.

What he didn't do was stare directly at her face. Beauty like Miss Peterson's elicited a reaction.

Thorne preferred to remain impassive.

She would be accustomed to some response, what with her perfectly round eyes and irises so dark blue they resembled the Mediterranean on the morning of a storm, full lips the color of a bruised rose petal, and cream-colored skin pulled taut over high cheekbones.

Fascinating how each person's face contained the exact same elements, but in one person, Miss Peterson for example, they were arranged so as to make a man stammer and blush, shuffle his feet, and work to wet his suddenly dry mouth.

Fascinating and dangerous.

Miss Peterson took her seat, and Thorne rang the bell for a servant to build up the fire and fetch another pot of hot water. When he judged Miss Peterson's bloodlust to have calmed, Thorne took a chair from against the wall and set it and himself in between Winthram and Miss Peterson.

"You must know Winthram from his days as the doorman at Athena's Retreat," Thorne said.

Miss Peterson sat straighter in her chair, clasping the strings of her reticule tight in her hands as she shot a worried glance at Winthram, who held up a hand to ward off her concern.

"The agents at Tierney's already knew about the club before I came to work here," Winthram assured her. "They've worked with Lord Greycliff and Mr. Kneland before."

That would be the Viscount Greycliff. His stepmother, the former Lady Greycliff, had used the money left to her by Greycliff's late father and converted a series of outbuildings behind her town house into a club. Most of London believed it to be a ladies' social club where women with an interest in the natural sciences would gather for tea and listen to lectures on subjects as varied as the proper means of cultivating orchids or how to use botanicals for better housekeeping.

Behind closed doors, however, women scientists used three floors of hidden laboratories to further their work in fields as varied as organic chemistry, ornithology, and experimental physics. When Lady Greycliff had come under threat last year, a former counter-assassin, Arthur Kneland, had been hired to protect her.

Much to Thorne's amusement, the intimidating man not only had gone and gotten himself shot for the umpteenth time, but had also fallen in love with the lady and now tried desperately to keep the scientists from wreaking havoc on the club and one another. On occasion, Kneland would help Winthram with small missions both to keep himself sharp and to pass on some of his skills to the younger man.

Having poached Winthram from the duties of doorman to

serve as one of its employees, Tierney's had not entirely reckoned with the fact that the women scientists who had relied on
Winthram to help them with their experiments now came to
him for help with other quandaries.

Women scientists lived highly eventful lives.

"I use the laboratories of the Retreat since our space at the
apothecary is taken up by our supplies and treatment room,"
Miss Peterson said now. "For *years* I worked to create the formula for a throat lozenge that reduces the swelling of a putrid
throat as well as soothes the pain. I planned on patenting the
formula, but—"

Despite his best effort, Thorne let his gaze rest on Miss Peterson's face, perhaps assuming the anguish contained in her
voice would diminish the luminosity of her beauty. In fact, it
added to it, and Thorne redirected his eyes to her clenched
hands and listened to her tremulous voice and any clues it
might provide.

"Before I could bring the formula to market myself," Miss
Peterson continued, "I showed it to Duncan Rider. The son in
Rider and Son Apothecary."

Unexpectedly, she launched from her chair and began pacing the room. Accustomed to the demure responses of the occasional gentlewoman or the humility of the domestic servants
who sought Tierney's services, Thorne was taken aback by the
ferocity in her manner.

Winthram showed no sign of surprise, and Thorne pre-
sumed this behavior was common among women scientists.

"Once I realized what that fungus-sucking tumor of a man
had done to me"—Thorne swallowed a laugh and nearly
choked while Winthram nodded his head in appreciation of
the insult—"patenting *my* formula, I pleaded with him to do

the right thing and either put my name on the patent or fulfill his promise to marry me. He did neither. I was tempted then to do him bodily harm, but I refrained."

"Most likely for the best," Winthram offered.

Miss Peterson stopped midstride, pointed a finger at the poor boy's head, and leveled a ferocious glare at him.

"Do you think so, Winthram?" Her voice rose now, and she advanced on Winthram, who sensibly leaned back in his chair, realizing it would have been better to keep his mouth shut until the end.

"Do you think so? Let me tell you, as bad as it is that that thieving pustule now makes a fortune from my hard work, to-day I learned something even worse. He has somehow come into my home and once *again* stolen my work. My formula for a new croup salve has disappeared."

Photo by Asa Shutts

Elizabeth Everett lives in upstate New York with her family. She likes going for long walks or (very) short runs to nearby sites that figure prominently in the history of civil rights and women's suffrage. Her writing is inspired by her admiration for rule breakers and her belief in the power of love to change the world.

VISIT ELIZABETH EVERETT ONLINE

ElizabethEverettAuthor.com

 ElizabethEverettAuthorBooks

 ElizabethEverettAuthor

Ready to find
your next great read?

Let us help.

Visit prh.com/nextread

Penguin
Random
House